ALSO BY LEN DEIGHTON

SPY HOOK

SPY
HOOK

a novel by

Len Deighton

ALFRED A. KNOPF
NEW YORK
1989

THIS IS A BORZOI BOOK
PUBLISHED BY ALFRED A. KNOPF, INC.

Copyright © 1988 by B. V. Holland Copyright Corporation

Library of Congress Cataloging-in-Publication-Data

Deighton, Len, [*date*]
Spy hook / by Len Deighton.
p.   cm.
ISBN 0-394-55178-8 :

I. Title.
PR6054.E37S67   1988
823'.914—dc19   88-11461
                                                CIP

Manufactured in the United States of America

Published December 14, 1988
Reprinted Once
Third Printing, February 1989

SPY HOOK

Chapter 1

When they ask me to become president of the United States I'm going to say, "Except for Washington, D.C." I'd finally decided while I was shaving in icy-cold water without electric light, and signed all the necessary documentation as I plodded through the uncleared snow to wait for a taxicab that never came, and let the passing traffic spray Washington's special kind of sweet-smelling slush over me.

Now it was afternoon. I'd lunched, and I was in a somewhat better mood. But this was turning out to be a long, long day, and I'd left this little job for the last. I hadn't been looking forward to it. Now I kept glancing up at the clock, and through the window at the interminable snow falling steadily from a steely-gray overcast, and wondering if I would be at the airport in time for the evening flight back to London, and whether it would be canceled.

"If that's the good news," said Jim Prettyman with an easy American grin, "what's the bad news?" He was thirty-three years old, according to the briefing card, a slim, white-faced Londoner with sparse hair and rimless spectacles who had come from the London School of Economics with an awesome reputation as a mathematician and qualifications in accountancy, political studies, and business management. I'd always got along very well with him—in fact, we'd been friends—but he'd never made any secret of the extent of his ambitions, or of his impatience. The moment a faster bus came past, Jim leaped aboard; that was his way. I looked at him carefully. He could make a smile last a long time.

So he didn't want to go to London next month and give evidence. Well, that was what the Department in London had expected him to say. Jim Prettyman's reputation said he was not the sort of fellow who would go out of his way to do a favor for London Central—or anyone else.

I looked at the clock again and said nothing. I was sitting in a huge, soft beige leather armchair. There was that wonderful smell of new leather that they spray inside cheap Japanese cars.

"More coffee, Bernie?" He scratched the side of his bony nose, as if he was thinking of something else.

"Yes, please." It was lousy coffee, even by my low standards, but I suppose it was his way of showing that he wasn't trying to get rid of me, and my ineffectual way of disassociating myself from the men who'd sent the message I was about to give him. "London might ask for you officially," I said. I tried to make it sound friendly, but it came out as a threat, which I suppose it was.

"Did London tell you to say that?" His secretary came and peered in through the half-open door—he must have pressed some hidden buzzer—and he said, "Two more—regular." She nodded and went out. It was all laconic and laid-back and very American, but, then, James Prettyman—or, as it said on the oak-and-brass nameplate on his desk, Jay Prettyman—was very American. He was American in the way that English emigrants are in their first few years after applying for citizenship.

I'd been watching him carefully, trying to see into his mind, but his face gave no clue as to his real feelings. He was a tough customer; I'd always known that. My wife, Fiona, had said that, apart from me, Prettyman was the most ruthless man she'd ever met. But that didn't mean she didn't admire him for that and a lot of other things. He'd even got her interested in his time-wasting hobby of trying to decipher ancient Mesopotamian cuneiform scripts. But most of us had learned not to let him get started on the subject. Not surprising he'd ended his time running a desk in Codes and Ciphers.

"Yes," I said, "they told me to say it." I looked at his office, with its paneled walls that were made of some special kind of plastic on account of the fire department's regulations. And at the stern-faced president of Perimeter Security Guarantee Trust framed in gold, and the fancy reproduction-antique bureau that might have concealed a drinks cupboard. I'd have given a lot for a stiff Scotch before facing that weather again.

"No chance! Look at this stuff." He indicated the trays laden with paperwork, and the elaborate work station with the video screen that gave him access to one hundred and fifty major data bases. Alongside it, staring at us from a big solid silver frame, there was another reason: his brand-new American wife. She looked about eighteen but had a son at Harvard and two ex-husbands, to say nothing of a father who'd been a big shot in the State Department. She was standing with him and a shiny Corvette in front of a big house with cherry trees in the garden. He grinned again. I could see why they didn't like him in London. He had no eyebrows and his eyes were narrow, so that, when he grinned those superwide mirthless grins with his white teeth just showing, he looked like the commander of a Japanese prison camp complaining that the POWs weren't bowing low enough.

"You could be in and out in one day," I coaxed.

He was ready for that. "A day to travel; a day to travel back. It would cost me three days' work and, quite frankly, Bernie, those goddamned flights leave me bushed."

"I thought you might like a chance to see the family," I said. Then I waited while the secretary—a tall girl with amazingly long red tapering fingernails and a great deal of silvery-yellow wavy hair—brought in two paper cups of slot-machine coffee and put them down very delicately on his huge desk, together with two bright-yellow paper napkins, two packets of artificial sweetener, two packets of "nondairy creamer," and two plastic stirrers. She smiled at me and then at Jim.

"Thank you, Charlene," he said. He immediately reached for his coffee, looking at it as if he was going to enjoy it. After putting two sweetener pills and the white "creamer" into it, and stirring energetically, he sipped it and said, "My mother died last August, and Dad went to live in Geneva with my sister."

Thank you, London Research and Briefing, always there when you need them. I nodded. He'd made no mention of the English wife he'd divorced overnight in Mexico, the one who had refused to go and live in Washington, despite the salary and the big house with the cherry trees in the garden; but it seemed better not to pursue that one. "I'm sorry, Jim." I was genuinely sorry about his mother. His parents had given me more than one sorely needed Sunday lunch and had looked after my two kids when the Greek au pair had had a screaming row with my wife and left without notice.

I drank some of the evil-tasting brew and started again. "There's a lot of money—half a million, perhaps—still unaccounted for. Someone must know about it. Half a million. Pounds!"

"Well, I don't know about it." His lips tightened.

"Come along, Jim. No one's shouting 'fire.' The money is somewhere in Central Funding. Everyone knows that, but there'll be no peace until the bookkeepers find it and close the ledgers."

"Why you?"

Good question. The true answer was that I'd become the dogsbody who got the jobs that no one else wanted. "I was coming over anyway."

"So they saved the price of an air ticket." He drank more coffee and carefully wiped the extreme edge of his mouth with the bright-yellow paper napkin. "Thank God, I'm through with all that penny-pinching crap in London. How the hell do you put up with it?" He drained the rest of his coffee. I suppose he'd developed a taste for it.

"Are you offering me a job?" I said, straight-faced and open-eyed. He frowned and for a moment looked flustered. The fact was that, since my wife had defected to the Russians a few years before, my bona fides was dependent upon my contract with London Central. If they dispensed with my services, however elegantly it was done, I might suddenly start finding that my "indefinite" U.S. visa for "unlimited" visits was not getting me through to where the baggage was waiting. Of course, some really powerful independent corporation might be able to face down official disapproval, but powerful independent organizations, like these friendly folks Jim worked for, were usually hell-bent on keeping the government sweet.

"Another year like last year and we'll be laying off personnel," he said awkwardly.

"How long will it take to get a cab?"

"It's not as if my drag-assing over to London would make a difference to you personally. . . ."

"Someone told me that some cabs won't go to the airport in this kind of weather." I wasn't going to crawl to him, no matter how urgent London was pretending it was.

"If it's for you, say the word. I owe you, Bernie. I owe you." When I didn't react, he stood up. As if by magic, the door opened, and he told his secretary to phone the car pool and arrange a car for me. "Do you have anything to pick up?"

"Straight to the airport," I said. I had my shirts and underwear and shaving stuff in the leather bag that contained the faxed accounts and memos that the embassy had sent round to me in the middle of the night. I should have been showing them to Jim, but showing him papers would make no difference. He was determined to tell London Central that he didn't give a damn about them or their problems. He knew he didn't have to worry. When he'd told them he was going to Washington to work, they'd taken his living accommodation to pieces and given him a vetting of the sort that you never get on joining—only on leaving. Especially if you work in Codes and Ciphers.

So Jim clean-as-a-whistle Prettyman had nothing to worry about. He'd always been a model employee: that was his *modus operandi*. Not even an office pencil or a packet of paper clips. Rumors said the investigating team from K-7 were so frustrated that they'd taken away his wife's handwritten recipe book and looked at it under ultraviolet light. But Jim's ex-wife certainly wasn't the sort of woman who writes out recipes in longhand, so that might be a silly story: no one likes the people from K-7. There were lots of silly stories going round at the time; my wife had just defected, and everyone was nervous.

"You work with Bret Rensselaer. Talk to Bret: he knows where the bodies are buried."

"Bret's not with us any more," I reminded him. "He was shot. In Berlin . . . a long time back."

"Yeah; I forgot. Poor Bret; I heard about that. Bret sent me over here the first time I came. I have a lot to thank him for."

"Why would Bret know?"

"About the slush fund Central Funding set up with the Germans? Are you kidding? Bret masterminded that whole business. He appointed the company directors—all front men, of course—and squared it with the people who ran the bank."

"Bret did?"

"The bank directors were in his pocket. They were all Bret's people, and Bret briefed them."

"It's news to me."

"Sure. It's too bad. If half a million pounds took a walk, Bret was the man who might have pointed you in the right direction." Jim Prettyman looked up to where his secretary stood at the door again. She must have nodded or something, for Jim said, "The car's there. No hurry, but it's ready when you are."

"Did you work with Bret?"

"On the German caper? I okayed the cash transfers when there was no one else around who was authorized to sign. But everything that I did had already been okayed. I was never at the meetings. That was all kept behind closed doors. Shall I tell you something? I don't think there was ever one meeting held in the building. All I ever saw was cashier's chits with the authorized signatures: none of them names I recognized." He laughed reflectively. "Any auditor worth a damn would immediately point out that every one of those damned signatures might have been written by Bret Rensselaer. For all the evidence I have, there never was a real committee. The whole thing could have been a complete fabrication dreamed up by Bret."

I nodded soberly, but I must have looked puzzled as I picked up my bag and took my overcoat from his secretary.

Jim came with me over to the door, and through his secretary's office. With his hand on my shoulder he said, "Sure, I know. Bret didn't dream it up. I'm just saying that's how secret it was. But when you talk to the others, just remember that they were Bret Rensselaer's cronies. If one of them put his hand in the till, Bret will probably have covered it for him. Be your age, Bernie. These things happen: only rarely, I know, but they happen. It's the way the world is."

Jim walked with me to the elevator and pushed the buttons for me, the way Americans do when they want to make sure you're leaving the building. He said we must get together again, have a meal, and talk about the good times we had together in the old days. I said yes, we must, and thanked him, and said goodbye, but still the lift didn't come.

Jim pressed the button again and smiled a crooked little smile. He straightened up. "Bernie," he said suddenly, and glanced around us and along the corridor to see that we were alone.

"Yes, Jim?"

He looked around again. Jim had always been a very careful fellow: it was the reason he'd got on so well. One of the reasons. "This business in London . . ."

Again he paused. I thought for one terrible moment that he was going to admit to pocketing the missing money, and then implore me to help him cover it up, for old times' sake. Or something like that. It would have put me in a damned difficult position, and my stomach turned at the thought of it. But I needn't have worried. Jim wasn't the sort who pleaded with anyone about anything.

"I won't come. You tell them that in London. They can try anything they like, but I won't come."

He seemed agitated. "Okay, Jim," I said. "I'll tell them."

"I'd love to see London again. I really miss the smoke. . . . We had some good times, didn't we, Bernie?"

"Yes, we did," I said. Jim had always been a bit of a cold fish: I was surprised by this revelation.

"Remember when Fiona was frying the fish we caught and spilled the oil and set fire to the kitchen? You really flipped your lid."

"She said you did it."

He smiled. He seemed genuinely amused. This was the Jim I used to know. "I never saw anyone move so fast. Fiona could handle just about anything that came along." He paused. "Until she met you. Yes, they were good times, Bernie."

"Yes, they were."

I thought he was softening, and he must have seen that in my face, for he said, "But I'm not getting involved in any bloody inquiry. They are looking for someone to blame. You know that, don't you?"

I said nothing. Jim said, "Why choose you to come and

ask me? . . . Because, if I don't go, you'll be the one they finger."

I ignored that remark. "Wouldn't it be better to go over there and tell them what you know?" I suggested.

My reply did nothing to calm him. "I don't know anything," he said, raising his voice. "Jesus Christ, Bernie, how can you be so blind? The Department is determined to get even with you."

"Get even? For what?"

"For what your wife did."

"That's not logical."

"Revenge never is logical. Wise up. They'll get you, one way or the other. Even resigning from the Department—the way I did—makes them mad. They see it as a betrayal. They expect everyone to stay in harness forever."

"Like marriage," I said.

"Till death do us part," said Jim. "Right. And they'll get you. Through your wife. Or maybe through your father. You'll see."

The car of the lift arrived, and I stepped into it. I thought he was coming with me. Had I known he wasn't, I would never have left that reference to my father go unexplained. He put his foot inside and leaned round to press the button for the ground floor. By that time it was too late. "Don't tip the driver," said Jim, still smiling as the doors closed on me. "It's against company policy." The last I saw of him was that cold Cheshire Cat smile. It hung in my vision for a long time afterwards.

When I got outside in the street, the snow was piling higher and higher, and the air was crammed full of huge snowflakes that came spinning down like sycamore seeds with engine failure.

"Where's your baggage?" said the driver. Getting out of the car, he tossed the remainder of his coffee into the snow, where it left a brown-ridged crater that steamed like Vesuvius.

He wasn't looking forward to a drive to the airport on a Friday afternoon, and you didn't have to be a psychologist to see that in his face.

"That's all," I told him.

"You travel light, mister." He opened the door for me, and I settled down inside. The car was warm; I suppose he'd just come in from a job, expecting to be signed out and sent home. Now he was in a bad mood.

The traffic was slow, even by Washington weekend standards. I thought about Jim while we crawled out to the airport. I suppose he wanted to get rid of me. There was no other reason why Jim would invent that ridiculous story about Bret Rensselaer. The idea of Bret being a party to any kind of financial swindle involving the government was so ludicrous that I didn't even give it careful thought. Perhaps I should have done.

The plane was half empty. After a day like that, a lot of people had had enough, without enduring the tender, loving care of any airline company plus the prospect of a diversion to Manchester. But at least the half-empty First Class cabin gave me enough legroom. I accepted the offers of glasses of champagne with such enthusiasm that the stewardess finally left the bottle with me.

I read the dinner menu and tried not to think about Jim Prettyman. I hadn't pressed him hard enough. I'd resented the unexpected phone call from Morgan, the D-G's personal assistant. I'd planned to spend this afternoon shopping. Christmas had passed, and there were sale signs everywhere. I'd glimpsed a big model helicopter that my son, Billy, would have gone crazy about. London was always ready to provide me with yet another task that was nothing to do with me or my immediate work. I had the suspicion that this time I'd been chosen not because I happened to be in Washington but because London knew that Jim was an old friend who'd respond more readily to me than to anyone else in the Department. This afternoon, when Jim had proved recalcitrant, I'd rather enjoyed the idea of passing his rude message back to that stupid man Morgan. Now it was too late, I was beginning to have second thoughts. Perhaps I should have taken up his offer to do it as a personal favor to me.

I thought about Jim's warnings. He wasn't the only one who thought the Department might still be blaming me for my wife's defection. But the idea that they'd frame me for embezzlement was a new one. It would wipe me out, of course. No one would employ me if they made something like that stick. It was a nasty thought, and even worse was that throwaway line about getting to me through my father. How could they get to me through my father? My father didn't work for the Department any more. My father was dead.

I drank more champagne—fizzy wine is not worth drinking if you allow the chill to go off it—and finished the bottle before closing my eyes for a moment in an effort to remember exactly what Jim had said. I must have dozed off. I was tired: really tired.

The next thing I knew, the stewardess was shaking me roughly and saying, "Would you like breakfast, sir?"

"I haven't had dinner."

"They tell us not to wake passengers who are asleep."

"Breakfast?"

"We'll be landing at London Heathrow in about forty-five minutes."

It was an airline breakfast: shriveled bacon, a plastic egg with a small, stale roll, and powdered cream for the coffee. Even when starving hungry, I found it very easy to resist. Oh well, the dinner I'd missed was probably no better, and at least the threatened diversion to sunny Manchester had been averted. I vividly remembered the last time I was forcibly flown to Manchester. The airline's senior staff all went and hid in the toilets until the angry, unwashed, unfed passengers had been herded aboard the unheated train.

But soon I had my feet on the ground again in London. Waiting at the barrier there was my Gloria. She usually came to the airport to meet me, and there can be no greater love than that which brings someone on a voluntary visit to London Heathrow.

She looked radiant: tall, on tiptoe, waving madly. Her long, naturally blond hair and a tailored tan suede coat with its big fur collar made her shine like a beacon amongst the line of weary welcomers leaning heavily—like drunks—across the rails in Terminal Three. And if she did flourish her Gucci handbag a bit too much and wear those big sunglasses even at breakfast time in winter, well, one had to make allowances for the fact that she was only half my age.

"The car's outside," she whispered as she released me from the tight embrace.

"It will be towed away by now."

"Don't be a misery. It will be there."

And it was, of course. And the weathermen's threatened snow and ice had not materialized either. This part of England was bathed in bright early-morning sunshine, and the sky was blue and almost completely clear. But it was damned cold. The weathermen said it was the coldest January since 1940, but who believes the weathermen.

"You won't know the house," she boasted as she roared down the Motorway in the yellow, dented Mini, ignoring the speed limit, cutting in front of angry cabbies, and hooting at sleepy bus drivers.

"You can't have done much in a week."

"Ha ha! Wait and see."

"Better you tell me now," I said with ill-concealed anxiety. "You haven't knocked down the garden wall? Next door's rose beds . . ."

"Wait and see: wait and see!"

She let go of the wheel to pound a fist against my leg, as if making sure I was really and truly flesh and blood. Did she realize what mixed feelings I had about moving out of the house in Marylebone? Not just because Marylebone was convenient and central, but also because it was the first house I'd ever bought, albeit with the aid of a still-outstanding mortgage that the bank only agreed to because of the intervention of my prosperous father-in-law. Well, Duke Street wasn't lost forever. It was leased to four American bachelors with jobs in the City. Bankers. They were paying a handsome rent that not only covered the mortgage but gave me a house in the suburbs and some small change to face the expenses of looking after two motherless children.

Gloria was in her element since moving into the new place. She didn't see it as a rather shabby semidetached suburban house with its peeling stucco and truncated front garden and a side entrance that had been overlaid with concrete to make a place to park a car. For Gloria, this was her chance to make me see how indispensable she was. It was her chance to get us away from the shadow of my wife, Fiona. Number 13 Balaklava Road was going to be our little nest, the place into which we settled down to live happily ever after, the way they do in the fairy stories that she was reading not so very long ago.

Don't get me wrong. I loved her. Desperately. When I was away I counted the days—even the hours sometimes—before we'd be together again. But that didn't mean that I couldn't see how ill-suited we were. She was just a child. Before me her boyfriends had been schoolkids: boys who helped with logarithms and irregular verbs. Sometime she was going to realize suddenly that there was a big wide world out there waiting for her. By that time perhaps I'd be depending on her. No perhaps about it. I was depending on her now.

"Did it all go all right?"

"All all right," I said.

"Someone from Central Funding left a note on your desk . . . half a dozen notes, in fact. Something about Prettyman. It's a funny name, isn't it."

"Nothing else?"

"No. It's all been very quiet in the office. Unusually quiet. Who is Prettyman?" she asked.

"A friend of mine. They want him to give evidence . . . some money they've lost."

"And he stole it?" She was interested now.

"Jim? No. When Jim puts his hand in the till, he'll come up with ten million or more."

"I thought he was a friend of yours," she said reproachfully.

"Only kidding."

"So who did steal it?"

"No one stole anything. It's just the accountants getting their paperwork into the usual chaos."

"Truly?"

"You know how long the cashier's office takes to clear your expenses. Did you see all those queries they raised on last month's chit?"

"That's just your expenses, darling. Some people get them signed and paid within a week." I smiled. I was glad to change the subject. Prettyman's warnings had left a dull feeling of fear in me. It was heavy in my guts, like indigestion.

We arrived at Balaklava Road in record time. It was a street of small Victorian houses with large bay windows. Here and there the fronts were picked out in tasteful pastel colors. It was Saturday: despite the early hour, housewives were staggering home under the weight of frantic shopping, and husbands were cleaning their cars, everyone demonstrating that manic energy and determination that the British devote only to their hobbies.

The neighbor who shared our semidetached house—an insurance salesman and passionate gardener—was planting his Christmas tree in the hard-frozen soil of his front garden. He could have saved himself the trouble—they never grow. People say the dealers scald the roots. He waved with the garden trowel as we swept past him and into the narrow side entrance. It was a squeeze to get out.

Gloria opened the newly painted front door with a proud flourish. The hall had been repapered—large mustard-yellow flowers on curlicue stalks—and had new carpet too. I admired the result. In the kitchen there were some primroses on the table, which was set with our best chinaware. Cut-glass tumblers stood ready for orange juice, and rashers of smoked bacon were arranged by the stove alongside four brown eggs and a new Teflon frying pan.

I walked round the whole house with her and played my appointed role. The new curtains were wonderful; and if the brown leather three-piece was a bit too low and so difficult to climb out of, with a remote control for the TV, what did it matter? But by the time we were back in the kitchen, a smell of good coffee in the air, and my breakfast spluttering in the pan, I knew she had something else to tell me. I decided it wasn't anything concerning the house. I decided it was probably nothing important. But I was wrong about that.

"I've given in my notice," she said over her shoulder while standing at the stove. She'd threatened to leave the Department not once but several hundred times. Always until now she'd made me the sole focus of her anger and frustration. "They promised to let me go to Cambridge. They promised!" She was getting angry at the thought of it. She looked up from the frying pan and waved the fork at me, before again jabbing at the bacon.

"And now they won't? They said that?"

"I'll pay my own way. I have enough if I go carefully," she said. "I'll be twenty-three in June. Already I'll feel like an old lady, sitting with all those eighteen-year-old schoolkids."

"What did they say?"

"Morgan stopped me in the corridor last week. Asked me how I was getting along. 'What about my place at Cambridge?' I said. He didn't have the guts to tell me in the proper way. He said there was no money. Bastard! There's money enough for Morgan to go to conferences in Australia and that damned symposium in Toronto. Money enough for jaunts!"

I nodded. I can't say that Australia and Toronto were high on my list of places to jaunt in, but perhaps Morgan had his reasons. "You didn't tell him that?"

"I damned well did. I let him have it. We were outside the Deputy's office. He must have heard every word. I hope he did."

"You're a harridan," I told her.

She slammed the plates on the table with a snarl and then, unable to keep up the display of fierce bad temper, she laughed. "Yes, I am. You haven't seen that side of me yet."

"What an extraordinary thing to say, my love."

"You treat me like a backward child, Bernard. I'm not a fool." I said nothing. The toast flung itself out of the machine with a loud clatter. She rescued both slices before they slid into the sink and put them on a plate alongside my eggs and bacon. Then, as I began to eat, she sat opposite me, her face cupped in her hands, elbows on table, studying me as if I was an animal in the zoo. I was getting used to it now, but it still made me uneasy. She watched me with a curiosity that was disconcerting. Sometimes I would look up from a book or finish talking on the phone to find her studying me with that same expression.

"When did you say the children would be home?" I asked.

"You didn't mind them going to the sale of work?"

"I don't know what a sale of work is," I said, not without an element of truth.

"It's at the Church Hall in Sebastopol Road. People make cakes and pickles and knit tea cosies and donate unwanted Christmas presents. It's for Oxfam."

"And why would Billy and Sally want to go?"

"I knew you'd be angry."

"I'm not angry, but why would they want to go?"

"There will be toys and books and things too. It's a jumble sale really, but the Women's Guild prefers to call it their New Year Sale of Work. It sounds better. I knew you wouldn't bring any presents back with you."

"I tried. I wanted to, I really did."

"I know, darling. That wasn't why the children wanted to be here when you arrived. I told them to go. It's good for them to be with other children. Changing schools isn't easy at that age. They left a lot of friends in London; they must make new ones round here. It's not easy, Bernie." It was quite a speech; perhaps she'd had it all prepared.

"I know." I was still examining the awful prospect of her taking a place at the university next October, or whenever it was the academic year started in such places. What was I going to do with this wretched house, far away from everyone I knew? And what about the children?

She must have seen my face. "I'll be back every weekend," she promised.

"You know that's impossible," I told her. "You'll be working damned hard. I know you; you'll want to do everything better than anyone's ever done it before."

"It will be all right, darling," she said. "If we want it to be all right, it will be. You'll see."

Muffin, our battered cat, came and tapped on the window. Muffin seemed to be the only member of the family who'd settled into Balaklava Road without difficulties. And even Muffin stayed out all night sometimes.

Chapter 2

There was another thing I didn't like about the suburbs: getting to work. I braved the morning traffic jams in my aging Volvo, but Gloria seldom came with me in the car. She enjoyed going on the train; at least she said she enjoyed it. She said it gave her time to think. But the 7:32 was always packed with people from even more outlying suburbs by the time it arrived, and I hated to stand all the way to Waterloo. Second, there was the question of my assigned parking place. Already the hyenas were circling. The old man who ran Personnel Records had started hinting about a cash offer for it as soon as I registered my new address. You'll come in on the train now, I suppose? No, I said sharply. No, I won't. And apart from a couple of days when the old Volvo was having its transmission fixed, I hadn't. I calculated that five consecutive days in a row would be all I'd need to find my hard-won parking space reassigned to someone who'd make better use of it.

So on Monday I went by car and Gloria went by train. She arrived ahead of me, of course. The office is only two or three minutes' walk from Waterloo Station, whereas I had to drag through the traffic jams in Wimbledon.

I got into the office to find alarm and despondency spread right through the building. Dicky Cruyer was there already, a sure sign of a crisis. They must have phoned him at home and had him depart hurriedly from the leisurely breakfast he enjoys after jogging across Hampstead Heath. Even Sir Percy Babcock, the Deputy D-G, had dragged himself away from his law practice and found time to spare for an early-morning session.

"Number Two Conference Room," the girl waiting in the corridor said. She whispered in a way that revealed her pent-up excitement: as if this was the sort of day she'd been waiting for, ever since beginning to type all those tedious reports for us. I suppose Dicky must have sent her to stand sentry outside my office. "Sir Percy is chairing the meeting. They said you should join them as soon as you arrived."

"Thanks, Mabel," I said, and gave her my coat and a leather case of very unimportant nonclassified paperwork that I hoped she'd mislay. She smiled dutifully. Her name wasn't Mabel, but I called them all Mabel, and I suppose they'd got used to it.

Number Two was on the top floor, a narrow room that seated fourteen at a pinch and had a view right across to where the City's ugly tower blocks underpinned the low gray cloud base.

"Samson! Good," said the Deputy D-G when I went in. There was a notepad, a yellow pencil, and a chair waiting for me, and two more pristine pads and pencils that may or may not have been waiting for others who were arriving at work hoping their lateness would not be noted. Bad luck.

"Have you heard?" Dicky asked.

I could see it was Dicky's baby. This was a German Desk crisis. This wasn't a routine briefing for the Deputy, or a conference to decide about annual-leave rosters or more questions about where Central Funding have put the odd few hundred thousand pounds that Jim Prettyman authorized for Bret Rensselaer and Bret Rensselaer never got. This was serious. "No," I said. "What's happened?"

"Bizet," said Dicky, and went back to chewing his fingernail.

I knew the group; at least, I knew them as well as a desk man sitting in London can know the people who do the real nasty dangerous work. Somewhere near Frankfurt an der Oder, right over there on East Germany's border with Poland. "Poles," I said, "or that's how it started. Poles working in some sort of heavy industry."

"That's right," said Dicky judiciously. He had a folder and was looking at it to check how well my memory was working.

"What's happened?"

"It looks nasty," said Dicky, unvanquished master of the nebulous answer on almost any subject except the gastronomic merits of expensive restaurants.

Billingsly, a bald-headed youngster from the Data Centre, tapped the palm of his hand with his heavy horn-rimmed spectacles and said, "We seem to have lost more than one of them. That's always a bad sign."

So even in the Data Centre they knew that. Things were looking up. "Yes," I said. "That's always a bad sign."

Billingsly looked at me as if I'd slapped his face. Uncordial now, he said, "If you know anything else we can do . . ."

"Have you put out a contact string?" I asked.

Billingsly seemed to be unsure what a contact string—a roll call for survivors—was. But eventually Harry Strang, an elderly gorilla from Operations, stopped scratching his cheek with the eraser end of his brand-new yellow pencil for enough time to answer me: "Early yesterday morning."

"It's too soon."

"That's what I told the Deputy," said Dicky Cruyer, nodding deferentially to Sir Percy. Dicky was looking more tired and ill every minute. He usually came down with something totally incapacitating in this sort of situation. It was the thought of making a decision, and signing it for all to see, that affected him.

"Mass," said Harry Strang.

"They see each other at Sunday-morning Mass," explained Dicky Cruyer.

"No out-of-contact signals?" I asked.

"No," said Strang. "That's what makes it worrying."

"Damn right," I said. "What else?"

There was a moment's silence. If I'd been paranoid, I could easily have suspected that they wanted to keep me ignorant of the confirmation.

"Odds and ends," said Billingsly.

Strang said, "We have something from inside. Two men picked up for interrogation in the Frankfurt area."

"Berlin."

"Berlin? No, Frankfurt," said Billingsly.

I'd had enough of Billingsly by that time. They were all like him in the Data Centre: they thought we all needed a couple of megabytes of random-access memory to get level with them.

"Don't act the bloody fool," I told Strang. "Is your information from Berlin or from Frankfurt?"

"Berlin," said Strang. "Normannenstrasse." That was the big gray stone block in Berlin-Lichtenberg from which East Germany's Stasi—State Security Service—intimidated their world and poked their fingers into ours.

"Over a weekend," I said. "Doesn't sound good. If Frankfurt Stasi put that on the teleprinter, they must think they have something worthwhile."

"The question we're discussing," said the Deputy with the gentle courtesy that barristers show when leading a nervous defendant into an irreversible admission of guilt, "is whether to follow up." He looked at me and tilted his head to one side, as if seeing me better like that.

I stared back at him. He was a funny, bright-eyed, plump little man with a shiny pink face and hair brushed close against his skull. Black jacket, a waistcoat full of ancient pens and pencils, pinstripe trousers, and the tie of some obscure public school held in place by a jeweled pin. A lawyer. If you'd seen him on the street, you'd have thought him a down-at-heel solicitor or a barrister's clerk. In real life—which is to say, outside this building—he ran one of the most successful law firms in London. Why he persevered with this unrewarding job I couldn't fathom, but he was only one step away from running the whole department. The D-G was, after all, on his last legs. I said, "You mean, should you put someone in to follow up?"

"Precisely," said the Deputy. "I think we'd all like to hear your views, Samson."

I played for time. "From Berlin Field Unit?" I said. "Or from somewhere else?"

"I don't think BFU should come into this," said Strang hastily. That was the voice of Operations.

He was right, of course. Sending someone from West Berlin into such a situation would be madness. In a region like that, any kind of stranger is immediately scrutinized by every damned secret policeman on duty and a few that aren't. "You're probably right," I said, as if conceding something.

Strang said, "They'd have him in the slammer before the ink was dry on the hotel register."

"We have people nearer," said the Deputy.

They were all looking at me now. This is why they'd waited for me to join them. They knew what the answer was going to be, but they were going to make sure that it was me, an ex–field man, who would say it out loud. Then they could get on with their work, or their lunch, or doze off until the next crisis.

"We can't just leave them to it," I said. They all nodded. We had to agree on the wrong answer first; that was the ethic of the Department.

"We've had good stuff from them," Dicky said. "Nothing big, of course—they are only foundry workers—but they've never let us down."

"I'd like to hear what Samson thinks," said the Deputy. He had a slim gold pencil in his hand. He was leaning back in his chair, arm extended to his notepad. He looked up from whatever he was writing, stared at me, and smiled encouragement.

"We'll have to let it go," I said finally.

"Speak up," said the Deputy in his housemaster voice.

I cleared my throat. "There's nothing we can do," I said, rather louder. "We'll just have to wait and see."

They all turned to see the Deputy's reaction. "I think that's sound," he said at last. Dicky Cruyer smiled with relief at someone else's making the decision. Especially a decision to do nothing. He wriggled about and ran his hand back through his curly hair, looking round the room and nodding. Then he looked over to where a clerk was keeping an account of what was said, to be sure he was writing it down.

Well, I'd earned my wages for the day. I'd told them exactly what they wanted to hear. Now nothing would happen for a day or so, apart from a group of Polish workers having their fingernails torn out under hygienic conditions with a shorthand writer in attendance.

There was a knock at the door, and a tray with tea and biscuits arrived. Billingsly, perhaps because he was the youngest and least arthritic of us, or because he wanted to impress the Deputy, distributed the cups and saucers and passed the milk and the teapot along the polished tabletop.

"Chocolate oatmeal!" said Harry Strang. I looked up at him and he winked. Harry knew what it was all about. Harry had spent enough time at the sharp end to know what I was thinking.

Harry poured tea for me. I took it and drank some. It turned to acid in my stomach. The Deputy was leaning towards Billingsly to ask him something about the excessive "down time" the computers in the Yellow Submarine were suffering lately. Billingsly said that you had to expect some trouble with these "electronic toys." The Deputy said, not when you paid two million pounds for them, you didn't.

"Biscuit?" said Harry Strang.

"No, thanks."

"You used to like chocolate oatmeal, as I remember," he said sardonically.

I leaned over to see what the Deputy had written on his notepad, but it was just a pattern: a hundred wobbly concentric circles with a big dot in the middle. No escape; no solution; no nothing. It was the answer he wanted to his question, I suppose, and I had given it to him. Ten marks out of ten, Samson. Advance to Go and collect two hundred pounds.

It was only when the Deputy had finished his tea that protocol permitted even the busiest of us to take our leave. Just when the Deputy was moving towards the door, Morgan —the D-G's most obsequious acolyte—came in, flush-faced and complete with melton overcoat, carrying, like an altar candle, one of those short folding umbrellas. He said, in his singsong Welsh accent, "Sorry I'm late, sir. I had the most awful and unexpected trouble with the motorcar." He bit his lip. Exertion and anxiety had made his face even paler than usual.

The Deputy was annoyed but allowed no more than a trace of it to show. "We managed without you, Morgan," he said.

As the Deputy marched out, Morgan looked at me with a deep hatred that he made no attempt to hide. Perhaps he thought his humiliation was all my fault, or perhaps he blamed me for being there when it happened. Either way, if the Department ever needed someone to bury me, Morgan would be an enthusiastic volunteer. Perhaps he was already working on it.

I went downstairs, relieved to get out of that meeting even if it meant sitting in my cramped little office and trying to see over the top of the uncompleted paperwork. I stared at the cluttered table near the window, and more specifically, at two boxes in beautiful Christmas wrappings. One marked "Billy" and the other "Sally." They'd been delivered by the Harrods van together with cards that said, "With dearest love from Mummy," but not in Fiona's handwriting. I should have given them to the children before Christmas, but I'd left them there and tried not to look at them. She'd sent presents on previous Christmases, and I'd put them under the tree. The children had read the cards without comment. But this year we'd spent Christmas in our new little home, and somehow I didn't want Fiona to intrude into it. The move had given me a chance to get rid of Fiona's clothes and personal things. I wanted to start again, but that didn't make it any easier to confront those two bright boxes waiting for me every time I went into my office.

My desk was a mess. My secretary, Brenda, had been covering for two filing clerks who were sick or pregnant or some damned thing, so I tried to sort out a week of muddle that had accumulated on my desk in my absence.

The first things I came across were the red-labeled "urgent" messages about Prettyman. My God, last Thursday there must have been new messages, requests, assignments, and words of advice landing on my desk every half-hour. Thank heavens, Brenda had enough sense not to forward it all to Washington. Well, now I was back in London, and they could get someone else to go and bully Jim Prettyman into coming back here to be roasted by a committee of time-serving old flowerpots from Central Funding who were desperately looking for some unfortunate upon whom to dump the blame for their own inadequacies.

I was putting it all into the classified waste when I noticed the signature. Billingsly. Billingsly! It was damned odd that Billingsly hadn't even mentioned it to me this morning in Number Two Conference Room. He hadn't even asked me what had happened. His passion, if not to say obsession, for getting Prettyman here had undergone some abrupt traumatic

change. That was the way it went with people like Billingsly
—and many others in the Department—who alternated dis-
plays of panic and amnesia with disconcerting suddenness.

I threw the notes into the basket and forgot about it.
There was no point in stirring up trouble for Jim Prettyman.
In my opinion, he was a fool to suddenly get on his high horse
about something so mundane. He could have testified and
been the golden boy; he could have declined without upset-
ting them. But I think he liked confrontation. I decided to
smooth things over as much as I could. When it came to
writing the report, I wouldn't say he'd refused point-blank: I'd
say he was thinking about it. Until they asked for the report,
I'd say nothing at all.

I didn't see Gloria until we had lunch together in the
restaurant. Her fluent Hungarian had recently brought her a
job downstairs: promotion, more pay, and much more responsibility. I suppose they thought that it would be enough to
make her forget the promises they'd made about paying her
wages while she was at Cambridge. Her new job meant that
I saw much less of her, and so lunch had become the time
when our domestic questions were settled: Would it look too
pushy to invite the Cruyers for dinner? Who had the receipt
for the dry cleaning? Why had I opened a new tin of catfood
for Muffin when the last one was still half full?

I asked her if anything more had been said about her
resignation, secretly hoping, I suppose, that she might have
changed her mind. She hadn't. When I broached the subject
over the "mushroom quiche with winter salad," she told me
that she'd had an answer from a friend of hers about some comfortable rooms in Cambridge that she could probably rent.

"What am I going to do with the house?"

"Not so loud, darling," she said. We kept up this absurd
pretense that our co-workers—or such of them as might be
interested—didn't know we were living together. "I'll keep
paying half the rent. I told you that."

"It's nothing to do with the rent," I said. "It's simply that

I wouldn't have taken on a place out in the sticks so I could sit there every night on my own, watching TV and saving up my laundry until I've got enough to make a full load for the washing machine."

That produced the flicker of a grin. She leaned closer to me and said, "After you find out how much dirty laundry the children have every day, you won't be worrying about filling up the machine: you'll be looking for a place where you can get washing powder wholesale." She sipped some apple juice with added vitamin C. "You've got a girl for the children. You'll have that nice Mrs. Palmer coming in every day to tidy round. I'll be back every weekend; I don't know what you are worrying about."

"I wish you'd be a little more realistic. Cambridge is a damned long way away from Balaklava Road. The weekend traffic will be horrendous, the railway service is even worse, and in any case you'll have your studying to do."

"I wish I could make you stop worrying," she said. "Are you ill? You haven't been yourself since coming back from Washington. Did something go wrong there?"

"If I'd known what you were going to do, I would have made different plans."

"I told you. I told you over and over." She looked down and continued to eat her winter salad as if there was no more to be said. In a way she was right. She had told me time and time again. She'd been telling me for years that she was going to go to Cambridge and get this honors degree that she'd set her heart on. She'd told me so many times that I'd long since ceased to give it any credence. When she told me that she'd actually resigned, I was astounded.

"I thought it would be next year," I said lamely.

"You thought it would be never," she said curtly. Then she looked up and gave me a wonderful smile. One thing about this damned business of going to Cambridge. It had put her into an incomparably sunny mood. Or was that simply the result of seeing me discomfited?

Chapter 3

It was Gloria's evening for visiting parents. Tuesday she had an evening class in mathematics, Wednesday economics, and Thursday evening she visited her parents. She apportioned time for such things, so that I sometimes wondered if I was one of her duties, or time off.

I stayed working for an extra hour or so until there was a phone call from Mr. Gaskell, a recently retired artillery sergeant-major who'd taken over security duties at reception. "There is a lady here. Asking for you by name, Mr. Samson." The security man's hoarse whisper was confidential to the point of being conspiratorial. I wondered if this was in deference to my professional or social obligations.

"Does she have a name, Mr. Gaskell?"

"Lucinda Matthews." I had the feeling that he was reading from the slip that visitors have to fill out.

The name meant nothing to me, but I thought it better not to say so. "I'll be down," I said.

"That would be best," said the security man. "I can't let her upstairs into the building. You understand, Mr. Samson?"

"I understand." I looked out of the window. The low gray cloud that had darkened the sky all day seemed to have come even lower, and in the air there were tiny flickers of light: harbingers of the snow that had been expected all day. Just the sight of it was enough to make me shiver.

By the time I'd locked away my work, and checked the filing cabinets, and got down to the lobby, the mysterious Lucinda had gone.

"A nice little person, sir," Gaskell confided when I asked what the woman was like. He was standing by the reception desk in his dark-blue commissionaire's uniform, tapping his fingers nervously upon the pile of dog-eared magazines that were loaned to visitors who spent a long time waiting here in the drafty lobby. "Well turned out; a lady, if you know my meaning."

I had no notion of his meaning. Gaskell spoke a language that seemed to be entirely his own. He was especially cryptic about dress, rank, and class, perhaps because of the social no-man's-land that all senior NCOs inhabit. I'd had these elliptical utterances from Gaskell before, about all kinds of things. I never knew what he was talking about. "Where did she say she'd meet me?"

"She'd put the car on the pavement, sir. I had to ask her to move it. You know the regulations."

"Yes, I know."

"Car bombs and that sort of thing." No matter how much he rambled, his voice always had the confident tone of a regimental orderly room: an orderly room under his command.

"Where did she say she'd meet me?" I asked yet again. I looked out through the glass doors. The snow had started and was falling fast and in big flakes. The ground was cold, so that it was not melting: it was going to lay. It didn't need more than a couple of cupfuls of that sprinkled over the metropolis before the public-transportation systems all came to a complete halt. Gloria would be at her parents' house by now. She'd gone by train. I wondered if she'd now decide to stay overnight at her parents', or if she'd expect me to go and collect her in the car. Her parents lived at Epsom; too damned near our little nest at Raynes Park for my liking. Gloria said I was frightened of her father. I wasn't frightened of him, but I didn't relish facing intensive questioning from a Hungarian dentist about my relationship with his young daughter.

Gaskell was talking again. "Lovely vehicle. A dark-green

Mercedes. Gleaming! Waxed! Someone is looking after it, you could see that. You'd never get a lady polishing a car. It's not in their nature."

"Where did she go, Mr. Gaskell?"

"I told her the best car park for her would be Elephant and Castle." He went to the map on the wall to show me where the Elephant and Castle was. Gaskell was a big man, and he'd retired at fifty. I wondered why he hadn't found a pub to manage. He would have been wonderful behind a bar counter. The previous week, when I'd been asking him about the train service to Portsmouth, he'd confided to me—amid a barrage of other information—that that's what he would have liked to be doing.

"You told me all that, Mr. Gaskell. I need to know where she's meeting me."

"Sandy's," he said again. "You knew it well, she said." He watched me carefully. Ever since our office address had been so widely published, thanks to the public-spirited endeavors of "investigative journalists," there had been strict instructions that staff must not frequent any local bars, pubs, or clubs, because of the regular presence of eavesdroppers of various kinds, amateur and professional.

"I wish you'd write these things down," I said. "I've never heard of it. Do you know where she means? Is it a café, or what?"

"Not a café I've ever heard of," said Gaskell, frowning and sucking his teeth. "Nowhere near here with a name like that." And then, as he remembered, his face lit up. "Big Henry's! That's what she said: Big Henry's."

"Big Henty's," I said, correcting him. "Tower Bridge Road. Yes, I know it."

Yes, I knew it, and my heart sank. I knew exactly the kind of "informant" who was likely to be waiting for me in Big Henty's: an ear-bender with open palm outstretched. And I had planned an evening at home alone with a coal fire, the carcass of Sunday's duck, a bottle of wine, and a book. I looked at the door and I looked at Gaskell. And I wondered if the sensible thing wouldn't be to forget about Lucinda, and whoever she was fronting for, and drive straight home and ignore the whole thing. The chances were that I'd never hear from the mysterious Lucinda again. This town was filled with people who knew me a long time ago and suddenly remembered me when they needed a few pounds from the public purse in exchange for some ancient and unreliable intelligence material.

"If you'd like me to come along, Mr. Samson . . ." said Gaskell suddenly, and allowed his offer to hang in the air.

So Gaskell thought there was some strong-arm business in the offing. Well, he was a game fellow. Surely he was too old for that sort of thing; and certainly I was.

"That's very kind of you, Mr. Gaskell," I said, "but the prospect is boredom rather than any rough stuff."

"Whatever you say," said Gaskell, unable to keep the disappointment from his voice.

It was the margin of disbelief that made me feel I had to follow it up. I didn't want it to look as if I was nervous. Damn it! Why wasn't I brave enough not to care what the Gaskells of this world thought about me?

Tower Bridge Road is a major South London thoroughfare that leads to the river, or, rather, to the curious neo-Gothic bridge which, for many foreigners, symbolizes the capital. This is Southwark. From here Chaucer's pilgrims set out for Canterbury; a couple of centuries later, Shakespeare's Globe Theatre was built upon the marshes. For Victorian London this shopping street, with a dozen brightly lighted pubs, barrel organs, and late-night street markets, was the center of one of the capital's most vigorous neighborhoods. Here filthy slums, smoke-darkened factories, and crowded sweatshops stood side by side with neat leafy squares where scrawny clerks and pot-bellied shopkeepers asserted their social superiority.

Now it was dark and squalid and silent. Well-intentioned bureaucrats nowadays sent shop assistants home early, street traders were banished, almost empty pubs sold highly taxed watery lager, and the factories were derelict: a textbook example of urban blight, with yuppies nibbling the leafy bits.

Back in the days before women's lib, designer jeans, and deep-dish pizza, Big Henty's snooker hall, with its "ten full-size tables, fully licensed bar, and hot food," was the Atheneum of Southwark. The narrow doorway and its dimly lit staircase gave entry to a cavernous hall conveniently sited over a particularly good eel-and-pie shop.

Now, alas, the eel-and-pie shop was a video rental "club" where posters in primary colors depicted half-naked film stars firing heavy machine guns from the hip. But in its essentials Big Henty's was largely unchanged. The lighting was exactly the same as I remembered it, and any billiards hall is judged on its lighting. Although it was very quiet, every table was in use. The green baize tabletops glowed like ten large aquariums, their water still until suddenly across them brightly colored fish darted, snapped, and disappeared.

Big Henty wasn't there, of course. Big Henty died in 1905. Now the hall was run by a thin white-faced fellow of about forty. He supervised the bar. There was not a wide choice: these billiard-playing men didn't appreciate the curious fizzy mixtures that keep barmen busy in cocktail bars. At Big Henty's you drank whisky or vodka; strong ale or Guinness with tonic and soda water for the abstemious. For the hungry there were "toasted" sandwiches that came soft, warm, and plastic-wrapped from the microwave oven.

"Evening, Bernard. Started to snow, has it?" What a memory the man had. It was years since I'd been here. He picked up his lighted cigarette from the Johnnie Walker ashtray and inhaled on it briefly before putting it back into position. I remembered his chain-smoking, the way he lit one cigarette from another but put them in his mouth only rarely. I'd brought Dicky Cruyer here one evening long ago, to make contact with a loud-mouthed fellow who worked in the East German embassy. It had come to nothing, but I remember Dicky describing the barman as the keeper of the sacred flame.

I responded, "Half of Guinness . . . Sydney." His name came to me in that moment of desperation. "Yes, the snow is starting to pile up."

It was bottled Guinness, of course. This was not the place where a connoisseur of stout and porter would come to savor beverages tapped from the wood. But he poured it down the side of the glass, holding his thumb under the point of impact, to show he knew the folklore, and he put exactly the right-size head of light-brown foam upon the black beer. "In the back room." Delicately he shook the last drops from the bottle and tossed it away without a glance. "Your friend. In the back room. Behind Table Four."

I picked up my glass of beer and sipped. Then I turned slowly to survey the room. Big Henty's back room had proved its worth to numerous fugitives over the years. It had always been tolerated by authority. The CID officers from the Borough High Street police station found it a convenient place to meet their informants. I walked across the hall. Beyond the tasseled and fringed lights that hung over the billiards tables, the room was dark. The spectators—not many this evening— sat on wooden benches along the walls, their gray faces no more than smudges, their dark clothes invisible.

Walking unhurriedly, and pausing to watch a tricky shot, I took my beer across to Table Four. One of the players, a man in the favored costume of dark trousers, loose-collared white shirt, and unbuttoned waistcoat, moved the scoreboard pointer and watched me with expressionless eyes as I opened the door marked "Staff" and went inside.

There was a smell of soap and disinfectant. It was a small storeroom with a window through which the billiards hall could be seen if you pulled aside the dirty net curtain. On the other side of the room there was another window, a larger one, which looked down upon Tower Bridge Road. From the street below came the sound of cars slurping through the slush.

"Bernard." It was a woman's voice. "I thought you weren't going to come."

I had sat down on the bench before I recognized her in the dim light. "Cindy!" I said. "Good God, Cindy!"

"You'd forgotten I existed."

"Of course I hadn't." I'd only forgotten that Cindy Prettyman's full name was Lucinda and that she might have reverted to her maiden name. "Can I get you a drink?"

She held up her glass. "It's tonic water. I'm not drinking these days."

"I just didn't expect you here," I said. I looked through the net curtain at the tables.

"Why not?"

"Yes, why not," I said, and laughed briefly. "When I think how many times Jim made me swear I was giving up the game forever." In the old days, when Jim Prettyman was working alongside me, he taught me to play snooker. He played an exhibition-class game, and his wife, Cindy, was something of an expert too.

Cindy was older than Jim by a year or two. Her father was a steelworker in Scunthorpe: a socialist of the old school. She'd got a scholarship to Reading University. She said she'd never had any ambition but for a career in the civil service since her schooldays. I don't know if it was true, but it went down well at the Selection Board. She wanted Treasury but got Foreign Office, and eventually got Jim Prettyman, who went there too. Then Jim came over to work in the Department, and I saw a lot of him. We used to come here, me, Fiona, Jim, and Cindy, after work on Fridays. We'd play billiards to decide who would buy dinner at Enzo's, a little Italian restaurant in the Old Kent Road. Invariably it was me. It was a joke, really—my way of repaying him for the lesson. And I was the eldest and making more money. Then the Prettymans moved out of town, to Edgware. Jim got a raise and bought a full-size table of his own, and then we stopped coming to Big Henty's. And Jim invited us over to his place for Sunday lunch, and a game, sometimes. But it was never the same after that.

"Do you still play?" she asked.

"It's been years. And you?"

"Not since Jim went."

"I'm sorry about what happened, Cindy."

"Jim and me. Yes, I wanted to talk to you about that. You saw him on Friday."

"Yes. How do you know?"

"Charlene. I've been talking to her a lot lately."

"Charlene?"

"Charlene Birkett. The tall girl we used to let our upstairs flat to . . . in Edgware. Now she's Jim's secretary."

"I saw her. I didn't recognize her. I thought she was American." So that's why she'd smiled at me: I'd thought it was my animal magnetism.

"Yes," said Cindy, "she went to New York and couldn't get a job until Jim fixed up for her to work for him. There was never anything between them," she added hurriedly. "Charlene's a sweet girl. They say she's really blossomed since living there and wearing contact lenses."

"I remember her," I said. I did remember her: a stooped, mousy girl with glasses and frizzy hair, quite unlike the shapely Amazon I'd seen in Jim's office. "Yes, she's changed a lot."

"People do change when they live in America."

"But you didn't want to go?"

"America? My dad would have died." You could hear the Northern accent now. "I didn't want to change." Then she said solemnly, "Oh, doesn't that sound awful. I didn't mean that exactly."

"People go there and they get richer," I said. "That's what the real change is."

"Jim got the divorce in Mexico," she said. "Someone told me that it's not really legal. A friend of mine—she works in the American embassy—she said Mexican marriages and divorces aren't legal here. Is that true, Bernard?"

"I don't imagine that the Mexican ambassador is living in sin, if that's what you mean."

"But how do I stand, Bernard? He married this other woman. I mean, how do I stand now?"

"Didn't you talk to him about it?" My eyes had become accustomed to the darkness now, and I could see her better. She hadn't changed much; she was the same tiny bundle of brains and nervous energy. She was short with a full figure but had never been plump. She was attractive in an austere way, with dark hair that she kept short so it would be no trouble to her. But her nose was reddened, as if she had a cold, and her eyes were watery.

"He asked me to go with him." She was proud of that, and she wanted me to know.

"I know he did. He told everyone that you would change your mind."

"No. I had my job!" she said, her voice rising as if to repeat the arguments they'd had about it.

"It's a difficult decision," I said, to calm her. In the silence there was a sudden loud throbbing noise close by. She jumped almost out of her skin. Then she realized that it was the freezer cabinet in the corner, and she smiled.

"Perhaps I should have done. It would have been better, I suppose."

"It's too late now, Cindy," I said hurriedly, before she started to go weepy on me.

"I know; I know; I know." She got a handkerchief from her pocket but rolled it up and gripped it tight in her red-knuckled hand, as if resolving not to sob.

"Perhaps you should see a lawyer," I said.

"What do they know," she said contemptuously. "I've seen three lawyers. They pass you on, one from the other, like a parcel, and by the time I was finished paying out all the fees, I knew that some law books say one thing and other law books say different."

"The lawyers can quote from the law books until they are blue in the face," I said. "But eventually people have to sort out the solutions with each other. Going to lawyers is just an expensive way of putting off what you're going to have to do anyway."

"Is that what you really think, Bernard?" she said.

"More or less," I said. "Buying a house, making a will, getting divorced. Providing you know what you want, you don't need a lawyer for any of that."

"Yes," she said. "What's more important than getting married? You don't go to a lawyer to do that."

"In foreign countries you do," I told her. "Couples don't get married without signing a marriage contract. They never have this sort of problem that you have. They decide it all beforehand."

"It sounds a bit cold-blooded."

"Maybe it is, but marriage can be a bit too hot-blooded too."

"Was yours?" She released her grip on the tiny handkerchief and spread it out on her lap to see the colored border and the embroidered initials "LP."

"My marriage?" I said. "Too hot-blooded?"

"Yes."

"Perhaps." I sipped my drink. It was a long time since I'd had one of these heavy bitter-tasting brews. I wiped the froth from my lips; it was good. "I thought I knew Fiona, but I suppose I didn't know her well enough."

"She was so lovely. I know she loved you, Bernard."

"I think she did."

"She showed me that fantastic engagement ring and said, Bernie sold his Ferrari to buy that for me."

"It sounds like a line from afternoon television," I said, "but it was a very old, battered Ferrari."

"She loved you, Bernard."

"People change, Cindy. You said that yourself."

"Did it affect the children much?"

"Billy seemed to take it in his stride, but Sally . . . She was all right until I brought a girlfriend home. Lots of crying at night. But I think she's adjusted now." I said it more because I wanted it to be true than because I believed it. I worried about the children, worried a lot, but that was none of Cindy's business.

"Gloria Kent, the one you work with?"

This Cindy knew everything. Well, the FO had always been Whitehall's gossip exchange. "That's right," I said.

"It's difficult for children," said Cindy. "I suppose I should be thankful that we didn't have any."

"You're right," I said. I drank some Guinness and sneaked a look at the time.

"But, on the other hand, if we'd had kids, perhaps Jim wouldn't have wanted to go so much. He wanted to prove himself, you see. Lately I've wondered if he blamed himself that we never were able to have children."

"Jim was talking about that time when the kitchen caught fire," I said.

"Jim spilled the oil. He's always been clumsy."

"Fiona didn't do it?"

"She took the blame," said Cindy with a sigh. "Jim could never admit to making a mistake. That was his nature."

"Yes, Fiona took the blame," I said. "She told me Jim did it but she really took the blame . . . the insurance . . . everything."

"Fiona was a remarkable woman, Bernard, you know that. Fiona had such self-confidence that blame never touched her. I admired her. I would have given almost anything to be like Fiona, she was always so calm and poised."

I didn't respond. Cindy drank some of her tonic water and smoothed her dress and cleared her throat and then said, "The reason I wanted to talk to you, Bernard, is to see what the Department will do."

"What the Department will do?" I said. I was puzzled.

"Do about Jim," said Cindy. I could see her squeezing the handkerchief in repeated movements, like someone exercising her hands.

"About Jim." I blew dust from my spectacle lenses and began to polish them. They'd picked up grease from the air, and polishing just made them more smeary. The only way to get them clean was to wash them with kitchen detergent under the warm tap. The optician advised against this method, but I went on doing it anyway. "I'm not sure I know what you mean, Cindy."

"Will they pay me or this American woman, this so-called wife?" she said angrily.

"Pay you?" I put my glasses on and looked at her.

"Don't be so difficult, Bernard. I must know. I must. Surely you can see that."

"Pay you what?"

Her face changed. "Holy Mary!" she said in that way that only churchgoing Catholics say such things. "You don't know!" It was a lament. "Jim is dead. They killed him Friday night, when he left the office after seeing you. They shot him. Six bullets."

"Last Friday."

"In the car park. It was dark. He didn't stand a chance. There were two of them; waiting for him. No one told you?"

"No."

"Don't think me callous, Bernard. But I want to put in a claim for his pension before this other woman. What should I do?"

"Is there a pension, Cindy? I would have thought all that would have been wound up when he left."

"Left? He's never stopped working for the Department."

"You're wrong about that, Cindy," I said.

She became excited. "Do you think I don't know! By God, I saw . . ." She stopped suddenly, as if she might be saying something I wasn't entitled to know.

"I was there in Washington asking him to come to London to give evidence. He wouldn't come," I explained quietly.

"That was the cover-up, Bernard," she said. She had her temper under control now, but she was still angry. "They want him in London, but it was going to be done as if he came under protest."

"It fooled me," I said.

"Jim got into very deep water," she said. "Was it the money you had to talk to him about?"

I nodded.

"Jim arranged all that," she said sadly. "Millions and millions of pounds in some secret foreign bank account. A lot of people were empowered to sign: Jim was one of them."

"You're not saying that Jim was killed because of this, are you, Cindy?"

"What was it, then, robbery?" she said scornfully.

"Washington is a rough place," I told her.

"Two men; six bullets?" she said. "Damned funny thieves."

"Let me get you a proper drink, Cindy. I need time to think about all this."

Chapter 4

I was in Dicky Cruyer's very comfortable office, sitting in his Eames chair and waiting for him to return from his meeting with the Deputy. He'd promised to be no more than ten minutes, but what the Deputy had to say to him took longer than that.

When Dicky arrived he made every effort to look his youthful carefree self, but I guessed that the Deputy had given him a severe wigging about the Bizet crisis. "All okay?" I said.

For a moment he looked at me as if trying to remember who I was and what I was doing there. He ran his fingers back through his curly hair. He was slim; and handsome in a little-boy way which he cultivated assiduously.

"The Deputy has to be kept up to date," said Dicky, allowing himself to express a measured amount of condescension about the Deputy's inexperience. As long as Sir Henry, the Director-General, had been coming in regularly, the Deputy, Sir Percy Babcock, had scarcely shown his face in the building. But since the old man's attendance had become intermittent, the Deputy had taken command with all the zeal of the newly converted. The first major change he'd wrought was to tell Dicky to wear clothes more in keeping with his responsibilities. Dicky's extensive wardrobe of faded designer jeans, sneakers, tartan shirts, and the gold medallion that he wore at his neck had not been seen recently. Now, in line with the rest of the male staff, he was wearing a suit every day. I found it difficult to adjust to this new, sober Dicky.

"You weren't at Charles Billingsly's farewell gathering last night," said Dicky. "Champagne . . . very stylish."

"I didn't hear about it," I said. Billingsly—German Desk's more-or-less useless Data Centre liaison man—wasn't a close friend of mine. I suppose he thought I might drink too much of his expensive fizz. "Are we getting rid of him?"

"A super-hush-hush assignment to Honkers. Forty-eight hours' notice is all they gave him. So he didn't let you know about the party? Well, it was all a rush for him."

"What would Hong Kong need him for?"

"No one knows, not even Charles. Hurry and wait. That's how it goes, isn't it?"

"Maybe the Deputy just wanted to get rid of him," I suggested.

Dicky's eyes glittered. After his little session on the carpet, it probably made him wonder if he might not one day find himself on a fast plane to distant places. "Get rid of Charles? Why?"

"I've no idea," I said.

"No. Charles is a good sort."

Unbidden, Dicky's secretary arrived with a large silver-plated tray bearing the Spode chinaware and a large pot of freshly ground coffee made just the way Dicky liked it. I suppose she hoped it would put Dicky into a better frame of mind, as sometimes a heavy shot of caffeine did. He bent over it and gave low murmurs of approval before pouring some coffee for himself. He went and sat down behind the big rosewood table that he used as his desk before he tasted the coffee appreciatively. "Damn good!" he pronounced and drank some more. "Pour yourself a cup," he said when he was quite sure it was okay.

I took one of the warmed cups, poured some for myself, and added cream. It always came with cream, even though Dicky drank his coffee black. I often wondered why. For a moment we drank our coffee in silence. I had the feeling that Dicky needed a few minutes to recover from his meeting.

"He's become an absolute despot lately," said Dicky at last. Having devoured a large cup of coffee, he took a small cigar from his pocket, lit it, and blew smoke. "I wish I could make him understand that it's not like running his law business. I can't get a book down from the shelf and read the answers to him."

"He'll get the hang of it," I said.

"In time, he will," agreed Dicky. "But by then I'll be old and gray." That might be quite a long time, for Dicky was young and fit and two years my junior. He flicked ash into the big cut-glass ashtray on his desk and kept looking at the carpet as if lost in thought.

I pulled my paperwork from its cardboard folder and said, "Do you want to run through this stuff? " I brandished it at him, but he continued to stare at the carpet.

"He's talking about vertical reorganization."

I said, "What's that?"

Dicky, short-listed for the Stalin Prize in office politics, said, "Jesus Christ, Bernard. Vertical planning! Dividing the German Desk up into groups, region by region. He told me that I'd have Berlin, as if that would make me overjoyed. Berlin! With other desks for Bonn and Hamburg and so on. A separate unit would liaise with the Americans in Munich. Can you imagine it!"

"That idea has been kicking around for ages," I said. I began to sort out the work I'd brought for him. I knew that getting him to look at it would be difficult in his present agitated mood, so I put all the papers that required a signature on top. There were five of them.

"It's ridiculous!" said Dicky, so loudly that his secretary looked in through the door to see if everything was all right. She was a new secretary, or she would have made herself scarce when there was a chance of encountering Dicky's little tantrums.

"It will happen sooner or later, I suppose," I said. I got my pen out so that Dicky could sign while he talked about something else. Sometimes it was easier like that.

"You'd heard about it before?" said Dicky incredulously, suddenly realizing what I'd said.

"Oh, yes, a year or more ago, but it had some other name then."

"Ye gods, Bernard! I wish you'd told me."

I put the papers on his desk and gave him the ball-point pen and watched him sign his name. I hadn't heard of the vertical-planning scheme before, of course, but I guessed that the Deputy had simply invented something that would goad Dicky into more energetic action, and I thought it better not to let the old boy down. "And these you should look at," I said, indicating the most important ones.

"You'll have to go and see Frank," he said as he signed the final one, then plucked at the corners of the rest of the stuff to see if anything looked interesting enough to read.

"Okay," I said. He looked up at me. He'd expected me to object to a trip to Berlin, but he'd caught me at a good time. It was a month or more since I'd been to Berlin, and there were reasons, both official and social, for a trip there. "And what do I tell Frank?" I wanted to get it quite clear, because we had this absurd system in which Dicky and Frank Harrington—the Berlin Resident and as old as Methuselah—had equal authority.

He looked up from the carpet and said, "I don't want to rub Frank up the wrong way. It's not up to me to tell him how to run his Berlin Field Unit. Frank knows more about the Operations side of his bailiwick than all the rest of us put together." That was all true, of course, but it wasn't often the line Dicky took.

"We're talking about Bizet, I take it?"

"Right. Frank may want to put someone in. After all, Frankfurt an der Oder is only a stone's throw from where he is."

"It's not the distance, Dicky. It's . . ."

He immediately held up his hand in defense. "Sure. I know, I know, I know."

"Are you hoping he'll have done something already?"

"I just want his advice," said Dicky.

"Well, we both know what Frank's advice will be," I said. "Do nothing. Just the same advice that he gives us about everything."

"Frank's been there a long time," said Dicky, who had survived many a crisis and reshuffle by following "do-nothing" policies.

I made sure Dicky had signed everything in the right place. Then I drank the coffee and left it at that for a bit. But this seemed a good opportunity to quiz him about the Prettyman business. "Remember Prettyman?" I said as casually as I could manage.

"Should I?"

"Jim Prettyman: ended up in 'black boxes.' Left and went to America."

"Codes and Ciphers, downstairs?" It was not a region into which Dicky ever ventured.

"He was on the Special Operations Committee with Bret. He was always trying to organize holidays where you could look at tombs and no one ever put their name down. Wonderful billiards player. Don't you remember how we went down to Big Henty's one night and he made some fantastic break?"

"I've never been to Big Henty's in my life."

"Of course you have, Dicky. Lots of times. Jim Prettyman. A young fellow who got that job in Washington."

"Sometimes I think you must know everyone in this building," said Dicky.

"I thought you knew him," I said lamely.

"A word to the wise, Bernard." Dicky was holding a finger aloft, as if testing for the direction of the wind. "If I was in this room talking to you about this Prettyman fellow, you'd change the subject to talk about Frank Harrington and the Bizet business. No offense intended, old chum, but it's true. Think about it."

"I'm sure you're right, Dicky."

"You must try and concentrate upon the subject in hand. Have you ever done any yoga?" He pushed aside the papers that I'd suggested he should read.

"No, Dicky," I said.

"I did a lot of yoga at one time." He ran a finger across the papers, as if reading a contents list. "It trains the mind: helps the power of concentration."

"I'll look into that," I promised, taking from him the signed papers that he had decided not to read, and stuffing them into the cardboard folder.

When I stood up, Dicky, still looking at the carpet, said,

"My mother's cousin died and left me a big lion skin. I was wondering whether to have it in here."

"It would look just right," I said, indicating the antique furniture and the framed photos that covered the wall behind him.

"I had it in the drawing room at home, but some of our friends made a bit of fuss about shooting rare animals and that sort of thing."

"Don't worry about that, Dicky," I said. "That's just because they're jealous."

"That's just what I told Daphne," he said. "After all, the damned thing's dead. I can't bring a lion back to life, can I?"

Chapter 5

Many civilians have a lifelong obsession about what it would be like to be in the army. Some like the idea of uniforms, horses, trumpets, and flags; others just want clearly expressed orders, and a chance to carry them out in exchange for hot meals on the table every day. For some men the army represents a challenge they never faced; for others a cloistered, cozy masculine retreat from reality.

Which of these aspects of the soldier's life Frank Harrington found attractive—or whether it was something entirely different—I never knew. But whenever Frank was not in his office, or in the splendid Grunewald mansion that he'd arranged should be one of the "perks" of being the Berlin Resident, I knew I'd find him in some squalid dugout, sitting in the middle of a bunch of begrimed infantry officers looking thoroughly happy as he told them how to fight their war.

This day, dressed in borrowed army togs with mud on his

knees and elbows, he was delivered to the Grunewald house in a big army staff car.

"I'm awfully sorry, Frank," I said.

"I was only playing soldiers," he said in that disarming way he had. "And Dicky said it was urgent."

He looked as if he was going to conduct me straight into his study. "It's not so urgent that you can't change and take a shower," I said. I gave him the report from London.

He took it and shook it at his ear to listen for its rattle. He grinned. We both knew Dicky. "Go into the drawing room and get yourself a drink, Bernard," he said. "Ring for Tarrant if you can't find what you want. You're going to eat with me, I hope?"

"Yes. I'd like that, Frank."

He was a wellspring of cheer after his day with the soldiers. Halfway up the stairs he turned to say, "Welcome home, Bernard," knowing how delighted I would be at such a greeting. For, no matter where I went or what I did, Berlin would always be home for me. My father had been Resident long ago —before they were provided with a grand mansion in which to live and an entertainment allowance—and Berlin held all my happy childhood recollections.

When, after thirty minutes or more, Frank returned, he was dressed in what for him were informal clothes: an old gray herringbone-tweed jacket and flannels, but the starched shirt and striped tie wouldn't have disgraced any mess. Just as I was able to make new clothes look shabby, so Frank was able to invest even his oldest garments with a spruce look. His cuffs emerged just the right amount, and there was a moiré kerchief in his top pocket and hand-sewn oxfords that were polished to perfection. He went across to the drinks trolley and poured himself a large Plymouth gin with a dash of bitters. "What have you got there?" he asked.

"I'm all right, Frank," I said.

"Wouldn't you rather have a real drink?"

"I'm trying to cut back on the hard stuff, Frank."

"That bottle must have been on that trolley for years. Is it still all right?" He picked up the bottle I'd poured my drink from, and studied the label with interest, and then he looked at me. "Vermouth? That's not like you, Bernard."

"Delicious," I said.

He came and sat opposite me. His face had the war-painted look that dedicated skiers wore at this time of year. His skin was dark, with pale surrounds where his goggles had been. Frank knew a thing or two about the good life. I didn't ask after his wife. She spent most of the time at their house in England nowadays. She had never liked Berlin, and rumors said there had been a row when Frank accepted the invitation to stay on past his official retirement date.

He'd read the interim report in his bath, he told me. We knew that it had been roughly cobbled together in London, and we both knew it was just a lengthy way of saying nothing at all. He flicked through it very quickly again and said, "Does Dicky want me to deposit someone in there?"

"He's going to great pains not to say so," I said.

"I'll do anything for the poor bastards who are in trouble," he said. "But this is Berlin. I can't think of anyone here who could go to Frankfurt an der bloody Oder and do anything to help them." He touched his blunt military mustache. It was going very gray.

"They don't like to sit in London doing nothing," I said.

"How do they think I like it?" said Frank. Just for a moment his face and his voice revealed the strain of the job. I suppose there were plenty of agents being picked up all the time, but it was only when there was monitored Soviet radio traffic about them that London got interested and concerned. "The army have got wind of it," said Frank. "They're keen to try their hand."

He must have seen my face go white, and my teeth clench, or whatever happened when I became so terrified that I wanted to scream. "The army?" I said, holding tight to my drink and keeping my voice under control.

"The Brigadier was reminding me about the Military Mission staff we have with the Russian army headquarters. They are able to move about a little more freely nowadays."

"What else did your Brigadier say?"

"He was quoting the behavior of these GRU bastards our chaps have to put up with at Bünde. Counting those with the French army at Baden-Baden, and those with the Yanks, there are about fifty Soviet Military Mission staffers. GRU agents every one, and many of them with scientific training. They wear leather jackets over their uniforms and deliberately muddy their car registration plates so they're not recognized while they go pushing their way into, and photographing, everything that interests them." He grinned. " 'What about tit for tat?' That's what the Brigadier says."

"You didn't tell your army pal about Bizet?"

"I'm not senile, Bernard."

"The idea of some keen young subaltern sniffing around in Frankfurt an der Oder is enough to give me a nightmare."

"I shouldn't have mentioned it."

"You said the army had wind of it," I reminded him.

"Did I? I should have said that the army know we have a crisis of some sort." He looked at me and added, "They have a good radio-monitoring service, Bernard."

"For listening to Russian-army signals," I said.

"Along the border, that is true. But here in Berlin—right in the middle of the DDR—they hear all the domestic stuff. They monitor GRU and KGB traffic; they like to know what's going on. I would never object to that, Bernard. In an outpost like this, the army need to keep a finger on the pulse."

"Maybe I will have something stronger," I said. But at that moment Frank's German maid came in to say that dinner was served.

I pushed all my worries about what Frank might have said

to his army cronies to the back of my mind. We sat in the grand dining room, just me and Frank, at one end of the long polished table. He'd had someone decant a bottle of really good claret: the empty bottle was on the sideboard. It was something of an honor. Frank kept his best wines for people either important enough to merit them, or choosy enough to notice. He poured some for me to taste when the egg-and-bacon tart arrived. The portions were very small. I suspected that the cook was trying to eke out Frank's meal and make enough for me. Frank seemed not to notice. He wanted to hear all the latest gossip from the Department, and I told him how the Deputy was slowly but surely changing the Department to his own wishes.

From my own point of view, I rather welcomed the new ideas. It was time the old gang were shaken up a bit. Frank agreed, but with less enthusiasm.

"I'm too old to welcome change just for the sake of change, Bernard. I was in the Department with your father back in 1943. I did a training course with Sir Henry Clevemore —'Pimples,' we called him—a damned great hulking kid. He fell into a drainage ditch on one of the assault courses. It needed four of us to haul him out." He drank some more wine, and after a reflective pause added, "My wife says I've given my life to the Department, and a large chunk of her life too!" It was a heartfelt declaration of pride, resentment, and regret.

He went on talking about the Department through the cottage pie, the bread-and-butter pudding, and the cheddar cheese. No matter how long he lived here, and how assimilated he became, the output from Frank's kitchen remained defiantly British public-school. I was happy to listen to him, especially when he mentioned my father. He knew that, of course, and all the stories he told showed my father in such a glorious light that I knew he was just putting it on for me. "Your dad sat for days and days in some filthy apartment here in Berlin-Wedding with only this German fellow for company: arguing and swearing most of the time, according to your dad's account. They were waiting for news of Hitler's assassination. When the news came that the assassination attempt had failed, in came this Gestapo agent. Your dad was all ready to jump out of the window, but it turned out that it was the other chap's brother. . . . I'm probably getting it all muddled," said Frank with a smile. "And I'm sure it was all just one of your father's yarns. But whenever your dad could be persuaded to tell that story he'd have me, and everyone else, in fits of laughter." Frank had some more wine and ate some cheese. "None of the rest of us had ever been in Nazi Germany, of course. We hung on your dad's every word. Sometimes he'd be pulling our leg mercilessly."

"The other day someone hinted that the Department might get to me through my father," I said, as casually as I could.

"Pressure you?"

"That was the implication. How could they do that, Frank? Did Dad do anything . . ."

"Are you serious, Bernard?"

"I want to know, Frank."

"Then may I suggest you seek clarification from whoever gave you this bizarre idea."

I changed the subject. "And Fiona?" I asked, as casually as I was able.

He looked up sharply. I suppose he knew how much I still missed her. "She keeps a very low profile."

"But she's still in East Berlin?"

"Very much so. Flourishing, or so I hear. Why?"

"I was just curious."

"Put her out of your mind, Bernard. It's all over now. I suffered for you, but now it's time to forget the past. Tell me about the new house. Do the children like having a garden?"

Our conversation was devoted to domestic small talk. By the time we went back to the drawing room to drink coffee,

Frank was in a mellow mood. I said, "Remember the last time we were together in this room, Frank?"

He looked at me and after a moment's thought said, "The night you came over asking me to get Bret Rensselaer off the hook. Is it really that long ago? Three years?"

"You were packing your Duke Ellington records," I said. "They were all across the floor here."

"I thought I was retiring and going back to England." He looked round, remembering it all, and said, "It changed my life, I suppose. By now I would have been pensioned off and growing roses."

"And been Sir Frank Harrington," I said. "I'm sorry about the way it all worked out, Frank." It was generally agreed that the debacle resulting from my intervention had deprived Frank of the Knighthood he'd set his heart on. London Central had been saved from humiliation by my warning and Frank's unilateral action, but they'd still not forgiven either of us. We'd been proved right, and in the eyes of the mandarins of the Foreign Office that was a rare and unpardonable sin.

"It must be nearer four years," he said, unrolling his tobacco pouch and stuffing his Balkan Sobranie tobacco into the bowl of a curly pipe. Oh God, was Frank going to smoke that pipe of his? "I was disappointed at the time, but I've got over it now."

"I suppose Bret got the worst of it."

"I suppose so," said Frank, lighting his pipe.

"Last I heard, he was having night-and-day nursing care and sinking fast," I said. "He's not still alive?"

Frank took his time getting his pipe going before he replied. Then he said, "Bret hung on for a long time, but now he's gone." He smiled in that distant way of his and started puffing contentedly. I moved back from him. I could never get used to Frank's pipe. He said, "That's not to be repeated. Perhaps I shouldn't have told you. I was told in confidence; the Department have said nothing yet."

"Poor Bret. That night I flew out of Berlin, there was a roomful of men in white coats swearing he couldn't live beyond the weekend."

"His brother arrived with some damned American general in tow. Bret was hauled aboard a U.S. Air Force plane and flown out. I heard they'd put him into that hospital in Washington where they treat the U.S. presidents. He was in all kinds of hospitals for a long time: you know what the Americans are like. And then he went to convalesce in a house he owns in the Virgin Islands. He sent me a postcard from there: 'Wish you were here,' palm trees, and a beach. Berlin was deep under snow, and the central heating was giving trouble. I didn't think it was so funny at the time. I wondered if he meant that he wished I'd stopped the bullet that he'd taken. I don't know. I never will know, I suppose."

I said nothing.

There was a lot of prodding at the tobacco. Frank had a special little steel device for pushing it around. He tended that pipe like some Scots engineer at the boiler of an ancient and well-beloved tramp steamer. And it gave him time to think about what he was going to say. "I've never been told officially, of course. I thought it was funny, the way that Bret always made such a big performance of being English. And then he's injured and he's off to America." Another pause. "As I say, Bret never died officially; he just faded away."

"Like old soldiers," I said.

"What? Oh, yes, I see what you mean."

Then the conversation moved to other matters. I asked about Frank's son, an airline pilot who'd recently gone from British Airways to one of the domestic airlines. He was flying smaller planes on shorter routes, but he was at home with his wife almost every night and making more money too. In the old days Frank's son had often got to Berlin, but nowadays it was not on any of his routes, and Frank admitted that sometimes he felt lonely.

I looked around. The house was all beautifully kept up,

but it was a dark, echoing place for one man on his own. I remembered how, many years ago, Frank told me that marriage didn't fit very well with men "in our line of business; women don't like secrets to which they are not a party." I'd thought about it ever since.

Frank asked about mutual friends in Washington, D.C., and after talking about some of them I said, "Do you remember Jim Prettyman?"

"Prettyman? No," said Frank with conviction. Then he asked if everything was all right between me and Gloria. I said it was, because the ever-growing fear that I had, about becoming too dependent upon her, seemed too trivial and childish to discuss.

"Not thinking of marrying again?" Frank asked.

"I'm not free to marry," I reminded him. "I'm still legally married to Fiona, aren't I?"

"Of course."

"I have a nasty feeling she'll try for custody of the children again," I said. I hadn't intended to tell him, but I'd got to the point where I had to tell someone.

"I hope not, Bernard."

"I had a formal letter from my father-in-law. He wants regular access to the children."

He took his pipe from his mouth. "And you think he's in touch with Fiona?"

"I'm not going to rule it out; he's a two-faced old bastard."

"Don't meet trouble halfway, Bernard. What does Gloria think?"

"I haven't told her yet."

"Bernard, you are an ass. You must stop treating her as if she's half-witted. A woman's point of view, Bernard."

"You're right," I said.

"Yes, I am. Stop brooding. Talk to her. She must know the children by now."

"I'd better get going, Frank," I said. "It's been like old times."

"I'm glad you stayed to dinner. I wish I'd known you were coming, I could have laid on some decent grub for you."

"It was just like home," I said.

"Have you got a car?" he asked.

"Yes, thanks."

"I wish you wouldn't rent cars at the airport. It's not good security."

"I suppose you're right," I admitted.

His pipe was burning fiercely now, its smoke so dense that Frank's eyes were half closed against it. "Staying with Frau Hennig?" He always called her Frau Hennig. I don't think he liked her very much, but he hid his emotions about her, as he did about a lot of other things.

"Yes," I said. Out of the corner of my eye I saw Tarrant glide in, scowling. Frank's longtime valet always materialized like the ghost of Hamlet's father. I swear he listened at the door. How else could he always appear at the exactly right— or sometimes no less exactly wrong—moment?

When Frank turned to him, Tarrant said, "Colonel Hampshire phoned to say headquarters won the tournament."

I looked at Frank, who took the pipe from his mouth, smiled at me, and said, "Bridge."

So I'd dragged Frank from some damned officers'-mess bridge final. No doubt the meal we'd eaten was Tarrant's supper. But appearances could be deceptive. Tarrant's big eyebrows were always lowered menacingly, like a bull about to charge. Perhaps he wasn't hungry and resentful: maybe he was drunk.

"Thank you, Tarrant. You can go to bed. I'll see Mr. Samson out."

"Very good, sir."

"Don't go," said Frank to me. "Let's open a bottle of tawny and make a night of it."

Frank's choice in vintage port was always a temptation, but I declined. "I must put my head round the door before Lisl goes to sleep," I said, looking at my watch.

"And what time is that?"

"Pretty damned late," I admitted.

"You heard she's closing down?"

"The hotel? No more than that. Werner wrote me one of his cryptic notes, but that's all he said."

"It's too much for her," said Frank, "and those bloody people who work for her turn up only when they feel like it."

"You don't mean Klara?" Klara was Lisl Hennig's maid and had been for countless ages.

"No, not Klara, of course not. But Klara is very old now. They're a couple of very old ladies. They should both be in a nursing home, not trying to cope with all the problems of a broken-down hotel."

"What will Lisl do?"

"If she takes the advice everyone is giving her, she'll sell the place."

"She's borrowed on it," I said.

He prodded the pipe. "If I know anything about the mentality of bank managers, the bank won't have loaned her more than half of what it will fetch on the market."

"I suppose you're right."

"She'd have enough cash to live her last few years in comfort."

"But the house means such a lot to her."

"She can't have it both ways," said Frank.

"I can't imagine coming to Berlin and not being able to go to Lisl's," I said selfishly. My father had been billeted in that house, and eventually my mother took me there to join him. We lived there all through my schooldays and my youth. Every room, every stick of furniture, every bit of frayed carpet held memories for me. I suppose that was why I was pleased that so little was done to bring it up to date. It was my private museum of nostalgia, and the thought of being deprived of it filled me with dread. It was tantamount to someone's wrenching from me memories of my father.

"Just one?" said Frank. He laid his pipe on the ashtray with reverential care and went to the drinks trolley. "I'm opening the bottle anyway."

"Yes, thanks," I said, changing my mind and sitting down again while Frank poured a glass of his tawny port for me. I said, "The last time I was at Lisl's, only three rooms were occupied."

"That's only half of the trouble," said Frank. "The doctor said running that place is too much for her. He told Werner that he wouldn't give her more than another six months if she doesn't rest completely."

"Poor Lisl."

"Yes, poor Lisl," said Frank, handing me a brimming glass of port wine. There was a sardonic note in his voice: he usually called her Frau Hennig.

"I know you never liked her," I said.

"Come, Bernard. That's not true." He picked up his pipe and got it going again.

"Isn't it?"

"I said she was a Nazi," he said in a measured way, and smiled to acknowledge his dissembling.

"That's nonsense," I said. She was like a second mother to me. Even if Frank was like a second father, I wasn't going to let him get away with such damaging generalizations about her.

"The Hennigs were social climbers in Hitler's time," said Frank. "Her husband was a member of the Party, and a lot of the people she mixed with were damned shady."

"For instance?"

"Don't get so defensive, Bernard. Lisl and her friends were enthusiastic Hitler supporters right up to the time when the Red Army started waving a flag from the Brandenburger Tor." He sipped. "And even after that she only learned to keep her political opinions to herself."

"Maybe," I said grudgingly. It was true that Lisl had always had a quick eye for any failings of socialism.

"And that Lothar Koch . . . Well, we've been through all that before."

Frank was convinced that Lothar Koch, an old friend of Lisl's, had some sort of Nazi past. One of Frank's German pals said Koch was a Gestapo man, but there were always stories about people's being Gestapo men, and Frank had said the same thing about many other people. Sometimes I thought Frank spent more time worrying about the Nazis than he did about the Russians. But that was something common to a lot of the old-timers.

"Lothar Koch was just a clerk," I said. I emptied my glass and got to my feet. "And you're just a romantic, Frank, that's your problem. You're still hoping that Martin Bormann will be discovered helping Hitler to type his memoirs in a tin hut in the rain forest."

Still puffing his pipe, Frank got to his feet and gave me one of his "we'll-see-one-day" smiles. When we got to the door he said, "I'll acknowledge Dicky's memo on the teleprinter, and we'll get together late tomorrow so you can take a verbal back to him. Will that suit you?"

"Just right! I wanted to have a day sightseeing," I said.

He nodded knowingly and without enthusiasm. Frank didn't approve of some of my Berlin acquaintances. "I thought you might," he said.

It was about one-thirty when I got back to Lisl Hennig's little hotel. I'd arranged that Klara should leave the door unlatched for me. I crept up the grand front staircase under crippled cherubs that were yellowing and cobwebbed. A tiny shaded table lamp in the bar spilled its meager light across the parquet floor of the salon, where the enormous Baroque mirrors —stained and speckled—dimly reflected the tables set ready for breakfast.

The pantry near the back stairs had been converted to a bedroom for Lisl Hennig when her arthritis made the stairs a torment to her. There was a wedge of yellow light under her door and a curious intermittent buzzing noise. I tapped lightly.

"Come in, Bernd," she called with no hint in her voice of the frailty I'd been led to expect. She was sitting up in bed, looking as perky as ever, cushions and pillows behind her and newspapers all over the red-and-green quilt. Reading newspapers was Lisl's obsession.

Parchment lampshades cast a rich golden light that made a halo of her disarranged hair. She had a small plastic box in her hands, and she was pushing and pulling at it. "Look at this, Bernd! Just look at it!"

She fiddled with the little box again. A loud buzz with a metallic rattle came from behind me. I was visibly startled, and Lisl laughed.

"Look at it, Bernd. Careful, now! Isn't that wonderful!" She chuckled with delight. I jumped aside as a small olive-colored Jeep came rattling across the carpet, but it swerved aside and rushed headlong at the fireplace, then hit the brass fender with a loud clang before reversing and swinging round —antenna wobbling—to race across the room again.

Lisl, who was wrestling with the levers and steering of this little radio-controlled toy, was almost hysterical with joy. "Have you ever seen anything like it, Bernd?"

"No," I said, not wanting to tell her that every toy shop in the Western world was awash with such amusements.

"It's for Klara's nephew's son," she said, although why Lisl should be playing with it in the small hours was left unexplained. She put the control box alongside a glass of wine on the bedside table where the wind-up gramophone, and a pile of old 78 records, stood at her elbow. "Give me a kiss, Bernd!" she ordered.

I rescued the little toy Jeep from where it had come to a halt on the rumpled carpet and gave her an affectionate hug and kiss. She smelled of snuff, a heavy spicy mixture that she'd spilled down the front of her bed jacket. The idea of losing this crazy old woman was a terrible prospect. She was no less dear to me than my mother.

"How did you get in?" she said, and glared at me. I moved back from her, trying to think of a suitable answer. She put on her glasses so that she could see me better. "How did you get in?"

"I . . ."

"Did that wretched girl leave the door on the latch?" she said angrily. "The times I've told her. We could all be murdered in our beds." She hit the newspaper with her loose fingers, so that it made a loud smack. "Doesn't she read the papers? People are murdered for ten marks in this town nowadays. . . . Muggers! Heroin addicts! Perverts! Violent criminals of all kinds. You only have to go a hundred meters to the Ku-Damm to see them parading up and down! How can she leave the door wide open? I told her to wait up until you arrived. Stupid girl!"

The "stupid girl" was almost Lisl's age and would be up at the crack of dawn collecting the breakfast rolls, making coffee, slicing the sausage and the cheese, and boiling the eggs that are the essential constituents of a German breakfast. Klara deserved her sleep, but I didn't point this out to Lisl. It was better to let her simmer down.

"Where have you been?"

"I had dinner with Frank."

"Frank Harrington: that snake in the grass!"

"What has Frank done?"

"Oh, yes, he's an Englishman. You'd have to defend him."

"I'm not defending him. I don't know what he's done to upset you," I said.

"He's all schmaltz when he wants something, but he thinks only of himself. He's a pig."

"What did Frank do?" I asked.

"Do you want a drink?"

"No thanks, Lisl."

Thus reassured, she drank some of her sherry, or whatever it was, and said, "My double suite on the first floor had a new bathroom only a year or two ago. It's beautiful. It's as good as anywhere in any hotel in Berlin."

"But Frank's got his big house, Lisl."

She waved her hand to tell me I'd got it wrong. "For Sir Clevemore. He stayed here long ago when your father was here. That's before he became a 'sir,' and he'd be happy to stay here now. I know he would."

"Sir Henry?"

"Clevemore."

"Yes, I know."

"Frank got him a suite at the Kempi. Think of the expense. He would have been happier here. I know he would."

"When are we talking about?"

"A month . . . two months ago. Not more."

"You must have made a mistake. Sir Henry has been sick for nearly six months. And he hasn't been in Berlin for about five years."

"Klara saw him in the lobby of the Kempi. She has a friend who works there."

"It wasn't Sir Henry. I told you: he's sick."

"Don't be so obstinate, Bernd. Klara spoke with him. He recognized her. I was so angry. I was going to ring Frank Harrington, but Klara persuaded me not to."

"Klara got it wrong," I said. I didn't like to say that it was the sort of story that Klara had been known to invent just to needle her autocratic and exasperating employer.

"It's a beautiful suite," said Lisl. "You haven't seen that bathroom since it was done. Bidet, thermostatic control for the taps, mirrored walls. Beautiful!"

"Well, it wasn't Sir Henry," I said. "So you can sleep easy on that one. I would know if Sir Henry came to Berlin."

"Why would you know?" she said. She grinned from ear

to ear, delighted to catch me out in a self-contradiction, for I'd always kept up the pretense that I worked for a pharmaceutical company.

"I get to hear these things," I said unconvincingly.

"Good night, Bernd," she said, still smiling. I kissed her again and went upstairs to bed.

As my foot touched the first stair there came a sudden blast of sound. A Dixieland band, with too much brass, giving "I'm Forever Blowing Bubbles" a cruel battering. The volume was ear-splitting. No wonder Lisl's hotel wasn't overcrowded.

I had my usual garret room at the top of the house, the room I'd had as a child. It was a cramped room, overlooking the back of the house and the courtyard. It was chilly at this time of year. The effects of the hot-water pump didn't seem to reach up to the top of the house nowadays, so the massive radiator was no more than tepid. But the indomitable Klara had put a hot-water bottle between the crisp linens of my bed, and I climbed into it content.

Perhaps I should have been more restrained when drinking my way through Frank's big pot of strong coffee, for I remained awake for hours thinking about Fiona, who would by now be tucked up in bed somewhere just a few blocks away. In my mind's eye I saw her so clearly. Would she be alone, or were there two people in that bed? A deluge of memories came flooding into my mind. But I forced myself to think of other matters. Lisl and what would become of the old house after she sold it. It was a valuable site: so near the Ku-Damm. Any speculator would do what all speculators do everywhere: chase out the residents and the family-owned shops and old-fashioned eating places, bulldoze everything in sight to build ugly concrete-and-glass offices that yielded high rent for landlords and high taxes for the government. It was a depressing thought.

And I thought about Klara's provocative little story about spotting the Director-General in the Hotel Kempinski. It didn't make sense, for a number of reasons. First, the D-G was sick and had been for months. Second, he hated to travel anywhere outside England. The only official trip he'd done, apart from the odd conference in Washington, D.C., was to the Far East. As far as I could remember, the D-G hadn't visited Berlin for at least five years. And, third, had he come he wouldn't have taken a room in a big Berlin hotel: he'd have been Frank's houseguest or, if it was official, been a guest of the general commanding the British forces. But where Klara's story really rang false was saying that the D-G recognized her. The D-G couldn't remember the name of his own Labrador dog without having Morgan—his faithful attendant—prompt him.

I tried to sleep, but sleep didn't come. There was so much to think about. And I couldn't help noticing the promptness with which Frank had denied knowing Jim Prettyman. He hadn't hemmed and hawed or asked why I'd mentioned his name. It was a flat no and a change of subject. It wasn't like Frank's normal behavior to be so lacking in curiosity: in fact, it wasn't like anyone's normal behavior.

Chapter 6

I told Willi not to put that damned machine in here," Werner said, looking up from his big plate of beef to where two white-coated surgeons were poking screwdrivers deep into the entrails of an old jukebox that had clearly been kicked into silence. Willi Leuschner, the proprietor, watched, as grim-faced as any grieving relative. Apparently certain pop-music aficionados of the late-evening hours voted with their feet.

We were sitting in one of the booths near the window. When we were kids we had all firmly believed that the people in the window seats got bigger portions, to attract passersby. I still don't know whether it's true or not, but it wasn't something that either of us wanted to take a chance on. "You can't trust music critics," I said. "Toscanini could have told him that."

"I'll bet that his jukebox is not insured," said Werner. He had the sort of mind that thought in terms of expenditure, percentages, interest rates, risk, and insurance.

"It was offered cheap," I explained. "Willi thought it would bring more teenagers."

"He'd make a lot of money from penniless teenagers, wouldn't he," said Werner with heavy irony. "He should be glad they keep away, not trying to find a way of attracting them."

Even after a lifetime's friendship, Werner could still surprise me. It was his often expressed view that juvenile delinquency was to be blamed on TV, single-parent families, unemployment, or too much sugar in the diet. Was this new reactionary stand against teenagers a sign that Werner was growing old, the way I'd been all my life?

Werner made his money by avalising, which means he financed East European exports to the West with hard currency borrowed from anywhere he could get it. He paid high interest and he lived on narrow margins. It was a tough way to make a living, but Werner seemed to flourish on the hazards and difficulties of this curious by-water of the financial world. Like many of his rivals, he had no banking experience, and his formal education went no further than the legerdemain that comes from prodding a Japanese calculator.

"I thought you liked young people, Werner," I said.

He looked at me and scowled. He was always accusing me of being intolerant and narrow-minded, but on the issue of keeping my haunts *Jugend-frei* I was with him, and so were a lot of Berliners. You don't have to walk far down Potsdamer Strasse before starting to believe that universal military conscription for teenagers might be a good idea.

There was something different about Werner today. It wasn't his new beard—a fine full-set with mustache—when it was fully grown he'd look like a prosperous Edwardian beer baron or some business associate of Sir Basil Zaharoff. It wasn't just that he was noticeably overweight—he was always overweight between his dedicated slimming regimes—or the fact that he'd arrived absurdly early for our appointment. But he was unusually restless. While waiting for the meal to arrive, he'd fidgeted with the salt and pepper as well as tugging at his earlobes and pinching his nose and staring out of the window as if his mind was somewhere else. I wondered if he was thinking of some other appointment he had, for Werner, in his tailor-made suit and silk shirt, was not dressed for this sort of eating place.

We were in Café Leuschner, a once famous and fashionable café near Potsdamer Platz. It was shabby now and almost empty. It had been like this for many years, for the great expanse of Potsdamer Platz—once the busiest traffic intersection in all Europe—was now a still and silent place where armed sentries patrolled constantly between the massed barbed wire and, with a compassion not extended to their fellow countrymen, carefully restrained their attack-trained dogs from running into the mine fields. And as the district became a backwater, Café Leuschner became the sort of place where men were cautious what they said to strangers, and policemen came regularly to inspect everyone's identity papers.

Once great luxury hotels stood here, adjacent to the mighty Anhalter railway terminal, which was the biggest in the world. The posters in the museum listed one hundred and forty-five trains arriving each day, eighty-two of them long-distance luxury expresses that came complete with cocktail bars, sleeping compartments, and diners. Beneath the road, by means of a specially constructed tunnel, baggage porters, laboring under steamer trunks and cases made of the hides of crocodile and pig, and smartly dressed pages conducted the arriving passengers under the swirling traffic, directly into the plush foyer of the famous Excelsior Hotel next door. Here they would be conveniently close to the fine shops of Leipziger Strasse, the embassies, palaces, and grand houses that adjoined the Tiergarten, and the government offices of the newly created German Reich and the Palace of its Emperor. By day the traffic seemed never-ending, and the nightlife continued until breakfast was served free to any reveler who was still awake.

Now the Anhalter Bahnhof is gone, except for a large section of old yellow brickwork that used to be the ticket hall. In summer it is lost amid a tangle of weeds. Behind it, as Werner and I had discovered in our schooldays, there is a vast no-man's-land of rusting rails, collapsed roundhouses, skeletons of old sleeping cars, and signal boxes complete with handles that could be pulled. No one has passed this way since the last train left for Magdeburg in April 1945. It remains empty except for a few tramps and fugitives who spend a night sheltering in the wrecked buildings but find them too inhospitable even for their stark needs.

Grimy and neglected, this is a neighborhood of derelict bombed buildings, roofless façades that might look like some phony cityscape built for a film, except that they are so filthy. Now this place, which once seemed like the center of all Europe, is nothing. It is just a place past which traffic hurries to get to the newspaper offices of Kochstrasse, or to Checkpoint Charlie, which is only a short distance away along this garbage-littered thoroughfare that skirts the Wall.

But Café Leuschner remains. Willi Leuschner, despite such lapses as installing a jukebox, knows how to tap a glass of strong Berlin beer, and his Austrian wife still produces once a week the best *Tafelspitz* in town. And the tender boiled beef comes with little potato dumplings, and the cabbage is cooked in drippings and has caraway seeds to flavor it.

As Werner came to the end of his huge portion of beef, dipping the final forkful into rather too much horseradish, it was time to tackle again the subject I'd come here to talk to him about. I said, "Well, I thought Lisl looked awfully well."

"You only saw her for five minutes," said Werner, wiping the final smear of horseradish from his plate with a crust of bread roll. Frau Leuschner's powerful horseradish did not affect Werner as it did me.

"She was sleeping this morning, so I didn't want to disturb her." I put the prongs of my fork into the horseradish I'd abandoned, and tasted it again. It was very, very hot.

"She's a stupid old woman," said Werner with a sudden paroxysm of uncharacteristic bitterness. It was a measure of his frustration. "The doctor told her again and again to lose weight and take things easy. She drinks, she smokes, she gets excited, she argues and loses her temper. It's absurd." Perhaps it wasn't bitterness so much as grief that I heard in his voice.

"You say she had a stroke?"

"The hospital gave her tests and said they couldn't be sure." He put the last piece of bread in his mouth and chewed it. "But either way she'll have to have a complete rest."

"Who will arrange about selling the house?" Even as I said it, I realized what a big task was involved. There would be meetings with the property agents and with the bank, a lawyer, and a tax accountant too, plus all the form-filling and petty bureaucratic rigmarole that makes such simple transactions a nightmare. "It would be better if we could persuade Lisl to go away until it's all done. Perhaps we could find a place in Baden-Baden. She's always talked about taking a holiday in Baden one day."

He looked at me and gave a twisted little smile. "And which of us is going to explain all this to Lisl?" he asked.

Willi Leuschner came over to the table to clear the plates. "What are you two having now?" said Willi. "Bread pudding?" Willi was my age, but his head was bald, and the big curly mustache that he'd grown as a joke was gray with age and yellow with nicotine.

He used the familiar *du*, for all three of us had been to school together, and we understood each other better than we understood our wives. In my case much better than I understood my wife. Certainly Willi knew that Werner and I could eat unlimited amounts of the old wartime recipe that Frau Leuschner had elevated to haute cuisine by the addition of eggs and cream. He didn't wait for an affirmative. He wiped the plastic table with a cloth and balanced the mustard pot and beer glasses on top of the plates and cutlery with the skill of long practice. Willi's father had commanded a forbidding maître d', a dozen waiters in tailcoats and bow ties, and white-jacketed youngsters to assist them. Now Willi and his brother had only a couple of young draft dodgers to help, and both those helpers were apt to arrive in the morning glassy-eyed and trembling.

"I know what you're thinking, Werner," I said, once Willi had gone.

"What am I thinking?" He was looking through the big plate-glass windows at the almost deserted street. Yesterday's snow had gone, but the temperature had dropped, and every Berliner could recognize that low gray sky from which much more snow would come.

"You think it's easy for me to come breezing into town and talk about Lisl, and then I go home, leaving you to do the things that have to be done."

"It's not the same for you, Bernie," he said. "Lisl is my problem, not yours."

"She's only got us," I said. "Whatever has to be done,

we'll do it together. I'll get leave." Werner nodded mournfully, so I tried to be brisk. "Selling the house shouldn't be too difficult. But we'll have to arrange somewhere for Lisl to go. Somewhere she'll like," I added vaguely.

"I'm a Jew," said Werner suddenly. "I was born in the war. My name is Jacob, like my grandfather, but they called me Werner because it was more Aryan. Lisl hid my parents. She made no money out of it; my parents had no money. She risked her life. The Nazis put people into camps for much less. I don't know why she took such a risk. Sometimes I ask myself if I'd do the things she did to help comparative strangers. And, to tell you the truth, I'm not sure. But Lisl hid them, and when I was born she hid me. And when my parents died Lisl brought me up as if I was her own child. Now do you understand?"

"We do it together," I said.

"Do what?"

"Sell the house. Get Lisl into some nice residential home. Klara too."

"Are you crazy?" said Werner. "You'd never get her out of that house in a million years."

I looked at him. He had that inscrutable expression he'd developed as a schoolboy. "So what are you saying? Are they going to pull the house down around her?"

"I'm going to run the hotel," said Werner. He stared at me defensively, as if expecting strenuous opposition or a burst of laughter.

"Run the hotel?"

He became defensive in the face of my amazement. "I grew up with her, didn't I? I used to do the accounts. I know enough."

"She'll not let you change anything," I warned him.

"I'll run it my way," he said quietly. It was so easy to forget the hard center inside that sugar coating. But Werner could be tough too.

"And make it pay?"

"It only has to tick over."

"And what about the avalising? What about your own work?"

"I'm winding it up."

"You'd better think it over, Werner," I said in alarm as the implications struck me.

"I've made my decision."

"Where will you live?"

He smiled at my consternation; perhaps that was the only compensation for him; maybe he'd been looking forward to it. "One of those upstairs rooms. I'm moving out of my apartment."

"What about Zena?" I asked. I couldn't imagine his young, tough, snobbish wife adapting to one of Lisl's upstairs rooms, or even to the suite with the refurbished bathroom of which Lisl was so proud.

"It's difficult for Zena to understand," said Werner.

"I imagine it is."

"Zena says she has no debt to Lisl, and in a way she's right," he said sadly.

"For richer or poorer . . . with all my worldly debts . . . Or is it different now there's women's lib?"

"I wish you'd got to know Zena better. She's not selfish. Not as selfish as you think," he amended it as he realized just what he was claiming.

"So what's Zena going to do?"

"She'll stay in the apartment in Dahlem. It's just as well, really, when you think of all that furniture we have there. We couldn't move it to Lisl's, could we?"

"It's a big step, Werner." He was giving up his work and his luxury apartment and, by the sound of it, losing his wife too. He'd lost her before; Zena's constancy to Werner wasn't something the poets wrote sonnets about. Limericks, maybe. I suppose that's why I detested her so much.

"There's no alternative, Bernie. If I did anything less for Lisl, I'd never be able to face myself again, would I?"

I looked at him. Werner was a good man. Perhaps he was the only truly good person I'd ever met. What could I say except, "You're right, Werner. It's the only thing to do."

"Maybe it will work out very well," said Werner, trying desperately to see the best side of it. "If the hotel could get some more holiday bookings, I could pay off the bank loan. I'm going to talk to some of the travel companies."

He seemed serious about it. Didn't he know that travel companies want only cheap, bleak two-hundred-room shoe boxes, run by sixteen-year-old high-school dropouts who don't speak any known language? What would a travel company do with a small, comfortable hotel run by humans? "Good idea, Werner," I said.

"Of course, I can't wind up my business overnight," he said. "I have a few deals outstanding."

"How often do you go over there nowadays?" I asked. Werner's business required regular visits to DDR government officials in East Berlin. I didn't ask him whether he was still reporting back to our people in Frank's office. It was better that I didn't know.

"Not so often. Nowadays I can sometimes arrange a few of the preliminaries on the phone."

"Is it getting better?"

"Not better; different. They are better at covering up than they used to be; better too at understanding what upsets the Western press." It was a harsh verdict coming from Werner, who tried always to be objective in such off-the-cuff remarks about the East.

"How is Normannenstrasse these days?"

"Very happy," said Werner.

"Tell me more."

"The East Germans are number one on Moscow's hit

parade. Prague is no longer the center of Russian penetration of the West, and our friends in Normannenstrasse are rubbing their hands in glee."

"I heard the Stasi was getting a big shake-up over there."

"One by one the old gang are being got rid of. The same with the administration. It's a smaller and better organization these days."

"Okay."

"Of course, the KGB monitors it from day to day. If things are not going well, Moscow makes its displeasure known."

"Ever hear anything about that fellow Erich Stinnes?"

"He's the Moscow liaison. He got a big promotion."

"Stinnes?"

"The KGB is riding high: no financial cutbacks for them. And the Americans are still running their networks from their embassies, and all U.S. embassies are bugged from roof to cellar. They never learn."

"Is my wife involved in this reorganization?" I asked.

"Isn't that who we're talking about?" said Werner. "She helped you with that 'Structure Report,' didn't she?"

I didn't reply. For ages now, many had been saying that our networks should be organized quite separately from the embassies and other diplomatic organizations. I'd spent a long time on a report about it, on the bottom of which Dicky Cruyer gladly signed his name. A lot of people, me included, thought that it would mean another big promotion for Dicky. It was the best work of that kind I'd ever done, and I was proud of it. Some said that it must inevitably lead to a reorganization. But we reckoned without the Foreign Office. Even getting the D-G to submit the report was difficult. When the mandarins at the Foreign Office read it, they stamped on it with such force that the whole building trembled. The Secret Intelligence Service was going to stay a part of the Foreign Office, its submissions rated no more important than those from a medium-size embassy in Africa. Our offices would remain inside embassies, and if that meant that everyone knew where to find us, too bad, chaps! It was a depressing thought. And Fiona knew the whole story.

We sat in silence, watching the street, where traffic raced past and some people waiting to cross the road were hunched against the bitter-cold wind. "There is the matter of inheritance," I said finally. I suppose we'd both been thinking of Lisl all the time.

"The hotel?" said Werner.

"You might work yourself to death and then find she's left the place to a dogs' home."

"Dogs' home?" said Werner, puzzled. It was, of course, an entirely English concept: old German ladies were unlikely to bequeath their entire estates for the welfare of unwanted canines.

"To some charity," I explained.

"I'm not doing it to get the house," said Werner.

"No need to get irritable," I said. "But it's something you should settle before you start."

"Don't be stupid, Bernie. How can I sit down with Lisl and tell her to write her will in my favor?" I didn't try to answer through the sudden bellow of discordant sound that came from the jukebox. But after a few bars to test it, the mechanic switched it off and started to replace the colored panels.

"She has no other relatives, does she?"

"Yes, she has," said Werner. "There was a sister who died in the war and another—Inge Winter—even older than Lisl. She used to live in France. Childless, and probably dead by now. Lisl said I met her once when she came to Berlin, but I don't remember it. She has some sort of claim to the house. Lisl once told me that her father left it to both daughters but only Lisl wanted to live in it. But it was half Inge Winter's. And apart from the sister, there could be relatives of Lisl's late husband, Erich. I must talk to her again."

"If Lisl said half the house belonged to her sister, the sister might be a signatory for the bank loan."

"I know," said Werner, rubbing his mustache. "I was wondering if that's why the sister came to Berlin."

"You'd better ask the bank," I said.

"The bank won't reveal anything to me without Lisl's permission." He rubbed his mustache again. "It itches," he explained.

"It will have to be sorted out," I said. "I'll talk to her."

"No, you won't," said Werner immediately. "It would spoil everything. It's got to look as though I *want* to go and run the place. It's got to seem as though she's doing *me* the favor. Surely you see that?"

It was a long time before I nodded. But Werner was right. He must have spent a lot of sleepless nights working it all out. "Shall I find out if the sister is still alive?" I offered to do it more because I wanted to appease my conscience than because I thought it would lead anywhere, or be of any practical use.

Perhaps Werner understood what my motives were. He said, "That would be really useful, Bernie. If you could find out about the sister, that would be the most important problem solved. I've got the last address she used in France. I got it out of that big green address book Lisl keeps in the office. I don't know when it dates back to." He looked across to the bar counter, where Willi Leuschner had been operating the chrome espresso machine, and said, "Willi's coming with the bread pudding."

"And about time."

"He'll want to sit down and chat," Werner warned. "Don't mention anything about the hotel for the time being. I'll phone and give you the sister's address."

"Take a day or so to think it all over," I suggested. Willi was coming this way now, carrying the desserts and the coffees and some *Kipferl*—sweet crescent-shaped biscuits—which always marked the end of any of Werner's diets. "It's a big step."

"I've thought it over," said Werner firmly and with just a trace of sadness. "It's what I've got to do."

France, I thought. Why do I have to say such silly things? How the hell am I going to get time off and go to France to trace the sister, who is undoubtedly long since dead and gone? And, anyway, wasn't one Lisl in my life enough?

Chapter 7

We could have bought a microwave oven," said Gloria suddenly and spontaneously.

"Is that what you want? A microwave oven?"

"With the money this damned flight is costing us," she explained bitterly.

"Oh," I said. "Yes." She was making a list in her head. She did this sometimes. And the longer the list got, the more bitter hatred she had for the airline and its management. Fortunately for the airline's management, none of them were sitting in the seat next to Gloria on the flight to Nice. I was sitting there. "It's a rip-off," she said.

"Everyone knows it's a rip-off," I said. "So drink the nice warm *café,* unwrap your processed *fromage,* and enjoy the *ambiance.*"

The Plexiglas windows were scratched, so that even the dense gray cloud looked cross-hatched. Gloria did not respond, or eat the items set before her on the tiny plastic tray. She got nail varnish from the big handbag she always carried and began doing something with her fingernails. This was always a dire portent.

I suppose I should have told her, right from the beginning, that our journey was made to fulfill a promise I'd made about finding Lisl Hennig's sister. I should have realized that Gloria would be angry when the truth was revealed, and that I'd have to tell her sooner rather than later.

Looking back on it, I don't know why I chose the airport departure lounge to tell Gloria the real reason for the trip. She was unhappy to hear that this was not actually the "mad lovers' weekend" that I'd let her think of it as. She called me names, and did it so loudly that some people on the next seat took their children out of earshot.

It was at times like that that I tried to analyze the essence of my relationship with Gloria. My contemporaries—married men in their forties—were not reluctant to give me their own interpretations of my romance with this beautiful twenty-two-year-old. Sometimes these took the form of serious "talks," sometimes anecdotes about mythical friends, and sometimes they were just lewd jokes. Oddly enough, it was the envious comments that offended me. I wished they would try to understand that such relationships are complex and this love affair was more complex than most.

Sitting on the plane, with no work to do, and nothing to read except the "flight magazine," I thought about it. I tried to compare this relationship with Gloria to the one I'd had with Fiona, my wife, whose fortieth birthday would be coming up soon. She'd always said she dreaded her fortieth birthday. This "dread" had begun as a sort of joke, and my response was to promise that we'd celebrate it in style. But now she'd be celebrating it in East Berlin—with Russian champagne, no doubt, and perhaps some caviar too. Fiona loved caviar.

Would I have got as far as London Heathrow with Fiona and still been trying to pretend that we were embarking on some madcap romantic escapade? No. But the fact of the matter was that such a romantic escapade would have had a very, very limited appeal to my wife, Fiona. Wait a moment! Was that true? Surely the real reason I wouldn't have told her that this was a "surprise getaway" was that my wife would not have believed for one instant that a sudden invitation to fly to Nice would be a romantic escapade. My wife, Fiona, knew me too well; that was the truth of it.

But at Nice the sun was shining, and it did not take very much to restore Gloria to her usual lighthearted self. In fact, it took no more than my renting a car for our trip to the last known address of Inge Winter. At work, Gloria had seen me dictating and conversing in German, and sometimes my imperfect Russian was used too. So she was ill-prepared for my halting French.

It went wrong right from the start. The beautifully coiffured young Frenchwoman at the car-rental desk was understandably irritated when I tried to interpose news about my need for a car into a private conversation she was having with her female colleague. She didn't hide her irritation. She spoke rapidly and with a strong Provençal accent that I couldn't follow.

When finally I appealed to Gloria for help in translating this girl's rapid instructions about finding the vehicle, Gloria's jubilation knew no bounds. *"No compree!"* she said, and laughed and clapped her hands with joy.

Despite Gloria's uncooperative attitude, we found the car, a small white Renault hatchback that must have been sitting in the rental-car pound for many winter days, for it did not start easily.

But once away, and on the Autoroute heading west, all was well. Gloria was laughing, and I was finally persuaded that it had all been very amusing.

We were only a few minutes along the Autoroute before we reached the Antibes exit. On this occasion, determined not to provide more laughs for Gloria, I had a handful of small change ready to pay the Autoroute charge. Now, with Gloria bent low over a map, we began to thread our way through the back roads towards Grasse.

Once off the Autoroute, you find another France. Here in

this hilly backwater there is little sign of the ostentatious wealth that marks the coastline of the Riviera. Rolls-Royces, Cadillacs, and Ferraris are here replaced by brightly painted little vans and antique Ladas that bump over the large potholes and splash through the ocher-colored pools that are the legacy of steady winter rain. Here is a landscape where nothing is ever completed. Partly built houses—their innards skeletal gray blocks, fresh cement, and ganglia of wiring—stand alongside half-demolished old farm buildings. Ladders, broken bidets, and abandoned bathtubs mark the terraces of olive trees. Heaps of sand—eroded by the rainstorms—are piled alongside bricks, sheets of galvanized metal, and half-completed scaffolding. The fruit of urban squalor litters the fields, where the most profitable cash crop is the *maison sécondaire.*

But Les Mas des Vignes Blanches was not such a place. Here, on the south-facing brow of a hill, there was a Prussian interlude in the Gallic landscape. The house had once been a place from which some lucky landowner surveyed his vineyards. Now the hillsides were disfigured with a pox of development, an infection inevitably rendered more virulent by the thin crescent of Mediterranean, which shone pale blue beyond the next hill.

The house was surrounded with a box hedge, but the white wooden gates were open, and I drove up the well-kept gravel path. The main building must have been well over a hundred years old. It wasn't the grim rectangular buildings that Northern landowners favored. This was a house built for the Provençal climate, a two-story building with shuttered windows, vines climbing across the façade, some mature palm trees—fronds thrashing in the wind—and a gigantic cactus, pale green and still, like a huge prehensile sea creature waiting to attack.

At the back of the house I could see a cobbled courtyard, swept and scrubbed to a cleanliness that is unusual hereabouts. From the coachhouse jutted the rear ends of a big

Mercedes and a pale-blue BMW. Behind that there was a large garden with neatly pruned fruit trees espaliered on the walls. I noticed the lawns in particular. In this part of the world—where fierce summer sunshine parches the land—a well-tended lawn is the sign of eccentric foreign tastes, of a passionate concern for gardens, or wealth.

On the small secluded front terrace was a selection of garden furniture: some fancy metal chairs arranged around a large glass-topped table and a couple of recliners. But, despite the sunshine, it was not a day for sitting outside. The wind was unrelenting, and here on the hill even the tall conifers whipped with each gust of it. Gloria turned up her collar as we stood waiting for someone to respond to the jangling bell.

The woman who answered the door was about forty years old. She was attractive-looking in that honest way that country people sometimes are, a strong, big-boned woman with quick intelligent eyes and graying hair that she'd done nothing to darken. "Frau Winter?" I said.

"My name is Winter," she said. "But I am Ingrid." She opened the door to us and, as if needing something to say, added, "It is confusing that I have the same initial as my mother." Having noted our cheap rented car, she gave all her attention to Gloria, and was no doubt trying to guess our relationship. "You want Mama. Are you Mr. Samson?" Her English was excellent, with an edge of accent that was more German than French. Her dress was a green, floral-patterned Liberty fabric cut to an old-fashioned design with lacy white high collar and cuffs. It was hard to know whether she was poor and out of style, or whether she was following the trendy ideas that are *de rigueur* at smart dinner parties in big towns.

"That's right," I said. I'd written to say that I was an old friend of Lisl, a writer, researching for a book that was to be set in Berlin before the war. Since I would be in the neighborhood, I wondered if she would allow me to visit her and perhaps share some of her memories. There had been no reply to the letter. Perhaps they had hoped that I wouldn't show up.

"Let me take your coats. It's so cold today. Usually at this time of year we are lunching outside." Her nails were short and cared for, but her hands were reddened, as if with housework. There was an expensive-looking wristwatch and some gold rings and a bracelet, but no wedding ring.

I murmured some banalities about the winters getting colder each year, while she got a better look at us. So there was a daughter. She didn't look anything like Lisl, but I remembered seeing an old photo of Lisl's mother in a large hat and a long dress with leg-of-mutton sleeves: she was a big woman too. "How is your mother?" I asked, as Gloria took the opportunity to look at herself in the hall mirror and tease her hair out with her fingertips.

"She goes up and down, Mr. Samson. Today is one of her better days. But I must ask you not to stay too long. She gets tired."

"Of course."

We went into the large drawing room. Several big heating radiators kept the room warm, despite large windows that provided a view of the front lawn. The floor was of the red tile that is common in this region; here and there some patterned carpets were arranged. On the wall was one big painting that dominated the room. It was a typical eighteenth-century battle scene; handsome officers in bright uniforms sat on prancing chargers and waved swords, while far away serried ranks of stunted anonymous figures were killing each other in the smoke. Two white sofas and a couple of matching armchairs were arranged at one end of the room, and an old woman in a plain black dress sat in the ugly sort of high chair from which people with stiff joints find it possible to get up.

"How do you do, Mr. Samson," she said, as her daughter went through the formalities with us, and studied Gloria carefully before nodding to her. Lisl's sister was not at all like Lisl.

She was a slight, shriveled figure, with skin like speckled yellow parchment, and thinning white hair that looked as if it might have been specially washed and set for this visit. I looked at her with interest: she was even older than Lisl; goodness knows how old that would make her. But this was a woman who had come to terms with aging. She hadn't dyed her hair or painted her face or stuck onto her eyelids the false lashes that Lisl liked to wear if visitors came. Yet, despite all the differences, there was no mistaking the facial resemblance to her sister. She had the same determined jaw and the large eyes and the mouth that could go so easily from smile to snarl.

"So you are a friend of my sister?" Her words were English, her pronunciation stridently American, but her sentences were formed in a mind that thought in German. I moved a little closer to her so she did not have to raise her voice.

"I've known her a long time," I said. "I saw her only a couple of weeks ago."

"She is well?" She looked up at the daughter and said, "Are you bringing tea?" The younger woman gave a filial smile and went out of the room.

I hesitated about the right way to describe Lisl's health. I didn't want to frighten her. "She might have had a slight stroke," I said tentatively. "Very slight. Even the hospital doctors are not sure."

"And this is why you have come?" I noticed her eyes now. They were like the eyes of a cat: green and deep and luminous. Eyes of a sort I'd never seen before.

This old woman certainly didn't beat about the bush. "No," I said, "but it means she'll have to give up the hotel. Her doctor insists it's too much for her."

"Of course it is. Everyone is telling her that at some time or other."

"It was your father's house?" I said.

"Sure. It has many wonderful memories for me."

"It's a magnificent old place," I said. "I wish I could have seen it in your father's time. But the entrance steps make it difficult for Lisl. She needs to live somewhere where everything is on the ground floor."

"So. And who is caring for her?"

"Have you heard of Werner Volkmann?"

"The Jew?"

"The boy she brought up."

"That Jew family she hid away on the top floor. Yes, my sister was completely crazy. I was living in Berlin until 1945. Even me she never told! Can you believe that from her own sister she'd keep such a thing secret? I visited her there; it was partly my house."

"It's astonishing," I said dutifully.

"So the Jewish kid she raised is looking after her." She nodded.

"He's not a kid any more," I said.

"I guess not. So what's he getting out of it?"

"Nothing," I said. "He feels he owes it to Lisl."

"He figures he's going to inherit the house. Is that it?" She gave a malicious little chuckle and looked at Gloria. Gloria was sitting on a carved wooden chair: she shifted uncomfortably.

"Not as far as I know," I said defensively. So bang goes the whole purpose of coming all the way here. Did this vituperative old woman deliberately maneuver me into that denial? I couldn't decide. I was still thinking about it when the daughter arrived with tea and that sort of open apple tart in which the thin slices of fruit are carefully arranged in fanlike patterns.

"Ingrid made that," said the old woman when she saw the way I was looking at it.

"It looks wonderful," I said, without adding that after the "light meal" on the plane almost anything would have looked wonderful. Gloria made appreciative noises too, and the daughter cut us big slices.

During tea I asked the old woman about life in Berlin before the war. She had a good memory and answered clearly and fully, but the answers she gave were the standard answers that people who lived under the Third Reich gave to foreigners and strangers of any kind.

After forty-five minutes or so I could see she was tiring. I suggested that we should leave. The old woman said she wanted to go on longer, but the daughter gave me an almost imperceptible movement of the head and said, "They have to go, Mama. They have things to do." The daughter could also show a hard edge.

"Are you just passing through?" Ingrid asked politely while she was handing us our coats.

"We are booked into the big hotel on the road this side of Valbonne," I said.

"They say it's very comfortable," she said.

"I'll write up my notes tonight," I said. "Perhaps, if I have any supplementary questions, I could phone you?"

"Mama doesn't have many visitors," she said. It was not meant to sound like an encouragement.

When we reached the hotel, we found it was not the "honeymoon hotel" that I'd described to Gloria. It was at the end of a long winding road—broken-surfaced and potholed, as are all local roads in this region—and behind it there was an abandoned quarry. In a bold spirit of enterprise, someone seemed to have fashioned a car-park gate from two cartwheels, but on closer inspection it was a prefabricated plastic contraption. A few genuine old wine barrels were arranged across the patio, and in them some rhododendrons and camellias were struggling to stay alive. The hotel was a pink stucco building with shiny plastic tiles.

At the far end of the car park was an outbuilding in which some derelict motor vehicles of indeterminate shape and marque were rusting away, undisturbed by human hand. We parked beside a new Peugeot station wagon and a van that carried advertisements for a butcher shop in Valbonne. A large sign said that all cars were parked at owners' risk, and another pointed the way to an empty swimming pool which was partly repainted in a vivid shade of cerulean blue.

But inside everything looked up. The dining room was clean and rather elegant, set with starched cloths and shining glass and cutlery. And there was a big log fire in the bar.

Gloria went straight upstairs to bathe and change but I went into the bar and warmed my hands at the fire and tried the Armagnac, which the barman said was especially good. Gloria didn't enjoy alcohol: she preferred orange juice or yogurt or even Seven-Up. It was another manifestation of the generation gap, I suppose. Concurring with the barman's verdict, I took a second Armagnac up to our room, where Gloria had just finished taking her bath. "The water is hot," she called happily. She walked across the room stark naked and said, "Have a shower, darling. It will cheer you up."

"I'm cheered up already," I said, watching her.

All the way from Les Mas to the hotel, she'd kept quiet, giving me time to think about the Winter woman. But when I said, "So what did you think of her?" Gloria was ready to explode with indignation.

"What a cow!" she said, dabbing herself with a towel.

"If I have to be knocked out in the first round, it's a consolation to know it's done by a world champion," I said.

"She trapped you."

"And you have to admire the skill of it," I said. "She sensed what we'd come for even before we started talking. It was quick and clever. You have to admit that."

"What a vicious old moo," said Gloria.

"Are you going to put some clothes on?"

"Why?"

"It's distracting."

She came and kissed me. "You smell of booze," she said, and I stretched out my arms to embrace her. "Well, that's very reassuring, darling. Sometimes I think I've lost the art of being distracting."

I reached for her.

"No, no, no! What time's dinner? Stop it! There's no time. I said what time's dinner."

"It's too late to think of that now," I said. And it was.

Afterwards, when we were sitting quietly together, she said, "What are you, Bernard?"

"What do you mean?"

"Are you English, or German, or nothing? I'm a nothing. I used to think I was English, but I'm a nothing."

"I used to think that I was a German," I said. "At least I used to think that my German friends thought I was a Berliner, which is even better. Then one day I was playing cards with Lisl and an old man named Koch, and they just took it for granted that I was an Englishman and had never been anything else. I was hurt."

"But you wanted it both ways, darling. You wanted your English friends to treat you like an Englishman, while your German friends think of you as one of them."

"I suppose I did."

"My parents are Hungarian, but I've never been to Hungary. I grew up in England and always thought of myself as one hundred percent English. I was a superpatriot. Being English was all I had to hang on to. I learned all those wonderful Shakespeare speeches about England and chided anyone who said a word against the Queen or wouldn't stand up for the national anthem. Then one day one of the girls at school told me the truth about myself."

"Truth?"

"You Hungarians, she said. All the other girls were there watching us; I wasn't going to let it go. She knew that. I told her I was born in England. She said, If you were born in an orange box, would that make you an orange? The other girls laughed. I cried all night."

"My poor love."

"I'm a nothing. It doesn't matter. I'm used to the idea now."

"Here's to us nothings," I said, holding the last of my Armagnac aloft before draining it.

"We'll miss dinner unless you hurry," she said. "Go and have a shower."

Chapter 8

There was no breakfast room, of course. In this sort of French hotel there never is. And, unlike Gloria, I don't like eating food in bed. Thus she was propped up in bed, the tray balanced on her thighs, and I was halfway through my second cup of coffee, and eating Gloria's second brioche—"You are a fool, darling. You've had two already"—when the phone rang.

I knew it would be the Winter woman. No one else knew where I was. Contrary to regulations, I'd not left a contact number at the office. People who left overseas contact numbers were likely to find themselves answering questions about where they'd been and why.

"This is Ingrid Winter. Mama is feeling rather fit today. She wonders if you'd like to join us for lunch."

"Thank you; I would." Gloria had used the extra earpiece that all French phones have, and was waving a hand, in case her violently shaking head escaped my attention. "But Miss Kent has an appointment in Cannes. She could drop me and pick me up, if you'd suggest convenient times."

"Eleven and three," said the daughter without hesitation. The Winter family seemed to have answers ready for everything.

Gloria dropped me at the gate a few minutes early. It was better that way when dealing with Germans. "So! Exactly on time," said Ingrid Winter as she opened the door to me. It was a statement of warm approval. We went through the same formalities as before, talking about the weather as I gave her my coat, but today she proved far more affable. "Let me close the door quickly: that yellow dust gets everywhere when the wind is from the south. The sirocco. It's hard to believe that the sand could be blown all the way from the Sahara, isn't it?"

"Yes," I said.

She locked my raincoat away in a closet painted with big orange flowers. "My mother is a very old lady, Mr. Samson." I said yes, of course she was, and Ingrid Winter looked at me as if to convey some special meaning, apprehension almost. Then she said, "A very old lady." She paused. *"Komm!"*

With that she turned and walked not into the drawing room we'd used the previous afternoon but along a tiled corridor, hung with old engravings of ancient German cities, to a room at the back.

It had not always been a bedroom, of course. Like Lisl, she'd had a downstairs room converted to her use. Few people of Inge Winter's age want to go upstairs to bed.

She was not in bed. She was wearing the sort of gray woolen dress provided to impecunious patients in state hospitals, and sitting in a large angular armchair with a heavy cashmere shawl draped round her thin shoulders. "Sit down," she told me. "Do you want a drink of any sort?"

"No, thank you," I said. Well, now I understood Ingrid's fears. This wasn't a bedroom, it was a shrine. It wasn't simply that Inge Winter had surrounded herself with pictures and mementos of times past—many old people do that —it was the ones she'd chosen that provided the surprise. The top of a large side table was crowded with framed photos, the sort of collection that actors and actresses seem to need to reassure themselves of the undying affection that their colleagues have promised them. But these were not film stars.

The large silver-framed photo of Adolf Hitler had been carefully placed in a commanding position. I'd seen such photos before: it was one of the sepia-toned official portraits by Hoffmann that Hitler had given to visiting dignitaries or old comrades. But this one was not just perfunctorily signed with the scratchy little abbreviated signature normally seen on such likenesses. This was carefully autographed with greetings to Herr and Frau Winter. It was not the only picture of Hitler. There was a shiny press photo of a handsome middle-aged couple standing with Hitler and a big dog on a terrace, with high snow-capped mountains in the background. Berchtesgaden probably, the Berghof. Prewar, because Hitler was not in uniform. He was wearing a light-colored suit, one hand stretched towards the dog as if about to stroke it. The woman was a rather beautiful Inge Winter, with long shiny hair, wearing the angular padded fashions of the 1930s. The man— presumably Herr Winter—slightly too plump for his dark pinstripe suit, had been caught with his mouth half open, so that he looked surprised and slightly ridiculous. But perhaps that was a small price to pay for being thus recorded consorting with the Führer. I couldn't take my eyes away from the collection of pictures. Here were signed photos of Joseph Goebbels with his wife and all the children; greetings from a black-uniformed blank-faced Himmler; a broadly smiling, soft-focused and carefully retouched Hermann Göring; and a flamboyantly inscribed picture of Fritz Esser, with whom Göring faced the judges at Nuremberg. The Winters had found welcome in the very top echelons of Nazi society. So where did that put her sister, Lisl?

"People usually do nowadays," said the old woman. "There's far too much drinking." Without giving me much of a chance to answer, she reached over for one of the pictures. Holding it in her hand, she looked at her daughter and said in rapid German, "Leave us alone, Ingrid. You can call us when lunch is ready."

"Yes, Mama."

When I said how pleased I was that she'd spared time to see me again, I automatically continued in German.

The old woman's face lit up in a way that I wouldn't have thought possible. "Such beautiful German . . . You are German?"

"I think I am," I said. "But my German friends seem doubtful."

"You are a Berliner?" She was still holding the photo, but she seemed to have forgotten about it.

"I grew up there."

"I hear you speak and I am drinking a glass of champagne. If only my daughter didn't have that dreadful Bavarian growl. Why didn't you tell me yesterday? Oh, how splendid that my daughter made me ask you back today."

"Your daughter made you ask me?"

"She thinks I am being too Prussian about the house." She smiled grimly, as one Prussian to another. "She thinks I should let Lisl give it to the wretched Jew, if that's what she wants to do. Poor Lisl was always the simpleton of the family. That's why she married that piano player." It was a relief to hear her speaking German instead of her uncertain English with its terrible accent, the sort of accent people only acquire when they come to a language late in life. I suppose that's how I spoke French. But Inge Winter's German was—apart from a few dated words and expressions—as clear and as fresh as if she'd come from Berlin yesterday.

She looked at me. I was expected to respond to her offer of the house. "That's very generous, Frau Winter."

"It makes no difference to me. Everything will be Ingrid's when I die. She might as well decide now."

"Lisl has borrowed money on the house, I believe."

She ignored that. "Ingrid says it's too much trouble for nothing. Perhaps she's right. She knows more than I do about these things."

"There will be taxes and so on. . . ."

"And Ingrid says it's better that we don't have to go to all the trouble of filing accounts and submitting tax forms. Who would I find here who knew about German taxes?"

I didn't answer. Considering how many rich Germans had big houses on the Riviera—and the fleets of huge German-registered yachts that crowded local ports and marinas—I would have thought it a not insurmountable problem.

"But I have things there in the house," she said. "Personal things."

"I can't think there would be any difficulty about that," I said.

"The ormolu clock. My mother was so insistent that I should have it. Do you remember seeing it?"

"Yes," I said. Who could forget it: a huge, horrid thing with angels and dragons and horses and goodness knows what else jumping about all over the mantelshelf. And if you missed seeing it, there was every chance that its resonant chimes would keep you awake all night. But I could see a complication just the same; Lisl had often expressed her fondness for that dreadful object.

"And some other oddments. Photos of my parents, a tiny embroidered cushion I had when I was a little girl. Some papers, keepsakes, diaries, letters, and things that belonged to my husband. I'll send Ingrid to Berlin to get them. It would be tragic if they were thrown away."

"Nothing will happen as quickly as that," I said. I was fearful that she'd phone Lisl before Werner had spoken to her. Then there would be a fearful rumpus.

"Just private papers," she said. "Things that are of no concern to anyone but me." She nodded. "Ingrid will find them for me. Then Lisl can have the house." She looked down at her hands and became aware of the photo she was holding. She passed it to me. "My wedding," she announced.

I looked at it. It had been an elaborate ceremony. She was standing on the steps of some grand building in a magnificent wedding gown—there were pages behind her to hold the train of it—and her husband was in the dress uniform of some smart Prussian regiment. Deployed on the higher steps was a sword-brandishing honor guard of army officers, each one accompanied by a bridesmaid, in the old German style. On either side the guests were arrayed: a handsome naval officer, high-ranking brownshirts and SS officers, richly caparisoned Nazi Party officials, and other elaborate uniforms of obscure Nazi organizations.

"Do you see Lisl there?" she said with an arch smile.

"No."

"She's with the civilian." It was easy to spot them now; he was virtually the only man there without a uniform. "Poor Erich," she said, and gave a snigger of laughter. Once, no doubt, her cruel joke against Lisl's piano-player husband had been a telling blow. But this old woman didn't seem to realize that history had decided in Erich Hennig's favor.

I slid the photo back into its narrow allotment of space on the table.

"Just private papers," she said again. "Things that are of no concern to anyone but me."

Promptly at one o'clock, her daughter called us for lunch in the small dining room, which looked onto the courtyard. The old woman walked there, slowly but without assistance, and continued to talk all through the meal. It was always about Berlin.

"I know Berlin not at all," said Ingrid, "but for my mother there is no other town like it."

It was enough to start another story about her happy prewar days in the capital. Sometimes the old woman's stories were told with such gusto that she seemed to forget I was there with her daughter. She seemed to be speaking to other people, and she larded her stories with ". . . and you remember that stuff that Fritz liked to drink . . ." or ". . . that table that Pauli and I always reserved at the Königin on the Ku-Damm . . ." Once, in the middle of a story about a gala ball she'd attended in 1938, she said to Ingrid, "What was the name of that place where Göring had that wonderful ball?"

"Haus der Flieger," said Ingrid. I must have looked puzzled, for she added, "I know all Mama's stories very well by now, Herr Samson."

After lunch her mother quietened. Ingrid said, "My mother gets tired. I think she should have a little sleep now."

"Of course. Can I help?"

"She likes to walk on her own. I think she's all right." I waited while Ingrid took her mother to her room again. There was still another quarter of an hour before Gloria was due to collect me, so Ingrid invited me to sit in the kitchen and share a second pot of coffee she was just about to make for herself. I accepted.

Ingrid Winter seemed a pleasant woman, who waved away my suggestions that forgoing a share in the house was a generous thing to do. "When Mama dies, and Tante Lisl dies," she said, not using any of the common euphemisms for death, "I will have no use for a house in Berlin."

"You prefer France?" I asked.

She looked at me for a moment before answering. "Mama likes the climate." There was no indication about her own likes and dislikes.

"Most people do," I said.

She didn't respond. She poured more coffee for me and said, "You mustn't take any notice of what Mama says."

"She's a wonderful old woman, considering her age."

"That may be true, but she is mischievous. Old people often like to make trouble. They are like children in that respect."

"I see," I said, and hoped she would explain.

"She tells lies." Perhaps seeing that these allegations had little effect upon me, she became more specific. "She pretends to believe everything, but her brain works like lightning. She pretends to believe that you're a writer, but she knows who you are." She waited.

"Does she?" I said in a bored voice and sipped some coffee.

"Exactly who you are. She knew before you arrived. She knew your father a long time ago: before the war, she said it was. She told me your father was an English spy. She says you're probably a spy too."

"She is a very old woman."

"Mama said your father killed her husband."

"She said that?"

"In those very words. She said, 'This man's father killed my darling husband,' and said I must be on my guard against you."

"You've been very frank, Fräulein Winter, and I appreciate it, but I truly can't fathom what your mother was referring to. My father was a British army officer, but he was not a fighting soldier. He was stationed in Berlin after the war; she might have met him then. Before the war he was a traveling salesman. It seems very unlikely that she could have met him before the war."

Ingrid Winter shrugged. She was not going to vouch for the accuracy of anything her mother said.

There was a peremptory toot on a car horn, and I got up to go. When Ingrid Winter handed me my coat, we were back to discussing the vagaries of the weather. As I said goodbye to her, I found myself wondering why her mother might have said "killed my darling husband" rather than "killed your father." I didn't know much about Inge Winter's husband except what I'd heard from Lisl: that Paul Winter had been some kind of civil servant working in one of the Berlin ministries, and that he'd died somewhere in southern Germany in the aftermath of the war. Now that I'd met Ingrid—this woman of whom her aunt Lisl knew nothing—I could only say that there were a lot of things about the Winter family that I didn't understand, including what my father might have had to do with them.

Chapter 9

We spent the last evening of that hectic weekend in Provence at the nearby home of Gloria's "uncle." Gloria's parents were Hungarian; this old friend wasn't actually a kinsman, except in the way that all Hungarian exiles are a family of crazy, congenial, exasperating individuals who, no matter how reclusive their mode of living, keep amazingly well informed about the activities of their "relatives."

Zu, he called her. All her Hungarian friends called her Zu. It was short for Zsuzsa, the name she'd been given by her parents. This "Dodo" lived in an isolated tumbledown cottage. It was on a hillside, sandwiched between a minuscule vineyard and the weed-infested grounds of an abandoned olive-oil mill. One small section of earth had been partitioned off to be Dodo's garden, where the final few leaves of last year's winter vegetables were being devoured by slugs. Perched precariously over a drainage ditch at the front was a battered *deux chevaux* with one headlight missing.

He was introduced to me as "Dodo" and, judging by the vigorous way he shook my hand, was happy enough to be called that. My first impression was of a man in his middle sixties, a short, fat, noisy fellow whom any casting director would engage to play the role of a lovable Hungarian refugee. He had a lot of pure-white hair that was brushed straight back, and a large unruly mustache that was somewhat grayer. His face was ruddy—the result, perhaps, of his drinking, for the whole house was littered with bottles, both full and empty, and he seemed quite merry by the time we arrived. To what extent his imbibing advanced his linguistic ability I'm not sure, but his English was almost accentless and fluent, and—apart from a tendency to call everyone "darling"—his syntax had only the imperfections of the natives.

He wore old brown corduroy trousers that had, in places, whitened and worn to the underfabric. His shaggy crimson turtleneck sweater came almost to his knees, and his scuffed leather boots had zipper sides and two-inch heels. He gave us wine and sat us down on the long, lumpy chintz-covered sofa, in front of the blazing fire, and talked without taking breath.

His house was about thirty kilometers from Les Mas, where the Winters lived, but he seemed to know all about them. "The Hitler woman," the locals called Inge Winter, for some talkative plumber had been there to fix a pipe and broadcast news of the old woman's photos of Hitler all round the neighborhood.

When he heard that we'd visited his mysterious neighbors he added to my knowledge, telling amusing stories about Inge's father-in-law—old Harald Winter—who'd been a rich businessman. Vienna abounded with all sorts of tales about him: his motorcars, his violent temper, his unrelenting vengeance, the titled ladies seen with him in his box at the opera, huge sums of money spent on amazing jewelry for women he was pursuing, his ridiculous duel with old Professor Doktor Schneider, the gynecologist who delivered his second son.

"In my father's time Harry Winter was the talk of Vienna; even now the older people still tell stories about him. Most of the yarns are nonsense, I suspect. But he did keep a very beautiful mistress in Vienna. This I know is true, because I saw her many times. I was studying chemistry in Vienna in 1942 and living with my aunt, who was her dressmaker for many years. The mistress was a bit down on her luck by that time: the war was on, the Nazis were running Austria, and she was a Jew. She was Hungarian, and she liked to gossip in her native language. Then one day she didn't turn up for a fitting; we heard later that she'd been taken off to a camp. Not all the money in the world could save you from the Gestapo." Having said this, he sniffed and went to stir something in the kitchen. When he returned, he heaved a big log onto the fire. It was wet and it sizzled in the red-hot embers.

Dodo's little home was as different as could be from the well-ordered good taste of the Winters' house. The Winter mansion had a Spartan luxury, but Dodo's "glory hole" was a wonderful squalor. Half the south-facing wall had been re-placed by sliding glass doors, and through them—just visible in the twilight—there was a ramshackle terrace. In retirement he'd become a painter. The only other sizable room in the house faced north, and he'd put a skylight into it and used it as a studio. He showed us around it. There were some half-finished canvases: landscapes, bold, careless, competent pas-tiches of van Gogh's Provençal work. Most of them were variations of the same view: his valley at dawn, at dusk, and at many of the stages between. He claimed to have a gallery in Cannes where his works were sold. Perhaps it wouldn't be too difficult to sell such colorful pictures to the rich tourists who came here in the holidays.

When we returned from our tour of the premises, the damp log in the living-room fireplace was oozing blue smoke that billowed into the room, further blackening the painted walls and irritating the eyes. Gloria set the table that was conveniently near the door of the kitchen. Behind it stood a massive carved wardrobe that almost touched the ceiling.

Its doors missing, it had been provided with unpainted shelves for hundreds of books. Philosophy, history, chemistry, art, dictionaries, detective stories, biographies, they were crammed together in anarchic disorder. Everything was worn, stained, bent, or slightly broken.

When we sat down at the big table, he pulled a wheelback chair into position for me, and the arm of it came away in his hand. He roared with laughter and thumped it back into position with a deftness that had obviously come from practice. He laughed often, and when he did his open mouth revealed gold molars only slightly more yellow than the rest of his teeth.

I knew, of course, that we'd come here because Gloria wanted to show me to Dodo, and that his approval would be important to her. And, in turn, important to me. *In loco parentis,* he eyed me warily and asked me the casual sort of questions that parents ask their beloved daughter's suitors. But his heart wasn't in it. That role was soon forgotten, and he was laying down the law about art:

"Titian loved reds and blues. Look at any of his paintings and you'll see that. That's why he was always painting auburn-haired models. Wonderful women: he knew a thing or two about women, eh?" A roar of laughter and a quick drink. "And look at his later work. . . . Never mind *The Assumption of the Virgin,* or any of that. . . . Look at the real Titians. He was putting the paint on with his fingertips. He was the first impressionist: that's the only word you can use. I'll tell you, darling, Titian was a giant."

Or on Gloria's interest in British higher education:

"You won't learn anything worth knowing at Oxford or Cambridge. But I'm glad to hear you're not going to study modern languages. I had a graduate here last year: he couldn't even read a menu, darling! What are *quenelles,* he asked me. Ignorant beyond belief! And his accent was unimaginable. The only people who can understand an Englishman speaking French are people who have been taught French in England."

Or about gambling:

"Use two dice and you change the odds, of course. Why, I've seen men backing the same odds on two as on six."

Gloria provided the cue. "Shouldn't they have?" she asked.

He swung round to the fire and, supporting himself with a hand on each armrest of his dining chair, he aimed a kick at the log, so that it exploded in sparks. "Naw! With two dice? No! You can throw six so many different ways. You can get it with two threes; with a four and a two; four and a two the other way; a five and a one; five and a one the other way. That makes five different ways. But you have only one chance to get two; both dice have to come up right for you. Same with getting twelve."

He swung back to face us and reverted to being Gloria's guardian. He looked at Gloria and then examined me, as if trying to decide if my motives were honorable. What he decided did not show on his face. He was remarkably good at concealing his feelings when he was so inclined.

Art and science and cookery and politics and weather forecasting and ancient Greek architecture, and every so often there came that penetrating stare. And so for the whole evening he was roaring down these motorways of conversation and then slamming on the brakes as he remembered that I was the man who was taking his old friend's little girl to bed every night.

It was during one of these abrupt pauses in the conversation that he suddenly extended his fist so it was only a few inches from my nose. I stared at him and made no move. Click! There was the handle of a flick knife concealed in his hand, and now its blade snapped forward so that its shiny point was almost touching my eye.

"Dodo!" Gloria yelled in alarm.

Slowly he drew his knife back and folded the blade back into the handle. "Ha ha. I wanted to see what this fellow had in him," he said, and sounded disappointed that I'd been able to conceal my alarm.

"I don't like that sort of joke," she said.

Gloria had bought two bottles of Hine brandy in the duty-free shop, and Dodo had got the cork out of the first one before we were far through his front door. I stuck to the local rosé wine, a light and refreshing drink, but Dodo favored the Hine through the black olives, the chicken and vegetable stew, the goat cheese, and the bowl of apples and oranges that followed. By the end of the meal he was uncorking the second bottle, and when we went out on his patio to see the view he was talking loud enough to be heard in Nice. The sky was clear, and every star in the sky was gathering over his house, but it was damned cold, and the chilly air had no discernible effect upon his ebullience. "It's cold," I said. "Damned cold."

"One hundred and fifty years," he answered, and wiped drink from his chin. "And the walls are a meter thick, darling."

Gloria laughed. "Shall we go back inside?" she said. I suppose she was used to him.

He held tight to the balcony to get back in through the sliding door. Even so he collided with the fly screen and banged his head on the door's edge.

Despite all his shouting about its not being necessary, Gloria went into the kitchen to wash the dishes. In an attempt to show him what a goodhearted and inoffensive fellow I was, I tried to follow her, but he pulled me aside with a rough tug at my sleeve.

"Leave her alone, darling," he said gruffly. "She'll do what she wants to do. Zu has always been like that." He poured more wine for me and topped up his tumbler of brandy. "She's a wonderful girl."

"Yes, she is," I said.

"You're a lucky man: do you know that?" His voice was soft but his eyes were hard. I was on my guard all the time, and he knew that, and seemed to enjoy it.

"Yes, I do."

He went suddenly quiet. He was staring out through the glass doors at the lights that wound up into the hills: orange lights and blue lights and sometimes the headlights of cars that shone suddenly and then disappeared like fireflies on a summer's evening. The wonderful view seemed to wreak some profound change upon him. Perhaps it has that effect upon people who spend most of their working days studying the same landscape, its colors, patterns, and contradictions. When he spoke again his voice was soft and sober. "Make the most of every minute," he said. "You'll lose her, you know."

"Will I?" I kept my voice level.

He sipped his brandy and smiled sadly. "She adores you, of course. Any fool could see that. I could see it in her eyes as soon as you walked into the house. Never takes her eyes off you. But she's just a child. She has a life ahead of her. How old are you? . . . Over forty. Right?"

"Yes," I said.

"She's determined on this university business. You'll not persuade her otherwise. She'll go to college. And there she'll meet brilliant people of her own age, and because they are at college they'll all end up sharing the same appalling tastes and the same half-baked opinions. We're old fossils. We're part of another world. A world of the dinosaurs." He swigged his brandy and poured more. There was a lot of spite in him. His friendly advice was really a way of hurting me. And it was a method difficult to counter.

I said, "Yes, thanks a lot, Dodo. But, the way I see it, you are indisputably an old tyrannosaurus, but I'm a young, dynamic, brilliant individual in the prime of life, and Gloria is an immature youngster."

He laughed loudly enough to rupture my eardrums, and he grabbed my shoulder to save himself from falling over.

"Zu, darling!" he shouted gleefully and loud enough for

her to hear him from the kitchen. "Where did you find this lunatic?"

She came from the kitchen, wiping her hands on a tea towel decorated with a picture of the *Mona Lisa* smoking a big cigar. "Are you on some sort of diet, Dodo?" she asked. "How can you eat three dozen eggs?"

For a moment words did not come, but then he stammered and said that they were the finest eggs he'd ever eaten and a nearby farmer supplied him but he had to take a lot at a time. "Have some," he offered.

"I'm not that fond of eggs," said Gloria. "They are bad for you."

"Rubbish, darling. Arrant rubbish. A newly laid soft-boiled egg is the most easily digested protein food I know. I love eggs. And there are so many delicious ways of cooking them."

"They won't be so newly laid by the time you get through three dozen of them," said Gloria with devastating feminine logic. She smiled. "We must be leaving you, Dodo."

"Sit down for a moment longer, darling," he pleaded. "I have so few visitors nowadays, and you haven't told me the latest news of your parents and all our friends in London."

For the next ten minutes or so they talked of the family. Small talk of Gloria's father's dental practice and her mother's charity committees. Dodo listened politely and with ever-more-glazed eyes.

At ten-twenty-five exactly—I looked at my watch to see the time—Dodo drew himself up to his full height, drank to the health of "Zu and her lunatic," and, having upended his glass, bent and fell full-length onto the floor with a horrifying crash. The tumbler broke, and there was a flare from the log fire as brandy splashed on the embers.

Gloria looked at me, expecting me to revive him, but I just shrugged at her. He groaned and moved enough to reassure us that he wasn't dead. Having stretched himself across the carpet before the fire, he began to snore heavily. Gloria's attempts to wake him failed.

"I shouldn't have brought the brandy for him," Gloria said. "He has liver trouble."

"And I can understand why," I said.

"We must try and get him onto his bed," she said. "We can lift him between us."

"He looks comfortable enough," I said.

"You're a callous swine," said Gloria. So I got his boots off and carried him into his bedroom and dumped him on his bed.

In his tiny bedroom one more surprise awaited us. A table had been hidden in here. It was laden with pots of color, a kitchen measuring spoon, a bottle of vinegar, and a bottle of linseed oil. Balanced on a jug was a muslin strainer through which raw beaten egg had been poured, and in the rubbish bin under the table there were half a dozen broken eggshells. Propped against the wall was another panel, unpainted, but smooth and shiny with its beautifully prepared chalk-gesso ground.

"What the hell is this?" I said, looking at the half-finished painting leaning against the table. It was quite different from anything we'd seen in the living room or the studio: a Renaissance street scene, a procession, painted on a large wooden panel about five feet long. The colors were weird but the drawings were exact. "What strange coloring," I said.

"It's just the underpainting," explained Gloria. "He'll put colored glazes over that to create deep, luminous colors."

"You seem to know all about it."

"I was an au-pair girl in Nice. I used to come up here on my afternoons off. Sometimes I helped him. He's a sweet man. Do you know what it is?" Gloria asked.

"Egg-tempera painting, I suppose. But why on long panels?"

"Renaissance marriage chests."

"I don't get it."

"He paints forgeries. He sells them through a dealer in Munich."

"And buyers are fooled?"

"They are authenticated by international art experts. Often famous museums buy them."

"And he gets away with that?"

"Now it's new . . . unfinished. It will be stained and varnished and damaged so that it looks very old."

"And fool museums?" I persisted.

"Museum directors are not saints, Bernard."

"And there goes another illusion! So Dodo's rich?"

"No, they take him a long time to do, and the dealers won't pay much: there are other forgers ready and willing to supply them."

"So why . . . "

". . . does he do it?" she finished the question for me. "The deception . . . the fraud, the deceit, is what amuses him. He can be cruel. When you get to know him better, perhaps you'll see what makes him do it."

The old man groaned and seemed about to wake up, but he turned over and went back to sleep, breathing heavily. Gloria bent over and stroked his head affectionately. "The dealers make the big profits. Poor Dodo."

"You knew all along? You were teasing him about the eggs in his refrigerator?"

She nodded. "Dodo is notorious. He claims to have painted a wonderful 'School of Uccello' marriage chest that ended up in the Louvre. Dodo bought dozens of colored postcards of it, and used them as Christmas cards last year. I thought he'd end up in prison, but no one knows whether that was just Dodo's idea of a joke. Hungarians have all got a strange sense of humor."

"I wondered about that," I said.

"He knows about chemistry. It amuses him to reproduce

the pigments, and age the wood and the other materials. He's awfully clever."

The old man stirred again and put a hand to his head where he'd banged it in falling. "Oh my God!" he groaned.

"You're all right," I told him.

"He can't hear you; he's talking in his sleep," said Gloria. "You do that sometimes."

"Oh, yes," I scoffed at the suggestion.

"Last week you woke me up. You were calling out crazy things." She put an arm round me in a protective gesture.

"What things?"

" 'They're killing him; they're killing him.' "

"I never talk in my sleep," I said.

"Have it your own way," said Gloria. But she was right. Three nights in a row I'd woken up after a nightmare about Jim Prettyman. "They're killing Jim!" is what I'd shouted. I remembered it only too well. In the dream, no matter how urgently I shouted at the passersby, none of them would take any notice of me.

"Look at these photos," said Gloria, unrolling some old prints that had been curled up on a cluttered side table. "Wasn't he a handsome young brute?"

A slim, youthful, athletic Dodo was in a group with half a dozen such youngsters and an older man whose face I knew well. Three of them were seated on wicker chairs in front of a garden hut. A man in the front row had a foot upon a board that said "The Prussians."

"Probably a tennis tournament," explained Gloria. "He was a wonderful tennis player."

"Something like that," I said, although I knew in fact that it was nothing of the kind. The older man was an old Berlin hand named John "Lange" Koby—a contemporary of my father—and his "Prussians" were the intelligence teams that he ran into the Russian Zone of Germany. So Dodo had been an agent.

"Did Dodo ever work with your father?" I asked her.

"In Hungary?" I nodded. "Intelligence gathering?" She had such a delicate way of putting things. "Not as far as I know." She took the photo from me. "Is that a team?"

"That's the American: Lange Koby," I said.

She looked at the photo with renewed interest now that she knew they were field agents. "Yes, he's much older than the others. He's still alive, isn't he?"

"Lives in Berlin. Sometimes I run into him. My father detested Lange. But Lange was all right."

"Why?"

"He detested all those Americans who Lange ran. He used to say, 'German Americans are American Germans.' He had an obsession about them."

"I've never heard you criticize your father before," said Gloria.

"Maybe he had his reasons," I said defensively. "Let's go."

"Are you sure Dodo will be all right?"

"He'll be all right," I said.

"You do like him, don't you?"

"Yes," I said.

At that first meeting I did like him; I must have been raving mad.

Chapter 10

"It went well, I thought," Dicky Cruyer said with a hint of modest pride. He was carrying illustration boards, and now he put them on the floor and leaned them against the leg of his fine rosewood table.

I came into his room, still trying to read the notes I'd scribbled during the babble, indignation, and dismay that were always the hallmark of Tuesday mornings. I wasn't giving my whole attention to Dicky, and that was the sort of thing he noticed. I looked up and grunted.

"I said," Dicky repeated very slowly, having given me a good-natured smile, "that I thought it all went very well." I must have looked puzzled. "In the departmental get-together." He tapped the brass barometer that he'd lately added to the furnishings of his working space. Or maybe he was tapping the temperature, or the time in New York City.

"Oh, yes," I said. "Very well indeed."

Well, why wouldn't it go to his satisfaction? What Dicky Cruyer, my immediate boss, called a "departmental get-together" took place in one of the conference rooms every Tuesday morning. At one time it had taken place in Dicky's office, but the German Station Controller's empire had grown since then: we needed a larger room nowadays, because Tuesday morning had become a chance for Dicky to rehearse the lectures he gave to the indefatigable mandarins of the Foreign Office. It was usually a mad scramble of last-minute paperwork, but today he'd used satellite photos and had pretty colored diagrams—pie charts, stacked bars, and line graphs—prepared in the new "art department," and an "operator" came and put them on the projector. Dicky prodded the screen with a telescopic rod and looked round the darkened room in case anyone had lit a cigarette.

The get-together was also the opportunity for Dicky to allocate work to his subordinates, arbitrate between them, and start thinking about the monthly report that would have to be on the Director-General's desk first thing on Friday morning. That is to say, he got me to start thinking about it, because I always had to write it.

"It's simply a matter of motivating them all," said Dicky,

sitting at his rosewood table and straightening out a wire paper clip. "I want them to feel . . ."

". . . part of a team," I supplied.

"That's right," he said. Then, detecting what he thought might be a note of sarcasm in my voice, he frowned. "You have a lot to learn about being part of a team, Bernard," he said.

"I know," I said. "I think the school I went to didn't emphasize the team spirit nearly enough."

"That lousy school in Berlin," he said. "I never understood why your father let you go to a little local school like that. There were schools for the sons of British officers, weren't there?"

"He said it would be good for my German."

"And it was," conceded Dicky. "But you must have been the only English child there. It made you into a loner, Bernard."

"I suppose it did."

"And you're proud of that, I know. But a loner is a misfit, Bernard. I wish I could make you see that."

"I'll need your notes, Dicky."

"Notes?"

"To do the D-G's report."

"Not much in the way of notes today, Bernard," he said proudly. "I'm getting the hang of these Tuesday-morning talks nowadays. I improvise as I go along."

Oh my God! I should have listened to what he was saying. "Any rough notes will do."

"Just write it the way I delivered it."

"It's a matter of emphasis, Dicky."

He threw the straightened wire clip into his large glass ashtray and looked at me sharply. "A matter of emphasis" was Dicky's roundabout way of admitting total ignorance. Hurriedly I added, "It's so technical."

Dicky softened somewhat. He liked being "technical."

Until recently Dicky's lectures had been a simple résumé of the everyday work of the office. But now he'd decided that the way ahead was the path of hi-tech. So he'd become a minor expert—and major bore—on such subjects as "photo-interpretation of intelligence obtained by unmanned vehicles." And "optical cameras, line-scan, and radar sensors that provide monochrome, color, false-color, or infrared imagery."

"I think I explained it all carefully," Dicky said.

"Yes, you did," I said, and bent over far enough to flip through the cardboard-mounted pictures he'd used, in the hope that they would all be suitably captioned. To some extent they were: "SLRR sideways looking reconnaissance radar," the first one said, and there was a neat red arrow to show which way was up. And "IRLS infrared line-scan photo showing various radiometric temperatures of target area at noon. Notice buildings occupied by personnel, and the transport vehicles at bottom right of photo. Compare with photo of same area at midnight."

"Don't take that material away with you," Dicky warned. "I'll need those pictures tomorrow, and I promised the people at Joint Air Reconnaissance that they'd have them back in perfect condition: no fingerprints or bent corners."

"No, I won't take them," I promised, and slid the illustrations back in place. I was hopeless at understanding such things. I began to wonder which one of Dicky's staff, present at this morning's meeting, might have remembered his discourse well enough to recapitulate and explain it to me. But I couldn't think of anyone who gave Dicky his undivided attention during the Tuesday-morning meetings. Our most assiduous note-taker, Charlie Billingsly, was now in Hong Kong, and Harry Strang, with his prodigious memory, had artfully contrived an urgent phone call that granted him escape just five minutes into Dicky's dissertation. I said, "But you used to be strongly opposed to all this stuff from JARIC and the satellite material too."

"We have to move with the times, Bernard." Dicky looked down at the appointments book that his secretary had left open for him. "Oh, by the bye," he said casually. Too casually. "You keep mentioning that fellow Prettyman. . . ."

"I don't keep mentioning him," I said. "I mentioned him once. You said you didn't remember him."

"I don't want to quibble," said Dicky. "The point is that his wife has been making a nuisance of herself lately. She cornered Morgan when he was in the FO the other day. Started on about a pension and all that kind of stuff."

"His widow," I said.

"Verily! Widow. I said 'widow.'"

"You said 'wife.'"

"Wife. Widow. What damned difference does it make."

"It makes a difference to Jim Prettyman," I said. "It makes him dead."

"Whatever she is, I don't want anyone encouraging her."

"Encouraging her to do what?"

"I wish you wouldn't be so otiose," said Dicky. He'd been reading *Vocabulary Means Power* again; I noticed that it was missing from the shelf behind his desk. "She shouldn't be buttonholing senior staff. It would serve her right if Morgan made an official complaint about her."

"She wields a lot of clout over there," I reminded him. "I wouldn't advise Morgan to make an enemy of her. He might end up on his arse."

Dicky wet his thin lips and nodded. "Yes. Well. You're right. Morgan knows that. Far better that we all close ranks and ignore her."

"Jim Prettyman was one of us," I said. "He worked downstairs."

"That was a long time ago. No one told him to go and work in Washington, D.C. What a place that is! My God, that town has some of the worst crime figures in the whole of North America." So Dicky had been doing his homework.

I said, "This is not official, then? This . . . this not encouraging Prettyman's widow?"

He looked at me and then looked out of the window. "It's not official," he said with measured care. "It's good advice. It's advice that might save someone a lot of trouble and grief."

"That's what I wanted to know," I said. "Shall we get the heading for the D-G's report?"

"Very well," said Dicky. He looked at me and nodded again. I wondered if he knew that Cindy Matthews—onetime Mrs. Prettyman—had invited me to dinner that evening.

"And by the way, Dicky," I said, "that lion looks very good on the floor in here."

Mrs. Cindy Matthews, as she styled herself, lived in considerable comfort. There was new Italian furniture, old French wine, a Swiss dishwasher, and the sort of Japanese hi-fi that comes with a thick instruction manual. They'd never faced the expense that children bring, of course, and I suppose the rise in London house prices had provided them with a fat profit on the big house they'd been buying in Edgware. Now she lived in a tiny house off the King's Road, a thoroughfare noted for its punks, pubs, and exotic boutiques. It was no more than four small rooms placed one upon the other, with the lowest one—a kitchen and dining room—below street level. But it was a fashionable choice: the sort of house that estate agents called "bijou" and newly divorced advertising men hankered after.

There were candles and pink roses on the dining table, and solid silver cutlery, and more drinking glasses than I could count. Through the front window we could see the ankles of people walking past the house, and they could see what we were eating. Which is perhaps why we had the sort of meal that women's magazines photograph from above. Three paper-thin slices of avocado arranged alongside a tiny puddle of tomato sauce and a slice of kiwi fruit. The second course was three thin slices of duck breast with a segment of mango and a lettuce leaf. We ended with a thin slice of Cindy's delicious homemade chocolate roulade. I ate a lot of bread and cheese.

Cindy had always been brimful of nervous energy, and arranging this dinner party had not lessened her restless anxiety. Now she fussed about the table, asking her guests whether they wanted more champagne, Perrier, or Chablis, wholemeal or white rolls, and making sure that everyone had a table napkin. There was a tacit sigh of relief when she finally sat down.

It was a planned evening. Cindy always planned everything in advance. The food was measured, the cooking times synchronized, the white wines chilled and reds at the right temperature. The rolls were warmed, the butter was soft, the guests were carefully prompted, and the conversation was predictable. It wasn't one of those evenings when you can hardly squeeze a word into the gabble, when the guests stay too late, drink too much, and lurch out of the house excitedly scribbling each other's phone numbers into their Filofax notebooks. It was dull.

Perhaps it was a tribute to Cindy's planning that she'd invited me on an evening when Gloria did a class in mathematics, part of her determination to do well at university, and so I went along to dinner on my own.

The evening started off very sedately, as evenings were likely to do when Sir Giles Streeply-Cox was the guest of honor. A muscular old man with bushy white Pickwickian sideburns and a florid complexion, "Creepy-Pox" had been the scourge of the Foreign Office in his day. Ministers and ambassadors went in terror of him. Since retirement he lived in Suffolk and grew roses while his wife made picture frames for all the local water-color artists. But the old man was still attending enough committees to get his fares and expenses paid when he came to London.

It was the first time I'd ever seen the fearful Creepy close to, but this evening he was on his best behavior. Cindy knew exactly how to handle him. She let him play the part of the charming old great man of Whitehall. He slipped into this role effortlessly, but there was no mistaking the ogre that lurked behind the smiles and self-deprecating asides. Lady Streeply-Cox said little. She was of a generation that was taught not to mention the food or the table arrangements, and talking about her husband's work was as bad as talking about TV. So she sat and smiled at her husband's jokes, which meant she didn't have much to do all evening.

There were two Diplomatic Corps people. Harry Baxter, a middle-aged second secretary from our embassy in Bern. His wife, Pat, had a heavy gold necklace and pink-tinted hair, and told jokes—with punch lines in *Schweizerdeutsch*—about bankers with unpronounceable names.

When Cindy asked Baxter what exciting things had been happening in Bern lately, old Streeply-Cox answered for him by saying the only exciting thing that happened to the diplomatic staff in Bern was losing their bread crusts in the fondue. At which both Streeply-Coxes laughed shrilly.

There was a young couple too. Simon, a shy chap in his early twenties who'd been teaching English in a private school in Bavaria. It was not an experience he'd enjoyed. "You see these mean little German kids and you understand why the Germans have started so many wars," he said. "And you see those teachers and you know why the Germans lost them." Now Simon had become a theater critic on a giveaway magazine and achieved a reputation as a perfectionist and connoisseur by condemning everything he wrote about. With him was a quiet girl with smudged lipstick. She was wearing a man's tweed jacket many sizes too big for her. They smiled at each other all through dinner and left early.

After dinner we all went upstairs and had coffee and drinks in a room with an elaborate gas fire that hissed loudly. Creepy had one demitasse of decaffeinated coffee and a chocolate mint; then his wife swigged down two large brandies and drove him home.

The couple from Bern stayed on for another half-hour or so. Cindy having indicated that she wanted a word with me, I remained behind. "What do you think of him?" she said after all the other guests had left.

"Old Creepy? He's a barrel of fun," I said.

"Don't take him for a fool," Cindy warned. "He knows his way around."

I had a feeling that Creepy was there to impress me with the sort of contacts she had, the sort of influence she could wield behind the scenes in the Foreign Office corridors if she needed a show of strength. "Did you want to talk to me?"

"Yes, Bernard, I did."

"Give me another drink," I said.

She got the bottle of Scotch from the side table and put it in front of me, on a copy of *Nouvelle Cuisine* magazine. On the cover it said, "Ten easy steps to a surefire chocolate roulade." She didn't pour the Scotch; she walked across to the fireplace and fiddled with something on the mantelpiece. "Ever since poor Jim was murdered . . ." she began without turning round.

I suppose I'd guessed—in fact, dreaded—what was coming, because I immediately tried to head it off. "Is 'murdered' the right word?" I said.

She rounded on me. "Two men wait for him and shoot him dead? Six bullets? What do you call it, Bernard? It's a damned bizarre way to commit suicide, isn't it?"

"Yes, go on." I dropped some ice into my glass and poured myself a generous drink.

"I asked about the funeral. I told them I wanted to go and asked them for the fare."

"And?"

"It's all over and done with. Cremated!" She used the word as if it was an obscenity, as perhaps for her it was.

"Cremated! Not a word to me about what I'd like done for my husband." Her voice was bitter. As a Catholic she felt herself doubly wronged. "Oh, and there's something for you."

She gave me a cardboard box. I opened it and found a pile of papers about ancient Mesopotamian tomb inscriptions. It was all neatly arranged and included ones that Fiona had worked on. I recognized her handwriting. "For me?" I said. "In Jim's will?"

"There was no will; just a letter Jim had left with his lawyer. Things to be done after he died. It's witnessed. It's legal, they say."

"Are you sure he wanted me to have it? I was never interested."

"Perhaps he wanted you to send it on to Fiona," she said. "But don't give it back to me. I've got enough on my mind without all the tricks and puzzles of the ancient world."

I nodded. She'd always been sarcastic about Jim's hobby, and I suppose I had too.

"I've been trying to find out more exactly what Jim was doing when he died," she said, and there was a significant pause.

"Tell me," I said. I knew she was going to tell me anyway.

"I started with the money," she said. I nodded. The Foreign Office handled our budget. It was one aspect of our work that she might have been able to pry into.

"Money?" I said.

"The money that's supposed to be missing. The money you went to Washington to ask Jim about."

"Just for the record, Cindy. I didn't go to Washington to ask Jim anything. That extra little job was dumped upon me after I got there."

She was unconvinced. "Maybe, maybe not," she said. "When we've got to the bottom of it you might find that it was all arranged right from the start."

"That what was arranged?"

"Having you in Washington at the right time to do that 'little extra job.' "

"No. Cindy . . ."

"Mother of God! Will you listen to me, Bernard, and stop interrupting. The fund that Jim arranged. There was a lot of money laundered through a couple of banks in Gibraltar and Austria. Backward and forward it went, so it's damned difficult to trace. It seems to have ended up in an account in Germany. All that money was moved and invested six months before your wife defected."

"So what?"

"Before!"

"I heard you."

"Don't you see?"

"See what?"

"Suppose I told you that this fund was set up by your wife, Fiona. Suppose I said that this was a KGB slush fund."

"A KGB what?" I said, rather more loudly than I intended. "And Jim could sign? You told me Jim could sign."

She smiled knowingly. "Exactly. That was the cunning of it. Suppose Fiona set up the funding of a KGB network and used SIS money and people to operate it. Do you see the elegance of it?"

"Frankly, no," I said. I wasn't going to make it easy for her. If she wanted to sell me her crackpot hypothesis, she'd have to take me through it theorem by theorem.

"Financing a secret network is the most difficult and dangerous part of any secret operation. You don't have to be working on your side of the river to know that, Bernard."

"Yes, I think I read that somewhere," I said. But sarcasm wasn't going to stop her.

"Don't be stupid, Bernard. I know how it all works."

I drank her whisky and didn't answer.

"I must have a cigarette," she said. "I'm trying to give them up, but I must have one now." She got an unopened pack from a brass bowl on the bookshelf and took her time lighting up. Her hands were shaking, and the flaming match emphasized the movement, but that might have been because she craved the cigarette. I watched her with interest. The people in the Foreign Office knew things that we never found out about until it was too late. She said, "If Fiona set up a clandestine bank account and had our own people run it under strict secrecy, it would be the best and most secret way to supply funds to enemy agents, wouldn't it?" She was calmer now that she was smoking the cigarette.

"But if you have found out about it, how secret is that?"

She had an answer. "Because Fiona defected. That upset everything."

"And you are saying that Jim went to Washington because Fiona defected? That Jim was a KGB agent?"

"Maybe." That was the weakest link: I could see it in her face. "I keep thinking about it. I really don't know."

"Not Jim. Of all people, not Jim. And even if you were right, why the hell would he run to America, the heartland of capitalism?"

"I only said maybe. More probably Fiona fooled everyone into thinking it was official. How could they guess it was money for the KGB?"

"But the money is missing," I pointed out.

"They can't find the account," she said. "The whole damned account. And they are only guessing at how much might be in it: one estimate said four million pounds. No one in the FO or the Department will admit to knowing anything about it. The cashier knows the money is missing, but that's all."

"That only means that he doesn't have the right piece of paper with an appropriate signature on it. That's what the cashier means by money missing."

"This was real money, Bernard, and someone got their hands on it."

I shook my head. It was beyond me. "Did you get all this from 'our man in Bern'?" I said, referring to the Baxters.

"They're old friends. He knows his way around, but he hasn't got anywhere so far."

"But there must be a departmental record of who was named as the account holder."

"Yes. Jim."

"And who else?"

She shrugged. "We don't even know where the account is," she said, and blew smoke hard through pursed lips. "I'm not going to let it go, Bernard."

"What will you do?"

"What do you suggest?" she said.

"The Deputy D-G is very energetic these days," I offered. "You might find some way of talking to him."

"How can we be sure it doesn't go up that far?"

For a moment I didn't follow her. Then I did. "Working for the KGB? The Deputy? Sir Percy Babcock?"

"No need to shout, Bernard. Yes, the Deputy. You read the newspapers. You know the score."

"If I know the score, it's not because I read the newspapers," I said.

"No one is above suspicion these days."

"You're going to talk to Five?" And already I was wondering whether it was better to jump out of the window or ring for an ambulance.

She was horrified at the idea. "MI5? The Home Office? No, no, no. They'd know nothing about our Central Funding. And I work for the Foreign Office. That would be more than my job's worth, Bernard."

"So what else can you do? You're not thinking of trying to lobby the Cabinet Office, are you?"

"Are you saying you won't help?"

So that was it. I drank some of my whisky, took a deep breath, and said, "What do you want me to do, Cindy?"

"We've got to go through the files and find the orders that created the account."

"You said you've tried that already," I pointed out.

"But not in the Data Centre," she said.

"The Yellow Submarine? Jesus Christ, Cindy! You're not serious. And, anyway, you're not allowed there." I could have bitten my tongue off.

"No," she said, "but you are, Bernard. You're always in and out of there." I'd walked right into it. I took a good mouthful of booze and swallowed it quickly.

"Cindy . . ."

Hurriedly she explained her theory. "The computer will have it in cross-reference. That's how computers work, isn't it? Instead of me rummaging through hundreds of files, we'd only have to give the computer one hard fact to access everything."

"And what hard fact could we give it?"

"Jim. Jim was a trustee or a signature or something. Key him into the computer and we'll get everything we need."

So this was why I'd been invited along. And Creepy was there to reassure me that Cindy had friends at court, just in case. "Well, wait a minute, Cindy," I said as the full, awful implications of it hit me.

She said, "We must see who else had access to it before they are murdered too."

It was then that I began to think Jim's death had deranged her. "You think Jim was murdered because he was a signatory to the bank account?"

"Yes. That's exactly what I think, Bernard," she said.

I watched her as she lit a cigarette. "I'll see what I can find out," I promised. "Maybe there's another way."

"The Data Centre is our only chance," said Cindy.

"We could both be fired, Cindy. Are you sure it's worth it?" I asked. Having been warned off by Dicky, I wanted to see if she had an explanation.

But she was like a woman possessed. "There's something damned odd going on," she said. "Everything to do with this bloody bank account is so damned well covered. I've handled some sensitive material, Bernard, but I've never heard of anything buried as deep as this one. There is no paper: no files on it, no memos, no records. No one knows anything."

"Don't know or won't tell? It might just have a very high clearance."

"Someone is damned scared. Someone in the Department, I mean. Someone is so damned scared that they had Jim murdered."

"We're not sure of that," I said.

"I'm sure," she said. "And no one is going to shut me up."

"Cindy," I said, and paused, wondering how to put it to her. "Don't be offended. But there's something you must tell me. Truly."

"Spit it out, Bernard."

"You're not just putting this pressure on the Department as a way to get Jim's pension, are you?"

She smiled one of her special *Mona Lisa* smiles. "They've agreed to that already," she said.

"They have?"

"They're paying a full pension to me and a full pension to this American woman who says she married Jim in Mexico."

"They admitted Jim was still working for the Department?" Now I was surprised.

"They admit nothing. It's one of those 'in-full-and-final-settlement' contracts: Sign here and shut up."

"That's unusual," I allowed.

"Unusual?" She chortled. "Jesus! It's bloody unprecedented. It's not the way the Department works, is it? They didn't hesitate, didn't confirm with anyone or check anything I said. Okay, they said. Just like that."

"Who authorized it?"

A scornful little laugh. "No one knows. They said it was in the file."

"How could it be in the file?" I said. There couldn't be anything in the file about paying out two pensions to two wives of someone who'd stopped working for the Department years before.

"Exactly," she said. "Someone is damned scared."

"Scared," I said, "yes." She was right: it was me.

Chapter 11

Thursday was not a good day. I had to go down into the Yellow Submarine. The Data Centre was just about the only part of the Foreign Office where even Cindy Matthews would not be able to stroll past the security guard with some casual chat about getting the tin of biscuits for the Minister's afternoon tea. They were fussy here: Uniformed guards with hats on. A photo-identity check at the ground-floor entrance, and more checks at the software-library level, and video at the third and deepest level, where the secrets were really kept under lock and key.

After my wife defected it was several weeks—nearly three months, in fact—before I was required to go down into the Submarine again. I had begun to believe that my security clearance had been downgraded and that I'd never see the inside of the place again, but then one day Dicky stayed at home with a head cold and something was wanted urgently and I was the only one in the office who knew how to work the consoles down there and they sent me. From that time onward everything was back to normal again, as far as I could tell. But with the Department you can never be sure. It's not like the

Michelin Guide: they don't publish a book each spring so you can find out how the inspectors feel about you.

So I was happy enough to sit at the keyboard and tell the machine my name, grade, and department and wait for it to come up with the request for my secret access number. It meant that I was still one of the nation's trusted. Once the machine had okayed my number, I spent a couple of hours sitting there, rolling around on one of those uncomfortable little typist's chairs, calling up answers on the display screen and producing yards of pale-green security printout for Dicky. When I had finished everything he wanted, I sat there for a moment. I knew I should get up and go straight back to the office. But I couldn't resist probing into the machinery just once. Just so I could go back to Cindy and tell her that I'd tried. And also to satisfy my own curiosity.

I keyed it in: PRETTYMAN, JAMES.

The machine gurgled before providing a menu from which I selected BIOG. More soft clattering came from deep inside the machine before Prettyman's twenty-two-page-long service biography came up on the screen. I pushed the control-arrow buttons to get to the end of it and found it ended with a summary of Prettyman's last report. This was the standard civil-service file, in which one's immediate superior comments on "judgment, political sense, power of analysis, and foresight," but it didn't say whether Prettyman had retired from the Department or continued to work for it. When I pressed the machine for supplementary material, I got only the word REVISE.

So I pursued PRETTYMAN J BIOG REVISE and got REFER FILE FO FX MI 123/456, which seemed an unlikely number for a file. I tried to access that file and found ACCESS DENIED ENTER ARCTIC NUMBER.

I couldn't tell the machine the "Arctic" number it wanted, because I didn't even know what an Arctic number was. I looked at my watch. I still had plenty of time to spare before my appointment with Dicky. Dicky had been in a very good mood for the last few days. The Bizet crisis seemed to have faded. There had been no hard news, but Dicky told the Deputy that the Stasi prosecution office were about to release our men because of insufficient evidence, and managed to imply that it was all his doing. It was a total fabrication, but when Dicky needed good news he never hesitated to invent some. Once, when I'd tackled him about it, he said this was the only way of getting the old man off his back.

Today Dicky had gone to lunch with his old friend and onetime colleague Henry Tiptree, who'd left his cozy Foreign Office desk for a job with a small merchant bank in the newly deregulated City. Morgan had gone to lunch with them too. Morgan used to be a hatchet man and general factotum for the Director-General, but since the D-G's appearances had become fewer and further between, Morgan had nothing to do but pass queries to the Deputy D-G's office and blow smoke at the ceilings of the City's private dining rooms. I suspected that Morgan and Dicky were cautiously investigating their chances of getting one of the six-figure City salaries that I kept reading about in *The Economist.* In any case, Tiptree, Morgan, and Dicky were not likely to finish judging the Havanas and old tawny port until three at the earliest, which is why I'd brought my packet of sandwiches to the Submarine.

So I tried again. I entered the company for which Prettyman worked in Washington. TRANSFER LOAD, then PERIMETER SECURITY GUARANTEE TRUST.

The machine purred contentedly, and then the screen filled. Here it all was: the address of the headquarters, computed world assets, stock-market price, and names of president and vice-presidents of the PSGT. This wasn't what I wanted, so I entered PRETTYMAN into the PSGT queries space. Hiccups. Then I got REFER FILE FO FX MI 123/456.

I went back to REGISTRY ONE and entered that file number. On the screen came the same message as before: ACCESS DENIED ENTER ARCTIC NUMBER. It was a merry-go-round. Had I not been seeking specific information, it would not have seemed sinister. Had I not chosen those particular subjects, it would not have produced the coincidence.

Now I tried another angle. The data bank held details of departmental employees, past and present. I entered the name of my wife, SAMSON, FIONA, and entered the UPDATE command for the final part of her file.

No surprise now. Up came that damned bogus number that couldn't possibly have come from the normal filing system; REFER FILE FO FX MI 123/456. And, of course, the subsequent keying was answered by the inevitable request for the ARCTIC NUMBER. So whatever the Arctic number was, it would give an inquirer answers about Jim Prettyman, his U.S. employers—almost certainly a front for some sort of illicit business—and whatever my wife, Fiona, was doing during those final weeks before her defection.

I went and walked around for a few minutes. Level Three was especially depressing. On one wall the huge open room had dark metal shelving packed with spools and huge twelve-platter disk packs, and other examples of sophisticated computer software. Another long wall was occupied with the work stations, and on the third wall was a series of desks and soft chairs that were allotted to senior staff. The last wall was of glass, and behind it the toilers came hauling trolleys piled with paper, which the machines consumed with terrible appetites.

I stretched my legs and racked my brains. I even drank some of the concoction that the "beverage dispenser" classified as coffee. I went to the toilet. For many months the question "Is there intelligent life in the Data Centre?" had been posed in neat handwriting on the wall there. Now someone had scrawled, "Yes, but I'm only visiting," below it. The graffiti were the only sign of real human life displayed anywhere, for the staff assigned here soon became as robotic as the machines they operated and serviced. I went back to my work station.

I continued for another hour, but it was no use. The

damned machine always defeated me. In the old days everything was in Registry; no matter that the files were grimy, and you had to take your own soap and towel down there—at least, if you couldn't find what you wanted, there was always someone to show you the bottom shelf where the missing file was put because it was too heavy, or the top shelf where it was put because it was never asked for, or the door it was put against because someone had stolen the wedge that kept the door open. I preferred Registry.

"Where did you have lunch today?" Gloria asked me in that cheerful, casual voice that she assumes when suspicion warps her soul. She wasn't visiting her parents this evening: they were at a dentists' convention in Madrid.

"The Submarine," I said. We were at home and about to have dinner. I was sitting watching the seven o'clock Channel Four news. Gale-force winds were "lashing the coastline" and bringing "chaos" and "havoc," in the way that the weather is apt to do when camera crews have no real news to record. As if to bring the news home to me, the windowpanes rattled and the wind howled loudly through the little trees in the garden. Gloria, on her way to the dining room, put two glasses of chilled white wine on the side table. She was trying to wean me off the hard liquor.

"In the Submarine?" she said with a slight smile and a voice brimming with that malicious one-sided delight for which the Germans coined the word *Schadenfreude*. "How perfectly awful!" She laughed.

"Rubber sandwiches from the Dinky Deli," I added, just to complete her pleasure.

"But you weren't back until nearly four," she called. I could see her in the dining room. She was setting the table for dinner. She did it with the same careful attention she gave to everything. Knives, forks, and spoons were aligned with the plastic place mats; serving spoons guarded the mustard, salt, and peppermill. The napkins were folded and put into position with mathematical accuracy. Satisfied with the table, she came back to where I was sitting, perched herself on the arm of the sofa, and took a small sip of her wine.

"I had a meeting at four . . . with Dicky." I switched off the TV. It was just a regurgitation of ancient happenings. I suppose the news has to be expanded to fit into its allotted time slot.

"The whole afternoon down there? Whatever were you doing?"

"I stayed on, tinkering with the files. I do sometimes."

"Jim Prettyman?"

She knew me too well. "That sort of thing," I admitted.

"Any luck?"

"The same all the time. Have you ever heard of an Arctic coding?"

"No, but there have been a dozen new coding levels in the past year. And there are new top-level data-bank names coming in every month these days."

"I kept getting the same 'access-denied' signal from everything I tried."

"You were trying different ways to get the same data?"

"I spent well over an hour at it."

"I wish you'd told me, darling," she said, her voice changing to one of concern.

"Why?"

"I know those machines. I spent a month down there until you rescued me. Remember?"

"I was working those machines . . ." I almost said before she was born, but the difference in our ages was not something I wanted to keep reminding myself about. ". . . years ago," I finished lamely.

"Then you should know about 'sneaky-peek,'" she said.

"Who or what in hell is sneaky-peek?"

"If you'd taken proper training, instead of just tapping away and hoping for the best, you'd not do silly things."

"What are you talking about?" I said.

"When you get any sort of 'access-denied' signal, the machine flags it and records your name and number."

"Does it?" I asked as she went into the hall and called upstairs to where Billy and Sally were supposed to be doing their homework under the supervision of Doris.

"Dinner, children! Are you ready, Doris?"

She came back into the room and added, "And that's not all. It lists every file you fail to access. When the Data Security clerks run their analysis program, they can see exactly what it is you were trying to get that is beyond your security clearance."

"I didn't know that."

"Obviously, darling." A kitchen timer sounded, and she uttered a muffled Hungarian curse that I'd learned to recognize, and went to the kitchen to get our dinner.

I got up and followed her and watched her getting bright, new pots from the oven and loading them onto the trolley. I said, "You don't know how often they run their security program, do you?"

"Make yourself useful," she said, and left me with the trolley. I pushed it into the dining room. "You can't erase it, darling. If that's what you're hoping for, forget it."

Sally and Billy came in, carrying their schoolbooks. Billy was fourteen and had suddenly grown tall. He had wire braces on his teeth. It must have been uncomfortable, but he never complained. He was a stoic. Sally was a couple of years younger, still very much a child, and still suffering from the loss of her mother. The truth was that both children missed their mother. They never said so; they kept their grief hidden deep inside, and I could find no way of even beginning to console them.

Gloria had made it a routine to check their homework after dinner each evening. She was wonderful with them. Sometimes they seemed to learn more from her in their half-hour of cheerful instruction than they learned all day at school. And Gloria had gained the children's confidence by means of these lessons, and that was no less important to all of us. And yet I sometimes wondered if the children didn't resent the happiness I'd found with Gloria. I suspected that they wanted me to bear my rightful share of their sorrow.

"Hands washed?"

"Yes, Auntie Gloria," they both chorused, their palms held high. Doris held her hands up too and smiled shyly. Newly slimmed, this quiet—and hitherto overweight—girl from a little village in Devon had been with the children a long time now. Having started as a nanny, she now shuttled them back and forth to their respective schools, gave Sally some lunch at home, did some shopping, and scorched my shirts. She was about Gloria's age, and sometimes I wondered what she really thought about Gloria's setting up home with me. But there would be little chance of her confiding any such thoughts to me. In my presence Doris was inscrutable, though with the children I could often hear her yelling merrily and joining in their noisy games.

"Billy can plug the trolley into the electricity socket for me," said Gloria. I sat down. Doris was fidgeting with the cutlery. Abstaining from eating chocolate seemed to have given her chronic withdrawal symptoms.

The trolley with the built-in warmer—to say nothing of the brightly colored casseroles and striped pot holders—was Gloria's idea. It was going to revolutionize our lives, as well as being wonderful when we gave dinner parties.

"Chipolata sausages!" I said. "And Uncle Ben's Rice! My favorites."

Gloria didn't respond. It was the third time in a week we'd had those damned pork sausages. Perhaps if I'd had a proper lunch I would have had sense enough to keep a civil tongue in my head.

Gloria didn't look at me; she was serving the children. "The rice is a bit burned," she told them. "But if you don't take it from the bottom, it will be all right."

She served two sausages to each of us. She'd had the heat too high, and they were black and shrunken. She put the rest of them back on the warmer. Then she gave us all some spinach. It was watery.

Having served the meal, she sat down and took an unusually large swig of her wine before starting to eat.

"I'm sorry," I said, in the hope of breaking her tight-lipped silence.

In a voice unnaturally high she said, "I'm no good at cooking, Bernard. You knew that. I never pretended otherwise." The children looked at Doris, and Doris looked down at her plate.

"It's delicious," I said.

"Don't bloody well patronize me!" she said loudly and angrily. "It's absolutely awful. Do you think I don't know it's all spoiled?"

The children looked at her with that dispassionate interest that children show for events outside their experience. "Don't cry, Auntie Gloria," said Sally. "You can have my sausage: it's almost not burned at all."

Gloria got to her feet and rushed from the room. The children looked at me to see what I would do.

"Carry on eating your supper, children," I said. "I must go and see Auntie Gloria."

"Give her a big kiss, Daddy," advised Sally. "That's sure to make everything all right."

Doris took the mustard away from Billy and said, "Mustard is not good for children."

Some days with Gloria were idyllic. And not just days. For week after week we lived in such harmony and happiness that

I could hardly believe my good fortune. But at other times we clashed. And when one thing went wrong, other discords followed like hammer blows. Lately there had been more and more of these disagreements, and I knew that the fault was usually mine.

"Don't switch on the light," she said quietly. I went into the bedroom expecting to face a tirade. Instead I found Gloria inappropriately apologetic. The only light came from the bedside clock-radio, but it was enough for me to see that she was crying. "It's no good, Bernard," she said. She was sprawled across the bed, the corner of an embroidered handkerchief held tightly in her teeth as if she was trying to summon up enough courage to eat it. "I try and try, but it's no use."

"It's my fault," I said, and bent over and kissed her.

She lifted her face to me, but her expression was unchanging. "It's no one's fault," she said sadly. "You try. I know you do."

I sat on the bed and touched her bare arm. "Living together is not easy," I said. "It takes time to adjust."

For a few moments neither of us spoke. I was tempted to suggest that we send Doris off to cooking classes. But a man who lives in a house with two women knows better than to sprinkle even a mote of dust upon the delicate balance of power.

"It's your wife," said Gloria suddenly.

"Fiona? What do you mean?"

"She was the right one for you."

"Don't talk nonsense."

"She was beautiful and clever." Gloria wiped her nose. "When you were with Fiona, everything was always perfect. I know it was."

For a moment I said nothing. I could take all this admiration of Fiona from anyone except Gloria. I didn't want Gloria implying that I'd been a lucky fellow; I wanted her to say how fortunate Fiona had been to capture me. "We had more help," I said.

"She was rich," said Gloria, and the tears came to her eyes again.

"It's better the way we are."

She seemed not to hear me. When she spoke, her voice came from very far away. "When I first saw you, I wanted you so much, Bernard." She sniffed. "I thought I'd be able to make you so happy. I so envied your wife."

"I didn't know you ever met my wife."

"Of course I saw her about. Everyone admired her. They said she was one of the cleverest women to ever come to work in the Department. People said she would be the first woman D-G."

"Well, people were wrong."

"Yes. I was wrong too," said Gloria. "Wrong about everything. You'll never be happy with me, Bernard. You're too demanding."

"Demanding? What are you talking about?" Too late I recognized that it had been my cue to say how happy I was with her.

"That's right: get angry."

"I'm not getting angry," I said very quietly.

"It's just as well that I'm going to Cambridge."

She was determined to feel sorry for herself. There was nothing I could say. I gave her a kiss, but she didn't respond. Her grief was not to be assuaged.

"Perhaps Doris could help more," I said very tentatively.

Gloria looked at me and gave a bitter smile. "Doris has given notice," she said.

"Doris? Not Doris."

"She says it's boring here in the suburbs."

"Jesus Christ!" I said. "Of course it is. Why else does she think we came here?"

"She had her friends in central London. She went to discos there."

"Doris had friends?"

"Don't be a pig."

"She can go up on the train."

"Once a week. It's not much fun for her. She's still young."

"We're all still young!" I said. "Do you think I don't want to go with Doris's friends to discos?"

"Making jokes won't help you," said Gloria doggedly. "We'll be in a terrible mess when she goes. It won't be easy to get someone who will get on well with the children." Outside the rain kept coming down, thrashing through the apple tree and banging on the windows, while the wind buffeted against the chimney stack and screamed through the TV antenna. "I'm going to see what the agency can offer, but we might have to pay more around here. The woman in the agency says this is a particularly high wages area."

"I bet she did," I said.

Then the telephone rang on my side of the bed. I went to get it. It was Werner. "I've got to see you," he said. He sounded excited, or as near excited as the phlegmatic Werner ever got.

"Where are you?" I asked.

"I'm in London. I'm in a little apartment in Ebury Street, near Victoria Station."

"I don't understand."

"I flew to Gatwick."

"What's happened?"

"We must talk."

"We've got a spare room. Have you got wheels?"

"Better you come here, Bernard."

"To Victoria? It will take half an hour. More, perhaps." The idea of dragging up to central London again appalled me.

"It's serious," said Werner.

I capped the phone. "It's Werner," I explained. "He says he's got to see me. He wouldn't say that unless it was really urgent."

Gloria gave a little shrug and closed her eyes.

Chapter 12

I didn't realize what had happened to some of those little hotels in Ebury Street. It used to be a no-man's-land, where the rucksack-laden hordes from the bus terminal met the smart set of Belgravia. In a curious juxtapositioning that is peculiarly English, Ebury Street provided Belgravia with its expensive little boutiques and chic restaurants and offered budget-conscious travelers cheap overnight lodging. But change was inevitable, and Werner had found a small but luxuriously appointed suite, "all major credit cards accepted," with twenty-four-hour service and security, rubber plants in the lobby, and Dom Perignon in the refrigerator.

"Have you eaten?" said Werner as soon as he opened the door to me.

"Not really."

"Good. I've booked a table for us. It's just round the corner. I read a rave review of it in a flight magazine coming over." He said this in a distracted way, as if his mind was really on something entirely different.

"Wonderful," I said.

"No," said Werner, "I think it might really be good." He looked at his watch. He was agitated; I knew the signs. "The magazine said the fresh salmon mousse is very good," he said, as if not totally convinced.

"How did you find this hotel, Werner?" He was my best friend, but I never really understood Werner in the way I understood other people I'd known for a long time. He was not just secretive: he masked his real feelings by assuming others. When he was happy, he looked sad. When he made a rib-tickling joke, he scowled as if resenting laughter. Winning, he looked like a loser. Was that because he was a Jew? Did he feel he had to conceal his true feelings from a hostile world?

"It's an apartment, a service apartment, not a hotel," he corrected me. The rich, of course, have more words than the rest of us, for they have more goods and services at their disposal. "A fellow I do business with at Kleinwort Benson keeps it as his London base. He said I could use it. Champagne? Whisky or anything?"

"A glass of wine," I said.

He stepped into the tiny kitchen. It was just a fluorescent-lighted box, designed to encourage the use of the "service" rather than as a place to do any proper cooking. He took a bottle of wine from the refrigerator. A Meursault, the bottle was full but uncorked, as if he'd guessed what I would like to drink and prepared for my arrival. He poured a good measure into a Waterford wineglass and put the bottle back again. The refrigerator's machinery began to purr, setting off a soft rattle of vibrating bottles.

"Happy days, Werner," I said before I drank.

He smiled soberly and picked up his wallet from a side table and made sure his credit cards were all there before putting it in his pocket. Meursault: it was a luxury I particularly enjoyed. I suppose Werner could have guzzled it all day long if he'd had a mind to.

Most people were hurtled through life on a financial switchback, a roller coaster that decided for them whether they must economize or splurge. Not Werner; Werner always had enough. He decided what he wanted—anything, whether it was a little place round the corner that did a good salmon mousse, or a splendid new car—and put his hand in his pocket and bought it. Mind you, Werner's needs were modest: he didn't hanker for yachts or private planes, keep mistresses, gamble, or throw lots of extravagant parties. Werner simply had money more than sufficient for his needs. I envied his unbudgeted easygoing life style; he made me feel like a money-grubbing wage slave, because, I suppose, that's exactly what I am.

I took my wine and sat down in one of the soft leather armchairs and waited for him to tell me what was distressing him so much that he would fly to London and drag me up here to talk with him. I looked round. So it was an apartment. Yes, I could see that now. It was not quite like a hotel suite; it looked lived in. Glenn Gould was playing Bach uncharacteristically softly on the CD player, and there were two big, hideous modern paintings on the walls, instead of the tasteful lithographs that architects and interior designers bought wholesale.

It was a place used by men who were away from home. You could tell that from the books. As well as year after year of outdated restaurant guides, street maps, and museum catalogs, there were the sort of books that help pass the time when all the work is done. Dog-eared detective stories of the sort that can be read over and over again without any feeling of repetition, very thin books by thin lady novelists who win prizes, and very thick ones by thick lady novelists who never win prizes. And a whole shelf full of biographies, from Mother Teresa to Lord Olivier, via *Streisand: The Woman and the Legend.* Long, long hours away from home.

Werner had responded to my toast by drinking some mineral water from a cut-glass tumbler. It had a lemon slice in it, and ice too. It was as if he wanted to pretend it was a real drink. He sank down into an armchair and sighed. The black beard—now closely trimmed—suited him. He didn't look like a hippie or an art teacher; it was more formal than that. But formality ended at his neck. His clothes were casual: a black long-sleeve woolen pullover, matching trousers, rainbow-striped silk shirt, and shiny patent shoes. His hair was thick and dark, his pose relaxed; only his eyes were worried. "It's Zena." He reached across to get a coaster from the shelf and moved my wineglass onto it, so it would not mark the polished side table. Werner was house-trained.

Oh, no, I thought. Not an evening of talking about that wife of his. It was more than even a best friend should be expected to endure. "What about Zena?" I said, trying to make my voice warm and concerned.

"More precisely, that damned Frank Harrington," said Werner bitterly. "I know what Frank means to you, Bernie, but he's a bastard. He really is." He watched me to see if I would take offense in Frank's behalf, and he pinched his nose, as he often did when distressed.

"Frank?" Frank Harrington was an amazingly successful womanizer. Linking Frank's and Zena's names meant only one thing to me. Some years back Frank and Zena had had a tempestuous affair. Like some nineteenth-century rake, he'd even set her up in a little house to await his visits. Then—the way I heard it—Zena got fed up with sitting waiting for Frank to find time for her. There was nothing of the nineteenth-century mistress about Zena. Since then I suspected that Zena had found other men, but always she returned to poor old Werner. In the long term he was the only one who would put up with her. "Frank and Zena?"

"Not like that," said Werner hurriedly. "He's using her for departmental work. It's dangerous, Bernie. Bloody dangerous. She's never done anything like that before."

"You'd better start at the beginning," I said.

"Zena has relatives in the East. She takes them food and presents. You know. . . ."

"Yes, you told me." I reached for the little bowl of salted

almonds, but there were only a couple of broken pieces left, buried under salt and bits of skin. I suppose Werner had eaten them while sitting here waiting for me and worrying.

"She went over there last week." In German "over there" —*drüben*—meant only one thing: it meant the other side of the Wall. "Now I've discovered that that bloody Frank asked her to look up someone for him."

"One of our people?" I said guardedly.

"Of course. Who else would they be, if Frank wants her to look them up for him?"

"I suppose so," I conceded.

"Frankfurt an der Oder," said Werner. "You know what we're talking about, don't you?" Despite the level voice, he was angry now—damned angry—and somewhere in the back of his mind he was implicating me in this development of which I knew nothing and preferred to know nothing.

"That's just speculation," I said, and waited to see if he'd say it wasn't.

"Why ask Zena?" His face was distorted as he bit his lip with rage and anxiety. "He has his own people to do that kind of work."

"Yes," I admitted.

"It's Bizet. He's trying to reopen a contact string."

"She'll be all right, Werner," I said. I sympathized with Werner's anger, but I'd been at the sharp end of Operations. From the field agent's point of view, it sometimes looked like good sense to send legitimate travelers, such as Zena, into these touchy situations. They were told nothing, so they knew nothing. Usually they got away scot-free.

My apparent indifference to Zena's plight made him angrier than ever, but as usual he smiled. He leaned well back on the sofa and stroked the house phone as if it were a pet cat. From the street outside there was the growling sound of the long-distance buses that had to turn into a narrow side street to get to the bus terminal. "I want you to do something," he said.

"What do you want me to do?"

"Get her out," he said. His fingers were twitching on the phone. He reached for the handpiece, called reception, and, without asking me what I wanted to eat, told them he wanted the restaurant dinner sent round for us. He spoke rapidly into the phone, ordering two portions of the very good salmon mousse and a couple of filet steaks—one rare and one well done—and whatever went with it, then put the phone down, turned, and looked at me. "It's getting late," he explained. "The kitchen will close soon."

I said, "You don't really want the Department to bring her out, do you? From what you've told me, there's nothing to suggest she's in any kind of danger. I imagine Frank just asked her to make a couple of phone calls, or knock at a door. If I go rushing into the office demanding a full-scale rescue attempt, everyone will think I've taken leave of my senses. And —quite honestly, Werner—it might be putting Zena into a worse position than she is." What I didn't add was that there was no chance at all that Dicky, or anyone in authority at the office, would countermand Frank's actions on my say-so. It sounded as if Frank had been made "file officer" and his word would be law.

"How dare Frank ask Zena to help him?" Was that the real focus of Werner's rage: Frank Harrington? They'd never seen eye to eye. Even before Frank stole Werner's wife, he'd eased Werner out of the Berlin Field Unit. Now there was no way to convince Werner that Frank was what he was: a very experienced departmental administrator, and an archetypal "English gentleman" who not only knew how to attract adventuresome young women but often fell prey to them.

And I could hardly tell Werner that his wife should have learned to stay away from Frank by now. So I said, "When is she due back?"

"Monday." He touched his beard. Glenn Gould finished playing, but after a couple of clicks, Art Tatum started. Werner liked the piano. In the old days he used to play at all the most rowdy Berlin parties. Seeing him now, it was difficult to believe the things we had done in Berlin back when we were young.

"She'll be all right," I said.

Unconvinced by my reassurances, he nodded without replying, and studied his glass of mineral water suspiciously before taking a sip of it. We sat for a moment in silence. Then he looked at me, gave a little shrug and a smile, and, noticing that my glass was empty, got up and went to the refrigerator and brought more wine for me.

I watched him carefully. There was more to it, some other aspect to the story. But I didn't press him for more details. His anger had peaked. It was better to let him simmer down.

There was a tap at the door and—as in some sort of well-rehearsed cabaret act—a uniformed man from the reception desk helped a restaurant waiter to set up two folding chairs, a folding table, and an array of tableware. There were steaks and some spinach keeping warm on a chafing dish. The portions of fish mousse, which the waiter insisted upon showing us, were under the heavy dome-shaped silver covers that are always needed to keep microscopic portions of food from escaping.

It wasn't until they'd gone and we were seated at the table, eating the mousse, that Werner mentioned Zena again. "I love her. I can't help that, Bernie."

"I know, Werner." The salmon mousse was sinking into a puddle of bright-green sauce: a pink, tilted slab with fragments of vegetable looking out of it, like passengers waiting for a rescue boat. I ate it quickly.

"So I worry," said Werner, and he shrugged in a gesture of resignation. I felt sorry for him. It wasn't easy to imagine being in love with Zena. That some man might murder her, or join the Foreign Legion to escape her, was simple to envisage. But love her? No. "She's the only woman for me." He said it defensively, almost apologetically.

Sometimes I thought he loved her because she was incapable of loving anyone. A friend of mine once explained the lifetime he'd given to the study of reptiles by saying that he was fascinated by their complete lack of any response to affection. And I think Werner's relationship with Zena was like that. She seemed to have no real feelings about anyone, alive or dead. People were all the same for her, and she dealt with them by means of a curious, highly developed sense of self-imposed and carefully apportioned "justice" that some of her critics had called "fascistic."

But it was no use talking to Werner about Zena. For him she could do no wrong. I remember him falling in love with girls at school. His love was boundless; the respect he showed for them usually earned only their withering contempt, until eventually Werner's ardor faded and died. So I thought it would be when Zena came along. But Zena wasn't so profligate with Werner's love. She welcomed his affection, encouraged him, and knew how to handle him, so that she could do almost anything with him.

Werner picked at the fish mousse. It was dry and completely tasteless; only the creamy watercress sauce had any flavor: it was salty. "Refrigerated and then warmed in a microwave," said Werner knowledgeably. He pushed the mousse aside and started on the steak, as I'd already done. "It looks as if you liked the mousse," he said accusingly.

"It was delicious," I said. "But I'm beginning to think that this is your well-done filet." By that time I'd already eaten some of his steak. Silently he passed the untouched underdone one to me and took what was left of the steak I'd half-eaten. "Sorry, Werner," I said.

"You eat everything," he said. "Even at school you ate everything."

"You won't like the underdone one," I told him, and offered it back to him.

He declined. "I know," he said.

To change the subject I said, "How is the hotel?"

"It's going all right," he said sharply. Then he added, "Did I tell you that that damned woman Ingrid Winter insists on coming to Berlin?"

"She wants some things," I said, keeping it vague.

"She wants to help," said Werner, as if this was the direst threat in his vocabulary.

"Tell her you don't need help," I said. It seemed simple enough.

"I can't stop her coming. She's Lisl's niece . . ."

". . . and she has a claim on the house. Yes, you'd better be nice to her, Werner, or she could upset the whole apple cart."

"Just as long as she doesn't get in the way," he said ominously. Werner was in a bad mood.

I decided I might as well face it. He wasn't going to simmer down. "Are you going to tell me about Zena?" I said as casually as I could.

"Tell you what?"

"You're not worried about what could happen to her for knocking on the wrong door in Frankfurt an der Oder, Werner. Not Zena—she'd talk her way out of that one with a paper bag over her head."

He looked at me with that impassive look I knew so well and then chewed a piece of steak before replying. "I should have given you some red wine," he said. "I've got some for you."

"Never mind the wine. What's the real story?"

He dabbed his lips with a dinner napkin and said, "Zena's uncle has a wonderful collection of very old books and crucifixes, icons, and things. . . ." He looked at me. I stared back at him and said nothing. Werner amended it to, "Maybe he buys them. . . . I'm not sure."

"And maybe he's not her uncle," I suggested.

"Oh, I think he's her— Well, yes, maybe an old friend.

Yes, sometimes he buys these things from Poles who come in-to East Germany looking for work. Bibles mostly: seventeenth-century. He's an expert on early Christian art."

"And Zena smuggles them back to the West, and they are sold in those elegant shops in Munich where orthodontists go to furnish their *Schlosse.*"

Werner wasn't listening. "Zena doesn't understand how they work," he said lugubriously.

"How who work?"

"The Stasi. If she goes calling, the way Frank has told her to, they'll just follow her day after day to see where she goes. But Zena won't realize that. The whole lot of them will go into the bag. They'll accuse her of stealing state art treasures or something."

"The people's art treasures," I corrected him. "Yes, well, they won't like the idea of her exporting antiques without a license." I tried to make it sound like a minor misdeed, a technical infraction of a customs regulation. "But Frank wouldn't know anything about that, of course."

Without answering, Werner got up and went to the tiny kitchen. He came back with the half-empty bottle of Meursault and a wineglass for himself. He poured more wine for me and some for himself too and set the bottle on the table, having put a coaster into position for it. I watched him drink. He pulled a face like a small child asked to swallow some nasty medicine. Werner knew a lot about wine, but he always treated it like sour grape juice. "Suppose Frank knew all about Zena and the antique books?" Werner said slowly and carefully. "After all, Frank is supposed to be running an intelligence service, isn't he?"

"Yes," I said, ignoring the sarcasm.

"And suppose Frank had reason to believe that, by deliv-ering poor Zena to the Stasi, he'd get them to lay off his Bizet people. Maybe let them get away?"

I said nothing. I sipped my wine and tried to conceal my

thoughts. Then bloody good for Frank, I thought. Yet it all sounded highly unlikely. I suspected that Frank was still too fond of Zena to throw her to the wolves. But if he'd worked out some bizarre deal that got two or three of our people off the hook, in exchange for a ring of cheap crooks who were running a racket involving religious antiques, books, and God knows what else—stuff that might well have been stolen in the first place—then good for Frank. I would be all in favor of a deal like that. So I said nothing.

"Don't forget it's Zena," said Werner.

No, don't forget it's Zena. That would make a swap like that a real public benefit. "No," I said. "It's her I'm thinking about."

"He's a bloody Judas," said Werner. He drank some more wine but seemed no more happy with the taste of it than he had been the first time.

"Have you got any reason to think so?" I asked.

"I feel it in my guts," said Werner in a voice I didn't recognize.

"Frank wouldn't do a thing like that," I said, more to calm Werner than because I completely believed it. Frank liked Zena, but Frank could be ruthless: I knew it and so did Werner. And so, if she had any brains, did the wretched Zena.

"Yes, Frank would!" snapped Werner. "It's just the sort of thing he would do. It's the sort of thing the English are notorious for. You know that."

"Perfidious Albion?" I said.

He didn't think that was funny. He didn't answer or even look at me. He just sat there with his face tight, his eyes watery, and his big hands clenched together so tight that the knuckles whitened.

I'd never seen him in such a state before. Whether it was concern for Zena or a burning hatred for Frank, it was eating him up. I watched him biting his lip with rage, and I worried about him. I'd seen men wound up this tight before; and I'd seen them snap. "I'll see what I can do," I said, but it was too late for such offers.

Through gritted teeth Werner said, "First thing tomorrow morning I'm going to the office. I'll find the D-G and make him do something. Make him!"

"I wouldn't advise that, Werner," I said anxiously. "No, Werner, I really wouldn't." The idea of this black-bearded Werner shouting and struggling in the lobby of London Central, with the redoubtable Sergeant-Major Gaskell trying to subdue him, and the questions that would inevitably be directed at me in consequence, was something I didn't care to contemplate. I tipped the rest of the Meursault into my glass. It was warm: I suppose he'd not put the bottle back into the refrigerator. All in all, Thursday was not a good day.

Chapter 13

I have always been a light sleeper: it's a part of the job. But it wasn't the low rumble of the motorcycle that awakened me—they come roaring past at all hours of the night—it was the silence that followed its engine's being switched off. By the time the garden gate clicked, I was fully awake. I heard the footsteps—high-heel boots on the stone paving—and I rolled out of bed before the brief ring of the doorbell awakened Gloria.

"Three-thirty!" I heard Gloria say sleepily as I went out of the bedroom. She sounded surprised; she had a lot to learn about the demands the Department made on its middle management. I went downstairs two steps at a time, to answer it before Doris and the children were disturbed. But before I got to the bottom of the stairs the caller tried again: more insistent this time, two long rings.

"Okay, okay, okay," I said irritably.

"Sorry, governor, I thought you hadn't heard." The caller was a tall, thin young man dressed entirely in shiny black leather, like some apparition from a bad dream. "Mr. Samson?" Over his arm he had a black shiny helmet, and there was a battered leather pouch slung from his neck.

"Yes?"

"Have you got something to identify yourself, sir?" he said, without saying what I was supposed to produce. That was the way regulations said it should be done, but I'd got used to a more vernacular style from the messengers I knew. So it was a new man.

"What about this?" I said and, from behind the half-open door, I brought the Mauser 9mm into view.

He grinned. "Yeah, I reckon that'll do," he said. He opened the pouch and from it took one of the large buff envelopes that the Department uses to circulate its bad news.

"Samson, B.," I said, just to get him off the hook. "Any verbal?"

"You're to open it right away. That's all."

"Why not," I said. "I'll need something to help me back to sleep."

"Good night, governor. Sorry to disturb you."

"Next time," I said, "don't ring the bell. Just breathe heavily through the letter box."

"What is it, darling?" asked Gloria, coming downstairs slowly like a chorus girl in a Busby Berkeley musical. She was not fully awake. Blond hair disarranged, she was dressed in the big fluffy white Descamps bathrobe that I'd bought her for Christmas. She looked wonderful.

"A messenger." I tore open the big brown envelope. Inside there was an airline ticket from London Heathrow to Los Angeles International by the flight that left at 9:00 a.m.—that is to say, in less than six hours' time—and a note, curt and typed on office paper bearing the usual rubber stamps:

Dear Bernard,

You'll be met on arrival. Sorry about the short notice, but the
Washington office works five hours later than we do, and someone
there arranged with the Deputy that this one should be down to
you, and only you,

Yours apologetically,
Harry (N.D.O. Ops.)

I recognized the sprawling handwriting. So poor old Harry
Strang was still on the roster for night duty in Operations. I
suppose he must have felt sorry for himself too, for he'd
scribbled on the bottom of the note, "Some people have
all the luck!" I guess, for someone sitting up all night in Operations and listening to the rain, the prospect of immediate transportation to sunny California must have seemed
attractive.

To me it didn't. At least, it didn't until I recalled Werner's
threat to go into the office this morning and tackle the D-G
head-on.

"They can't make you go," said Gloria, who had leaned
over my shoulder to read the note.

"No," I agreed. "I can always start drawing unemployment benefits."

"It doesn't even say how long you'll be away," she said,
in such a way as to leave me in no doubt about how she would
respond to such a peremptory command.

"I'm sorry," I said.

"You promised to look at the garage door."

"It just needs a new hinge," I told her. "There's a place
near Waterloo Station. I'll get it next week."

"I'll pack your bag." She looked at the clock on the mantelpiece. "It's not worth going back to bed."

"I said I'm sorry," I reminded her.

"The weekends are the only time we have together," she
said. "Why couldn't it wait till Monday?"

"I'll try and find something exciting for Billy's birthday."

"Bring yourself back," said Gloria, and kissed me tenderly. "I worry about you. . . . When they send you off on these urgent jobs with that damned 'Briefing-on-Arrival' rubber stamp, I worry about you."

"It won't be anything dangerous," I said. "I'll be sitting beside a pool all weekend."

"They've specifically asked for you, Bernard," she said.

I nodded. It was not a flattering assumption, but she was right. They hadn't asked for me on account of my social contacts or my scholarship. "I'll wear the water wings and stay away from the deep end," I promised.

"What will you do when you get there?"

"It's 'Briefing on Arrival,' sweetheart. That means they haven't yet decided."

"Seriously. How will you recognize them?"

"It doesn't work like that, darling. They'll have a photo of me. I won't know them until they come up to me and introduce themselves."

"And how will you know that person is the genuine contact?"

"He'll show me my photo."

"It's all carefully arranged," she said with a note of approval in her voice. She liked everything to be well arranged.

"It's all in the 'Notes and Amendments,' " I said.

"But always the same airline, Bernard? That seems bad security."

"There must be a reason," I said. "How about making me a cup of coffee while I pack my bag?"

"Everything's clean. Your shirts are on hangers in the wardrobe, so don't start shouting when you find the chest of drawers empty."

"I won't shout about shirts," I promised, and kissed her. "And if I do, rip more buttons off."

"I do love you, Bernard." She put both arms round me and hugged me tight. "I want to have you forever and ever."

"Then that's the way it will be," I promised, with the sort of unthinking impetuosity that I am prey to when rudely awakened in such early hours of the morning.

For a moment she just held me, crushing me so that I could hardly breathe; then, into my ear, she said, "And I love the children, Bernard. Don't worry about them."

The children missed their real mother, of course, and I knew how hard Gloria worked to replace her. It wasn't easy for her. Cambridge, just unremitting hard work, must have been an attractive prospect at times.

Almost every seat was taken in First Class. Wide-awake young men, with well-cut suits and large gold wristwatches, were shuffling papers that came from pigskin document cases, or tapping at tiny portable computers with hinged screens. Many of them declined the champagne, and worked right through the meal service: reading reports, ticking at accounts, and underlining bits of "projections" with colored markers.

The man in the seat next to mine was from the same mold but considerably less dedicated. Edwin Woosnam—"a Welsh name, although I've never been there: can you believe it?"—an overweight fellow with thick eyebrows, thin lips, and the sort of nose they create from putty for amateur productions of *Julius Caesar*. My desire to catch up on lost sleep was frustrated by his friendliness.

He was, he told me, the senior partner of a "development company" in Glasgow. His firm was building eight six-hundred-room hotels in towns around the world, and he told me all about it. "Outdoor pool, that's important. The hotel owners need a picture on the brochure that makes it look like the weather is good enough for swimming all year round." Throaty chuckle and a quick sip of champagne. "Penthouses at the top, leisure centers in the basement, and en-suite bathrooms throughout. Find a big cheap site—I mean really big—and after the hotel is up, shops and apartment blocks will follow. The neighborhood is upgraded. You can't go wrong on an investment like that. It's like money in the bank. As long as the local labor is cheap, it doesn't matter where you site the hotel; half these idiot tourists don't even know which country they're in."

But otherwise Mr. Woosnam proved a congenial companion, with an endless supply of stories. ". . . You can't tell the Greeks anything. I showed this foreman—Popopopolis or something, you know what those names are like—I showed him the schedule, and told him the eighth floor should be all complete by now. And he got angry. It was complete, he shouted. He shook his fist and waved his arms and went rushing along the girders, jumped through a doorway, and fell all the way into the basement. Eight stories! Killed, of course. We had terrible trouble getting a new foreman at that time of year. Another month and it wouldn't have mattered so much." He took a drink.

"Ha ha ha. Some people just won't listen. Perhaps you find that in your business too," said Woosnam, but before I could agree he was off again. "I was with one of our site surveyors in Bombay, and he was laughing and making jokes about the way the Indians build their lashed-up wooden scaffolding. I told him that he'd be laughing on the other side of his face when he put up steel scaffolding and the heat of the sun twisted it into a corkscrew and his project collapsed. Bloody architects! They come straight from college, and they know it all. That's the trouble nowadays. I'll give you another example. . . ." And so it went on. He was good entertainment, though his affability precluded all chance of slumber.

"Travel much?" he said as I began to doze.

"No," I said.

"I travel all the time. Flying across the Atlantic is exciting for you, of course, but it's just a bore for me." He looked at me to see my reaction.

"Yes," I said, and tried to look excited.

"And what line are you in? No, don't tell me. I'm good at guessing what people do for a living. Insurance?"

"Chemicals," I told him. I usually say that, because it's so vague, and also because I have a prepared line of chat about pharmaceuticals, should my bluff be called.

"All right," he said, reluctant to admit to error. "Not a salesman, though. You haven't got the pushy temperament you need for the sales side."

"No, not sales," I agreed.

"Keep an eye on my briefcase while I go to the toilet, will you? Once they start the meal service, everyone will jump up and want to go. It's always like that."

The toy meal came and went. The captain's carefully modulated voice recited the names of places that were hidden far beneath the clouds. The great aluminum tube droned on, its weary cargo of unwashed, red-eyed travelers numbed with alcohol and crippled with indigestion. Duty-free baubles were interminably hustled by stewardesses who went, eyes averted, past bawling babies and harassed mothers. Over the public-address system came more names of equally invisible towns. The shutters were closed against the daylight, and the cabin darkened. Blurred ghosts of tiny, unrecognizable actors postured on the pale screens while their strident voices assaulted the inner ear from plastic tubes. We raced after the sun and chased a never-ending day. Tortured by the poker-red glare of the sun, dazzled by the white clouds, one by one the heads of the passengers lolled and bent as they succumbed to their misery and sought escape in fitful sleep.

"This is your captain speaking. . . ."

We'd arrived at Los Angeles: now came the worst part. The lineup at U.S. Customs and Immigration. I spent well over an hour standing in line, disconsolately kicking my baggage forward a few inches at a time. But finally I was grudgingly admitted to America.

"Hi there! Mr. Samson? Did you have a nice flight?" He

was chewing gum, a suntanned man about thirty years old with patient eyes, stretch pants, a half-eaten hamburger, and a half-read paperback edition of *War and Peace:* everything necessary for meeting someone at LAX. We walked through the crowded concourse and into the melee of cabs and cars and buses that served this vast and trainless town.

"Buddy Breukink," the man introduced himself. He flicked a finger at the dented, unpainted metal case that I'd wrenched from the carousel. "Is this all your baggage?" If everyone kept saying that to me, I was going to start feeling socially disadvantaged.

"That's right," I said. He took my bag and the corrugated case. I didn't know whether I should politely wrest it from him. There was no way to discover if he was just a driver, sent to collect me, or a senior executive who was going to pick up the bills and give me my orders. The U.S. of A. is like that. He marched off, and I followed him. He hadn't been through the formalities, but I didn't press it. He didn't look the type who would regularly read and update the "Notes and Amendments."

"Hungry? We have more than an hour's ride." He had a sly gap-toothed smile, as if he knew something that the rest of the world didn't know. It wasn't to be taken personally.

"I'll survive," I promised. My blood sugar wasn't so low that I wanted an airport hamburger.

"The buggy's across the street." He was a coffee-shop cowboy: a tall, slim fellow with a superfluity of good large teeth, tan-colored tight-fitting trousers, short-sleeve white shirt, and a big brown Stetson with a bright band of feathers round it. In keeping with the outfit, Buddy Breukink climbed into a Jeep, a brand-new Wrangler soft-top, complete with phone, personalized plates—BB GUN—and roll bar.

He threw my baggage and Tolstoy into the back before carefully placing his beautiful Stetson in a box there. He got in and pushed a lot of buttons, a coded signal to activate his car phone. "Have to make sure none of these parking-lot jockeys make a long, long call to their folks in Bogotá," he said, as if a short freebie hello to Mexico City might be okay with him. He smiled to himself and cleared half a dozen audio cassettes from the passenger seat and dumped them into a box. When he turned the ignition key, the tape recorder started playing *Pavarotti's Greatest Hits* or, more specifically, "Funiculi, Funicula" delivered in ear-splitting fortissimos. "It's kind of classical," he explained with a hint of apology.

He gunned the engine impatiently. "Let's go!" he yelled, louder than Pavarotti; even before I was strapped in, the wheels were burning rubber and we were out of the car park and off down the highway.

I had arrived in the New World and was as bemused as Columbus. In this part of the world it was already spring; the air was warm and the sky was that pale shade of blue that portends a steep rise in temperature. The noisy downtown streets were crowded with black roaring Porsches and white Rolls-Royce convertibles, shouting kids rattled around on roller skates, and pretty girls preened in sun tops and shorts.

Up the ramp. On the Freeway that stretches across the city, the anarchy of the busy streets ended. Apart from some kids racing past in a dented pickup, restrained drivers observed lane discipline and moved at a steady pace. The wind roared through the Jeep's open sides and threatened to blow me from my seat. I huddled down to shelter behind the windscreen. Buddy turned the music louder and looked at me and grinned.

"Funiculi," sang Buddy between chewing. "Funicula."

Once clear of the "international airport," its *mañana*-minded airline staff and its hard-eyed bureaucrats, Southern California reaches out to its visitors. The warmth of the sun, the sight of the San Gabriel Mountains, dry winds from the desert, the bitter herbal smells of the brushwood flowers, the orange poppies in the bright-green landscape that has not yet suffered the cruel heat of summer—at this time of year all these things urge me to stay forever.

Racing along the road that is slung roof-high above the city, one has a view of the whole of Los Angeles, from the ocean to the mountains. Clusters of tall buildings at Century City, and more at Broadway, dominated a town of modest little suburban houses squeezed between pools and palms. Soon Buddy took an off ramp and cut across town to pick up the Pacific Coast Highway and go north, following the signs that point the way to Santa Barbara and eventually San Francisco. At Malibu the traffic thinned, and we sped past an ever-more-varied selection of elaborate and eccentric beach houses, until houses, and even seafood restaurants, ended, and the road followed the very edge of the continent. Here the Pacific Ocean relentlessly assaulted the seashore. Huge green breakers exploded into lacy foam and a mist of water vapor, and roared so loudly that the noise of them could be heard above the sound of the Jeep's engine, and that of the music.

Buddy took the gum from his mouth and pitched it out onto the road. "They told me you'd ask questions," he confided.

"No," I said.

"And they said I shouldn't tell you anything."

"It's working out just fine," I said.

He nodded, and dodged round a big articulated truck marked "Budweiser," before flattening the gas pedal against the floor and showing me what speed his Jeep would do.

We passed the place where agile figures dangling from hang gliders threw themselves off the high cliffs and did figure eights above the highway and the Pacific Ocean before landing on the narrow strip of beach that provided their only chance of survival. We passed the offshore oil rigs, standing like anchored aircraft carriers in the mist. By the time we turned off the Pacific Coast Highway into a narrow "seven-mile canyon," we were well past the county line and into Ventura. And I was getting hungry.

It was a private road, narrow and potholed. On the corner a tall wooden post was nailed with half a dozen signs in varying degrees of deterioration: "Schuster Ranch," "Greentops Quarterhorse Stud—no visits," "Ogarkov," "D and M Bishop," "Rattlesnake Computer Labs," and "Highacres." As the Jeep climbed up the dirt road into the canyon, I wondered which of those establishments we were going to. But as we passed all the mailboxes on the roadside, it became clear that we were heading up to some unmarked property nearer the summit.

We were about three miles up the canyon, and high enough to get glimpses of the ocean far below us, when we came to gates in a high chain-link fence that stretched on either side as far as I could see. Alongside the gate a sign said, "La Buona Nova. Private Property. Beware Guard Dogs." Buddy steered the Jeep to within reaching distance of a small box on a metal post. He pressed a red button and spoke into the box. "Hi there! It's Buddy with the visitor. Open up, will yuh?"

With a hesitant, jerky motion, and a loud grinding of hidden mechanical devices, the gates slowly opened. From the box a tinny voice said, "Hang in to see the gates click shut, Buddy. Last week's rain seems to have gotten to them."

We drove inside and Buddy did as he'd been told. I could see no buildings anywhere, but I had the feeling that we were being kept under observation by whoever the tinny voice belonged to. "Keep your hands inside the car," Buddy advised. "Those darn dogs run free in this outer compound."

We continued up the dirt road, always climbing, and leaving hairpins of dust on the trail behind us. Then suddenly, around a spur, another chain fence came into view. There was

another gate and a small hut. Inside this second perimeter
fence were three figures. At first they looked like a man with
his two children, but when I got closer I could see it was a huge
man with two Mexicans. They were guards. The white man
had his belt slung under a big gut. He wore a Stetson, starched
khakis, and high boots, and had a shield-shaped gold badge
on his shirt. In his hand he held a small transceiver. The
Mexicans wore dark-brown shirts, and one of them had a
shotgun. Like the chain-link fence, the men looked fresh and
well cared for. One of the Mexicans opened the gate, and the
big man waved us through.

It was still another mile or more to where a cluster of low
pink stucco buildings, with red-tiled roofs, sat tight just below
the summit of the hill. The buildings were of indeterminate
age, and designed in the style that Californians call Spanish.
After passing a couple of mud-spattered Japanese pickups,
Buddy parked the Jeep in a cool barnlike building which already held an old Cadillac Seville and a Lamborghini. Buddy
put on his Stetson, looked at himself in the wing mirror to
adjust the brim, and then took my bags. With my jacket over
my arm, and sweating in the afternoon heat, I followed him.
The main buildings were two stories high and provided views
westwards to the ocean. On the east side they sheltered a wide
patio of patterned tiles and a pool about twenty-five yards
long. The pool was blue and limpid, with just enough breeze
from the ocean to dimple the surface of the water. There was
no one to be seen except in the pool, where a slim middle-
aged woman was swimming in the gentle dog-paddle style that
ensures that your eye makeup doesn't get splashed. At the
side of the pool where she'd been sitting was a big pink towel,
bottles of sun oil and other cosmetics, a brush and comb, and
a hand mirror. Leaning against the chair was a half-completed
water-color painting of bougainvillea flowers. Beside it was a
large paint box and a jar of brushes.

"Hello, Buddy," called the lady in the pool without interrupting her swim. "What's the traffic like? Hi there, Mr. Samson. Welcome to La Buona Nova."

Without slowing his pace, Buddy called, "We came up the PCH, Mrs. O'Raffety, but if you're going to town, go through the canyon." He swiveled his head for long enough to give her one of his shy, gap-toothed smiles. I waved to her and said thanks but had to hurry to follow him.

He went up two steps to an arcaded passageway that provided shady access to, and held chairs and tables for, three guest suites, which occupied one side of the building. One of the outdoor tables still had the remains of breakfast: a vacuum coffeepot, a glass jug of juice, and expensive-looking tableware of a sort that Gloria would have liked. Buddy opened a door and led the way into the last suite. It was decorated in a theme of pink and white. On the walls were three framed landscape paintings, amateurish watercolors of local scenes that I was inclined to authenticate as O'Raffety originals.

"Mrs. O'Raffety is my mother-in-law," Buddy explained without being asked. "She's sixty years old. She owns this whole setup." He put the bags down and, opening the door of the huge green-and-white-tiled bathroom, said, "This is your suite. Switch the air to the way you want it." He indicated a control panel on the wall. "You've got time for a swim before lunch. Swimsuits in the closet and a slew of towels in the other room."

"Lunch? Isn't it a bit late for lunch?" The afternoon had almost gone.

"I guess, but Mrs. O'Raffety eats any time. She said she'd wait for you."

"That's very nice of her," I said.

The large brown-tinted windows gave a view of the patio area. Mrs. O'Raffety was still swimming slowly down the pool. There was a look of stern determination on her face. I watched her as she reached the deep end and steered round majestically, like the *Queen Elizabeth* coming into Southampton. I could see her more clearly from here. The swimming produced such a look of concentration on her face that, despite the trim figure, and the Beverly Hills beauty treatments, she looked every bit of her sixty years. "It's quite a place," I said, realizing that some such response was expected from me.

"She'd get three million dollars—maybe more—if she wanted to sell. There's all that land."

"And is she going to sell?" I said, hoping to find out more about my mysterious hostess, and why I had been brought here.

"Mrs. O'Raffety? She'll never sell. She's got all the money she needs."

"Do you live here too?" I asked. I was trying to guess at his position in the household.

"I have a beautiful home: three bedrooms, pool, Jacuzzi, everything. We passed it on the way up here: the place with the big palm trees."

"Oh, yes," I said, although I hadn't noticed such a place.

"My marriage went wrong," he said. "Charly—that's Mrs. O'Raffety's daughter—left me. She married a movie actor we met at a benefit dinner. He never seemed to get the right kind of parts, so they went to live in Florida. They have a lovely home just outside Palm Beach." He said it without rancor— or any emotion—as a man might talk of people he'd only read about in the gossip columns.

"But you stayed with Mrs. O'Raffety?"

"Well, I had to stay," said Buddy. "I'm Mrs. O'Raffety's attorney. I handle things for her."

"Oh, yes, of course."

"You have your swim, Mr. Samson. The water's kept at eighty degrees. Mrs. O'Raffety has to swim on account of her bad back, but she can't abide cold water." He stared through the window to watch her swimming. There was a fixed expression on his face that could have been concern for her.

"And who is Mr. O'Raffety?" I said.

"Who is Mr. O'Raffety?" Buddy was puzzled by my question.

"Yes. Who is Mr. O'Raffety? What does he do for a living?"

Buddy's face relaxed. "Oh, I get you," he said. "What does he do for a living. Well, Shaun O'Raffety was Mrs. O'Raffety's hairdresser: L.A., a fancy place on Rodeo Drive." Buddy rubbed his face. "Way back before my time, of course. It didn't last long. She gave him the money to buy a bar in Boston. She hasn't seen him in ten years, but sometimes I have to go and get him out of trouble."

"Trouble?"

"Money trouble. Woman trouble. Tax-return trouble. Bookies or fistfights in the bar, so that the cops get mad. Never anything bad. Old Shaun is an Irishman. No real harm in him. He just can't choose carefully enough: not his clients, his friends, or his women."

"Except in the case of Mrs. O'Raffety," I said.

For a moment I thought Buddy was going to take offense, but he contained himself and said, "Yeah. Except in the case of Mrs. O'Raffety." The smile was noticeably absent.

"Since you're Mrs. O'Raffety's attorney, Buddy, perhaps you could explain why I've been brought here."

He looked at me as if trying to help, trying to guess the answer. "Socializing isn't my bag," said Buddy. He was silent for a few moments, as if regretting telling me about his employer and mother-in-law. Then he said, "Mrs. O'Raffety has a social secretary to handle the invites: weekend guests and cocktails and dinner parties and suchlike."

"But just between the two of us, Buddy, I've never even heard of Mrs. O'Raffety."

"Then maybe you are here to visit one of Mrs. O'Raffety's permanent guests. Do you know Mr. Rensselaer? He lives in the house with the big bougainvillea."

"Bret Rensselaer?"

"That's correct."

"He's dead."

"No, sir."

Everyone knew Bret was dead. If Frank Harrington said he was dead, he was dead. Frank was always right about things like that. Bret died of gunshot wounds resulting from a gun battle in Berlin nearly three years ago. I was only a couple of yards away. I saw him fall; I heard him scream. "Bret Rensselaer," I said carefully. "About sixty years old. Blond hair. Tall. Thin."

"You've got him. White hair now, but that's him all right. He's been sick. Real bad. An auto accident somewhere in Europe. Mrs. O'Raffety brought him here. She had that guest house remodeled and fixed up a beautiful room with equipment where he could do his special exercises and stuff. He could hardly walk when he first arrived. One or another of the therapy nurses comes up here every day, even Sunday." He looked at the expression on my face. "You knew him in Europe, maybe?"

"I knew him very well," I said.

"Isn't that something." Buddy Breukink nodded. "Yeah, he's some kind of distant relation to Mrs. O'Raffety. Old Cy Rensselaer—the famous one they named the automobile for —was Mrs. O'Raffety's grandfather."

"I see." So Bret Rensselaer really was still alive and they'd brought me all this way to see him. Why?

Chapter 14

We ate lunch very late. Mrs. Helena O'Raffety didn't eat much. Perhaps she'd had lots of other lunches earlier in the day. But she kept her salad scared, moving it around the huge pink plate like a cop harassing a drunk.

"I'm a European," she said. She'd been explaining that she was, at heart, quite unlike her native Californian friends and acquaintances. "When I was very young, I always said that one day I'd buy a little apartment in Berlin, but when I got there, it seemed such a sad place. And so dirty. Everything I wore got sooty. So I never got around to it." She sighed and this time speared a segment of peeled tomato and ate it.

"It gets cold in Berlin," I told her. I looked at the sun glittering on the blue water of the pool beside us and the brightly colored tropical flowers. I smelled the wild sage, breathed the clean air off the ocean, and watched the hawks slowly circling high above us. We were a long way from Berlin.

"Is that right?" she said, exhibiting only mild interest. "I've only been twice; both times in the fall. I always take vacations in the fall. It stays warm, and the resorts are not so crowded." As if to offset the simplicity of her blue cotton beach dress, she wore lots of jewelry: a gold chain necklace, half a dozen rings, and a gold watch with diamonds around the face. Now she touched the rings on her fingers, twisting them as if they were uncomfortable, or perhaps to make sure they were all still there.

From the garage at the back there was the sudden sound of the Wrangler being started and gunned impatiently. I'd got used to Buddy Breukink's manner by now, and I recognized his touch. Varoom, varoom, varoom, went the engine. Mrs. O'Raffety looked up to the sky with a pained expression. It wouldn't require an overdeveloped imagination to see suppressed rage in just about everything that Buddy did.

"They quarreled about the education of my little grandson, Peter." No need for her to say who she was talking about. "Buddy has his own ideas, but my daughter wants him brought up in the Jewish faith." She drank some iced tea.

I was fully occupied with the elaborate "lobster salad" that had been put before me. Every salad vegetable I'd ever heard of—from shiitaki mushrooms to lotus root—made a decorative jardinière for half a dozen baby lobster tails in rich mayonnaise. On a separate pink plate there was a hot baked potato heaped with sour cream and garnished with small pieces of crispy bacon. Salads in California are not designed for weight loss. I looked up from my plate. Mrs. O'Raffety was looking at me quizzically. She waited until I nodded.

"It's solely a question of the female line," she explained, prodding at a radish that rolled over and escaped. "My mother was a Jew, so I am a Jew. Therefore my daughter is a Jew, and so her son is a Jew. Buddy just can't seem to understand that."

"Perhaps," I ventured, "it's difficult to reconcile with a mother-in-law named O'Raffety."

She looked at me with the stern expression I'd noticed when she was swimming. Her eyes were glacial blue. "Maybe it is," she conceded. "Maybe it is. Mind you, I'm not strict. We don't eat kosher. You can't with Mexican kitchen staff."

"And where is your little grandson now?"

"In Florida. Last week Buddy was taking lunch with a private detective. I'm frightened he's got some plan to take the child away somewhere."

"Kidnap him?"

"Buddy gets emotional."

"But he's a lawyer."

"Even lawyers get emotional," she said, dismissing the subject without entirely condemning such emotion. As the sound of Buddy's Jeep receded, she went back to the subject of being European. "I was born in Berlin," she told me. "I have relatives in Berlin. Maybe one day I'll seek them out. But then I ask myself: Who needs more relatives?" She toyed with a pack of Marlboro cigarettes and a gold lighter, as if trying to resist temptation.

"You came to America as a child?"

She nodded. "But lost the language. A few years back I started taking German lessons, but I just couldn't seem to get the hang of it. All those bothersome verbs . . ." She laughed. "More wine?"

"Thank you."

She plucked the bottle from the bucket. "A friend of mine —not far from here—makes it. His Chablis is excellent, the rosé is good—wonderful color—but the red doesn't quite come off, so I keep to the French reds." She poured the remainder of the wine into my glass. She called all white wines Chablis; everyone in California seemed to do that.

"What about you, Mrs. O'Raffety?" I said. She never invited me to call her by her first name, and I noticed that even her son-in-law addressed her in that same formal way, so she must have liked being Mrs. O'Raffety. She had, I suppose, paid enough for the privilege.

"I take only half a glass. Chablis affects the joints, you know; it's the uric acid."

"I didn't know that."

The bottle, dripping from the ice water, had made her fingers wet. Fastidiously she dried her hands on a pink towel before touching the cigarettes again. "You're easy to talk to," she said, looking at me through narrowed eyes, as if my appearance might explain it. "Did anyone ever tell you that? It's a gift, being a good listener. You listen but show no curiosity; I suppose that's the secret."

"Perhaps it is," I said.

"You can't imagine how excited Bret was to hear you were actually coming."

"I'm looking forward to seeing him again."

"He's with the physiotherapist right now. Miss a session and he's set back a week: that's what the doctor says, and he's right. I know. All my life I've suffered with this darn disc of mine." She touched her back as if remembering the pain.

When I finished the lobster salad, a servant magically appeared to remove the plates to a side table: mine totally cleaned and Mrs. O'Raffety's still laden with food.

"Do you mind if I smoke, Mr. Samson?"

The Mexican servant—a muscular middle-aged man with the tight skin and passive face of the Indian—waited for her orders. There was not only a dignity about him, there was an element of repressed strength, like a fierce dog that was awaiting the order to spring.

I felt like inviting Mrs. O'Raffety to call me Bernard, but she was the sort of woman who might decline such an invitation. "It's your home," I told her.

"And my lungs. Yes, that's what Buddy tells me." She gave a throaty little laugh and tugged a cigarette from the pack on the table. The servant bent over and lit it for her. "Now, Mr. Samson: Fresh strawberries? Raspberries? Cook's home-made blueberry pie? What else is there, Luis?" There was something disconcerting about the way California's menus defied the strictures of the seasons. "The pies are just gorgeous," she added, but didn't ask for any.

When I'd decided upon blueberry pie and ice cream, and the silent Luis had departed to get it, Mrs. O'Raffety said, "You'll notice the change in him. Bret, I mean. He's not the man he used to be." She looked at the burning tip of her cigarette. "He'll want to tell you how tough he is, of course. Men are like that, I know. But don't encourage him to do anything stupid, will you?"

"What sort of stupid thing is he likely to do?"

"The physician has him on drugs up to here." She held her hand up to her head. "And he has to rest in the afternoon too. He's sick."

"The surgeons in Berlin didn't expect him to survive," I said. "He's lucky to have you to look after him, Mrs. O'Raffety."

"What else could I do? The hospital bills were piling up, and Bret had some lousy British insurance scheme that didn't even cover the cost of his room." She smoked her cigarette. "I got Buddy to try getting more money from them, but you know what insurance companies are like."

"You were the good samaritan," I said.

"Who else did he have who would take him? And I was related to him in a crazy, roundabout way. Not kin. My grandfather married Bret's widowed mother. She changed the children's names to Rensselaer. Bret's real name was Turner."

"He was married," I said.

"Do you know his wife?" She flicked ash into the ashtray.

"No."

"I contacted her. I wrote and told her Bret was on the point of death. No reply. She never even sent a get-well card." Mrs. O'Raffety inhaled deeply and blew smoke in a manner that displayed her contempt. She reminded me of Cindy Matthews just for a moment. They were both women who knew what they wanted.

"Perhaps she'd moved house," I suggested.

"Buddy got someone on to that. She cashes her alimony check every month without fail. She got my letter all right. She's taken all that money from him and she doesn't give a damn. How can a woman behave that way?" She drank iced tea and waited while a huge portion of blueberry pie with ice cream and whipped cream was put on the table for me. Then she said, "Bret and I were kids together. I was crazy about him. I guess I always figured we'd be married. Then one day he went downtown and joined the navy. I waited for him. Waited and waited and waited. The war ended, but he never came back."

"Never came back?"

"Never came back to live hereabouts. London, Berlin. I got letters and cards from him. Long letters sometimes, but the letters never said the one thing I wanted to hear."

I started eating my pie.

"You didn't think you were going to hear the confessions of a lonely old lady. Well, I don't know what got me started. You knowing Bret, I suppose. The only other acquaintance Bret and I have in common is that bitch of a wife of his."

"So you know her?" She had spoken of her distantly, as if she existed only as a spender of Bret's money.

"Nikki? Sure, I know her. I knew what would happen to that marriage right from the start. Right from the moment she told me she was going to marry him. Sometimes I think she only went for him because she knew how much I would suffer."

"Is she from around here?"

"Nikki Foster? Her folks had a shoe store in Santa Barbara. She was at school with me. She always was a little bitch."

"How long did it last?"

"Eight long, miserable years they lived together, or so I understand. I've never spoken to Bret about her, and he never mentions her name."

"And he has a brother."

"Sheldon." She gave an enigmatic little chuckle. "Ever meet him?"

"No," I said.

"Big man in Washington, D.C. Big, big man. A nice enough guy, but always on his way to somewhere better: know what I mean?"

"I know what you mean."

She lowered her voice. "And none of them seem to have any money. What did they do with all that Rensselaer money? That's what I'd like to know. Old Cy Rensselaer must have been sitting on a fortune when he died. Surely Bret couldn't have given so much of it to that awful woman. But if not, where did it go?"

I don't know what I was expecting, but Bret Rensselaer, when I finally got to see him, looked far from fit and well. He was somewhere about sixty, a slim, tailored figure in white cotton slacks, white tee shirt, and white gym shoes. It could have been the height of fashion, but on his frail figure the outfit looked institutional. He smiled. He'd kept that tight-jawed smile, and he'd kept his hair.

But how he'd aged. His cheeks were drawn and his face wrinkled. And yet something of that former youth had been replaced with distinction, as a film star might age and become a president. He was doing some gentle arm exercises when I entered the room. "Bernard," he called amiably. His exertions had made him a little out of breath. "Sorry to be so elusive, Bernard, but there's no way they'll let me break this routine." He always put the accent on the second half of my name, and hearing him say it in that low, burring accent brought back memories. I looked around at this private gym. Someone had spent a lot of money on it: the upstairs room had been ripped out to make a "cathedral" ceiling, and there were polished wood bars right across one wall, a picture window in the other. The floor was wood blocks, and the room was equipped with an exercise bicycle, a rowing machine, and a big steel frame with a seat inside and weights and pulleys, like some instrument of torture. Bret was inside it, pulling and pushing levers. "It's time I finished," he said.

It was that moment of the late afternoon when nature comes to a complete standstill. Even up here on the hillside, there was no wind, not a leaf moved, and no birds flew. The afternoon sun—now low and far away over the Pacific Ocean—gilded everything, and the air was heavy and suffocating. It was at this moment that sunlight coming through the big window painted Bret—and the machine that encaged him—gold, so that he looked like the statue of a remote, wrinkled, and pagan god. "I hear they're getting you ready for the Decathlon."

Bret looked gratified by this silly compliment. He smiled the shy, fleeting smile that he'd used on the best-shaped girls from the typing pool, and rubbed his face. "Three hours a day, but it pays off. In just the last two months I'm really getting back into shape," he said. He climbed out of his machine and wiped his forehead with a towel.

"Sounds grim."

"And with an ex–Marine Corps medic to put you through it, it is grim," said Bret with that proud, masochistic relish that all men are prone to at times. "I even went skiing."

"Not bad!"

"Sun Valley. Just a weekend. Easy slopes: no black runs or double diamonds." He shook my hand and gripped it tightly. For a moment we stood looking at each other. Despite all our ups and downs I liked him, and I suppose he knew that. Three years ago, when he'd really been in trouble, it was me he came to, and for some stupid reason that I could not fathom I was proud of that. But Bret had spent too much of his life with the rich and powerful, and he'd developed the hard carapace that all such people use to hide their innermost feelings. He smiled as he let go of my hand, and he punched my arm gently. "Jesus Christ! It's good to see you, Bernard. How is everything in the Department?"

"We're managing, but only just."

"But Dicky never got Europe?"

"No."

"Well, that's just as well. He's not ready for that one yet. How are you getting along with the Deputy? I hear he's kicking ass." He indicated that I should sit down on the bench and I did so.

"We see a lot more of him," I admitted.

"That's good. A deputy with a Knighthood hasn't got so much to work for," said Bret. "I suppose he wants to show he's keen."

"He didn't get the K for working in the Department," I pointed out.

"Is that a cry from the heart?" said Bret, and laughed a sober little laugh that didn't strain his muscles.

I hadn't meant to criticize the Deputy's lack of experience, but it reminded me that a chat with Bret was like a session on a polygraph. And as soon as the subject of honors and titles came up, Bret's face took on a predatory look. It always amazed me that educated and sophisticated people such as Bret, Dicky, and Frank were so besotted by these incongruous and inconvenient devices. But that's how the system worked, and at least it cost the taxpayer nothing. "The Deputy will be all right," I said. "But a lot of people don't like new ideas, no matter who's selling them."

"Frank Harrington, for instance," said Bret.

He'd hit it right on the nose, of course. Frank—so near to retirement—would oppose change of any sort. "I get to hear things, Bernard. Even over here, I get to know what's going on. The D-G tells me what's what."

"The D-G does?"

"Not personally," said Bret.

"We hardly ever see him nowadays," I said. "Everyone says he's sick and going to retire early."

"And let the Deputy take over . . . Yes, I hear the same stories, but I wouldn't write the D-G out of the script too early. The old devil likes to be a back-seat driver."

"I should come out here and talk to you more often, Bret," I said admiringly.

"Maybe you should, Bernard," he said. "Sometimes an onlooker sees the game more clearly than the players."

"But do any of the team take advice from the stands?"

"That's the same old Bernard I used to know," he said in a manner which might, or might not, have been sarcastic. "And your lovely Gloria? Is that still going strong?"

"She's a good kid," I said, vaguely enough for him to see that I didn't want to talk about it.

"I heard you'd set up house with her."

Damn him, I thought, but I kept my composure. "I rented the town house and got a mortgage on a place in the suburbs."

"You can never go wrong with real estate," he said.

"I'll go wrong with it if my father-in-law turns nasty," I

said. "He guaranteed the mortgage. Even the bank doesn't know I'm renting it yet."

"That will be all right, Bernard. Maybe they'll inch your payments up, but they won't give you a bad time."

"Half the house belongs to Fiona. If her father claimed it on her behalf, I'd be into a legal wrangle."

"You did get legal advice?" he asked.

"No, I'm trying not to think about it."

Bret pulled a face of disapproval. People like Bret got legal advice before taking a second helping of carbohydrates. "The Department would help," said Bret in that authoritative way in which he was inclined to voice his speculations.

"We'll see," I said. I was in fact somewhat fortified by his encouragement, no matter how flimsy it was.

"You don't think Fiona might come back?" he said. He put on a cardigan. The sun had gone now, and there was a drop in the temperature.

"Come back!" I said. "How could she? She'd find herself in the Old Bailey."

"Stranger things have happened," said Bret. "How long has she been away?"

"A long while."

"Bide your time," said Bret. "You're not thinking of getting married again, are you?"

"Not yet," I said.

He nodded. "Come back to me," said Bret. "Any problem about the house or your father-in-law, or anything like that, you come back to me. Phone here; leave a number where I can reach you. Understand?"

"Why you, Bret? I mean thanks. But why you?"

"Ever hear of the Benevolent Fund?" said Bret and, without waiting for me to say no, I hadn't, added, "They recently made me the president of the Fund. It's an honorary title, but it gives me a chance to keep in touch. And the Fund is for this kind of problem."

"Benevolent Fund?"

"These problems are not of your making, Bernard. Sure, your wife defected, but there's no way that can be laid at your door. It's the Department's problem, and they'll do what they can." He stopped studying his fingernails for long enough to give me a sincere look, straight in the eyes.

I said, "I envy you your faith in the Department's charity and understanding, Bret. Maybe that's what keeps you going."

"It comes with being an Anglophile, Bernard." He put both hands in his pockets and grinned. "And, talking about your marriage, what do you hear about Fiona?"

"She's working for the other side," I said stolidly. He knew I didn't want to discuss any of this, but it didn't deter him.

"No messages? Nothing? She must miss the children."

I said, "She'd be crazy to have the children there with her. It wouldn't be good for them, and her new bosses would hold the children ransom if she ever strayed out of line."

"Fiona is probably trusted, Bernard. She gave up a lot: children, husband, family, home, career. She gave up everything. It's my guess they trust her over there." He fiddled with the controls of the exercise bicycle. It was like Bret: he always had to fidget with something. Always had to interfere, his critics said. He pushed the pedal down, so that the mechanism made a noise. "But a lot of people find it impossible to live over there. Don't give up hope yet."

"Well, I guess you didn't have me come all the way to California to talk about Fiona," I said.

He looked up sharply. Years back I'd suspected him of having an affair with Fiona. They seemed to enjoy each other's company in a way that I envied. I was no longer jealous—we'd both lost her—but my suspicion, and his awareness of it, cast a shadow upon our relationship. "Well, in a way, yes, I did." Big smile. "I had some papers for London. Someone had to come, and they sent you, which makes me very happy."

"Don't give me all that shit," I said. "I'm grown up now. If there's something to say, say it, and get it over with."

"What do you mean?"

"What do I mean? I'll tell you what I mean. First, Harry Strang, not being in on the joke, whatever the joke is, told me that I was assigned at the particular request of the Washington Field Unit. Second, when I get here and open my suitcase, I find that it's all been searched very carefully. Not hurriedly ransacked and turned over, the way a thief does it, or the orderly and systematic 'authorized' way customs do it. But turned right over, just the same."

"Airport security," said Bret sharply. "Don't be so paranoid, Bernard."

"I thought you'd say that, Bret. So what about my hand baggage? What about the chatty Mr. Woosnam or whatever his real name was, who just happens to get the seat next to mine and goes through my bag while I'm in the toilet?"

"You can't be sure," said Bret.

"Sure it happened? Or sure it was the Department?"

Bret smiled. "Bernard, Bernard, Bernard," he said, shaking his head in disbelief. I was paranoid: the matter of my baggage was another example of my foolishness. There was nothing to be gained from trying to pursue the subject. "Sit back, and let's talk."

I sat back.

"Years ago—before Fiona took a walk—I was given a job to do. Operation Hook, it was called. It was designed to move some money around the globe. In those days I was always liable to get saddled with those finance jobs. There was no one else upstairs who knew anything about nuts-and-bolts finance."

"With Prettyman?"

"Right. Prettyman was assigned to me to oversee the facts and figures."

"Prettyman was on the Special Operations Committee with you."

"I wouldn't make too much of that," said Bret. "It might have looked good on his CV, but as far as that committee was concerned, he was just a glorified bookkeeper."

"But he reported back to Central Funding," I said. "Reported directly back to them. In effect, Prettyman was their man on the committee."

"You have been doing your homework," said Bret, piqued that I should have known anything about it. "Yes, Prettyman reported back directly to Funding, because I suggested that we do it that way. It saved me having to sign everything, and answer routine questions, at a time when I was out of London a lot."

"Operation Hook? I've never heard of it."

"And why should you? Almost no one heard of it. It was very 'need-to-know.' . . . The D-G, me . . . Even Prettyman didn't know all the details."

I looked at him waving his hands about. "Prettyman signed the checks," I said.

"I don't know who told you that. It's true he countersigned the checks. But that was just a belt-and-braces device the D-G added, to monitor spending. The checks had the amount and the date filled in—so that Prettyman could watch the cash flow—but he wasn't a party to the rest of it, payees and so on."

"And suddenly Prettyman goes to Codes and Ciphers. Fiona defects. Prettyman goes to Washington. Is it all connected in some way I don't see? What was it all for?"

"It's still going," said Bret. "It's still damned hot."

"Going where?" I said.

He hesitated and wet his lips. "This is still very touchy stuff, Bernard."

"Okay."

Another hesitation and more chewing of the lip. "Embassy penetration."

"I thought Ravenscroft had taken all that embassy stuff across the river. He's got a dozen people over there. What do they do all day?"

"Hook is quite different. Ravenscroft knows nothing about it."

"So Ravenscroft and his people were moved because they were compromised?"

He shrugged. "I couldn't say. Embassy penetration work is constantly compromised. You know that. A defector goes, and they tighten up, and Ravenscroft's life becomes more tricky for a while." He looked at me. "But Hook is not in Ravenscroft's class. A lot of money is involved. Hook is for really big fish."

"I learn more from you in five minutes than I find out in the office after a year of asking questions."

"Because I want you to stop asking questions," said Bret. A new, firmer voice now, and not so friendly. "You're poking into things that don't concern you, Bernard. You could blow the whole show for us." He was angry, and his angry words turned into a cough, so that he had to pat his chest to recover his breath.

"Is that why I was sent here?"

"In a way," said Bret. He cleared his throat.

"Just let me get this straight," I said. "You set up a lot of companies and bank accounts for this 'Hook' business so you could move cash without Central Funding having any record?"

"Embassies," said Bret. "East European embassies. Not many people. Even I don't have the details. That's how it's run. And it makes sense that way. Because, if someone in Funding had the ledgers, every one of our sources could be endangered." I looked at him. "Big fish, Bernard . . ."

"And Prettyman knew about all this?"

"Prettyman knew only what he had to be told, plus whatever he could guess."

"And how much was that?"

"Only Prettyman can answer that one."

"And Prettyman is dead."

"That's right," said Bret. "He's dead."

"And you want me to forget the whole thing?"

"Some bloody fool of a bookkeeper got his figures wrong. Panic. And suddenly it seemed like getting Prettyman back to London was the best way to sort out the muddle."

"But now it's sorted out?"

"It was an accountant's mistake. A glitch like that happens now and again."

"Okay, Bret. Can I go now?"

"It's no use getting tough," warned Bret. "This business is nothing to do with you. I don't want you prying into it. I'm asking you to back off because lives are at stake. If you're too dumb to see there's no other way . . ."

"Then what?"

"This is official," he said. "It's not just me asking you on a personal basis, it's an official order."

"Oh, I've got that one written down and learned by heart," I said. "My baggage wasn't turned over because there was any chance of finding something I was hiding. I'm too long in the tooth for that one. My checked baggage was searched to show me that you were on the side of the angels. Right, Bret? Was that your idea, Bret? Did you ask London Central Operations to turn me over? Harry Strang, was it? Harry's a good enough fellow. Tough, efficient, and experienced enough to arrange a small detail like that. And near enough to his pension not to be tempted to confide in me that it was going to happen. Right, Bret?"

"You're your own worst enemy, Bernard."

"Not while you're around, Bret."

"Think it over, Bernard. Sleep on it. But make quite sure you know what's at stake." He turned his eyes away from me and found an excuse to fiddle with the bicycle.

"Innocent lives, you mean?" I asked sarcastically. "Or my job?"

"Both, Bernard." He was being tough now. All that Benevolent Fund script was shredded. This was the real Bret: steely-eyed and contemptuous.

"Is this the sort of ultimatum you put to Jim Prettyman?" I asked. "Was he his own worst enemy, until you came along? Did he give your 'official order' a thumbs down, so you had to have some boys from out of town blow him away in the car park?"

The shake of his head was almost imperceptible. Bret's expression had locked up tight. The gold had gone from the sunlight; he looked old and tired and wrinkled. He'd never come back and work in the Department again, I was certain of that. Bret's time had come and gone. His voice was little more than a whisper as he said, "I think you've said enough, Bernard. More than enough, in fact. We'll talk again in the morning. You're booked on the London flight tomorrow."

I didn't answer. In a way I felt sorry for him, doing his exercises every day, and trying to keep in touch with the Department, and even interfere in what went on there. Telling himself that one day it would all be like it was before, and hoping that his chance of a Knighthood wasn't irretrievably lost.

I stood up. So it was the stick and carrot. Play ball with Bret and I even get help with the mortgage; but keep looking into things that don't concern me and I'll lose my job, and maybe lose it the way Jim Prettyman lost his job. Feet first.

Or had I misunderstood him?

Chapter 15

Disoriented and jet-lagged, my mind reeling with memories, I slept badly that night. That damned house was never quiet, not even in the small hours. Not only were there the relentless whines and hums of machinery from somewhere close by, but I heard footsteps outside my open window and muttered words in that thick, accented Spanish that Mexican expatriates acquire in Southern California. I closed the window, but from behind the house came the sounds of the guard dogs crashing through the undergrowth and throwing their weight against the tall chain-link fence that surrounded the house and kept the animals in the outer perimeter. Perhaps the animals sensed the coming storm, for soon after that came the crash of thunder, gusting winds, and rain beating on the window and drumming against the metal pool-furniture on the patio.

The storm passed over rapidly, as storms out of the Pacific so often do, and about four o'clock in the morning a new series of the loud buzzes and resonant droning of some nearby machines began. It was no good; I couldn't sleep. I got up to search for the source of the noise. Dressed in one of the smart toweling robes that Mrs. O'Raffety thoughtfully provided for her guests, I explored the whitewashed corridor. Here were doors to the pantry, the larder, the kitchen, and various storerooms. The main lighting was not working— perhaps the storm had caused a failure—but low-wattage emergency lights were bright enough for me to see the way.

I passed the boiler room and the fuse boxes and the piled cartons of bottled water that Mrs. O'Raffety believed was so good for the digestion. The mechanical sounds grew louder as I got to the low wooden door next to the kitchen servery. The key was left in a big brassbound lock. By now I'd come far enough around the house to be behind the guest rooms.

I opened the door and stepped cautiously inside. The hum of machinery was louder now, and I could see a short flight of worn stone steps leading down into a low-ceilinged cellar. Along one wall were four control panels lit with flickering numbers and programs. The glimmer of orange light from them was enough to reflect in the large puddles that had formed on the uneven flagstones of the floor. It was the laundry room, with a battery of washing and drying machines. On the top of one of the dryers was an empty beer can and some cigarette butts. The machines were aligned along the wall that I guessed must back onto mine. From somewhere close by I heard a cough and an exclamation of anger. It was one of the Mexicans.

I went past the machines to find another room; the door was ajar and there was bright light inside. I opened the door. Four men were seated round a table playing cards: three Mexicans and Buddy. He was wearing his Stetson. It was tilted well forward over his brow. There was money on the table, some cans of beer, and a bottle of whisky. Propped against the wall was a pump-handle shotgun. The machinery sounded loud in here, but the men seemed to be inured to it.

"Hi there, Bernard. I knew it was you," murmured Buddy. He hadn't looked up from his cards. The three Mexicans had turned their heads and were studying me with a passive but unwelcoming curiosity. All three of them were men in their mid-thirties; tough-looking men with close-cropped hair and weather-beaten faces. "Want to sit in?"

"No," I said. "I couldn't sleep."

"I wouldn't go strolling around at this time of night," said Buddy, rearranging the cards he was holding. "The night-shift guards are too damned trigger-happy."

"Is that so," I said.

Now, for the first time, he looked up, and studied me with the same discontent that he'd given to his hand of cards. "Yes, Bernard. It is so." He wet his lips. "We had a break-in last month. Some young punk got past our little soldiers, over the outer fence, past the dogs, cut his way through the inner fence using bolt cutters, opened the security bolt on Mr. Rensselaer's office, and tried to lever open the goddamned desk. How do you like that! Mrs. O'Raffety fired the whole army. She said they were asleep or drunk or spaced out or something. She's wrong about that, but new brooms sweep clean. These new recruits are eager to do things right. Know what I mean?"

"I didn't know Mr. Rensselaer had an office," I said.

"A kind of sitting room," amended Buddy, and shrugged. "If you want to see my cards . . ."

"No," I said. "No, I don't."

"These guys are taking me to the cleaners," complained Buddy lightheartedly. He poured himself a drink and swallowed it quickly.

"What happened to the kid?" I said.

"The kid? Oh, the punk who got in. I'm not sure, but he won't be operating bolt cutters in the foreseeable future. An excited *soldado* with a shotgun was a bit too close. Both barrels. He'd lost a lot of blood by the time we got him to the hospital. And then, of course, there was a hassle about whether he had Blue Cross insurance before they'd take a look at him."

"That was a tough decision for you," I said.

"Nothing tough about it," said Buddy. "I'll make damn sure Mrs. O'Raffety doesn't find herself paying the medical bills for any stiff who comes up here to rob her. It was bad enough clearing up the blood, and repairing the damage he did. So I told the night nurse I found him bleeding on the highway, and I had these guys with me to say the same." He nodded at the three Mexicans.

"You think of everything, Buddy."

He looked up and smiled. "You know something, Bernard? That joker wasn't carrying a weapon, and that's darned unusual in these parts. He had a camera in his pocket. Olympus: a darned good camera too, I've still got it somewhere. A macro lens and loaded with slow black-and-white film. That's the kind of outfit you'd need to photograph a document. I said that to Mr. Rensselaer at the time, but he just smiled and said maybe."

"I'll try sleeping again."

"What about a shot of Scotch?"

"No thanks," I said. "I'm trying to give it up."

. . .

I went back to bed and put a pillow over my head to keep the sound of the machines from my ears. It was getting light when eventually I went to sleep. A deep sleep, from which I was roused by the buzzing of my little alarm clock.

The next morning brought a sudden taste of winter. The temperature had dropped, so that I went digging into my bag for a sweater. The Pacific Ocean was greenish-gray, with dirty white crests that broke off the waves to make a trail of spray. Overhead, the dark clouds were low enough to skim the tops of the hills, and even the water in the pool had lost its clarity and color.

Time passed slowly. The London plane was not due to depart until the early evening. It was too cold to sit outside, and there was nowhere to go walking, for beyond the wire the dogs ran free. I swam in the heated pool, which steamed like soup in the cold air. By ten o'clock the rain had started again. I drank lots of coffee and I read old issues of *National Geographic* magazine. The "family room" was big, with dark oak beams in the ceiling and a life-size painting, in Modigliani style, of Mrs. O'Raffety in a flouncy pink dress. Mrs. O'Raffety was there in person, and so were Bret and Buddy. There was not much talking. A large TV, tuned to a football game, had been wheeled into position before us. No one watched it, but it provided an excuse for not speaking.

We sat sprawling on long chintz-covered sofas, arranged around a low oak table. On it stood a gigantic array of flowers in an ornamental bowl that bore the gold sticker of a Los Angeles florist. In a huge stone fireplace some large logs burned brightly, their flames fanned by the wind that howled in the chimney and was still fierce enough to whip the palm fronds.

Both Mrs. O'Raffety and Bret missed lunch. Buddy and I ate hamburgers and Caesar salad from trays that we balanced on our knees as we all sat around the fire. They were huge burgers, as good as I've ever tasted, with about half a pound of beef in each one. But Buddy only picked at his meal. He said he'd slept badly. He said he was sick, but he managed to eat all his french fries.

Outside, the weather got worse and worse all morning, until the gray cloud reached down and enveloped us, cutting visibility to almost nothing, and Mrs. O'Raffety made Buddy phone the airport to be sure the planes were still flying.

For the rest of the afternoon Mrs. O'Raffety—in red trousers and long pink crocheted top—exchanged small talk with her son-in-law, politely including me in the exchanges whenever a chance came along. Bret turned his head, as if to show interest in what was said, but contributed very little. He looked older and more frail this morning. Buddy had confided that Bret had bad days, and this was obviously one of them. His face was lined and haggard. His clothes—dark-blue openneck linen shirt, dark trousers, and polished shoes—worn in response to the colder weather, emphasized his age.

Mrs. O'Raffety said, "Are you sure you can't stay another day, Mr. Samson? It's such a pity to come to Southern California and just stay overnight."

"Maybe Mr. Samson has a family," said Buddy.

"Yes," I said. "Two children, a boy and a girl."

"Do they swim?" said Mrs. O'Raffety.

"More or less," I said.

"You should have brought them," she said, in that artless way that rich people have of overlooking financial obstacles. "Wouldn't they just love that pool."

"It's a wonderful place you have here," I said.

She smiled and pushed back the sleeves of her open-work sweater in a nervous mannerism that was typical of her. "Bret used to call it 'paradise off the bone,' " she said sadly. It was impossible to miss the implication that Bret was not calling it that these days.

Bret made a real attempt to smile but got stuck about halfway through trying. "Why 'off the bone'?" I asked.

"Like fish in a restaurant," she explained. "Every little thing done for you. Enjoy, enjoy."

Bret looked at me: I smiled. Bret scowled. He said, "For God's sake, Bernard, come to your senses." His voice was quiet, but the bitterness of his tone was enough to make Mrs. O'Raffety stare at him in surprise.

"Whatever are you talking about, Bret?" she said.

But he gave no sign of having heard her. His eyes were fixed on me, and the expression on his face was fiercer than I'd ever seen before. His voice was a growl. "You goddamn pinbrain! Search your mind! Search your mind!" He got up from his low seat and walked from the room.

No one said anything. Bret's outburst had embarrassed Mrs. O'Raffety, and Buddy took his cues from her. They sat there looking at the flower arrangement, as if they'd not heard Bret and not noticed him get up and leave.

It was a long time before she spoke. Then she said, "Bret resents his infirmity. I remember him at high school: a lion! Such an active man all his life . . . It's so difficult for him to adjust to being sick."

"Is he often angry like this?" I asked.

"No," said Buddy. "Your visit seems to have upset him."

"Of course it hasn't," said Mrs. O'Raffety, who knew how to be the perfect hostess. "It's just that meeting Mr. Samson makes Bret remember the times when he was fit and well."

"Some days he's just fine," said Buddy. He reached for the coffeepot that was keeping hot on the serving trolley. "More?"

"Thanks," I said.

"Sure," said Buddy. "And some days I see him standing by the pool with an expression on his face so that I think he's going to throw himself in and stay under."

"Buddy! How can you say such a thing?"

"I'm sorry, Mrs. O'Raffety, but it's true."

"He has to find himself," said Mrs. O'Raffety.

"Sure," said Buddy hastily, trying to assuage his employer's alarm. "He has to find himself. That's what I mean."

We took the coast road back. Buddy wasn't feeling so good, and so one of the servants—Joey, a small belligerent little Mexican who'd been playing cards the previous night—was driving Buddy's Jeep, leaning forward, staring into the white mist, and muttering that we should have taken the canyon road and gone inland to the Freeway instead.

"Buddy should be doing this himself," complained the driver for the hundredth time. "I don't like this kind of weather." The fog rolled in from the ocean and swirled around us, so that sudden glimpses of the highway opened up and were as quickly gone.

"Buddy felt ill," I said. Car headlights flashed past. A dozen black leather motorcyclists went with suicidal disregard into the white wall of fog, and were swallowed up with such suddenness that even the sound of the bikes was gone.

"Ill!" said Joey. "Drunk, you mean." The rain was suddenly fiercer. The gray shapes of enormous trucks briefly appeared, each adorned with a multitude of little orange lights, like ships lit up for a regatta.

When I didn't respond, Joey said, "Mrs. O'Raffety doesn't know, but she'll find out."

"Doesn't know what?"

"That he's a lush. That guy puts down a fifth of bourbon like it's Coca-Cola. He's been doing that ever since his wife dumped him."

"Poor Buddy," I said.

"The sonuvabitch deserves all he gets."

"Is that so?" I said.

In response to my unasked question, Joey looked at me and grinned. "I'm leaving next week. I'm going to work for my brother-in-law in San Diego. Buddy can shove his job."

A few miles short of Malibu, we were stopped by a line of flares burning bright in the roadway. Half a dozen big trucks were parked at the roadside. A man in a tan-colored shirt emerged from the mist. "Los Angeles County Sheriff," said the badge on his arm. With him were two Highway Patrol cops in yellow oilskins: a big fellow and a girl. They were all very wet.

"Pull over," the cop told Joey, pointing to the roadside.

"What's wrong?" The slap and buzz of the wipers seemed unnaturally loud. "A slide?"

"Behind the white Caddie." The man from the Sheriff's Office indicated an open patch of ground where several patient drivers were parked and waiting for the road to be cleared. The cop's face was running with rainwater that dropped from the peak of his cap; his shirt was black with rain. He wasn't in the mood for a long discussion.

"We've got a plane to catch: international," said Joey.

The cop looked at him with a blank expression. "Just let the ambulance through." The cop squeegeed the water from his face, using the edge of his hand.

"What happened?"

The ambulance moved slowly past. The cop spoke like a swimmer too, in brief, breathless sentences. "A big truck—artic—jackknifed. No way you'll get past."

"Any other route we can take?" Joey asked.

"Sure, but you'd add an hour to your trip." The cop squinted into the rain. "LAX, you say? There are a couple of guys in a big old Lincoln limo. They said they were going to turn around and head back downtown. They'd maybe take your passenger."

"Where are they?"

"Other side of the wreck. Maybe they left already, but I could try." He switched on his transceiver. There was a burst of static, and the cop said, "That big dark-blue limo still there, Pete?"

There was a scarcely intelligible affirmative from the radio. The cop said, "Ask them if they'd take someone in a hurry to get to LAX."

With bag in hand, I picked my way past a line of cars and the monster-size truck that was askew across the highway and completely blocked the road both ways. I found the limousine waiting for me; by that time—despite my plastic raincoat—I was very wet too.

The man beside the driver got out into the heavy rain and opened the rear door for me, and that's the kind of thing you do only if you've got a job you are determined to keep. Now I could see the man in the back: a short, thickset man with a rotund belly. He wore an expensive three-piece dark-blue suit —gold pocket-watch chain well evidenced—and a shirt with a gold collar pin below the tight knot of a very conservative striped tie. It was too Wall Street for the Pacific Coast Highway, where pants and matching jackets went out of fashion with laced corsets and high hats.

"Bernie. Jump in," said the well-dressed man in the back. His voice was low, soft, and attractive; like his car.

I hesitated no more than a moment. Wet, stranded, and without transport, I was in no position to decline, and Posh Harry knew that. He smiled a welcome that had an element of smug satisfaction in it, and revealed a lot of teeth and some expensive dentistry. I climbed in beside him. Or as beside him as I had to be on a soft leather seat wide enough for four.

"What's the game?" I said. I was angry at the simple trick.

"Take Mr. Samson's bag," Posh Harry told the man in the front seat.

"It's valuable," I protested.

"Valuable," scoffed Harry. "What do you think is going to happen to it? You think I've got some dwarf hidden in the trunk to ransack your baggage on the way to the airport?"

"Maybe," I said.

"Maybe!" He laughed. "Did you hear that?" he asked the men in the front. "This guy is a real pro. From this one you could learn a thing or two." And then, in case they were taking him seriously, he laughed. "So nurse the bag, Bernie, if that's the way you prefer it. Let's go, driver! This man has a plane to catch."

"You didn't do all this just for me?" I asked cautiously. But how could they have collared me so neatly without positioning the truck as well?

"Not my style, baby," said Posh Harry. He paused before adding, "But my boss: it sure is her style!"

One of the men in the front laughed, softly enough not to interrupt but loud enough to be heard.

"Her?" I said.

"We got a female station chief here. You mean you hadn't heard? Yup. We've got a 'chieftess' running things." He laughed.

"A woman!"

He waved a manicured hand in a dismissive gesture of impatience. "You guys in London know all that stuff. It was in the monthly briefing last September."

"In London there were bets on which one of your L.A. men was calling himself Brigette," I said.

"You bastard!" said Harry. He sniggered.

The driver said, "Right on! Half those young guys in the office have got earrings and permanent waves. Faggots!"

"It was Brigette's idea," insisted Harry. "I told her I knew you. I wanted to phone Bret and keep it all cool, but she had her mind all made up. She said we'd have to pay for the truck rental anyway. The ambulance was her idea: a nice touch, huh? It was all fixed up by then, so she insisted we go ahead. Not like the old days, huh, Bernie?"

"Is that her real name: Brigette?"

"She's a hard-nosed little lady," said Harry with respect.

"She runs that office . . . I mean, those guys jump. Not like the old days, Bernie. I mean it."

"So what's this really all about, then?" I said, now that the mandatory exchange about the CIA's first female station chief was over and done with.

"It's about Bret," said Posh Harry. "It's about Bret Rensselaer." Delicately he scratched his cheek with the nail of his little finger, so that I saw his starched linen cuffs and the gold cuff links. His complexion was yellow enough to suggest Japanese blood, but his hands were paler. And his nails were carefully manicured. It was in line with his natty appearance. I'd never seen him anything but perfectly haircut and shaved with talc on his chin and a discreet smell of aftershave in the air. His clothes were always new-looking and a perfect fit, so that he was like a carefully assembled plastic toy. Perhaps it says more about me—or about the gangster films of my child-hood—that I always saw in his polished appearance a certain hint of menace.

"Yeah?" I said.

"The word is that you have some kind of feud—some kind of private vendetta—with Bret." Very serious now: the smile gone, hands loosely clasped across his belly like a temple Buddha taking a day off.

"And?"

"Private vendettas don't get the rent paid. Vendettas are turnoffs, Bernie. Bad news for Bret, bad news for you, bad news for London, and bad news for us."

"Who's 'us'?"

"Don't put me through the mangle, baby; the laundry's dried and aired. You know who 'us' is. 'Us' is the Company."

"And what in hell has it got to do with you?"

Hand raised in a gesture of pacification. "Did I handle this all wrong? Maybe we could start over? Right?"

"I'm not likely to get out and walk," I said.

"No. Sure." He sat well back in his seat and watched me

from under lowered eyelids as he picked up the pieces of goodwill and figured how to glue it all back together again. Posh Harry was pretty good at that kind of thing. For years he'd been a Mr. Fixit, working both sides of the street, and he got paid only when everyone was happy.

We drove on in silence. I put my bag between my feet and turned away to watch the rain falling on the millionaires' shacks that line this part of the beach. Here and there I saw groups of surfers in shiny black rubber wet suits. Anyone crazy enough to go looking for big waves in the Pacific Ocean was not deterred by bad weather.

I sat back in my seat and stole a glance at Posh Harry. I'd heard that he'd taken a permanent job with the CIA. Some said he'd never been anything but their paid mouthpiece, but I doubted that. I'd known him a long time. I'd watched him scratching a living in that shady world where secret information is bought and sold like gilts and pork bellies. He'd always been something of an enigma, a Hawaiian who'd taken to Europe in a way that few strangers ever do. Posh Harry's mastery of the German language—grammar, pronunciation, and idiom—belied the rather casual, relaxed demeanor he liked to display. Adult foreigners who will devote enough time and energy to acquire German like his have to be dedicated, demented, or Dutch.

"Why would you care?" I asked him. "What's Bret to you?"

"They like him," said Harry.

"Brigette, you mean?"

"I mean Washington," he said.

"Is Bret so important to the boys in Langley?" I asked very casually.

Like a scalded cat, he jumped aside from the implications of that one. "Don't get me wrong," said Harry. "Bret is not a CIA employee and he never has been." There was an old-fashioned formality about that statement and about the way he said it.

"Everyone keeps telling me that," I said. By "everyone" I meant Posh Harry. We'd been all through this years ago.

With demonstrated patience he said, "Everyone keeps telling you that because it's true."

"Washington?"

"Will you listen, Bernard? Bret is not—repeat, not—an Agency employee. We know nothing about what Bret does for you. I wish the hell we did."

"Did you put someone over the fence there last month, Harry? Was that one of your people trying to get a line on Bret?"

Harry looked at me for a moment and then said, "Someone got shot up there. An intruder was hurt bad. Yes, I heard about that."

"A friendly Agency gumshoe dropping in to pass the time of day? Off the record," I coaxed, "was that one of yours?"

But Harry would not be coaxed into an admission like that. "I'm not talking about the Agency; I'm talking about Capitol Hill. Bret's got some good friends there. His family deploy a lot of muscle in that town. They won't stand by while Bret is smeared."

"While Bret is smeared? Harry, I wish I knew what you're talking about," I said. "I didn't know Bret was still alive until I got here."

"Don't snow me, Bernie. Dead or alive, you've been bad-mouthing Bret Rensselaer. Don't deny it."

I felt a sudden pang of fear. There were three of them. There were plenty of lonely stretches of coastline nearby, and the desert. With more boldness than I felt I said, "Put away the brass knuckles, Harry. That's not your style." But rumors from long ago said it was exactly his style.

He smiled. "They said you were becoming paranoid."

"You get that way when jerks shanghai you on the highway and bury you under horse manure."

He ignored that and said, "This guy Woosnam, for instance. This guy is a kosher businessman."

"What?"

"Bret came through to the office last night and asked for an urgent checkup on the passenger you sat next to on the plane. He's a nothing, Bernard. A two-bit building contractor who made it big in real estate. That's what I mean about you being paranoid."

"Bret asked? About Woosnam?" I said.

"Sure. Bret came on the phone. The way I heard it, Bret was mad. He wanted to know if we'd put someone on the plane with you, but I knew we hadn't. We didn't even know you were coming until you'd arrived. Bret persuaded someone to make it a number-one priority. Dig out this Woosnam baby, and dig him out fast. So they made the airline go through the manifests. They dug people out of their beds and had them working all night. They weren't pleased, I can tell you. It being a weekend too."

"And Woosnam wasn't working for London Central?"

"Jesus Christ. Even now you don't believe me. I can see it in your face."

"Who cares," I said.

"I care. Bret cares. Everyone who likes you cares. We wonder what's happening to you, Bernard baby."

I made a noise to indicate that I didn't want to talk about the wretched Mr. Woosnam. Posh Harry nodded sagely and leaned forward to push a button that made the glass partition slide into position, so the men in front couldn't hear us. Although, if this was the kind of CIA limo I think it was, there would be a hidden tape-recorder button built into the upholstery so that Brigette, and God knows who else, would be able to refer to a transcript of what I said. Or was I becoming paranoid? "Let's talk turkey, Bernie. Let's cut out all the crap, okay?"

"Which crap was that, Harry?"

He ignored my question. He looked out of the car to see how near to L.A. International we were and decided to get to the point. "Listen," he said. "Big men in Washington hear you are running around trying to pin some old London screw-up on Bret. . . . Well, Washington gets touchy. They talk to your people in London Central. They say, Shit or get off the pot. What charges? they ask. Where's the evidence? they want to know, Bernard. Because they don't like the way Bret is expected to take all your lousy flak without getting a proper chance to answer." Just for a moment, there had been a glimpse of the real Posh Harry: the savage little guy inside this soft, smiling, cerebral Charlie Chan.

"If Bret thinks that . . ." I started to say.

"Hold the phone, Bernie." The amiable smile was back in place. "I'm saying that this is the way Washington sees it. Maybe they got it wrong, but that's the way it was looking to them, by the time they got on to London Central and started asking questions."

"And what did London say?" I said with genuine interest.

"London said just what Washington expected them to say. They said this was just Bernie Samson, on a one-man crusade that had no official authorization. London said they'd talk to Bernard Samson and cool him off a little."

"And how did Washington feel about that?"

"Washington said that was good. These big men in Washington said that if a little help was needed in cooling this maverick Brit off, they'd be happy to arrange for someone to break his arm in several places, just to show him that his extracurricular energies would be better employed with wine, women, and song."

"In a manner of speaking," I said.

"Sure, in a manner of speaking, Bernie." No smiles now, just blank face and cold stare, before Posh Harry turned away to look out at the neon signs and the restaurant forecourts that were packed with the cars of people who liked their lunch to go on till sundown. He touched the condensation that had formed on the windows and seemed surprised when a dribble of water ran down the glass. "Because these big men in Washington don't believe what your people tell them," said Harry, talking to the window. "They don't think London really have got some wild man who likes to go off to stir the dirt on his own time."

"No?"

"No. Washington think he's on assignment. They wonder if maybe those bastards in London Central are getting ready for the big reshuffle that their deck of marked cards has needed so long."

"Tell me more about that," I said. "I'd like to know."

He turned his head and gave me a slow, toothy smile. "They think your top guys are very clever at burying the bodies in a neighbor's yard."

Now I was beginning to see it. "London Central are going to blame some of their disasters on Bret?"

"It would be a way of handling it," said Harry.

"A bit farfetched, isn't it?"

Harry gave a tight-lipped smile and didn't answer. We both knew it wasn't farfetched. We knew it was exactly the way that our masters handled their difficulties. And, anyway, I didn't feel like working hard to convince him that London Central wouldn't do anything like that. The alternative would focus the wrath of Bret's Washington fan club upon me. And I have always been opposed to violence, even when it's in a manner of speaking.

Chapter 16

Sunday lunchtime; London Heathrow; no Gloria to meet me. It was not a warm homecoming. An overtired customs man demanded that the box of official papers that Bret had dumped on me should be opened for his inspection. My inclination was to hand it over, but I waited until the duty Special Branch officer finished his late breakfast of fried egg and sausages so that he could come down—egg on his tie—and explain to all concerned that I was permitted to enter the United Kingdom with the box closed and locked and its contents not scrutinized by Her Majesty's customs.

The unnecessary delay was especially galling because I was certain that the paperwork in the box was of no great importance or secrecy: my errand was the Department's excuse to have me cross the water and be rattled, wrung, and reassured by lovable Bret Rensselaer. Whether my encounter with Posh Harry was also a part of my Department's plan was something I hadn't yet decided, but probably not. They would not relish the message that Posh Harry conveyed to me.

And when I got to Number 13 Balaklava Road, the house was dark and empty. A hastily scribbled message stuck on the oven door said that Gloria's mother was sick and she'd had to go to see her. The word "had" underlined three times. The children were on a trip to the zoo with some "very nice" schoolfriends.

It was difficult for Gloria. She knew that I was likely to be examining her priorities in anything to do with my children. Her parents were not enthusiastic about our domestic arrangements. And I was very much aware of the fact that her mother was only three years older than I was. So were they!

Sunday lunch is a sacred ritual for Englishmen of my generation. You eat at home. With luck it's raining, so you can't work in the garden. You monitor the open fire diligently, while sipping an apéritif of your choice. Should a mood of desperate intellectuality overcome you, you might peruse the Sunday papers, reassured by the certainty that there will be no news in them. At the appointed time, with an appreciative family audience, you carve thin slices from a large piece of roasted meat and, if possible, cabbage, roasted potatoes, and Yorkshire pudding. You divide it unevenly amongst the family, according to whim. You eventually do the same with a sweet, stodgy cooked dessert that is accompanied by both custard and cream. You doze.

No matter how German some others said I was, no matter what my tastes were for foreign food, foreign heating systems, foreign cars, and foreign bodies, in the matter of Sunday lunch I was resolutely English.

That was why I was so unhappy at the idea of eating the cold ham and salad that Gloria had left for me. So I took the car and went to Alfonso's—a small Italian restaurant in Wimbledon. An establishment which, after taking the children to see *Cosí fan tutte,* our family called Don Alfonso's. Alfonso himself was, of course, Spanish and, although willing to tackle an Italian menu in Wimbledon, he was not so foolish as to offer British cooking of any sort. Certainly not a Sunday lunch.

That Sunday, Alfonso's was crowded with noisy people who didn't know that a home-cooked lunch is an established English tradition. There were lots of children in evidence, and two loaded dessert trolleys awaited the onslaught. From the amplifier came a scratchy rendition of "Volare" sung in an Italian falsetto with massed guitar accompaniment. It came around about every thirty minutes.

"Have the *aragosta fra diavolo,*" Alfonso advised, having

poured me a glass of white wine and twisted the bottle to reveal an impressive Soave label. "Drink! Drink! It's on the house, Mr. Samson." Only the most unperceptive of customers could have mistaken Alfonso for an Italian, despite his having lived in Rome for eight years. He had the lively and unscrupulous salesmanship of the Roman, incongruously coupled with the relentless melancholy of Iberia. I sipped the wine and kept my eyes down on the menu. "Lobster cooked in wine with tomato. Really delicious," he added persuasively.

"Frozen lobster?" I inquired. He watched one of his newest young waiters trying to prize baked lasagne from the metal dish to which it had stuck. It almost fell from his hands. Only with commendable self-control did Alfonso restrain himself from rushing across the room to do it himself.

He turned back to me, and his anxiety was manifested in his reply. "You think I wade through the paddling pool on Wimbledon Common to trap them? Frozen? Sure. Frozen."

"I don't like frozen lobster," I said. "And I don't like anything that's going to be '*diavolo.*'"

Zzzwhoof. Sharp intake of breath. "So what happened to you this morning? Get out of bed on the wrong side?"

"I didn't get out of bed: I haven't been to bed. I've been on a bloody aeroplane all night." Now we both watched the mad waiter as a gigantic serving spoon, heavily laden with pasta and sauce, made a perilous journey across the table to the plate. By a miracle it got there; no one got splattered. Alfonso breathed out and said, "Okay, okay, okay. Sorry I asked. Have a little more Soave. Shall I ask the chef to cook you a lovely half-lobster without the chili? Just a little melted butter?"

"What will frozen lobster taste of without the chili?" I asked.

"Oh dear! Oh dear! No lovely lady. That's the trouble. Is this what you're like when you're on your own?"

"I'm not on my own: I've got you here selling me a lunch."

"Something very light," he said. He always said "something very light," even if he was going to suggest pork and dumplings. I know, because he often suggested pork and dumplings, and I often ate it. "Fish. A beautiful unfrozen red mullet baked with olives. Green salad. Start with a half-portion of risotto."

"Okay."

"And a carafe of this Soave?"

"Are you crazy, Al? Everyone knows Italian restaurants manufacture their booze in a garden shed. Soave, maybe, but I'll have a bottle with a cork in it."

"You're a cynic, Mr. Samson," he said.

"And I'm paranoid with it," I said. "Everyone says so."

I ate my meal in solitude, watching my fellow customers getting drunk and noisy. The yellow dented Mini arrived when I was having coffee. She found a place to park immediately outside. She did it with style and economy of effort, even if one wheel did end up on the pavement.

Gloria entered the dining room with all the joyful energy of show biz: without arm-waving or shouting, she was able to ensure that no one failed to look up. Even drunk I could not have done it like her; perhaps that's what I found so attractive about her. She was everything I could not be. A big kiss and a hug. "I'm bloody starved, darling," she said. "How did it go in California?" Another kiss. "Did you swim?" Alfonso took her coat and pulled out a chair for her. She said, "Am I too late to eat, Alfonso darling?"

"How could I send you away hungry, beautiful lady?" He gave her coat to a waiter and reached for the cutlery from another table and arranged a setting before her with surprising speed.

After no more than a glance at the menu, Gloria said, "Could I have that delicious calves'-liver dish you do with the onions and sage? And start with the marinated mushrooms?"

She was like that: she could make up her mind very quickly about almost everything. I often wondered whether she had her answers prepared in advance. Or was it that she simply didn't care very much about the consequences of these things she was so quick to decide upon?

"Perfect," said Al as if no one had ever thought of such a meal before. And then, as he thought about it again, "Absolutely perfect!" He poured her some wine and held the bottle up to the light, as if worried that the wine left would be insufficient for us.

"How's your mother?" I said in an attempt to lower the temperature.

"She'll live."

"What was it?" I said.

"Poor Mummy is doing her dramatic-Hungarian number. She thinks Daddy is getting tired of her."

"And is he?"

"I suppose so. Good God! I don't know. They've been married for twenty-five years. It wouldn't be amazing if he was starting to feel a bit imprisoned. I've seen some gorgeous patients at his surgery. And they all adore him."

"Imprisoned by marriage?"

"It happens. They haven't got much in common."

I was surprised to find her so resigned. "But they are both expatriate Hungarians. They came here together and set up a new life."

"Now they both speak excellent English, and my sisters are away at school, and I have left home. There is not so much binding them together."

"And people say *I'm* a cynic."

"I'm not being cynical. I'm stating facts."

"Did you tell your mother this?"

"I wrapped it up a bit."

"I hope you wrapped it up a lot. She must be depressed beyond measure. And maybe your father is not chasing other women. Or even feeling imprisoned."

She sipped some wine, looked me in the eyes, and then gave me a slow smile. "You're a romantic, really, Bernard. An old-fashioned romantic. Perhaps that's why I fell for you so badly."

She smiled again. Her blond hair had been rearranged so that she had bangs to just above her eyebrows. She was so beautiful. "Your new hairdo looks good," I said.

She touched her hair. "Do you really like it?"

"Yes." I couldn't bear being separated from her, not even for a day or two. The prospect of her going to Cambridge was unendurable. She pursed her lips to offer a kiss.

"I love you, Gloria," I said without meaning to.

She smiled and fidgeted with the cutlery. She seemed slightly agitated, and I wondered if perhaps she was more worried about her mother than she was prepared to admit.

"I saw Bret Rensselaer," I said. "Everyone thought he was dead, but he's convalescing."

"You saw Bret Rensselaer?" she said. She wasn't as surprised by the news as I'd been, but, then, Bret Rensselaer had been gone for years.

"He was in a filthy temper. I suppose being chronically sick makes you moody."

"But he's recuperating?"

"He seems to have found a rich old lady. She said they were childhood sweethearts."

"How sweet," said Gloria.

"With a very nice little spread in Ventura County. I can't think why he'd want to get well."

"What a rotten thing to say, darling," she said. "That spoils everything; that's not romantic at all." Her marinated mushrooms arrived, and as she started eating she said, "Well, you chose exactly the right day to disappear, as usual."

"I did?"

"Friday morning. First your old friend Werner Volkmann arrived, tight-lipped and glaring. From what I can understand, he's accusing Frank Harrington of sending his wife off on a suicide mission to Frankfurt an der Oder. He was furious! I stayed out of sight."

"What happened?"

She continued eating and then said, "After a lot of toing and froing, and Dicky complaining of a headache and saying he would have to go to the doctor, it was decided that the Deputy would talk to Werner."

"The Deputy?"

"Well, he was demanding to see the bloody D-G, no less. Dicky told him the D-G was away sick, but Mr. Volkmann wasn't buying that one. It was obvious that seeing Dicky would only put his back up worse, so the Deputy offered to handle it."

"Good on the Deputy," I said.

"Sir Percy is all right. He's got guts and he's willing to make decisions."

"And there are not many people in London Central who answer that description."

"And meeting the Deputy calmed Werner down. It was when he thought they were trying to get rid of him that he got really angry."

"And an angry Werner is not a pretty sight."

"I was surprised. Dicky was too. I think it's that damned beard. Dicky was frightened of him. Dicky took refuge in Morgan's room and closed the door, not noticing that I was standing there. He said to Morgan that all these field agents are slobs. When he realized that I'd overheard him, he smiled as if to make it into a joke."

"What did the Deputy say to Werner?"

"No one knows. There were just the two of them. They were together for nearly an hour; I don't know whether that means they got along just fine or they were at each other's throats, but Volkmann came out all smiles, so I suppose the Deputy did a good job."

"I'm damned glad I missed it," I said.

"Did you know he was going along to raise hell?"

"He may have mentioned it."

"You bastard."

"What did I do?"

"You could have talked him round the other night. You let him come into the office and raise hell. That amused you, I suppose?" She said it without bitterness. In some ways I suspected that the notion of me as a troublemaker was not unattractive to her.

"Maybe I could have done, maybe not. But it's not as simple as it looks. This is part of Werner's ongoing feud with Frank Harrington. Werner has always hated Frank, and I'm determined not to be in the middle of any dispute between those two. I'd end up losing two good friends, and I haven't got enough friends to risk losing two of the best ones in order to smooth things along for Dicky and Morgan and the rest of them in the office."

"You were lucky to avoid it all. Then yesterday your friend Lucinda came to call."

"Cindy Prettyman?"

"Lucinda Matthews, she calls herself nowadays. She was most particular about that."

"She came to the office?"

"No, this was Saturday; she came to Balaklava Road. I was in and out with the car. I'd left the garage door open on account of that broken hinge, so she walked right in on me. I cursed. I was trying to get the children's laundry done so that Mrs. Palmer could help with the ironing."

"What did she want?"

"The usual. Her husband's 'murder' and the KGB slush fund and the conspiracy behind it. You know."

"Did she tell you all that?"

"I thought she'd never stop. Finally I said you'd get to-gether with her one day next week. Not at the office, she says, because someone might see you together. If you ask me, darling, she's off her head."

"Has something new happened?"

"She said I was to tell you that she has a new line on the money. And she wants a box of papers she gave you. She thinks they might contain a clue."

"She won't get much joy from that stuff," I said. "Unless she's suddenly taken up archaeology." Without intending to, I sighed deeply. I was not ready to face Cindy again.

"She said you'd want to know. She's heard of some money being moved. They are running scared, she says. They must realize that someone is on to them. All that sort of thing. She's bonkers."

"Cindy has been working hard."

Gloria wasn't too keen to endorse this praise for Cindy. "She doesn't know what she's talking about," said Gloria. "A lot of hot money is being pulled out of German banks and companies right now. It's because the Bonn government is bringing in new laws. The EEC have instructed them to bring German corporate balance sheets into line with those of other countries. Until now German private banks and private corporations haven't had to reveal their profits. By next year it won't be so easy to bury money in a bank or corporation. Central Funding are sure to be preparing for that change."

"I thought the German banks reported everything to the German tax authorities. I thought Germany didn't have hot money."

Gloria shook her head. "They only have to report their customers' money, darling. Their own money, and all the rich pickings they make, are kept secret. You know what all those bloody High Street banks are like: well, German banks are ten times worse."

"How do you know all this?"

"My economics classes. The West German financial markets are my special subject."

"Did you tell Cindy this?"

"She thinks I'm your dumb blonde. She didn't come round to talk to me." Gloria's grilled liver arrived. It looked good; I stole a piece of sautéed potato and let her eat her lunch in peace.

"I suppose eventually I'll have to talk to Cindy. I owe it to Jim."

"She says phone her at home and she'll meet you at the weekend." Gloria abandoned her liver and put her knife and fork down. It was a different tone of voice now: serious and concerned. "I really do think she's unbalanced, Bernard. She parked her car miles away, in front of Inkerman Villas. I told her it was private parking there and she might get towed away, but she wouldn't listen. She kept looking out of the window, as though someone might have followed her. When I asked her what was the matter, she said she was just admiring the view. She has a mad sort of look in her eyes. She's scary."

"I'll have to phone her," I said, while searching my mind for excuses not to. "But I wish she'd leave me out of it. I've already ruffled Bret's feathers, and I ask myself what for? I've got enough work, and enough enemies, without looking for more."

"You said you wanted to get to the bottom of it," said Gloria.

"But I just can't spare any time. It's another one of the Department's little secrets, and if they are so determined that it remains a mystery, then let it stay a mystery. Everything I encounter mystifies me; I don't need any more."

"Do I mystify you, my poor darling?" She reached out and stroked my hand.

"You especially," I said.

"Do you think Alfonso would give me a bag so I can take the rest of my liver home for Muffin?" she said without expecting a reply, and added, "Your friend Cindy won't let it go so easily."

"She has more spare time than I do, and she likes these 'causes.' Cindy's always been a bit like that. Animal welfare, women priests, diesel emission is killing the trees—she has to have a cause."

"I think she's abnormal," said Gloria in that flat, casual voice that suggested she didn't care one way or the other. She had switched off now. Gloria could do that. It was a knack I would dearly like to acquire. Suddenly she raised an arm and shouted, "Can I have some coffee, Alfonso?"

"Make that two," I called to him, but he gave no sign of having heard me.

"I'm sorry," she said. "I forgot that you don't like me to order things when I'm with you."

"Are you wrapping that liver up in your handkerchief. Ugh!"

"Muffin loves liver." She put the little parcel in her handbag as the coffee arrived.

"I shouldn't be drinking coffee," I said. "I need to go to bed."

"The children won't be home until after supper. Maybe I will go to bed too," she said artlessly.

"Race you home!"

Chapter 17

There was plenty of work waiting for me in the office. At the top of the pile, flagged and beribboned, was a Ministry of Defence request for details on Semtex, a Czechoslovakian explosive exported through the DDR and now being used in homemade "bean-can grenades" and causing casualties in Northern Ireland. Under it were some confidential questions about the Leipzig Trade Fair and—with only a number-one priority—some supplementaries from the Minister that must be ready for parliamentary question time.

It was one of the natural laws of departmental life that the sort of files that Dicky chose to keep on his desk, while he worried about his career and vacillated about expedient courses of action, were always the ones that ultimately required the most urgent response from me when he finally dumped them on my desk. My work was not made easier by the cryptic thoughts and instructions that Dicky shared with me as each fat file was dropped into my tray.

"Just keep it warm until we hear who's going to be on the committee," Dicky would say. Or "Tell the old bastard to get stuffed, but keep him sweet," "This might work out if they find the right people, but make sure it doesn't bounce back our way," and his standard reaction, "Find out what they really expect and maybe we'll be able to meet them halfway." These were the sort of arcane instructions I was trying to implement on Tuesday while Dicky was gone to wherever he went when there was work in the offing. And Dicky wanted everything done by the end of the day.

By the time a debonair Frank Harrington looked into my little office and invited me to go for a quick lunch, I was glassy-eyed. "You'll do yourself an injury if you try and work your way through this lot before going home," said Frank, running the tip of an index finger across the cover of a fat file for which some unfortunate had analyzed, in considerable detail, the various types of East European shops where only Western currency was accepted. Here were tables and estimates, comments and balance sheets, from Pewex in Poland, Tuwex in Czechoslovakia, Korekom in Bulgaria, compared point by point with Intershops in East Germany.

Without picking it up, Frank flicked open the file carefully, so as not to get his hands dirty. "Would you believe I saw this in the tray on the old man's desk on the day I got the Berlin job?"

"Of course I would," I said.

"It's got fatter over the years, of course," said Frank, who probably wanted to be congratulated on his phenomenal memory. He hooked his tightly rolled umbrella on the desk edge and then consulted his gold pocket watch, as if to confirm that it was lunchtime. "Heave all this aside, Bernard. Let me buy you a pint of Guinness and a pork pie." The illusion that Englishmen wanted a pub lunch every day was something that many expatriates cherished, so I smiled. Frank was looking very trim. He had been upstairs talking to the Deputy and was dressed in a three-piece gray worsted with gold watch chain, wide-striped Jermyn Street shirt, and new Eton tie, of which Frank seemed to have an inexhaustible supply.

My tie was plain and polyester, and my watch Japanese and plastic. I was weary, and my ears were ringing with the sound of Dicky's voice. I'd been listening to the dictating machine. Taking notes from a long, rambling disquisition that Dicky had passed to me to "get into shape." It was going to be a long job. Dicky was not good at getting his arguments into proper order, and those passages where he was consistent and logical were riddled with inaccurate "facts." I pushed the work aside and said, "What about next week, Frank? I'm in Berlin on Wednesday."

Frank didn't leave. "A very quick lunch, Bernard."

I looked up to see him standing in the doorway with a forced smile on his face. It wasn't until then that I realized how much such little things meant to him.

I knew, of course, that Frank had always looked upon me as a surrogate son. Several people had remarked on it, usually at times when I was being especially rude or making Frank's life difficult. Even Frank himself had more than once referred to some undefined responsibility he'd owed to my father. But Frank took it too seriously. More than once he'd risked his career to help me, and, to tell the truth, that made me uncomfortably indebted to him. Father-son relationships seldom run smoothly and, true to my role, I'd taken considerably more from him than I'd ever given, and I confess I resented being obliged to anyone, even Frank.

"You're right, Frank. To hell with it!" I took the tape cassette from the machine and locked it in my desk drawer. Maybe I should have sent it to the KGB to promote more confusion amongst the opposition. Frank reached for my coat.

Frank always had a car and driver during his visits to London. It was one of the desirable perks of his job in Berlin. We went off to a small City wine bar; but because this was Frank Harrington's idea, the bar was not in the City. It was south of the Thames, in that borough of London which is enigmatically called "the Borough." In a street of rundown Victorian houses off the Old Kent Road, its entrance was a doorway marked by only a small polished brass plate of the sort that mark the offices of lawyers and dentists. A long underground corridor eventually opened upon a gloomy cellar with heavy pillars and low vaulting. The brickwork was painted a shiny bottle-green. Small blackboards were chalked with tempting vintage wines that were today available by the glass. A bar counter occupied most of one wall of the largest "room," and in the adjoining areas spotlights picked out small tables where shrill businessmen drank their vintage clarets and ports, nibbled at their expensive cold snacks, and tried to look like tycoons avoiding the TV crews while concluding multimillion-dollar City deals.

"Like it?" said Frank proudly.

"Wonderful, Frank."

"Charming little place, eh? And no chance of meeting any of our people here; that's what I like about it." By "our" people he meant important Whitehall bureaucrats. He was right.

An old man dressed in appropriate winecellar style—white shirt, bow tie, and long apron—showed us to places set ready at the counter. Frank was obviously known and welcomed there, and when I saw how much he spent on a bottle of Château Palmer 1966 I could understand why. But Frank's discursive survey of the wine list, and its extravagant outcome, was part of the paternal role he had to demonstrate.

With due ceremony, the bottle was opened, the cork sniffed. Poured, swirled, and tasted. Frank puckered his lips, bared his teeth, and pronounced it "drinkable." We laughed.

It was another immutable aspect of Frank's character that, along with this superlative wine, he ate, without adverse comment, yellowing Stilton, a desiccated hunk of pork pie, and squashy white bread.

I could see he had something to tell me, but I contributed my share of office small talk and let him take his time. When he'd eaten his segment of pork pie—each mouthful spread with a large dollop of fierce English mustard—he poured a second glass of claret for both of us and said, "That bloody Zena." He said it quietly but with feeling. "I could kill her."

I looked at him with interest. In the past Frank had always indulged Zena. "Infatuated" was the only word for it. "Is she all right?" I asked casually between pieces of pork pie. "She was off to Frankfurt an der Oder, the last I heard of her. Werner was worried."

He looked at me as if trying to decide how much I knew, and then said, "She was running up and down on the Berlin-Warsaw express."

"The 'paradise train'? What for?" I asked, but I'd already guessed the answer.

"Black market. You've been on that train; you know."

Yes, I'd been on that train, and I knew. Once over the Polish border, it became an Oriental bazaar. Black-market traders—and, in the subtle nuances of Eastern Bloc social life, brown- and gray-market traders too—moved from compartment to compartment, buying and selling everything from Scotch whisky to Black & Decker power tools. I remembered loud Polish voices and hands waving bundles of dollar bills and suitcases almost bursting with pop-music records and cartons of Marlboro cigarettes. The "paradise train" would provide plenty of opportunities to buy rare artifacts and manuscripts. "What was Zena doing on the train?" I asked.

"They picked her up coming back . . . on the platform at Friedrichstrasse. It sounds as if they were tipped off."

"Where is she now?"

"They let her go."

"What did she have?"

"Old engravings. And an icon and a Bible. They confiscated everything and let her go."

"She was lucky," I said.

"She told them she'd happily take a receipt for only one item and they could divide the rest of it up between them."

"I still say she was lucky. An offer like that to the wrong man and she'd end up with ten years for attempted bribery."

Frank looked at me and said, "She's a good judge of men, Bernard."

There was no answer to that. I sipped the lovely Château Palmer and nodded. The wine was coming to life now, a wonderful combination of half-forgotten fragrancies.

The anger that the memory of Zena had regenerated now subsided again. "Silly little cow," he said with a measure of affection in his voice. He smiled. "What about a pudding, Bernard? I believe they do a splendid apple here."

"No thanks, Frank. Just coffee."

"Werner came to London. He went into the office on Friday and kicked up no end of fuss," said Frank. "I was in Berlin, of course. By the time the Deputy got through to me, I'd heard that Zena was safe at home. I was able to tell him that all was well. I came out of it smelling of roses."

"I wasn't in London," I said. "I was in California."

"I'll have a savory: angels on horseback; they do it rather well here. Sure you won't have something?" When I shook my head he called to the waiter and ordered it. "I must say, Sir Percy is doing a damned good job," said Frank.

But I wasn't going to let him steer the conversation round

to the Deputy's abilities or lack of them. "Did you know that Bret is alive? I saw him in California."

"Bret?" He looked me full in the eye. "Yes, the old man told me . . . a couple of days ago."

"Were you surprised?"

"I was damned annoyed," said Frank. "The old man had actually heard me say that Bret was dead and had never contradicted me or confided the truth of the matter."

"Why?"

"God knows. The old man can be a bit childish at times. He just laughed and said Bret deserved a bit of peace. And yet it was the old man who told me Bret was dead. It was a little supper party at the Kempi; there were other people present, outsiders. I couldn't pursue it. Perhaps I should have done."

"But why say he was dead? What was it all about?"

"You saw him, I didn't. What did Bret tell you?"

"I didn't ask him why he wasn't dead," I replied woodenly.

Frank preferred to see it as a harmless subterfuge. "Bret was at death's door. What difference did it make? Perhaps it was better security to say he was dead."

"But you don't know of any special reason?"

"No, I don't, Bernard." He drank some more wine, studied its color, and gave it great attention.

I said, "Posh Harry buttonholed me over there." Frank raised an eyebrow. "He wanted to tell me that, whatever Bret was doing, Washington like it."

"Well, Posh Harry would know. He's landed a cushy job," said Frank. "They use him like an errand boy, but his starting salary is more like a king's ransom."

"Sounds just like my job," I said, "apart from the salary."

"Why did Posh Harry buttonhole you?"

"He said I was asking too many questions."

"Mistaken identity. That doesn't sound at all like you," said Frank with his laborious sense of humor. "Questions about Bret?"

"Fiona was involved. Some kind of financial borehole. A lot of money. Prettyman was a signatory . . . probably a go-between for Central Funding."

"You're not still going around saying Prettyman was murdered, are you? I looked at the homicide figures for Washington—it's horrific—and I know the Deputy arranged for the FBI to take a special look at the Prettyman killing. There's nothing to support the idea of it being anything but the casual sort of murder that muggers commit over there. A miserable business, but nothing there to justify any further investigation."

"It seemed like a chance to find out more about Fiona."

"I thought we'd found out all there was to find out about Fiona."

"Her motives. Her accomplices. And so on."

"I'd imagine the Department followed up every lead, Bernard. For months afterwards they were sniffing around everyone who'd even heard of Fiona."

"Even you?"

"No one is above suspicion in that sort of inquiry, Bernard. I would have thought you'd know that better than anyone. The D-G had the Minister breathing down his neck for week after week. I think that was what made the old man ill."

"Is the D-G really ill?" I said. "Or is it just a stunt so he can retire early or do something else?" Frank and the old man had been together during the war; they were close friends.

"Sir Henry's not around very much, is he? They're probably letting him work out the contract for the sake of his pension. But I can't see him taking up the reins again."

"Will Sir Percy take over?"

"No one knows at present. They say the PM is very keen to have someone from outside . . . putting one of the younger Law Lords into the driver's seat might ease the pressure on her to have a parliamentary committee sitting in judgment on everything we do."

Frank's "angels on horseback" arrived: a couple of cooked oysters wrapped in fried bacon and balanced on a triangle of warm toast. Frank liked savories. At his dinner parties he stubbornly kept to the Victorian tradition of serving such salty, fiery tidbits after the dessert. "Clears a chap's palate for the port," he'd explained to me more than once. Now he ate it with a relish that he'd not shown for anything else except the claret, and said nothing until it was finished and the plate removed.

Then he wiped his lips with one of the huge linen napkins and said, "You're miffed, aren't you, Bernard?"

"Miffed?"

Frank grinned. "You're put out. Don't pretend you're not."

"Why would I be?" I insisted.

"I'm not such an old fool," said Frank. "You're remembering that recently I said Sir Henry hadn't been to Berlin for many years. Now I've told you that he was at the Kempi hosting a supper party and your ears are flapping. Right, Bernard?"

"It's not important," I said.

"Exactly. The 'need-to-know' principle: the only people told the secrets are those who need to know. Not those who simply want to find out." He lifted the wine bottle to pour more, but the waiter had done it already. The bottle was empty. "A dead soldier!" said Frank, holding the bottle aloft. "And dead men tell no tales, eh? So what about a glass of Madeira?"

"No more for me, Frank," I said, "or I'll fall asleep over my desk."

"Quite right. What was I saying? Yes, need-to-know."

"You were telling me not to put my nose into matters not my concern."

"Not at all. I was simply explaining to you the policy of the Department. I heard that you were on another of your crusades. I'm just trying to convince you that there's nothing personal about it. Any extracurricular activities of that sort, by any employee, worry Internal Security."

"Thanks."

"You're not still trying to find a mole?" He smiled again. Frank had a resolute faith in his superiors, providing they had attended the right schools or done well in the army. For him any such suspicions were genuinely comical.

"No, Frank. No, I'm not."

"I'm on your side, Bernard."

"I know you are, Frank."

"But you do have enemies—or perhaps, more accurately, rivals—and I don't want them to be given an excuse to clobber you."

"Yes."

"You're what"—he paused no more than a moment—"forty-four last birthday." So Frank even had my birthdays registered in his memory.

I grunted an affirmative.

"With those two lovely kids, you should be thinking more about your career, not seeing how many different ways you can upset the chaps on the top floor." Another pause, while that sank in. "That's just a word to the wise, Bernard." He dropped his napkin on the table and got to his feet to show me that his little lecture was at an end.

"Okay, Frank," I said. "Strictly need-to-know, from now onwards and forever more."

"That's a sensible fellow," said Frank. "Think of the children, Bernard. They rely on you now that Fiona's gone."

"I know they do, Frank."

I hadn't promised Frank Harrington anything I hadn't already promised myself. It seemed as if everyone in the Western world was keen to tell me that Bret Rensselaer was clean-cut, upright, and true. It would have been stupid, in the light of so many reassurances, to continue poking and probing into the work he had been doing before my wife, Fiona, defected.

That afternoon I went back to work with renewed vigor. By Thursday my desk—despite a second onslaught from Dicky's out tray—was virtually clear. To celebrate my new freedom from extracurricular detective work, I took Gloria and the children for a weekend in the country. It was Cathy's first weekend off, having worked for us for no less than six days. We started early Saturday morning. In a ten-acre field near Bath we visited a "Steam Engine Rally," a collection of ancient steam-powered machines: harvesters, roundabouts, tractors, and rollers. All working. The children adored every moment of it. Gloria seemed to become even younger and more beautiful. Despite the constant presence of the children, Gloria kept saying how wonderful it was to have me to herself. I think it was the first time that all four of us discovered that we were a family, a happy family. Even twelve-year-old Sally, who'd hitherto shown a certain reserve about Gloria, now embraced her in a way I'd almost stopped hoping for. Billy— usually so prosaic and self-contained—took Gloria for a walk and told her the story of his life, and gave her a few hints and tips on handling the new girl's "ratty" moods, which seemed to be frequent and varied. I was not optimistic about his new girl. Doris, I now realized, wasn't so bad after all.

On Saturday evening we found Everton, a pretty little village. We had dinner in the hotel. It was a long drive back to London, so on impulse we stayed there overnight. Gloria, with feminine foresight, had put some overnight things—including the children's toothbrushes and pajamas, and even the spare elastic bands Billy had to put on his wired teeth— into a bag in the back of the car. I remembered that weekend forever afterwards. Gloria's future education was not discussed. On Sunday morning we all went for a walk across the fields, without seeing another living soul. We followed a stream that was filled with fish, and ended up in a tiny riverside pub decorated with photos, theater programs, playbills, and other mementos of Maria Callas. We drank a bottle of Pol Roger. Billy got very muddy and Sally picked flowers. Gloria told me that it could be like this forever and ever, and I allowed myself to believe her.

The children were growing up so fast that I could hardly reconcile this tall young fellow walking alongside me with the child that Billy had been only a few months ago. "Girls don't understand about moving," he said as if continuing a conversation we'd already started, although in fact we'd been giving all our attention to the prospect of scrambling across a stream.

"Sally, you mean?"

"Yes. She had these special friends at her school in Marylebone."

"More special than your friends?" I said.

"It's all right now. She likes it at the new place. Girls only want to talk about clothes," said Billy, "so it hardly matters where she is."

"And what about you?"

"I'm going to join the Vintage Car Club."

I concealed my surprise. "Are you old enough? Don't you have to have a car?"

"They will probably let me help . . . fixing the engines and pumping up the tires." He looked at me. "I like our new house, Dad. So does Sally. So don't worry about us."

"I'll go first," I said, and I took his arm and swung him across the water. He was heavy, damned heavy. I would never carry him on my shoulder again.

Now it was Billy's turn to extend a hand to me. And when I'd negotiated the steep muddy bank he said, "I saw Grandpa the other day."

"Grandpa?"

"He's got a new car, a Bentley turbo, dark blue. He came to the school."

"You spoke with him?"

"He drove us home."

"I thought Cathy met you."

"She came too."

"I should have taken you to see him," I said.

"He said we could have a holiday with him. He's going to Turkey. He might drive there: drive all the way."

"Grandpa? You're not making this up, Billy?"

"Could we go, Daddy? Perhaps in the Bentley."

"Did you tell Auntie Gloria about this?"

Billy looked contrite. He stared down at his muddy shoes and spoke quietly. "She said I wasn't to tell you. She said you'd worry."

"No, it's all right, Billy. I'll have to see about it. Maybe I'll talk to Grandpa."

"Thank you, Daddy. Thank you, thank you!" Billy hugged me and said. "Do you think Grandpa would let me sit up front?"

"Turkey is a long way away," I said.

"There's Sally and Auntie Gloria," he shouted. "They must have found a way across the stream."

So it had started. If it was simply a matter of going on holiday, why hadn't Fiona's father come to me and asked? Turkey: the U.S.S.R. just a stone's throw away. The idea of my children being there with my meddlesome father-in-law filled me with dread.

But if Billy's little story cast a gray shadow across our idyll, it was that bloody old fool Dodo who caused all the trouble to start again for me. At our first meeting in France, I'd seen him as an amiable eccentric, a cultured old man who occasionally took too much to drink. Now I was to encounter the malicious, self-aggrandizing, belligerent old drunk that was really him.

Although it was never confirmed, I have no doubt that Gloria's mother had spoken on the phone with him and poured her heart out about being neglected and lonely. Gloria said that in some unspecified time in the distant past, the old man had always been fond of her mother. Dodo, however, told everyone he met in London that he was "on business." Whatever the reason, Dodo suddenly appeared in London, dressed up in an old but beautifully cut Glen Urquhart suit, and for the first week he was staying in the Ritz—a room with a view across the park.

He had contacts, of course. Not only expatriate Hungarians and the people he'd known during his time in Vienna, but "departmental" people too. For Dodo had been one of Lange's "Prussians," and for some people that was a commendation beyond compare. He'd also played some unrevealed part in the Budapest network of which Gloria's father had been a member before escaping across the border. And Dodo was a man who could be relied upon to keep in touch, so "old pals" from the Treasury and the Foreign Office took him to lunch at the Reform and the Travellers.

He liked to go to parties. He went to embassy parties, show-biz parties, "society" parties, and literary parties. How much time he spent with Gloria's parents, and whether they talked about me, and speculated upon the work I did, was never established. But by the time I encountered him again, Dodo was disturbingly well informed about me.

Dodo's invitation to have drinks with "friends of mine—Thursday, 6–8 p.m., or as long as people stay . . ." at a smart address in Chapel Street near Eaton Square was scribbled on Ritz notepaper and arrived in the post on Wednesday morning. It was not adequate preparation for what we met there. We arrived at a small town house typical of London South West One. Outside, in the street, there were expensive motor-cars, and a formally dressed butler opened the door. Many of the guests were in evening clothes, the women in long dresses. There was the sound of live music and loud laughter. Gloria cursed under her breath, for she was wearing a tweed suit that had been relegated to her working day, and she'd not had time to fix her hair.

The whole house was given over to the party, and there were guests in every room. In the first room we entered was a young man in evening clothes and two girls in party dresses, seemingly engrossed in a large illustrated book. We left them to their reading and went to the next room, where two men were dispensing drinks from behind a trestle table. "Hungarian wines," said the barman when I asked what they were. "Only Hungarian wines." I took the biggest measure and, with drinks in hand, we went upstairs in search of the gypsy band. "It's a zimbalon," said Gloria when she heard the strings. "Hungarian music. Wherever would Dodo find someone to play a zimbalon?"

"Now's your chance to ask him," I said.

Dodo was coming down the upper stairs with a drink in his hand and a happy smile on his face. His hair had been neatly trimmed, but the dinner suit he wore had seen better days, and with it he was wearing blue suede shoes with odd laces and red socks. He grinned even more as he caught sight of us. He was not the sort of man who felt disadvantaged by old clothes. On the contrary, he seemed to like old garments, as he liked old books and old wines, and he paid no regard to Gloria's distress at feeling so inappropriately dressed.

He'd already had a few drinks and wasted little time on greetings before telling us about some of the distinguished guests. "The chap you saw me with on the stairs is the power behind the scenes with Lufthansa. He used to have a room across the hall from me when I lived in that dreadful flea pit in Kohlmarkt. Now, of course, it's one of the most fashionable streets in Vienna." Dodo led us into the room where the gypsy band was playing. It was dark, with only candlelight flickering on the faces of the musicians and revealing the rapt expressions on the shadowed faces of the audience.

"Were they playing czardas?" Gloria said with such urgency that I suddenly saw a new aspect of her revealed.

"Of course, darling Zu," said Uncle Dodo.

"How clever you are," she told him, all worries about her clothes and hair forgotten. She gave him a sudden kiss and said something in Hungarian. He laughed. I felt excluded.

"Are you from Budapest?" I asked him, more to make conversation than because I truly wanted to know.

"All Hungarians are from Budapest," he said.

Gloria said, "Yes, we all love Budapest." She looked at Dodo and reflectively said, "You're right: all Hungarians feel at home in Budapest."

"Even you gypsies," said Uncle Dodo as the slow gypsy music started again, and Gloria began to sway with its rhythm.

"Did Zu ever tell you your fortune?" he asked me.

"No," I said.

"With the tarot cards?"

"No, Dodo," said Gloria. "Sometimes it's better not to know what the cards say." The subject was closed.

"Have you eaten?" he asked.

When told we hadn't, he took us down to the kitchen, where two frantic cooks were slaving to produce a tableful of exotic dishes. Gloria and Dodo vied to name for me the different dishes, and disputed the authentic recipes for them. I tried everything. Veal strips in sour cream, garlicky stewed beef cubes with rich red paprika. There were bread-crumbed fried-chicken pieces, boiled pork with horseradish, and river fish flavored with garlic and ginger. It was not the food I'd ever encountered in modern Hungary, a country where cooks render meat stew completely tasteless and measure each portion with government-issued hundred-gram ladles.

"So you like Hungarian food, eh?" said Dodo. The only really good meal I'd eaten in Hungary was at a big country house near Lake Balaton. The food came from Käfer in Munich, smuggled over the border. My host was a black-market dealer who had a security colonel as the guest of honor. But when Dodo said, as everyone has to say, that the Hungarians eat damned well nowadays and that Budapest is fast becoming a place for gourmets to journey to, I nodded and smiled and gobbled my food and said yes, it was.

After eating, we wandered off to find a place where we could sit in comfort. The rooms had emptied as the gypsy band drew many of the guests upstairs. In the corner of the room was a large table with posters and brochures advertising a new book called *The Wonderful World of Hungarian Cooking.* I realized that the egregious Dodo had simply helped us to gate-crash a particularly lavish publication party. He saw me looking at the display, and he smiled without offering any explanation. He was like that.

A waiter, in a smart white jacket and gold shoulder loops, came over to us and offered coffee and small jam-filled pancakes. Dodo declined the food so that he could go on with his stories about his youth in Vienna. "The landlady —as mean and venal as only Viennese landladies can be— had a Schiele charcoal portrait hanging in her kitchen. Her kitchen! She'd wrung it from the poor devil for some insignificantly small debt. She didn't even appreciate her good fortune. The old cow! She'd rather have had a colored one, she kept saying. Well, all those colored Schiele pictures had the colored wash applied long after the drawing was completed. Anyone with any taste at all would have preferred this delicate charcoal portrait . . . a young woman. It might have been Schiele's wife, Edith. That would have made it more valuable, of course." I tried not to listen to him. Another waiter looked into the room. Dodo hurriedly downed the rest of his whisky and waved an arm for more without even looking to see if the waiter had noticed. "Those were the days!" said Dodo, and sat back, red-faced and breathing heavily. It wasn't clear whether he was referring to Schiele's times in Vienna, or his own. I didn't ask. There were not many respites from Dodo's remorseless chatter, and I was beginning to get a headache.

But there was little chance of him remaining quiet for

more than a moment or two. In record time a double Scotch arrived, and Dodo was off on another story.

He was well oiled by the time the coffee waiter returned with offers of second helpings, and Dodo's cheerfulness had turned to his own jocular sort of sarcasm that was edged with hostility. He put a heavy hand on my shoulder. "We know— those of us who have had the honor to work for Her Majesty's government in positions of trust and danger—that fortune favors the brave. Right, Bernard, right?"

He'd made similar remarks earlier in the evening, and now I decided not to let it go. "I'm not sure I know what you mean," I said. Gloria glanced at him and at me, having heard the irritation in my voice.

"A field agent who is smart doesn't get paid off with an MBE and a big thank you. A clever field agent knows he can get a sackful of gold sovereigns, and knows there are more where they came from. See what I mean?"

"No," I said.

He hit my shoulder again in a gesture that he probably thought fraternal. "And so he should be. I'm not against that. Let the people at the sharp end make a bit of money. It's only right and fair."

"Do you mean Daddy?" Gloria asked. Her voice too had a note of warning, had he been sober enough to heed it.

He made a hissing sound and said, "Darling, what your dear father was paid—and what I got—was chicken feed compared with what those in the know can tuck away. If you haven't discovered that by now, Bernard will fill in the details."

"I never met any rich field agents," I said.

"Really, darling, no?" A slowly expanding artful grin illuminated his whole face.

"What do you mean?" I asked him.

"If you want to pretend you don't know what I'm talking about, then so be it." He drank his whisky, spilling some down his chin, and turned his head away.

"You'd better tell me," I said.

"Damn it!" Big smile. "You and that wife of yours."

"Me and that wife of mine . . . what?"

"Come along, darling." A knowing grin. "Your wife was in Operations, right? She was a trustee for some kind of 'sinking fund.' She disappeared and so did all the money. Don't tell me that you didn't get your hands on a few pounds, or that some of it wasn't put away in the children's names somewhere."

"Uncle Dodo, that's enough," said Gloria sharply.

"Let him go on," I said. "I want to hear more."

Like some cunning little animal's, his eyes went from one to the other of us. "Berlin, the Ku-Damm," he said meaningfully.

"What about it?"

"Schneider, von Schild und Weber."

"It sounds like a bank," I said.

"It is a bank," said Dodo with great satisfaction, as if his argument was already won. "It is a bank."

"So what?"

"You want me to go on, darling?"

"Yes, I do."

"Weber—grandson of the original partner—handles special financial matters for the British government. That's where your money came from." He recited it as if I was trying to make a fool of him.

"Money? What money? And how did I get it?" I asked, convinced now that he was crazy as well as drunk.

"You're a signatory to the account."

"Rubbish."

"It's a fact, and easily proved or disproved." The waiter came and put a small plate of chocolate mints on the table. Dodo didn't offer them round; he peeled the wrapping from one, inspected it, and popped it into his mouth.

"Who told you all this?" I said.

Still chewing the mint, Dodo said, "I've known young

Weber for years. When I was pensioned off from the Department, it was Weber's father who arranged everything for me."

I looked at him, trying to see into his mind. He chewed at the mint and stared at me with unseeing eyes.

"You're always in Berlin, darling. Go to the Ku-Damm and have a word with Weber."

"Maybe I shall."

"The money is sure to be held in short-term bonds. It's the way they do it. A dozen or more signatories to the account —no less!—but there have to be two different signatures. You and your wife, for instance."

"A dozen signatories?"

"Don't pretend to be so naïve, darling. That's a common device, we all know that." The malevolence was unbridled now.

"Bogus names?" said Gloria.

"No need to use bogus names. Use real names. It disguises the purpose of the fund, and can give an account a bit of class if someone comes snooping around. Providing the signatories don't find out about it."

"Perhaps that's how Bernard's name got there," said Gloria softly. She obviously believed Dodo's story.

Dodo's beady eyes were almost hypnotic. There was something frightening about him: a whiff of evil. "If you never got your hands on any of that loot, you've really been swindled, darling." He laughed softly enough to show that it wasn't a possibility he would spare much time pondering. Then he looked at Gloria, inviting her to join in the fun. When she looked away, he picked up his drink and swilled down a good mouthful of it. "Must go," he said. "Must go."

I didn't get up. I let the old fool heave himself to his feet and stagger off in the direction of the door. Gloria and I sat together in silence for a few minutes. Finally, in what was doubtless an attempt to pacify me about Dodo's offensiveness, she said, "He was in a funny mood tonight."

"And I needed a good laugh," I said.

Chapter 18

It was the day before I was due to pay my regular visit to Berlin that Werner phoned and asked me if I was coming with only hand baggage. I was. Such visits required only a document case big enough to hold pajamas and shaving gear.

"Could you bring a parcel for me? I wouldn't ask you, but Ingrid needs it urgently."

"Ingrid?" I said. "Who's Ingrid?"

"Ingrid Winter. She's helping me in the hotel."

"Oh, is she."

"It will be heavy," he said apologetically. "It's curtain material from Peter Jones, the department store in Sloane Square. Ingrid says she can't get the patterns she wants anywhere in Berlin."

"Okay, Werner. I said okay."

"Wait till you see the hotel. Almost everything is changed, Bernie. You'll never recognize the place."

Oh my God! I thought. "And how is Lisl taking to all the changes?"

"Lisl?" said Werner as if having difficulty in remembering who Lisl was. "Lisl loves the changes. Lisl says it's wonderful."

"She does?"

"We wouldn't do anything Lisl didn't like, Bernie. You know that. It's Lisl we're doing it for, isn't it?"

"And Lisl likes it?"

"Of course she does. I've just told you she does."

"See you tomorrow, Werner."

"And it's bulky too."

"Stop worrying, Werner. I said I'll bring it."

"If the customs want to charge, pay. Ingrid wants to get the curtain people started on the work."

"Okay."

"You'll stay the night? Here? We have room."

"Thanks, Werner. Yes, I'd like that."

"Ingrid cooks a great *Hoppel-Poppel.*"

"I haven't eaten *Hoppel-Poppel* in twenty years," I said. "Not a real one."

"With fresh herbs," said Werner, "that's the secret. Fresh eggs and fresh herbs."

"Sounds like Ingrid is not getting in the way," I said.

"Oh, no," said Werner. "She's not getting in the way at all."

I cursed Werner, Ingrid, and the roll of curtain material before I got to Berlin-Tegel. The customs man watched me struggling with it and just grinned. In Berlin even the customs men are human.

Werner struggled to get it into the back seat of his brand-new silver 7-series BMW, and even then the end of the roll of cloth protruded through the open window. "This isn't you, Werner," I said as he roared off into the traffic with an insolent skill that I'd never known he had. "This flashy new fashionable car with the big engine—it's not you, Werner."

"I've changed, Bernie," he said.

"Because of running the hotel?"

"That's right. Because I'm running the hotel." And he smiled at some secret joke as he went weaving through the fast-moving traffic that fills West Berlin at this time of the morning. The heater was on; there were gray clouds overhead, and it was beginning to rain. Berliners were still wrapped up in their heavy clothes. Spring doesn't hurry on its way to Berlin.

He dropped me at Frank Harrington's office. Once there,

I started to earn my pay. Frank, and a couple of his senior people, plodded with me through the latest London directives. Every few minutes there would be some expletive or a sharp intake of breath as I revealed a particularly impractical or ill-advised notion that had sprung from London Central's committees. I was only there to take the brunt of the Field Office objections, and everyone present recognized that as my role. So I smiled and shrugged and wriggled and prevaricated as they hit me over the head with their reasoned objections. And eventually the game ended and, our role-playing abandoned, I was allowed to resume the more comfortable persona of Bernard Samson, former Berlin Field Unit agent.

It was six-thirty by the time I finished work. The rain had come and gone, but there was still a drizzle. The offices had emptied and the streets were crowded. Like rivers of flame, the flashing signs made brightly colored reflections in the wet streets. An official car took me to Lisl Hennig's hotel. As I got out of it, I stood in the rain and examined the façade apprehensively, but whatever changes Werner had wrought, they were not to be seen from the street. This was the same old house that I'd known all my life. They were all the same, these Ku-Damm houses near the Zoo. They were built at the turn of the century by speculative builders for *nouveau-riche* businessmen, and the adornments of bearded gods and buxom nymphs were chosen from catalogs by those who wanted to customize their homes. Some of them were grotesquely overdone.

Since then the Red Army's artillery, and the Anglo-American bombing fleets, had added further distinguishing features to all the buildings of Berlin, so that Lisl's house was scarred and chipped with a pox of splinter damage. The fighting done, the roof had been renewed and the decorated window surrounds of the upper stories had been shoddily and hastily patched up. Real repairs were forty years overdue.

I pushed through the heavy doors and went up the front

stairs. The carpet was new, a rich ruby-red, and the brass handrail was polished so it shone like gold. There was a sparkling chandelier over the stairs, and the elaborate mirrors on the walls had been cleaned, so that they repeated my reflections a thousand times. No sooner had I started up the stairs than I heard the piano. "Embrace me, my sweet embraceable you. . . ." And then a sudden cascade of improvised harmonies. It was Werner at the keys. I would recognize his silky, ebullient style anywhere. Something almost spiritual happened to Werner when he sat down at the piano.

". . . my irreplaceable you." Someone had moved the grand piano so that it was in the center of the "salon." And either it had been painted white or it was a new piano. There were comfortable soft brown leather armchairs too. And all Lisl's signed souvenir photos of Berlin personalities of long ago had been cleaned and newly arranged, one close upon the other, to cover the whole wall. Who wasn't represented there? Here were Einstein, Furtwängler, Strauss, Goebbels, Dietrich, Piscator, Brecht, Weill, and the photos were signed with extravagant declarations of affection for Lisl or for her mother —Frau Wisliceny—who'd once played hostess to all Berlin.

There were not many hotel guests to be seen. Just a party of four Danes who were chatting animatedly, as if unaware of the music, and a desiccated couple sitting at the bar, drinking colorful cocktails and glaring at each other. I caught a brief glimpse of Ingrid Winter as she came downstairs with a tray. She was wearing another of her stylish "farmer's-wife-goes-to-church" dresses. This one had a high lacy neckline and a long ankle-length skirt. She smiled at me.

Werner looked up from the keyboard. He saw me and stopped playing. "Bernie! I told you to phone. I was going to come and fetch you. The rain is terrible. . . ." He looked at my wet coat.

"Frank arranged a ride."

From her chair in the corner Lisl called imperiously,

"What are you doing, Bernd? Come and give your Lisl a kiss!"
She was in good voice, whatever her infirmities. She was
dressed in a flowing red robe. Her face was carefully painted,
and she had false eyelashes, which she fluttered like a school-
girl. As I leaned over her, the smell of perfume was almost
overwhelming. "Your coat is wet, Bernd," she said. "Take it
off. Tell Klara to dry it in the kitchen."

"It's all right, Lisl," I said.

"Do as I say, Bernd. Don't be so stubborn." I took the
coat off and gave it to the aged Klara, who appeared from
nowhere. "And then go down to the boiler room. The pump
is giving trouble again. I told them you were always able to
mend it."

"I'll try," I promised without conviction. Lisl was determined to believe that I had spent my childhood performing all
kinds of mechanical miracles with the antiquated electricity
system and the heating. It wasn't true, of course. The idea that
Bernd would fix it had been Tante Lisl's way of deferring as
long as possible the inevitable replacement of aged and broken machinery.

"The hotel is looking wonderful, Lisl."

She grunted as if she hadn't properly heard me, but the
one-sided little smile she gave was enough to tell me how
pleased she was with Werner's refurbishment.

I could not really be expected to cure the pump of its
chronic arrhythmias: it was too far gone. Werner came with
me to the subterranean boiler room, and we examined the
incontinent old brute with its dribbled rust and flaking insula-
tion. In an attempt to justify Lisl's confidence in me, I gave the
meters a tap, rapped upon the pump casing, and repeatedly
touched warm pipes that should have been hot enough to
scorch the flesh. "It's not just the boiler. The whole system
will have to be renewed," said Werner. "But I'm praying that
it will hold out till next year."

"Yes," I said. We continued to look at it in the hope that

it would suddenly come to life. Then Ingrid Winter joined us. She said nothing. She just stood with us, staring at the boiler. I stole a look at her. She was a handsome woman with a lovely complexion and clear eyes that shone when she looked at you. She glowed with the quiet vocational self-assurance that you hope to see in a nurse.

"It's not only the money," explained Werner to no one in particular. "We'll have to change all the pipes and radiators. There will be dust and noise in every room. If we had to do that in the winter, it would mean closing the hotel completely. . . ."

"Couldn't you change the boiler first?" I suggested. "Then do the plumbing and piping piece by piece?"

"The plumber says we can't," said Werner. He knew my ignorance about such matters was profound, and the look he gave me let me know that he knew. "The sort of boiler we'll need for all the new bathrooms just wouldn't operate with the old plumbing. It's very old."

Ingrid Winter said, "Perhaps we should talk to some other heating engineer, Werner."

Her accent was the rounded one of southern Bavaria, but it was not one of those raw backcountry accents, just a slight burr. Yet there was some inflection in Ingrid Winter's voice, some tiny change of pitch or of tone, that made me look at Werner. He stared back at me and gave the same mirthless smile that I remembered from our schooldays together. Werner once confided that it was his "inscrutable" expression, but "guilty" would have been a better description.

Werner said, "Old Heinmuller knows the system very well, Ingrid. It was he and his father who got it going again after the bombing in the war."

"We'll have to do something, Werner dear," she said, and this time she was unable to conceal the intimacy in her voice. There existed between them that intuitive sympathy and unspoken understanding for which Goethe coined the word *Wahlverwandtschaften.*

"While we're here alone, Ingrid, tell Bernie about the Hungarian." He touched her arm. "Tell him what you told me, Ingrid."

She hesitated and then said, "Perhaps I shouldn't have said anything. . . . But the other evening I was telling Werner about my mother and about that awful Hungarian man who lives nearby."

"Dodo?" I said.

"Yes. He calls himself Dodo."

"What about him?"

"He's a pathetic little man," said Ingrid. "I've never liked him. I wish Mother wouldn't invite him to the house. He's always leering at me." She paused and looked closely at the lagging on the boiler pipes. "It should be cleaned anyway," she said. "I hate dirt."

"When was it last cleaned and serviced?" I said. She seemed ill at ease. I wanted to give her a chance to compose herself. "I remember once a fellow came and replaced a nozzle or something, and it started working perfectly again."

"We've tried nozzles," said Werner impatiently. To Ingrid he said, "Tell Bernie what they said about his father. And your father. It's better that he knows."

Ingrid looked at me, obviously not wanting to tell me anything at all.

"I'd like to hear, Ingrid," I said, trying to make it easier for her.

"You remember what I told you when you visited my mother?"

"Yes," I said.

"I upset you. I know I did. I'm sorry."

"No matter."

"Most of what I know comes from Dodo; he's not a reliable source."

"But tell me anyway."

"All we've ever been told officially is that Paul Winter was killed after the war ended. An accidental shooting."

"By the Americans," said Werner.

"Let me tell it, Werner."

"I'm sorry, Ingrid."

"They said he was escaping," she said. "But they always say that, don't they?"

"Yes," I said. "They always say that."

"It was Dodo who brought it all up again. He kept on at my mother about it. You probably know how he goes on. She listens to him. He was a Nazi; that's why he gets on so well with Mother."

"A Nazi?" I said.

Werner said, "He worked for Gehlen. The Abwehr recruited him at Vienna University. When the war ended, and Gehlen started working for the Americans, Dodo worked for Lange."

I looked at Werner and tried to guess where my father fitted into all this. Werner smiled nervously, wondering perhaps if he should have brought up the subject of my father. Ingrid said, "Dodo is a troublemaker. Some people are like that, aren't they?" She looked at me, expecting a response, so I nodded.

She said, "He is a troubled, morbid creature. And he drinks too much and becomes maudlin. Full of self-pity. Hungarians have the highest suicide rate in the world: four times as many as Americans, and still climbing." Ingrid broke off, doubtless remembering that Gloria was Hungarian too. Flushed with embarrassment, she turned back to the boiler and said, "We could get it cleaned and serviced and see what happens. Even when the pump keeps working, the water doesn't get really hot."

"Lisl should have fitted a bigger one when she had it renewed," I said. I reached out with both hands and slapped the boiler twice, encouragingly, as a Neapolitan platoon commander might slap the shoulders of a man ordered out on a dangerous mission. It made no difference.

For a moment I thought she'd decided to say no more; then she said, "Dodo urged my mother to sue the American army."

"That sounds like Dodo," I said.

"Get compensation for Paul Winter's death. It was a shooting accident."

"It's a bit late now, isn't it? And I thought you said he was shot while trying to escape," I said.

"Ingrid said that the Americans gave that as their excuse."

"Dodo told my mother the Americans would pay a lot of money. He said they wouldn't want it all dragged up."

I grunted to express my doubts about Dodo's theory.

"My uncle Peter was a colonel in the American army. He was shot in the same incident. Dodo says they were on a secret mission."

I said, "What's all this got to do with my father?"

"He was there," said Ingrid.

"Where?" I said.

"Berchtesgaden," said Ingrid. "The inquiry said that he was the one who shot my father."

"I think you must have made a mistake," I said. "Werner knew my father. He will tell you . . . anyone will tell you . . ." I shrugged. "My father wasn't a shooting soldier. He worked in intelligence."

"He shot Paul Winter," said Ingrid coldly and calmly. "Paul Winter was a war criminal . . . or so it was alleged. Your father was an officer on duty with the army that had conquered us. There probably was a cover-up. Such things happen when there are wars."

I said nothing. There was nothing to say. She obviously believed what she said, but she wasn't getting angry. She was more embarrassed than angry. I suppose she had no recollection of her father. He was no more than a name to her, and that's how she spoke of him.

When it seemed that Ingrid didn't want to tell me more, Werner said, "Dodo used the American Freedom of Information Act and had someone go through the U.S. Army archives. He didn't find much, except that an American colonel and a German civilian—both named Winter—died of gunshot wounds. It was night, and snowing. The court of inquiry recorded it as an accident. No one was punished."

"Are you sure my father was there? Berchtesgaden was in the American Zone. Why would my father be with the Americans?"

"Captain Brian Samson," said Ingrid. "He gave evidence at the inquiry. A sworn statement from him—and many other documents were listed—but Dodo couldn't get transcripts."

Werner said, "That damned Dodo is a dangerous little swine. If he's determined to make trouble . . ."

He didn't finish. He didn't have to. Werner knew me well enough to appreciate how much any kind of blemish on my father's career would hurt me. "I have no quarrel with Dodo," I said.

"He resents you," said Ingrid. "After your visit to him, he came to see Mama. Dodo really hates you."

"Why should he hate me?"

"She's Hungarian, isn't she?"

"Yes, she's Hungarian," I said.

"And Dodo's a close friend of her family," said Ingrid with that decisive finality with which women pronounce upon such relationships. "To him you are a meddlesome foreign intruder . . ." She didn't finish. There was no need to. I nodded. Ingrid was right, and I knew the rest of it. It was easy to see myself as a middle-aged lecher taking advantage of this innocent young girl. It would be more than enough to trigger an unstable personality like Dodo. If it was the other way round, if that dreadful Dodo was living with the young daughter of one of my old friends, I would be angry too. Angry beyond measure.

"Yes," I said.

"There is always electricity," said Ingrid.

"Is there?" I said.

"To heat the water," said Ingrid. "We could even have small electric heaters in each bathroom. Then water from the boiler would just be used by the kitchen."

I was angry at the injustice of it. I looked at the boiler and kicked it at the place where the water went into the pump. Nothing happened, so I kicked it again, harder. It gave a whirring sound. Ingrid and Werner looked at me with new respect. For a moment or two we watched to see if it would keep going, and Werner touched it to be sure it was getting hot again. It got hotter. "What about a drink?" said Werner.

"I thought you'd never ask," I said.

"And then Ingrid will cook the *Hoppel-Poppel*. She has everything ready. She cooks it in goose dripping."

"If you want to wash or anything, your top-floor bath-room will have plenty of hot water. It gets it straight from the tank."

"Thanks, Ingrid."

"Your room is just the same as it was. Werner wanted to have it repapered and refurnished as a surprise for you, but I said it would be better to ask you first. I said you might like it just the way it is." She looked at me, and her face said how sorry she was to have been the conveyor of unpleasant news to Werner's friend.

"I like it the way it is," I admitted.

"It was nice of you to bring the curtain material. Werner said you wouldn't mind."

"In goose dripping, eh?" I said. "Ingrid, you're some woman!"

Werner smiled. He was smiling a lot lately.

Chapter 19

Having returned to London with the malicious, drunken defamations of Dodo still ringing in my mind, I left a message for Cindy Prettyman or Matthews, as, despite the Prettyman pension, she was determined to be known. She called back almost immediately. I expected her to be annoyed that I'd not contacted her earlier, but she had no recriminations. She was sweet and elated. Friday evening would be just fine for her. A hotel in Bayswater? Any way you want to play it, Cindy. While she was saying goodbye, the line went dead. So she'd gone out of the office and called from a pay phone. Pay phone? And a hotel in Bayswater? Oh well, Cindy had always been a bit weird.

I had to talk to her. Dodo's various bombshells, whether true or entirely nonsense, made it all the more urgent. And delicate little assignments like nosing into the tight little empire of Schneider, von Schild and Weber were best done via the big anonymous facilities of the Foreign Office, rather than the parochial ones of my Department, where all concerned would know, or guess, that the request had come from me. I'd come out of it with a lot of explaining to do, if any of Dodo's exotic allegations proved true.

"I hate the idea of you confiding in that woman," said Gloria when I got home that night. "She's so . . ." Gloria paused to think of the word. ". . . cold-blooded."

"Is she?"

"When are you seeing her?"

"Friday evening, from the office."

"Can I come?" said Gloria.

"Of course."

"I'd be intruding."

"No, do come along. She won't be expecting dinner. A drink, she said." I watched Gloria carefully. In all our years together, my wife, Fiona, had never revealed a trace of jealousy or suspicion, but Gloria scrutinized every female acquaintance as a possible paramour. She especially examined the motives of unattached females, and those from my past. In all these respects Cindy loomed large.

"If you're sure," said Gloria.

"You might have to close your ears," I warned. I meant, of course, that there would be things said that I might later officially deny, that Cindy might later deny, and that, if Gloria was going to be there, she'd have to be prepared to deny too. Deny on oath.

I think Gloria understood. "I'll make a trip to the ladies'; that will give her a chance to say anything confidential."

In the event, Gloria decided not to come after all. I suppose she just wanted to see whether I'd say no, and how I would do it. I knew these little "tests" she gave me were all part of her insecurity. Sometimes I wondered whether her plan to go to university was a test, designed to push me into a proposal of marriage.

Meanwhile, that Friday evening, I went to meet Cindy alone. It was just as well. Cindy was not in the best of moods. She was rather distracted, and it would not have improved her humor to see Gloria tagging along behind me. Cindy regarded her as a very junior civil servant who had come trespassing on the old friendship.

"Your blonde interlude" is how Cindy referred to Gloria. It summed up what she thought of the relationship: its participants, its incongruity, its frivolity, and its impermanence.

I let it go. She smiled in a fashion that both gave emphasis to what she'd said, and noted my passive acceptance of the judgment she'd passed. Cindy was an attractive woman, sexy in the way that health and energy so often are. But I'd never envied Jim. Cindy was too devious and manipulative, and I was not good at handling her.

She was in a room on the second floor, sitting on the bed, smoking a cigarette. Beside her there was a tray with a teapot and milk and cup—just one cup—and a big Martini ashtray with lots of lipstick-marked cigarette butts. Cindy's attempt to give up smoking seemed to have been abandoned. She asked me if I wanted a drink. I should have said no, but I said I'd have a Scotch, and I gave the box with the photos of the tomb inscriptions and the deciphering attempts—or, rather, I tried to give it—to her. She waved it away with a world-weary flick of splayed fingers. "I don't want it."

"Gloria said . . ."

"I've changed my mind. Keep it."

"There's nothing there that will shed any light on Jim or his work," I told her. "I'll stake my life on that."

She shrugged and touched her hair.

We wasted a lot of time getting the hotel staff to supply drinks, and while we waited we passed the time talking about nothing in particular. It was not my idea of an enjoyable evening out. Cindy had chosen the venue: The Grand & International, a seedy old hotel standing on the northern edge of Kensington Gardens, and hiding behind the Chinese restaurants of Queensway.

She'd coped with getting the room—paying in advance and arranging to occupy it without luggage and entertain a male visitor for an hour or so. I looked at her in her smart green-and-black-plaid jacket and matching skirt. A boxy imitation-fur coat was thrown across the bed. She wasn't tall and graceful in the way that Gloria was, but she had a shapely figure, and the way she was lounging across the pillows did everything to emphasize it. I wondered what they made of her downstairs at the desk. Or had reception clerks in this part of town stopped wondering about their clients?

It was probably one of their best rooms, but it was a

squalid place by any standards. A flyblown mirror surmounted a cracked blue china sink. The bed was big, with a quilted headboard and gray sheets. Cindy said it was suitably anonymous, but I think she was confusing anonymity with discomfort; many people did. But if The G & I, an amalgamation of two Victorian monoliths, was somewhere where Cindy was in no danger of seeing anyone she knew, the same could not be said for me.

I'd been in this place many times. I'd brought a lovely old Sauer automatic pistol to the bar there back in 1974. I'd sold it to a man named Max who died saving my life during the last "illegal" border crossing I ever made. It was a good little gun; its blueing had worn, but it had been little used. At the time its double action was better than anything else manufactured, but I suspect that Max selected it because during the war it had been the favored side arm of high-ranking German officers. Max was as anti-Nazi as anyone I knew, but he had a healthy respect for their choice of weapons.

There was hardly a day went by when I didn't think of Max. Like Dodo, Max had been one of "Koby's Prussians," an American Prussian in this case, for Max was one of those curious men who drift from place to place and from job to job. And somehow the towns they go to are all trouble spots, and the jobs they find are always violent and dangerous jobs, and usually illegal too. But Max was different from all the others, an ex–New York police detective who fretted and worried and looked after everyone he worked with, especially me, the youngest member of his team.

Max had the most amazing memory for poetry, and his quotes ranged from Goethe to Gilbert and Sullivan librettos. I could usually keep up with his Goethe—*"Kennst du das Land, wo die Zitronen blühen?"*—but his Gilbert was what I always remembered him for:

> *When you're lying awake, with a dismal headache,*
> *and repose is taboo'd by anxiety,*

I conceive you may use any language you choose
to indulge in, without impropriety.

And, of course, sung with verve and derision, for Max was not an uncritical admirer of his British allies:

For he might have been a Russian, a French, or Turk, or Prussian,
Or perhaps Itali-yan!
But in spite of all temptations,
To belong to other nations,
He remains an Englishman!

Some of Gilbert's phrases were too cryptic for Max. As the only Englishman with whom Max was regularly in contact, I was expected to decipher all the "Britishisms" and explain such Gilbertian inexplicables as "A Sewell & Cross young man, a Howell & James young man." Poor Max, I never did find out for him.

And yet there was nothing so inexplicable as Max himself. He was his own worst enemy, if my father was to be believed, but my father detested Max. In fact he detested "Lange" Koby and all what he called "the American freebooters" in Berlin. That's why my father stayed clear of them.

"Are you listening, Bernard?" I was jolted from my memories by Cindy.

"Yes, Cindy, of course I am." I suppose I hadn't nodded and smiled frequently enough while listening to her small talk.

"I'm going to Strasbourg," she said suddenly, and she had all my attention. With the cigarette still in her hand, she made a movement that left a thin trail of smoke. Then she touched her hair; it was shiny and curly and looked as if she'd been to the hairdresser. Her hair always looked like that.

"On holiday?"

"God-a-mercy! Don't be stupid, Bernard. Who would go

to Strasbourg on holiday?" She waved the cigarette in the air, and a long section of ash fell on the bedcover.

"A job?"

"Don't be so dense, Bernie. The bloody European Parliament is there, isn't it?" As if angry about the marked bedcover, she stubbed her cigarette into the ashtray, pushing it down in a punitive action that deformed its shape and left it bent and broken.

"And that's who you'll be working for?" I wondered why the hell she hadn't mentioned it earlier, when we'd been talking about the weather and how difficult it was to get seats for the Royal Opera House unless you knew someone. But then I realized that she didn't want to tell me until I'd had a drink.

"The pay is terrific, and I'll have no trouble selling my place in London. The estate agent is putting an ad in next Sunday's papers. He says I'll have hordes of people after it. He said that if I spent a bit of money on the kitchen and bathroom he could get another fifteen grand, but I just don't have the time."

"I see."

"You're not interested, I suppose?"

"Interested in what?"

"What's wrong with you tonight, Bernie? Are you interested in buying my house? I'd sooner it went to a friend."

"I've just moved," I said. "I couldn't go through packing and unpacking again."

"Yes, I forgot. You're in the sticks. I couldn't live in the suburbs again. It's a slow death."

"Yes, well, I'm not in a hurry," I said. I felt as if I'd just been given a swift kick in the guts. I'd come here believing that Cindy was even more determined than I was to get to the bottom of the mystery, and now I found she wasn't interested in anything but selling her bloody house. Tentatively, and keeping Dodo out of it, I said, "I think I might have had a breakthrough on the matter of the German bank account."

She had started rummaging through the expensive crocodile handbag that never left her side. "Good," she said, looking down into the handbag and showing little or no interest
in anything I might have discovered.

I persisted. "I hear it's a bank called Schneider, von
Schild and Weber. I found it in the Berlin phone book. We'll
need more details."

"I'll be in Strasbourg beginning the end of next week."
From the handbag she brought her pack of cigarettes and a
gold lighter.

"That's damned sudden."

Without hurrying, she lit her cigarette, blew a lot of
smoke high into the air, and said, "Sir Giles put my name in."

"Creepy-Pox strikes again."

She gave a fixed smile to show that she didn't think it was
amusing but wasn't going to make an issue of it.

"It's a plum job. The vacancy came up out of the blue.
That's why I got it. The fellow there now has AIDS. Two
others short-listed for the job are both family men with children at school. They wouldn't move at such short notice. No,
I have to be there next week."

I swallowed the angry words that first came to mind and
said, "But the last time we talked, you said that no one was
going to shut you up. You said you weren't going to let it go."

"I've got my life to lead, Bernard."

"So now you want me to forget it?"

"Don't shout, Bernie. I thought you'd be pleased and
wish me good luck. I'm not telling you what to do, Bernie. If
you want to continue and solve your whodunnit, I'm not going
to stop you."

Patiently and quietly I said, "Cindy, this isn't a whodunnit. If it's what I think it is—what we both think it is—it's the
biggest KGB penetration of our Department ever."

"Is it?" She didn't give a damn. It was as if I was talking
to a stranger. This wasn't the woman who'd vowed to uncover
the truth about the murder of her ex-husband.

"Even if I'm wrong," I said, "we're still talking about embezzlement on a mammoth scale: millions!"

"I thought the same at first," she said, very calmly and very condescendingly. "But when you consider it more carefully, it's difficult to sustain the notion that there's some gigantic financial swindle, and that the D-G is in on it." She smiled one of her saccharine smiles to emphasize the absurdity of that suggestion.

"The D-G has virtually disappeared." I was exaggerating only slightly; he was very seldom in the office these days.

"Is the disappearance of the D-G all part of this plot?" she said with that same stupid smile on her face.

"I'm not joking, Cindy," I said. Only with considerable difficulty did I resist telling the stupid bitch that she was the one who'd started all this.

"I'm not joking either, Bernie. So just answer my question: are you saying there is a conspiracy in which Bret Rensselaer, Frank Harrington, the Deputy, and maybe Dicky Cruyer are all implicated?"

It was such an absurd misrepresentation of anything I'd ever thought that I didn't know where to start refuting it. I said, "Let us suppose that just one really irreproachable individual . . ."

"The D-G," she said, like a particularly haughty member of the audience choosing a card for an amateur conjurer.

"Okay. For the sake of argument, let's say the D-G is a party to some big swindle. Surely you see that the structure of the Department is such that no one would believe it. Frank, Dicky, Bret, and all the others would simply stand firm and say everything's fine."

"And you're the little boy telling the Emperor he has no clothes?"

"Just because everyone says there is nothing wrong, we shouldn't refuse to examine it more closely. Strange things happen in the place where I go to work. I'm not talking about the Ministry of Education or the Department of Health and

Social Services, Cindy. I'm talking about the place where the rough stuff is arranged."

"If you want my advice . . ." She slid off the bed and stood up. Having eased her shoes half off her feet, she squeezed back into them, putting all her weight on first one foot, then the other. "You should stop beating your head against a brick wall."

"You make it sound like I enjoy beating my head against a brick wall."

She smoothed her lapels and reached for her coat. "I think you want to destroy yourself. It's something to do with Fiona leaving you. Perhaps you feel guilty in some way. But all these theories you dream up . . . I mean, they never come to anything, do they? Don't you see that inside you there is some kind of worm that is eating you up? I suppose you desperately want to believe that all the world is wrong, and only Bernard Samson is right." She snapped her handbag lock closed. "Forget all this crap, Bernard. Life is too short to rectify all the world's wrongs. It took me a long time to see that, but from now on I live my life. I'm not going to change the world."

"There's one small thing you could do before you go to Strasbourg."

"Not before I go, and not after I get there either. I don't want to know, Bernie. Do I have to draw a diagram for you?"

I looked at her and she stared back. She was not in any way hostile, not even tough. She was just a woman who'd made up her mind. There was no way to change it. "Okay, Cindy. Have a good time in Strasbourg."

She smiled, visibly relieved by my friendly tone of voice. "God willing, I'll find some nice young sexy Frenchman and get married." She drew the window curtain aside to see if it was raining. It was. She buttoned up her coat. "Do you want to buy the Mercedes, Bernard? Dark-green 380 SE. It's only two years old; it does twenty-five to a gallon."

"I can't afford it, Cindy."

"That's on the motorway, of course. In town, more like twenty." When she got to the doorway she stopped. Just for one moment I thought she was going to say she'd help after all, but she said, "The steering is on the wrong side for the Continent, and I can buy a tax-free car when I'm there, so I'll have to sell it."

We walked down the stairs in silence. When we got to the brightly lighted foyer, she stopped and delved into her handbag until she found a white plastic rain hat. There was no one there; even the reception desk was unmanned. Cindy walked over to look in a mirror and be sure her hair was tucked away. "Everything else I'm taking with me," she said while still looking at herself in the mirror. "Furniture and TV and video and hi-fi. That sort of thing is very expensive in France."

"Your TV won't work in France," I said. "They have a different system."

She didn't look at me. She turned and pushed the main door open and went out into the night without saying good-bye. The heavy doors slammed behind her with a soft thud. She thought I was trying to annoy her.

It was a long walk to where I'd left the car. The street was noisy and crowded with people and cruising traffic of all kinds. Young couples, skinheads, punks, freaks, whores of all sexes, cops and robbers too. Painted faces whitened under the bright neon. I found my car still in one piece. No sooner had I pulled away from the curb than another car was taking my place in the narrow parking slot.

The rain got heavier. My old Volvo stuttered and choked in the heavy downpour. Maybe they didn't have rain in Sweden. So I thought about Cindy's Mercedes all the way home: British racing green; paintwork waxed so that even Mr. Gaskell approved, and a V-8 engine. I wondered what she was asking for it.

When I got to Balaklava Road, the downstairs lights were

out. The children were in bed, and Cathy was watching a TV play in her room. Gloria wasn't there. I'd forgotten that she'd changed the night for visiting her parents to Friday. She probably never had the slightest intention of joining me and Cindy for our little drink and discussion in town. Gloria knew she could depend upon me to forget which evenings she went out.

I opened a tin of sardines and a bottle of white Burgundy. I put a tape of *Citizen Kane* in the video and ate my supper from a tray on my knees. But I spent all the time thinking about Bret Rensselaer's anger, Jim Prettyman's murder, Dodo's diatribe, and Cindy Matthews's sudden change of mind.

By the time Gloria got home I was in bed. I wasn't surprised that she was late. I guessed that it was something to do with this "crisis" that her mother said threatened their marriage. Whatever domestic crisis she'd attended, Gloria didn't arrive back low-spirited. In fact, she was bubbling with excitement. I knew what she'd be like even before she came into the house. Her old yellow Mini could only just be fitted into the space between the kitchen and the fence to which our neighbor's cosseted wisteria clung. Even then it meant squeezing out on the passenger side. This tricky feat was not something that Gloria always felt willing to attempt, but on this night I heard her bump over the curb and, with no slackening of speed, onto the garden path, and stop with a squeal of brakes. She gave the accelerator a little jab of satisfaction before switching off the ignition. I could visualize the smile on her face.

"Hello, darling," she said as she tiptoed into the bedroom, still carrying the plastic bag that I knew contained one of her mother's Hungarian walnut cakes and a tub of homemade liptoi cheese, pickles, and all sorts of other things that her family felt she needed regular supplies of when not living at home. "How was Mrs. Prettyman?"

"Suddenly silent."

Gloria looked at me, trying to read the expression on my face. "Has someone put a gun at her head?"

I laughed. "Right," I said. "A golden gun. Suddenly she's been offered a plum job with the Strasbourg bureaucrats, lots more money, little or no tax. God knows what else."

"You don't think . . ."

"I don't know."

"I wouldn't like to be trying to bribe her," said Gloria.

"Because she'd ask for more than you had to offer?"

"No, I don't mean that. I just think she'd be touchy. I'd worry that she might write it all down and take it to the newspapers."

"It's just a soft job in Strasbourg," I said. "Not even the reporters from the tabloids could make that into a bribe, unless Cindy declared herself so incompetent that the offer was ridiculously inappropriate."

"I suppose so." She put the bag of Hungarian delicacies on the dressing table and began to undress.

"What is it?" I asked, for she had the sort of self-satisfied grin on her face that usually meant I'd done something careless, like locking the cat in the broom closet or absent-mindedly picking up the milkman's money and putting it in my pocket.

"Nothing," she said, though I could tell by the wanton abandon with which she disrobed and threw aside her clothes that there was some kind of joke to share. But I thought it would be something about her parents, or the latest about the egregious Dodo, who'd now been given temporary rent-free use of a comfortable little house near Kingston upon Thames.

"That bank," she said as she got between the sheets and huddled against me. "Guess who owns that bank."

"Bank? Schneider, von Schild . . ."

". . . and Weber," she supplied, still grinning at her cleverness and at the joke that was to come. "Yes, that's the bank, my darling. Guess who owns it."

"Not Mr. Schneider, Mr. von Schild, and Mr. Weber?"

"Your precious Bret Rensselaer, that's who."

"What?"

"I knew that would bring you fully awake."

"I was already fully awake."

"At least, it belongs to the Rensselaer family."

"How did you find out?"

"I didn't have to raid the Yellow Submarine, darling. It's public knowledge. Even German banks have to make owner-ship declarations. My teacher at the economics class got it from an ordinary data-bank listing. He phoned me back in half an hour and had its history."

"I should have checked that out."

"Well, you didn't; I did." She chuckled like a baby.

"You're such a clever girl," I said.

"So you've noticed?"

"That you're a girl? Yes, I've noticed."

"Don't do that. . . . At least, don't do it yet."

"The Rensselaer family?"

"Are you ready for the details? Hold on to your hat, lover; here goes. Back in 1925 a man named Cyrus Rensselaer bought shares in a California banking group. Bret and his brothers worked for them; I guess they had directorships or something. I can get more details. . . . Then, sometime in the Second World War, the old man died. Under the terms of his will, the shares went into a trust, of which Bret's mother was the beneficiary. In a complicated share issue and merger in 1953, the California bank became a part of CALIBANK (INTER-NATIONAL) SERCO, which began large-scale buying of other banks. One shareholding they acquired gave them a majority holding in Schneider, von Schild and Weber."

"Anything else?"

"Anything else, he says! My darling, you're insatiable. Has anyone ever told you that?"

"I plead the Fifth Amendment," I said.

Chapter 20

Only desperation would have provoked me to set out on a journey to see Silas Gaunt that Saturday. He'd retired from the Department many years before, but he remained one of the most influential individuals in what Dicky Cruyer delicately called "the intelligence community." "Uncle" Silas knew everything and knew everyone. He had been close to my father over many years, was distantly related to my mother-in-law, and was Billy's godfather.

Perhaps I should have visited him more regularly, but he was devoted to my wife, Fiona, and her departure had distanced Silas from me. He wasn't likely to appreciate my arriving arm in arm with Gloria, and yet it was a damned long journey to do alone. But I did it alone, and as I drove through a pale, prostrate landscape that had still not loosened the shackles of winter, I had a chance to think about what I might say to him. How did I start? Jim Prettyman was dead and Bret Rensselaer was suddenly alive, but neither metamorphosis was going to help me. Dodo was telling anyone who'd listen that I'd been conspiring with Fiona to swindle the Department, while my prime helper, Cindy Prettyman, was suffering the selective amnesia that valued promotion sometimes brings.

Uncle Silas lived at Whitelands, a middle-size farm in the Cotswolds, a picturesque place of tan-colored stone with ill-fitting doors, creaking floorboards, and low beams that split the skulls of the tall and unwary. Silas must have been exceptionally wary, for he was a giant of a man and so fat that he was scarcely able to squeeze through some of the narrower doors. Some nineteenth-century tycoon had redone the interior to his own taste, so that there was a surfeit of mahogany and ornamental tiles and a scarcity of bathrooms. But it suited Silas, and somehow it was difficult to imagine him in any other environment.

In the daytime he kept busy. There were discussions with his farm manager, and his housekeeper, Mrs. Porter, and with the lady from the village who came in to deal with his mail but who seemed unable to deal with any telephone caller without coming downstairs and dragging Silas upstairs to the one and only phone.

I was sitting waiting for Silas to return from upstairs. The narrow stone-framed windows let in only a thin slice of gray afternoon light. The log fire burning brightly in the big stone hearth filled the air with a smoky perfume and provided the light by which to see the drawing room with its battered old sofa and uncomfortable chairs, their shapes only vaguely apparent under the baggy chintz covers. In front of the fire was a tray with the remains of our tea: silver teapot, the last couple of Mrs. Porter's freshly made scones and a pot of jam with a handwritten label saying "Whitelands—strawberry." It might have been a hundred years ago but for the big hi-fi speakers that stood in the far corners of the room. This was where Silas spent his evenings, listening to his opera records and drinking his way through his remarkable cellar.

"Sorry about these interruptions," he said as he fiddled to close the ancient brass door latch. He clapped his hands and then went to warm them at the fire. "Fresh tea?"

"I've had enough tea," I said.

"And it's too early for a drink," said Silas.

I didn't reply.

"You tell me a lot of things," he said, pouring the last tepid remains of the tea into his cup. "And you want me to make them fit together nicely, like pieces of a jigsaw." He sipped the cold tea, then pulled a face and abandoned it. "But I don't see any causal connection." Sniff. "Either it's much colder today or I'm getting flu . . . or maybe both. So this accountant fellow Prettyman was killed in Washington by some hooligan, and now his wife has been promoted? Well, jolly good, I say. Why shouldn't the poor woman be promoted? I've always thought we should look after our own people to the best of our ability."

There was a long, silent rumination until I helped him remember the rest of it. "And then there was Bret Rensselaer," I said.

"Yes, poor Bret. An awfully good chap, Bret; injured on duty. An episode in the very best traditions of the service, if I may say so. Yet you seem indignant that he's survived."

"I was damned surprised to see him arise from the dead."

"I can't see what you're getting at," said Uncle Silas. "Aren't you pleased by that either?" He scratched his crotch un-selfconsciously. He was a strange old devil; fat and disheveled, with a coarse humor and biting wit that was not funny to those who found it directed at them.

"There are too many things happening . . . funny things."

"I really don't follow your reasoning, Bernard." He shook his head. "I really don't." Uncle Silas had always been able to twist the facts to suit a hypothesis. He said, "It's not a bit of good you sitting there glaring at me, dear boy." He paused to take out a big red cotton handkerchief and blow his nose violently. "I'm trying to prevent you making a bloody fool of yourself."

"By doing what?"

"By bursting in on poor old Dodo and giving him the third degree." Old Silas must have been the last living person still using expressions like "third degree."

"Did you know him well?"

"Yes, I remember him well," said Silas, sitting back in his armchair and staring into the fire. "His real name was Theodor—Theodor Kiss—so he preferred to be Dodo. A keen worker: bright as a button. A good science degree at Vienna University and a good administrative knack. Lots of languages and dialects too. Dodo could effortlessly pass himself off as a German. Or as an Austrian. Effortlessly!"

"Amazing," I said.

"Oh, I know, you can do the same thing, Bernard. But it's quite an unusual feat. Not many Germans can do it, as I know to my cost. Yes, Dodo was a remarkable linguist."

"He worked for Gehlen," I said, to remind Silas that this paragon was an ex-Nazi.

"Most of the best ones had worked for him. They were the only experienced people available for hire. Of course, I never used any of them," said Silas, perhaps wanting to deflect my wrath. "Not directly. I stayed clear of Gehlen's ex-employees. Lange Koby took him away with the rest of his gang. . . . What did he call them . . . ?"

"Prussians," I supplied.

"Yes, 'Koby's Prussians'; that's right. How could I forget that? My memory is going wonky these days."

I said nothing.

"Your father too. He wouldn't go near any of them. He was upset when you worked for Lange Koby."

"I teamed up with Max," I said. "Koby came as part of the deal."

Silas sniffed. "You should have stayed with your father, Bernard."

"I know," I said. He'd touched a nerve.

We sat silent for a few minutes. "Your Dodo is all right," said Silas, as if he'd been thinking deeply about it. "Perhaps a bit too keen to demonstrate his valor, but so were all the ones who'd changed sides. But Dodo, when he settled down, he became a loyal, sensible agent—the sort of fellow I would have expected you to be specially sympathetic towards. A man like that must be excused an indiscretion now and again, what?" He got out his handkerchief and wiped his nose.

"Indiscretion?"

"I'd say the same for you, Bernard," he added before my indignation boiled over. "Have said it, in fact," he added, to make sure I knew I was indebted to him.

He stopped, perhaps waiting for some gesture of appreciation or agreement. I nodded without putting too much into it. Ever since arriving here, I had been considering ways to ask him about the mad allegations concerning my father. Silas had known my father as well as anyone still alive. They'd served together in Berlin, and in London too. Silas Gaunt could solve just about any mystery that arose out of my father's service if he wanted to. If he wanted to: there's the rub. Silas Gaunt was not a man much given to revealing secrets, even to those entitled to know. And this wasn't the time to ask. That much was clear just from looking at the old man's face. He was not enjoying my visit, despite all the smiles and nods and pleasantries. Perhaps he was just worried about me. Or about Fiona, or about my children. Or about Dodo. "I know you have, Silas," I said. "I appreciate it."

"I want you to promise not to go in there ranting and raving," said Silas. "I want you to promise to go along there and talk to him in a conciliatory manner that will make him see your point of view."

"I'll try," I said.

"We all have a lot of old comrades in common: the Gebhart twins; 'Baron' Busch, who took you to Leipzig; Oscar Rhine, who said he could swim across Lübeck Bay but couldn't. . . ." Silas had tried to make light of his list of departed colleagues but couldn't maintain the levity. He wiped his nose and tried again. "We all grieve for the same old friends, Bernard: you, me, Dodo. . . . No sense in quarreling amongst ourselves."

"No," I said.

"He's been in the business even longer than you have," said Silas, "so don't start talking down to him." This was Silas at his avuncular worst. Sometimes I wondered if he'd ever spoken to the D-G like this, for I knew that Silas regarded all of us as children attempting the man's job at which he'd excelled.

"No, Silas," I said, and I must have allowed some trace of my skepticism to show, for there was a twitch of the face that I'd learned to recognize as a sign of anger to come.

But the anger didn't come, or at least it didn't show. "Tell me again about Bret Rensselaer; is he coming back to work?"

"No chance," I said. "He's too sick and too old."

"They say he wanted Berlin," said Silas.

"Yes," I said. "At the time the rumors said Frank would get his K and retire, and Bret would get Berlin."

"And then Bret would get a K and retire," said Silas, completing the scenario that everyone had said was inevitable up to the time when things went wrong and Bret got shot. "So what was the long-term plan for Berlin?"

I looked at him and wondered what everyone in the Department must have wondered at some time or other: why Silas Gaunt had never got the Knighthood that usually came with such retirements. "Come along, Silas," I said. "You know more about what goes on in the minds of the men on the top floor than I will ever get to find out. You tell me."

"Seriously, Bernard. What do you think was the plan? If Frank had been bowler-hatted and replaced by Bret, Bret could only have had that job until his retirement came up. And they could hardly have asked for special dispensation to keep Bret there."

"I suppose you are right," I said. "I never get to thinking about such long-term possibilities."

"Then that's a pity," said Silas, lowering his voice as if saying something confidential and important, a trick he'd developed from his briefing days. "Perhaps, if you gave your mind to such things, you wouldn't be getting yourself into such deep water as you are now in."

"Wouldn't I?"

"Could Dicky Cruyer hold down the Berlin job?" His voice was still soft.

"He wants it," I said.

"Dicky has no German contacts, does he? None that are worth a damn anyway. The Berlin job must have someone with a flair, someone with a feeling for the streets, someone who can smell what's going on, quite apart from the departmental input."

"Someone like Frank?"

"Frank, like your father, was a protégé of mine. Yes, Frank has done well there. But age slows a man down. Berlin is a job for someone more resilient, someone younger, who gets out and about. Frank spends too much time at home, playing his damned gramophone records."

"Yes," I said, and nodded seriously. Gramophone records? Silas knew about Frank's extramarital amours as well as I did, but he preferred to tell the story his way. He was always like that.

"I get the idea, Silas," I said. The idea was that, if I was a good little chap, and didn't keep spreading alarm and despondency with my extracurricular questions, I might get Berlin. I didn't believe it.

"Do you? I'm so glad," he said. I got to my feet. "As a favor to me, Bernard. Could you hold off for a couple of days or so . . . ? On the Dodo fellow."

"I was going over there tonight. He's always home on a Saturday evening," I said. "There's some program he watches on TV."

"Just until next week. A cooling-off period, eh? Better for all concerned, dear boy."

I looked at Silas. He was giving me good advice, but I was wound up tight and ready to confront the little swine. He stared at me, not giving an inch. "If you insist," I said reluctantly.

"You won't regret your decision," said Silas. "I'll talk to the old man about it. And about you."

"Thanks for giving me your time, Silas."

"Why don't you hang on for supper? We'll have a game of billiards." He held his handkerchief in front of him as if transfixed. For one awful moment I thought he was having a heart attack or some other serious affliction, but then his nose twitched and he sneezed.

"You should be in bed, Silas," I said. "You've got flu."

He didn't persist. Silas was old and set in his ways. He didn't like visits at short notice, and he didn't want unscheduled dinner guests. He wiped his nose and said, "No news from your wife?"

"Nothing."

"It must be difficult for you, but don't give up," said Silas. "When are you going to bring the children to see me?"

I looked up in surprise. It had never occurred to me that Silas would welcome such an intrusion into his jealously guarded little world. "Any time," I said awkwardly. "Today week? Lunch?"

"Splendid!" He looked out of the window and said, "I'll tell Mrs. Porter to be sure the sirloin is underdone. And a Charlotte Russe to follow? Billy likes that, doesn't he?"

The old man's eye for detail could still astound me. So he'd noticed Billy's appetite for Mrs. Porter's rare roast beef and the Charlotte Russe. "Yes, we all do," I said.

"We don't have to tempt you; you like everything," said Silas dismissively. "Sometimes I wish you were more selective."

I took it this was a comment upon aspects of my life other than my appetite for Charlotte Russe, but I didn't pursue it.

At the time I undertook not to see Dodo, I meant it. But it was a resolve hard to stick to as I drove back to London, turning over in my mind everything that had happened.

By the time I got to the outer suburbs, I had decided to

disregard Silas's request to lay off Dodo. All my instincts told me to go for him and go now.

Dodo had emerged as a truly remarkable freeloader. So I was not surprised that he'd obtained the rent-free use of a house. It belonged to a Hungarian couple he'd met through Gloria's parents who were having a winter holiday in Madeira. It was an elegant old house in Hampton Wick. Positioned between the river and the grounds of Hampton Court Palace, it stood in a quiet back street of early Victorian houses varying in shape and size.

It was growing dark by the time I arrived, the sky purple with that hazy moon that is said to portend rain. The street-lamps showed that Number 18 stood alone and back from the road. Rising over its eight-foot-tall garden wall I could see its intricate ironwork balcony, complete with curving pagoda-style top. The contrived seclusion, and the delicacy of the design, immediately suggested it as the sort of villa in which some alluring concubine might have passed her long, lonely days.

The wrought-iron gate gave onto a small front garden. I stood there a moment and looked again at the house. The curtains were carelessly closed, so that chinks of light were to be seen in almost every window. It was a bitterly cold night, and the only sounds to be heard came from cars going along the main road, towards Kingston Bridge.

I went up the steps to the bright-green front door. There was no doorbell, so I hammered loudly, using a big brass lion's-head knocker. There was a long time before I heard movement inside. I had the feeling that someone might have gone to one of the upstairs windows to see who it was. Eventually the door opened to reveal Dodo. He was dressed in a white sweater, gray cotton jacket, gray cord slacks, and loafers with leather tassels. "Ahhh! Good evening!" he said. "So you tracked me down."

"Can I come in?"

He didn't answer immediately. He clung to the door edge and looked me up and down. "Very well," he said without much enthusiasm. "Come in and have a drink."

He led the way through the hall, past the bentwood coatrack and the big mirror. He didn't suggest that I should take off my overcoat. He ushered me into a room at the back. It was a large room with a grand piano, a couple of easy chairs, and some small antique tables cluttered with an array of snuffboxes and chinaware. The Victorian wallpaper provided a jungle of printed vegetation, and the only light came from a brass fixture that directed all its rays upon the sheet music displayed on the piano.

The room smelled musty and unused, the window was shuttered, and the piano wore a gray sheen of dust. Dodo turned to face me. "Now, what is it?" he said. His voice was hard and belligerent, and his eyes glittered fiercely. I guessed he'd been on the booze, but you could never be sure of anything with Dodo.

"Listen, Dodo," I said. "We'd better get one thing straight. . . ."

He had moved as if reaching past me, but smoothly and without warning he straightened, and bringing his fist forward slammed me in the guts with enough force to wind me. As I bent forward, choking for air, the edge of his hand came down upon the side of my neck. It was a well-placed karate chop, and the pain of it set fire to every nerve in my body.

As I doubled over and coughed up my dinner, he lashed out with a vicious kick, but with my head down, I saw his foot coming and lurched aside so that his shoe only grazed my arm.

My overcoat had protected me against the full effect of his blows; had Dodo got me to take off my overcoat in the hall, I would have been laid out by now. Another kick, but wide of the mark this time. I reached out in the hope of grabbing his foot, but he was too fast for me. Too fast and too experienced. I had underestimated Dodo all down the line: underestimated his brains, his influence, his malevolence, and his sheer physical strength.

Still in pain, I straightened up, backing away from him, and felt the piano behind me. Welcoming the support it provided, I rested a moment against it and waited for Dodo's next move. The light from the piano was fully in his eyes. His kicks and punches had tired him a little, but he was reluctant to give me any chance to recover. He came at me again, slower this time, his hands high and his feet well apart. I took a deep breath; if he placed them right, a couple of those chops would put my lights out.

"Gaah!" He gave a sudden cry and lunged at me. Or was it just a feint to see how I'd react? I sank down a little and kicked at his belly but didn't connect. My foot made an arc in empty air, but the threat of it made him hesitate. Then he ducked his head and reached out with a jab that struck my arm and sent pain down to my hand. I went for him then, going in close, swinging my fist, embracing him with a punch that landed in his kidney and produced an angry little grunt. For a moment we stood grappling like partners on the dance floor; then he pushed away, hammering a couple of blows at my chest as we broke.

When he stepped back, he was almost lost in the shadows of the dark room. We stood apart, panting heavily and staring at each other. The element of surprise was gone, and I was getting his measure. Dodo was no boxer—if I could get him toe to toe, trading blows, I could knock him unconscious. But that was a big if. From the street came the sound of a car moving slowly. Dodo cocked his head to listen, but after a moment or two the car revved up and moved on.

Click! A flick knife was in his hand, and as he inched forward, the light shone on its blade. He was holding the knife low, point upwards, the way you hold one when you mean business. "I'll teach you a lesson, Samson," he promised in that low growl that he produced when being especially venomous. "Slice you up!" His face was flushed and he was over-salivating.

I moved sideways. Now the support that the piano had provided became a trap. I didn't want to be impaled. I dragged my scarf from my neck and flipped it around my hand to provide a flimsy glove. I edged further sideways. From the corner of my eye I chose the largest glass ornament within reach, a big cut-glass pineapple with silver leaves. I grabbed it and threw it with all my force. It hit him in the chest, and he grunted and reeled back, banging against a table so that a dozen pieces of chinaware went crashing to the floor. But it didn't provide me with the chance I was hoping for. Dodo swore softly, some Hungarian curse, and kept his balance without looking round to see what he'd done.

When he came at me again, I was trying to unlock the old-fashioned shutters and get to the French windows that opened onto the garden. I turned back to face him and kicked high, trying to knock the knife from his hand, but he was ready for that and avoided the blow, smiling with satisfaction.

He closed again. My back crashed against the shutter and behind it a pane of glass cracked like a pistol shot. Dodo's knife came at me, ripping through my coat. I grabbed at his wrist and for a moment held it. We were close—he stank of whisky—then he wrenched hard to get free, and desperately I butted him in the face. "Bastard!" he called as he escaped my grip and backed away. A tiny red worm crawled from his nostril, slid over his mouth, and dripped from his chin. "Bastard!" he said again. He moved the flick knife to his left hand and reached under his jacket. Now there was a gun in his hand, a silly little toy designed for a lady's handbag, but it would be enough to settle things.

That was the moment I realized I couldn't beat him. And it was also the moment I got the feeling that Dodo had known I was coming. He was prepared for me. He hadn't wanted to talk, hadn't asked me what I was there for. He had put a gun and a knife in his belt and waited for me to arrive. But how could he have guessed that I was on my way?

"Say your prayers, Samson." With studied glee he took the gun in his left hand. He wanted me to understand what he meant by it. The gun was to be his insurance policy: Dodo was going to use the knife on me. He moved closer, but he was wary now; he wouldn't be caught again by my kicks or jabs. I tried to guess his intentions. He would have to cripple me with the knife to get me from wrenching the gun away from him. "Say your prayers," he whispered softly.

I was frightened, and he could see it. There was no way I could tackle him: he'd chosen his position well. There were no more handy objects for me to throw at him, no rugs under him, no doors or windows to escape through. And the only light was no longer in his eyes; it was in mine. That was why I didn't see clearly what happened next.

Over Dodo's shoulder I could make out a figure coming silently through the door behind him, a slim man wearing a short black car coat and a close-fitting cap. Like a dancer, he raised his hand high in the air, as if trying to touch the ceiling, and then brought it down in a graceful, vertical movement that ended with the thud of something hard hitting Dodo's skull.

Dodo gave a gasp like the air escaping from a balloon and collapsed, to sprawl senseless upon the carpet. Then suddenly the dark room seemed to be full of men. Someone pushed me flat against the wall and frisked me, while others were searching the house and searching Dodo's body too.

"Sit down, Bernie. Sit down and catch your breath." Someone handed me a glass of whisky, and I drank gratefully.

"That was a close one, eh?"

I knew the voice. Prettyman. "Jim!" I said. "Jesus! Is it really you, Jim? What . . . ? Why . . . ?"

I looked at him, but he gave no sign of friendliness. "Deep cover, Bernie."

"Cindy thinks you're dead. What's it all about?" Outside, in the hall, I could hear the squawks and hisses of a two-way radio. Upstairs someone was tramping about noisily. Drawers were being pulled open and doors closed. "What in hell is it all about?"

"You know better than to ask me that, Bernie."

"For the Department?" He didn't answer.

He stared at me. His skin was white and his face hard, like a waxwork figure. He said, "I've got to get you out of here. Can you drive yourself home?"

I couldn't resist leaning forward and touching his arm. "Is this why you sent me that box of ancient scripts and stuff? To keep for you? Was I supposed to guess that you weren't really dead?"

He flinched away from my touch. He got up and looked round the shadowy room. "Maybe," he said. He was near the piano. Reflectively he reached down and picked out a few bass notes. The room was dark, so that the lamp on the piano made a hard light upon the keyboard and his seemingly disembodied fingers.

"Jim," I said, "who ordered you to disappear? Is it something to do with Fiona?"

Unhurriedly he hit a few more notes, to complete a doleful little melody. Then he looked up and said, "Bernie, it's time you realized that the Department isn't run for your benefit. There's nothing in Command Rules that says we have to clear everything with Bernard Samson before an operation is okayed."

"I'm talking about my wife, Jim," I said angrily.

"Well, I'm not talking about her: not to you, not to anyone. Now, shut up and get out of here. Go home and forget everything, and leave me to sort out this bloody mess you've created."

"Or else?"

There was a pause. I met his gaze. "Or else I include you

in the report. You were told not to contact Dodo, but you just can't leave anything alone, can you, Bernie? You've just got to keep poking that nose of yours into everything."

"So Silas Gaunt sent you here?"

He played a minor chord and held it. "I told you to get going, so get going." He closed the piano. "Think you can drive?"

I gulped the rest of the whisky and got to my feet. I was still shaky. "Okay, Jim," I said.

"Just for old times' sake, I'll keep you out of it. Don't forget, now. If anyone wants to know—and I do mean anyone —you went straight home." He was watching me and now, for the first time, he smiled, but he didn't put a lot of energy into it. "Don't drop me into it." I thought he would offer his hand, but he turned away and prodded Dodo's inert shape with the toe of his shoe. "Come on, Dodo," he said. "The fight is over."

Chapter 21

Go to jail!" It was not unexpected. There is a measure of inevitability to every game of chance.

I sometimes wonder if the reservations and doubts that my generation showed for capitalism were the legacy of being bankrupted and humiliated by our parents in those Sunday-afternoon Monopoly games. Billy and Sally will not be similarly assailed; for them Monopoly games are simply a time when family discussions, reminiscences, stories, and jokes (Waiter, waiter, this Pekin Duck is rubbery. Chinese waiter: Thank you, sir) are punctuated by desultory throws of the dice.

"Go to jail, go directly to jail. Do not pass Go. Do not collect two hundred pounds." Oh well.

This was my family now: three children, in effect, for to see Gloria with my children was to recognize how she was just a grown-up child, with all the sudden changes of mood that children believe normal. I looked at her that Sunday afternoon. It was a promise of the spring to come; the sun shone from a blue sky, and we sat in the dilapidated conservatory that, more than any other thing, had made Gloria want to live in Balaklava Road. The potted plants and flowers that filled every shelf had been bought at the local garden center, but the effect was green and luxuriant, and for Gloria effect was everything.

The sun gave new life to Gloria, as it does to so many women, and I had never seen her looking more beautiful than she did that day. The sunshine had turned her blond hair to the color of pale butter. Her high cheekbones and wonderful teeth made her broad smile infectious, and despite my misery —or perhaps because of it—I fell in love with her all over again.

Not once but often I had wondered how I would have survived that terrible time after Fiona's defection without Gloria there at my side. Apart from working all week, studying for university, and attending to the household chores, she cared for my children and worried about me. Most of all, she renewed my self-respect at a time when my male ego was badly bruised by Fiona's departure.

I suppose I should have told her all this, but I never did. At the bad times, when I needed her most, I had no stamina for such tributes, and when things were going well between us, there seemed to be no need of them.

"You can't move, you're in jail," said Sally. "You have to throw a double six."

"Yes, I'm in jail," I said. "I forgot."

Sally laughed.

I wondered if the children were aware of the difficulties

that their mother's defection had brought. They were always polite to Gloria and occasionally affectionate, but there was no way that she could replace their mother. At best they treated her as an elder sister, and the authority they granted her was on that basis. I worried about them, and work was not going well. Dicky Cruyer complained that I was not working hard enough to clear my desk. I countered that I was getting too many messenger-boy trips to Berlin, but Dicky laughed and said that the Berlin jaunts were one of the best perks of the job. And Dicky was right. I liked the trips to Berlin. I'd be desolated to be deprived of the chance to see my friends there.

Were all the people I'd always trusted and depended upon working against me? Perhaps I was beginning to go mad; or maybe I was far gone! At nights I stayed awake, trying to figure out what might be going on. I went to a pharmacy and bought sleeping tablets that had no discernible effect. Something more powerful would have required a prescription from a doctor, and regulations for senior staff said that any medical consultations of any sort have to be reported. Better to stay awake. But I felt more and more exhausted. By Wednesday I had decided that the only possible way of escaping from this nightmare was to talk to someone at the very top. Since the Deputy was a new boy and something of an unknown quantity, this meant the Director-General, Sir Henry Clevemore. The only remaining task was to locate him; I was determined to do this before my next Berlin trip.

Apart from some spells in a nursing home, Sir Henry lived in a big stockbroker-Tudor mansion near Cambridge. In the distant past I had taken urgent papers there. Once I'd even been given lunch by the old man, a privilege so rarely granted to anyone but his immediate associates that Dicky interrogated me afterwards and wanted to know every word uttered.

How often Sir Henry came to London nowadays, no one on my floor seemed to know. As far as the staff were concerned, he was only to be glimpsed now and again emerging from—or disappearing into—the car of the express lift that took him to his top-floor office, his face gloomy and his back hunched.

Sir Henry's office was still there and still unchanged: a desperate muddle of old books, files, ornaments, mementos, and souvenirs too cheap and ugly to be enshrined in his richly furnished home, but too imbued with memories to be thrown away.

The irrepressible and ever-enchanting Gloria provided an answer to my problem when she invited a friend of hers to sit down with us in the canteen for lunch. Peggy Collier, a prematurely gray-haired lady who'd befriended Gloria right from the first day she'd come to work here, said something that indicated that Sir Henry must be in London every Friday. Peggy said that every Friday at noon she had a box of "current-and-vital" papers ready and waiting for the D-G. It was delivered to The Cavalry Club in Piccadilly. Also, I remembered that the Operations logbook showed The Cavalry Club as the contact number for the Deputy D-G every Friday afternoon.

Peggy said a special messenger brought the document box back to the office at varying times between 5:00 and 7:00 p.m. It was poor old Peggy who had to wait for the box to arrive, and then refile all the documents the D-G had been looking through. Sometimes—in fact, quite frequently—this meant that Peg did not get home in time to prepare a proper meal for her husband, Jerry—spelled with a "J" because it is short for Jerome not Gerald—who worked as a fully qualified accountant for the local office of the Inspector of Inland Revenue and so was always home early, not having the train journey which Peggy had to endure from the office on account of the absurd rents they charge anywhere near the center of town, and anyway wasn't the rent they paid out in the suburbs, where they lived next door to Jerry's mother, enough. And who wants a cold meal at night after a long day's work, although by the time you've dished up a cold meal it has taken almost as long as cooking. And who can afford the price you have to pay in the little shop just along the road from the bus stop that stays open to midnight—it's run by foreigners, but no matter what you say, those people don't mind hard work, and that's something you can't say about some of the English people Peg knows—but really the prices they charge for ready-prepared food. They have pork pies, cooked chicken, or those foreign sausages that are all meat and Jerry likes but which Peg finds funny-tasting on account of the way they are full of chemicals, or anyway that's what the papers say; still, you can't believe everything you read in the papers, can you?

"Who takes the box?" I asked.

"Anyone cleared to carry 'Top Secret,' " said Peg.

"I see," I said.

"And his dog," said Peggy. "The driver takes the box and the dog. The dog walks in Green Park."

The Cavalry Club is not one of those "gentlemen's clubs" which have been infiltrated by advertising men and actors. The only time outsiders gained access to these sacred portals was in January 1976, when members of the newly closed Guards' Club were allowed in. The quiet dignity of this old house at the Hyde Park Corner end of Piccadilly fits well with its elite and clannish membership. Reminded of their reputation for consuming more French champagne than any comparable establishment, these clubbable cavalrymen are likely to account for it by the popularity their premises enjoy as a venue for regimental events and the private cocktail parties that are so often to be heard even in the quiet of the library.

Sir Henry Clevemore was in the otherwise unoccupied writing room when I took his document box to him. He always chose this room, which was on the ground floor. It is different from all the other rooms in the club, for it can be entered from the street, without passing through the main entrance and answering questions from the men behind the desk. Here were stored cocktail-party chairs and a billiards table that the committee didn't want to throw away. The room smelled of ancient leather and scented polish, and Sir Henry was alone there. There were no cocktail parties to be heard, only the sound of buses crawling along the rainswept street outside. Sir Henry was sitting before a writing desk at the window, with a frantic wide-nostriled charger of the Light Brigade thundering through the oil paint above him. Beneath the vivid painting—framed and reverently positioned—were pressed flowers collected from the "Valley of Death" and a lock of hair from Wellington's favorite charger.

"Oh, it's you," said Sir Henry vaguely, his arms extended to take the document box.

"Yes, Sir Henry," I said as I handed it to him. "I was hoping that you'd grant me a few minutes of your time."

He frowned as I put the box on the table in front of him. It was not done, of course. Decent chaps didn't bamboozle their way into a fellow's club and then corner him for a chat. But he managed a brief and mandatory smile before reaching into his pocket and bringing out a key on a long silver chain.

"Of course, of course. Splendid! My pleasure entirely." He was still hoping that he'd misheard, that I would say goodbye and go away and leave him to his paperwork.

"Samson, sir. German Desk."

He raised his eyes to me and rubbed his face, like a man coming out of a deep sleep. Eventually he said, "Ummmm. Brian Samson. Of course." He was a strange old fellow, a gangling, uncoordinated, emaciated teddy bear, the bruinlike effect heightened by the ginger-colored rough tweed jacket he was wearing, and his long hair. His face was more wrinkled than I remembered, and his complexion had darkened with that mauvish color that sickness sometimes brings.

"Brian Samson was my father, sir. My name is Bernard Samson." The D-G put on his spectacles and for a moment he stared at me quizzically. This action disarranged his hair, so that demoniacal tufts appeared above each ear. The lenses glinted in the light from the window. The frames were incongruously small for his long droopy face and did not fit properly upon his nose.

"Bernard Samson. Yes, yes. Of course it is." He unlocked the box and opened it to get a glimpse of the papers. He was excited now, like a child with a box of new toys. Without looking up—and without much conviction—he said, "If we can find that waiter we'll get you a cup of coffee . . . or a drink."

"Nothing for me, thank you, Sir Henry. I must get back to the office. I'm going to Berlin this afternoon." I reached out for the lid of the box and firmly and gently closed it.

He looked up at me in amazement. Such insubordination was like a physical assault, but I enjoyed the shining armor of the self-righteous innocent. He did not voice his anger. He was a luminary of the expensive end of the British education system, which specializes in genial, courteous philistines. So, concealing his impatience, he invited me to sit down and take as long as I wished to tell him whatever I had to say.

There were plenty of stories that said the old man was *non compos mentis,* but any concern I had about explaining my worries to a batty boss were soon gone. I decided to leave out my visit to Dodo in Hampton Wick and my strange encounter with Jim Prettyman. If the Department said Jim was dead, then dead he would remain. As soon as I began, Sir Henry was bright-eyed and alert. As I told him what I had discovered about the funds passed over to Bret Rensselaer's company, and what I could guess about the way in which the money had been moved from place to place before going to the Berlin bank, he interrupted me with pertinent comments.

At times he was well ahead of me, and more than once I was unable to understand fully the import of his questions. But he was an old-timer and too much of a pro to reveal the extent of his knowledge or the degree of his fears. This didn't surprise me. On the contrary, I fully expected any director-general to deny stolidly suggestions of treason or malfeasance, or even a possibility that any member of the staff might be getting a second biscuit with his or her afternoon tea.

"Do you garden?" he said, suddenly changing the subject.

"Garden, sir?"

"Damn it man, garden." He gave a genial smile. "Dig the soil, grow flowers and shrubs and vegetables and fruit?"

I remembered Sir Henry's twenty-acre garden and the men I'd seen laboring in it. In his lapel he wore a small white rose, a mark of the rural Yorkshire upbringing of which he was so proud. "No, sir. I don't garden. Not really."

"A man needs a garden; I've always said so." He looked at me over his spectacles. "Not even a little patch?"

"I have a little patch," I admitted, remembering the wilderness of weeds and nettles at the rear of Balaklava Road.

"July is my favorite month in my garden, Simpson. Can you guess why?" He raised a finger.

"I don't think I can, sir."

"By July everything that's coming up is up. Some lovely things are ready for cropping: raspberries, red currants, and cherries, as well as your beans and potatoes. . . ." He paused and fixed me with his eye. "But if any of them haven't appeared aboveground, Simpson; if your seeds failed to germinate or got washed out in the rains or frozen by late frosts" —his finger pointed—"there's still time to plant. Right? July. Nothing you can't plant in July, Simpson. It's not too late to start again. Now, do you follow me?"

"I see what you mean, sir," I said.

"I love my vegetable garden, Simpson. There's nothing finer than to eat the crop you've planted with your own hands. I'm sure you know that."

"Yes, I do, sir."

"*Our* world is like an onion, Simpson," he said with heavy significance, his voice growing hoarser by the minute. "The

Department, I mean, of course. I told the PM that once, when she was complaining about our unorthodox methods. Each layer of the onion fits closely upon its neighbor, but each layer is separate and independent: *terra incognita*. Follow me, Simpson?"

"Yes, Sir Henry."

Thus reassured, he said, *"Omne ignotum pro magnifico.* Are you familiar with that splendid notion, Simpson?" Characteristically unwilling to take a chance, he explained it in a soft aside. "Anything little known is assumed to be wonderful. The watchword of the service, Simpson . . . at least, the watchword of the appropriations wallahs, eh?" He laughed.

"Yes, sir," I said. "Tacitus, wasn't it?"

His eyes flickered behind the spectacle lenses: a glass-eyed old teddy suddenly come to life. He cleared his throat. "Awww! Yes. Read Tacitus, have you? Remember any more of it, Simpson?"

"Omnium consensu capax imperii nisi imperasset," I quoted and, after giving him a moment to digest it, I took a leaf out of his book and told him what it meant. "Everyone thought him capable of exercising authority until he tried it."

The watery eyes gave me a steady stare. "Haw! A palpable hit! I take your point, young man. You're wondering if I am capable of exercising my authority. Is that it?"

"No, Sir Henry, of course I'm not."

He scratched his nose. "Exercising it forcefully enough to explore the substance of your fears and concerns." He turned his head and coughed in a quiet, gentlemanly way.

"No, sir." I got to my feet to take leave of him.

He looked up at me. "Have no fear, my boy. I'll act on your information. I'll root through every aspect of this matter until no shadow of a doubt remains."

"Thank you, sir." He heaved himself up to offer his hand in farewell, and his spectacles fell off. He caught them in mid-fall. I suppose it happened to him a lot.

Once outside in Piccadilly, I looked at my watch. I had more than enough time to pick up my case from the office, take the car to Ebury Street, and pick up Werner, who'd been in London shopping and was booked on the same plane back to Berlin-Tegel. So I walked towards Fortnum's and the prospect of a cup of coffee. I wanted just a moment to myself. I needed time to think.

There were dark clouds racing over the treetops of Green Park, and the drizzle of rain had now become spasmodic heavy showers and gusting winds. Tourists trudged through the downpour with grim determination. On the park side of the street, the artists who displayed their paintings there had covered them with sheets of plastic and gone to find shelter behind the colonnade of the Ritz Hotel. As I passed Green Park tube station, a woman's umbrella was blown inside out, and a man's wide-brimmed felt hat went flying away into the traffic. The hat bounced; a car swerved to avoid it, but a bus rolled on over it, and a man selling newspapers laughed grimly. There was a rumble of thunder. It was cold and wet; it was a thoroughly miserable day; it was London in winter.

For some there is a perverse satisfaction to walking in the rain; it provides a privacy that a stroll in good weather does not. Passersby bowed their heads and butted into the downpour, oblivious of anything but their own discomfort. I recalled my conversation with the Director-General and wondered if I had handled it right. There was something curious about the old man's demeanor. Not that he wasn't concerned: I'd never seen him more disturbed. Not that he wasn't prepared to listen: he weighed my every word. But something . . .

I turned into Fortnum's entrance and went through the food store to the tea shop at the back. It was crowded with ladies with blue hair and crocodile handbags, the sort of ladies who have little white dogs waiting for them at home. Perhaps I'd chosen a bad time. I sat at the counter and had a cup of coffee and a Danish pastry. It was delicious. I sat there thinking for some time. When I finished that coffee I ordered another. It was then that I realized what I'd found odd about my conversation with the Director-General. No matter how outrageous my story and my theories might have sounded to him, he had shown no indignation, no anger; not even surprise.

I must have lost track of time, for I suddenly looked at my watch and realized that my schedule was tight. But I hurried, and by the time I got to Ebury Street I was only a few minutes late. Werner—with that dedicated punctuality that is inherently German—was waiting for me on the pavement, briefcase packed, bills paid, black Burberry raincoat buttoned, and umbrella up. At his feet was a large carton marked "Chinaware Very Fragile." "Sorry, Werner," I said in apology for my late arrival. "Everything took a bit longer than expected."

"Plenty of time," said Werner. The driver opened the door for him and then heaved the carton of chinaware into the trunk. It looked damned heavy. Werner made no comment about this huge and cumbersome item of baggage. He reached over to put his umbrella in the front seat, alongside the driver, and then took off his trilby hat to make sure his ticket was inside it. Werner kept tickets and things in his hatband. He was the only person I knew who did that.

The car dropped us at Victoria Station so that we could catch one of the direct trains for Gatwick Airport. A porter took the carton of chinaware on a barrow, with Werner fussing around to make sure it didn't get knocked. The train was almost empty. We had no difficulty finding a place to ourselves. Werner was wearing a new suit—a lightweight gray mohair—and looking rather more rakish than the sober fellow I'd known so well. But he hung his umbrella so it would drain onto the floor, carefully folded his raincoat, and placed his hat and his briefcase on the rack. No matter how rakish he looked, Werner had been house-trained by the indomitable Zena. "Plates and cups and so on," said Werner, touching the carton delicately with the toe of his polished shoe.

"Yes," I said. I could think of nothing to add.

Once the train started its journey, he said, "In Berlin I suppose you'll be going to see Koby?"

"Lange Koby? Maybe." Koby lived in a squalid apartment near Potsdamer Platz and held court for foreign journalists and writers who were writing about "the real Berlin." I didn't enjoy my visits there.

"If this Dodo worked for him, Lange might be able to tell you something."

I didn't tell Werner that I'd seen Prettyman or grappled with Dodo; I hadn't told anyone. "Perhaps. But that was all a long time ago, Werner. Dodo was just a nasty little spear-carrier. I don't see how Lange can know anything about Bret and the money and all the things that really matter."

"Lange usually knows all the scandal," said Werner without admiration.

I leaned forward to him and said, "I told the old man everything I know . . . damn nearly everything," I amended it. "From now onwards it's the D-G's problem, Werner. His problem, not my problem."

Werner looked at me and nodded, as if thinking about it. "Does that mean you're going to drop the Bret business?"

"I might," I admitted.

"Let it go, Bernard. It's eating you up."

"If only I knew what part Fiona played in that fiddle."

"Fiona?"

"She had her hands on that money, Werner. I remember seeing the bank papers—statements—in the drawer where she kept her household accounts and money for Mrs. Dias, our cleaning woman."

"Before Fiona defected, you mean?"

"Yes, years ago. I was looking for the car keys. . . . Schneider, von Schild und Weber . . . I knew that damned name was familiar, and last night I remembered why."

"Why would Fiona have the Berlin bank accounts?"

"At the time I thought it was some stuff from the office . . . forgeries, even. There were a lot of zeros on those sheets, Werner. Millions and millions of deutschemarks. Now I realize it was real and the money was hers. Or at least in her keeping."

"Fiona's money? A secret account?"

"Banks send the statements to the account holder, Werner. There is no getting away from that."

"It's too late now," said Werner. "She's gone."

"I told the old man everything I know," I said again, as if to remind myself of what I'd done. "From now onwards it's his problem, Werner. His problem, not my problem."

"You said that already," said Werner.

"I left Ingrid out of it. There was no point in telling him all that rigmarole about her mother and Dodo."

"Nor the stuff about your father," said Werner.

"That's right," I said. "Do you think I should have told him that?"

"Either the Department authorized what Bret has been doing with the money, or Bret and Fiona have been stealing it," said Werner, with his usual devastating simplicity. "Didn't the old man give any indication of knowing?"

"Perhaps he's the greatest actor in the world, but it seemed like he was hearing it all for the first time."

"They say he's meshuggeh."

"No sign of that today."

"You did the right thing, Bernie. I'm sure of it. Now forget it and stop brooding."

I looked at his big package. "So what did you buy in London that I couldn't be trusted with?"

He smiled. "We felt we couldn't use you like a courier service."

"I'm in Berlin every week, the way things are now. I'll bring whatever you need."

"Ingrid wants the hotel to look more homely. She likes all these English fabrics and English china—little floral patterns. She says the hotel is too inhospitable-looking, too institutional."

"It's a Berlin hotel; it looks German."

"Times change, Bernie."

"I thought Lisl told you her sister was childless?" I said. "What did she say when Ingrid arrived here?"

He nodded and then said, "Lisl knew about Ingrid, but Ingrid is illegitimate. She has no legal claim on the hotel."

"Are you in love with Ingrid?"

"Me? In love with Ingrid?"

"Don't stall, Werner. We know each other too well."

"Yes, I'm in love with Ingrid," said Werner somewhat apprehensively.

"Does Zena know?" I asked.

"Zena will be all right," said Werner confidently. "I'll give her a lot of money and she'll be satisfied."

I said nothing. It was true, of course. This was a bleak comment on Zena and her marriage, but there was no arguing with it.

"Zena's in Munich. I keep hoping she'll meet someone. . . ." Werner looked at me and smiled. "Yes, me and Ingrid . . . We're happy together. Of course it will all take time. . . ."

"That's wonderful, Werner."

"You never liked Zena, I know."

"Ingrid is a very attractive woman, Werner."

"You do like her?"

"Yes, I do."

"She's never been married. She might find it difficult to adjust to married life at her age."

"You're both young, Werner. What the hell . . ."

"That's what Ingrid says," said Werner.

"Gatwick Airport," said the voice of the train conductor over the speakers; the train was slowing.

"Thanks, Bernie," he said. "You've helped me."

"Any time, Werner."

The plane took off on time. It was a small private company, Dan Air, and the stewardesses smile and give you real coffee. Once we were above the clouds, the sun shone brightly. Despite the emptiness of the train, the plane was filled. I asked Werner about his progress with Lisl's hotel, and I unleashed a long and enthusiastic account of his hopes and hard work. And Werner wasn't too selfish to include Ingrid Winter's contribution. On the contrary, his praise and admiration for her were very apparent. At times he seemed to be giving her too much credit, but I listened patiently and made the right noises at appropriate times. Werner was in love, and people who are in love are good company only for their beloved.

I looked at the landscape passing below. Germany: there was no mistaking it. The people of Europe may grow more and more alike in their choice of cars, their clothes, their TV programs, and their junk food, but our landscapes reveal our true nature. There is no rural West Germany. The German landscape is ordered, angular, and built upon, so that cows must share their *Lebensraum* with apartment blocks, and forest trees measure the factory chimneys. Towns are allotted foliage under which to hide their ugly shopping plazas, but huntsmen must stalk their prey between the parked cars and swimming pools of an unending suburbia.

Yet across the East-West frontier the landscape is lonely and tranquil. The Democratic Republic enjoys an agricultural landscape not yet sullied by shiny cars and new houses. Here the farms are old and picturesque. Big breeds of horses have stubbornly resisted the tractors, and men and women still do the hard work.

It was a lovely evening when we landed in Berlin, this

glittering little capitalist island, with its tall concrete office blocks and sparkling streets, set in a vast green ocean of grassy communism. The sun was low and orange-colored. Tall cumuli dominated the eastern skies, while to the west the gray storm clouds were smudged and streaked across the sky, as if some angry god had been trying to erase them.

I came down the steps from the plane carrying Werner's briefcase while he staggered under the weight of the china-ware. Ahead of us the other passengers straggled on their way to customs and immigration.

Berlin-Tegel is in the French Sector of occupied Berlin. This small airport is technically under the control of the French air force. So the incongruous presence of four British military policemen was especially noticeable, if not to say disturbing. They were dressed in that unnaturally perfect way that only military policemen can manage. Their shoes were gleaming, their buttons bright; their khaki had knife-edge creases in all the places where creases were supposed to be.

And if the incongruous presence of British "redcaps" was not enough, I now noticed that one of them was a captain. Such men are not commonly seen standing and staring in public places, for MP captains do not patrol airports to make sure there are no squaddies going around improperly dressed. A quick glance round revealed two British army vehicles—a khaki car and a van—drawn up on the apron. Behind them there was a blue van bearing the winged badges of *l'armée de l'air*. A few yards behind that was a civilian police car too. Inside it were a couple of cops in winter uniforms. Quite a police presence for a virtually empty airport.

As we walked across the apron, the four British MPs straightened up and stared at us. Then the captain strode forward on a path that intercepted us.

"Excuse me, gentlemen," said the British captain. He was a diffident young man with a large mustache that was less than bushy. "Which of you is Mr. Samson?"

Always afterwards I wondered exactly what made Werner unhesitatingly say, "I'm Bernard Samson. What is it, Captain?"

Werner could smell trouble; that's why he said it. He could smell trouble even before I got a whiff of it, and that was very quick indeed.

"I'll have to ask you to come with me," said the captain. He glanced at the sergeant—a burly forty-year-old with a pistol on his belt—and the looks they exchanged told me everything I needed to know.

"Come with you?" said Werner. "Why?"

"It's better if we sort it out in the office," said the captain with a hint of nervousness in his voice.

"I'd better go with him, Werner," said Werner, continuing the act.

I nodded. Surely the soldiers could hear Werner's German accent. But perhaps they hadn't been told that Bernard Samson was English.

As if demonstrating something to me, Werner turned to the captain and said, "Am I under arrest?"

"Well . . ." said the captain. He'd obviously been told that arresting a man in public was something of a last resort, something you only did when sweet talk failed. "No. That is . . . only if you refuse to come."

"We'll sort it out at your office," said Werner. "It's a stupid mistake."

"I'm sure it is," said the captain with marked relief. "Perhaps your friend will take the package."

"I'll take it," I said.

The captain turned to one of the corporals and said, "Help the gentleman, Corporal. Take the parcel for him."

I had Werner's briefcase in my hand. It contained his passport and all sorts of other personal papers. If they took Werner to their police office, it might take an hour or two before they discovered that he was the wrong man. So I followed the corporal and Werner's parcel of chinaware and left Werner to his fate.

With the military policeman acting as my escort, my passage through customs and immigration got no more than a nod. In the forecourt there were lines of taxicabs. My cab driver was an unshaven youngster in a dirty red tee shirt with the heraldic device of Harvard University crudely printed on the front. "I want an address in Oranienburger Strasse. I know it by sight. . . . Go to the Wittenau S-Bahn station." I said it in slow German, in earshot of the soldier. It would give them a confusing start, for Oranienburger Strasse stretches across town from the airport to Hermsdorf. Not the sort of street in which you'd want to start a door-to-door inquiry.

Once the taxi was clear of the airport, I told the driver that I'd changed my mind: I wanted to go to Zoo Station. He looked at me and gave a knowing smile that was inimitably *berlinerisch.*

"Zoo Station," he said. It was a squalid place, the Times Square of West Berlin. *"Alles klar."* In that district there was no shortage of people who would help a fugitive to hide from authority of any kind. The cab driver probably thought I was outsmarting the army cops, and he approved.

Yes, I thought, everything is clear. No sooner had I finished talking to him than the bloody D-G had signaled Berlin to have me arrested. It was artful to do it in Berlin. Here the army was king. Here I had no civil liberties that couldn't be overruled by regulations that dated from wartime. Here I could be locked away and forgotten. Yes, *alles klar,* Sir Henry. I am hooked.

Chapter 22

D on't ask me what I hoped to achieve. I don't know what I was trying to do, beyond gain time enough to collect my thoughts and see some way of extricating myself from this mess.

My mind worked frantically. I dismissed the idea of picking up the Smith & Wesson snub-nosed .38 and five hundred pounds' worth of mixed-currency small-denomination paper money that I used to keep in Lisl's safe but now kept in a twenty-four-hour safe-deposit box in the Ku-Damm. Neither ready cash nor flying lead would help me if the Department were after my blood. I dismissed too the Austrian passport that was sewn into the lining of a suitcase in a room in Marienfelde. I could become Austrian, if I raised my voice an octave and kept a tight grip on my nose. But what for? By Monday they would have good recent photos of me circulated, and being a phony Austrian wouldn't help.

A taxi took Werner's box of china round to the hotel with a note for Ingrid Winter that I'd gone with Werner to the cinema. For anyone who knew us well, the idea of such an excursion was absurd. But Ingrid didn't know us very well, and it was the only excuse I could think of that would prevent her making inquiries about us for two or three hours.

Some of my actions were less well reasoned. As if driven by some demon from my overactive past, I took a second cab and asked for Checkpoint Charlie. It was almost night by now, but my world was tilting towards the sun, and it was not dark. My cab edged through the traffic as battalions of weary tourists wandered aimlessly around the neon-and-concrete charms of the Europa Centre and chewed popcorn and "curry-wurst."

"Checkpoint Charlie?" said the driver again, just to be sure.

"Yes," I said.

Once clear of the crowds, we headed for the Canal. This quiet section of the city provides the shortest route to Checkpoint Charlie. No tourists walked the gently curving banks of the Landwehr canal, and yet there was more history in this short stretch than in the entire length of the Kurfürstendamm.

It had not always been such a neglected backwater. The street names of yesterday tell their own story. Bendlerstrasse, from which the Wehrmacht marched to conquer Europe, is now named after Stauffenberg, architect of the failed anti-Nazi putsch. But is there some militaristic ambition burning deep inside the town planners who keep Bendler Bridge still Bendler Bridge?

Here on the canal bank is the building where Admiral Canaris, Hitler's chief of military intelligence, sat in his office plotting against his master. And into these murky waters the battered body of Rosa Luxemburg was thrown by the army's assassins.

Soon the dark tree-lined canal was left behind, and the taxi was in Kreuzberg, speeding past Café Leuschner and along Kochstrasse—Berlin's Fleet Street—and to the Friedrichstrasse intersection that provides a view into the heart of East Berlin.

I paid off the cab and made a point of asking the American soldier on duty in the temporary hut that has been positioned there for forty years what time the checkpoint closed. It never closed, he told me; never! This was enough to make sure he remembered my passing through. If I was going to leave a trail that the MPs would follow, it would be better to make it wide and deep. The Department would not be fooled, but, judging by past performance, it would take a little time to get them into action. A Friday evening: Dicky Cruyer would have to be got back to his office from somewhere where the fishing and shooting were good and the telephoning demonstrably bad.

On the western side of Checkpoint Charlie you'll find only a couple of well laid-back GIs lounging in a hut, but the eastern side is crowded with gun-toting men in uniforms deliberately designed in the pattern of the old Prussian armies. I gave my passport to the surly DDR frontier guard, who showed it to his senior officer, who pushed it through the slot under the glass window. There it was photographed and put under the lights to reveal any secret marks that previous DDR frontier police might have put there. They gripped my passport with that proprietorial manner that all bureaucrats adopt towards identity papers. For men who man frontiers regard passports and manifests as communications to them from other bureaucrats in other lands. The bearers of such paper are no more than lowly messengers.

As a thinly disguised tax, all visitors are made to exchange Western money for DDR currency at an exorbitant rate. I paid. Guards came and went. Tourists formed a line. Buses and private cars crawled through and were examined underneath with the aid of large wheeled mirrors. A shiny new black Mercedes, flying the flag of some remote and impoverished African nation, was halted at the barrier behind a U.S. Army jeep that was demonstrating the victorious armies' right to patrol both sides of the city. The DDR guards did everything with a studied slowness. It all takes time: here everything takes time. And some of the victors have to be kept in their place.

East Berlin is virtually the only place to find a regime staunch and wholehearted in its application of the teachings of Karl Marx. Why not? Who could have doubted that the Germans, who had given such unquestioning faith and loyalty —not to mention countless millions of lives—to Kaiser Wilhelm and Adolf Hitler, would soldier on, long after Marxism had perished at its own hand and been relegated to the leveled Führerbunker of history?

The taller buildings around the shantytown of huts that is Checkpoint Charlie give the feeling of being in an arena. So do the banners and the slogans. But the bellicose themes have gone. It is a time of retrenchment. The communist propaganda has abandoned the promises of outstripping the West in prosperity or converting it politically. Now the messages stress continuity and security and tell the proletariat to be grateful.

Emerging from Checkpoint Charlie, you can see all the way to Friedrichstrasse Station. There a steel bridge crossing the street cuts a pattern in the indigo sky. Across that bridge go the trains that connect Paris with Warsaw and eventually Moscow, but the bridge itself is also the Friedrichstrasse Station platform of the elevated S-Bahn, the commuter line that runs through both East and West Berlin.

The sight of the bridge gives the impression that the station is only a short walk away, but the distance is deceptive, and as I walked up Friedrichstrasse—past the blackened and pockmarked shells of bombed buildings that people said were owned by mysterious Swiss companies that even the DDR did not wish to offend—I remembered too late that it's worth getting a cab that short distance when one is in a hurry.

The S-Bahn station at Friedrichstrasse provides another demonstration of the enormous work force that the DDR devotes to manning the Wall. I went through its agonizingly slow passport control—there are even more checks on people leaving than on those entering—and eventually went through the tunnel and up to the platform.

The station is a huge open-ended hangarlike building with overhead gantries patrolled by guards brandishing machine guns. The S-Bahn's rolling stock, like the stations and the track, are ancient and dilapidated. The train came rattling in, its windows dirty and the lights dim. I got in. It was almost empty: those privileged few permitted to cross the border are not to be found traveling westwards at this time of evening. It took only a few minutes to clatter over the Wall. The "antifascist protection barrier" is particularly deep and formidable here, where the railway crosses the Alexander Ufer; perhaps the sight of it is intended to be a deterrent.

There is an almost audible sigh of relief from the passengers who alight at Zoo Station. I had to change trains for Grunewald, but there was only a minute or two to wait, and it was quicker than taking a cab and getting tangled up in the Ku-Damm traffic, which would be thick at this time.

From the station I walked to Frank Harrington's home. I approached it carefully, in case there was anyone outside waiting for me. It seemed unlikely. The standard procedure was to cover the frontier-crossing points—those for German nationals as well as the ones for foreigners—and the airport. On a Friday night at short notice that would provide more than enough problems. Frank, as the Berlin chief, was already given special protection by the civil police. My guess was that whoever was allotting the personnel would decide that Frank couldn't be afforded a car and a three-shift watch. They would describe me as a fugitive special category three: "possibly armed but not dangerous."

It was Axel Mauser—one of the kids at school here—who had first shown me the proper way to climb drainpipes. Until then I'd been using my hands and getting my clothes into a terrible state. It was Axel who'd said, "Climb ropes with your hands, drainpipes with your feet," and shown me how the burglars did it without getting their hands dirty. I don't know who had shown Axel how to do it: his father probably. His father, Rolf Mauser, used to work in the hotel for Lisl. Rolf Mauser was an unscrupulous old crook. I'd believe almost anything of Rolf.

I was remembering all that as I climbed into the upstairs master bathroom of Frank's big house in Grunewald. There were no burglar alarms at the back. I knew where all the burglar alarms were. I'd helped Frank decide where to put them. And Frank always kept the bathroom window ajar. Frank was a fresh-air fiend. He'd often told me it was unhealthy to close the bedroom windows, no matter how cold it was. Sometimes I think that's why his wife doesn't like living with him: she can't stand those freezing-cold bedrooms. I told Fiona that once; she said, Don't be ridiculous, but it didn't seem ridiculous to me. I can't stand cold bedrooms: I prefer unhealthy warmth.

Frank wasn't in bed, of course; I knew he wouldn't be. That's why I got in upstairs. I got through the window and then had to stand there, carefully removing from the sill about three hundred bottles, tubes, and sprays of bath oil, shaving soap, hair shampoo, toothpaste, and God knows what. What could Frank ever want with all that stuff? Or was it the unredeemed property of Frank's girlfriends?

Finally I made a footspace on the windowsill, and from there I could step down into the bath and . . . Jesus, there was water in the bath. Lots of water! What did that bloody Tarrant do if he couldn't even make sure the bath was drained properly? My shoe was full of soapy water. How disgusting! I didn't like Frank's valet, and the feeling was mutual. I suppose, if I was to examine my feelings closely, the principal reason I didn't just knock on Frank's front door was that I wouldn't trust that bloody man Tarrant as far as I could throw him. In a jam like the one I was now in, I would give Tarrant just three minutes before catching sight of me and getting on the blower and reporting me. Less than three minutes: thirty seconds.

Frank was downstairs. I knew where he was. I'd known it even when I was on the back lawn, looking up at the drainpipes. He was sitting in the drawing room playing his Duke Ellington records. That's what Frank usually did when he was alone in the house. Volume up really loud, so that you could hear the drums and brass section halfway along the street.

Frank said the only way you could really appreciate these old records was to have them as loud as the original band had been when making them, but I think Frank was going deaf.

It was the 1940 band—the best Ellington band ever, in my opinion, although Frank didn't agree—playing "Cotton Tail." No wonder Frank didn't hear me come into the room. I could have been driving a combine harvester and still he wouldn't have heard me above the surging beat of the Ellington band.

Frank was sitting in a chair positioned exactly in line with his two giant speakers. He was dressed in a yellow sweater with a paisley-patterned silk scarf tucked into his open-neck shirt. It was all very Noel Coward except for the big curly pipe in his fist and the clouds of fierce-smelling tobacco smoke that made me want to cough. He was bent low, reading the small print on a record label. I waited for him to look up. I said, "Hello, Frank," as casually as I could say it.

"Hello, Bernard," said Frank, and held his pipe aloft to caution me. "Listen to Ben Webster."

Listen to him. How could I do anything else? The tenor-sax solo went through my head like a power drill. But when the immortal Webster had finished, Frank turned the volume down so it was merely very loud.

"Whisky, Bernard?" said Frank. He was already pouring it.

"Thanks," I said gratefully.

"I enjoy seeing you any time, Bernard. But I wish you'd just knock on the front door, the way other visitors do."

If Frank knew there was a warrant out for me, he was staying very cool. "Why?" I said, and drank some whisky. Laphroig: he knew I liked it.

"So you don't make such a mess on the carpet," said Frank with a fleeting grin to offset his complaint.

I looked at the carpet. My wet shoe had left marks all the way to the door, and right through the house probably. "I'm sorry, Frank."

"Why do you have to do everything arse upwards, Bernard? It makes life so difficult for your friends." Frank had always taken his paternal role seriously, and his way of demonstrating it was to be there when I needed him. Sometimes I wondered what kind of man my father must have been to have made a friendship so deep and binding that I was still drawing upon its capital. "You're too old now for tricks like climbing up to that damned bathroom. You used to do that when you were very young. Remember?"

"Did I?"

"I left the light on in the bathroom so you wouldn't fall off the ledge and break your neck."

"You heard what happened?" I said, not being able to endure another moment of Frank's small talk.

"I knew you'd come to me," Frank said, walking towards me with the whisky bottle. He couldn't resist it. It was the sort of complacent statement my mother made. Why did he have to be such an old woman? Couldn't he see how it spoiled everything? I let him pour me another drink. It was a wonder he was able to resist telling me I drank too much, but he'd probably find some way to work it into the conversation before long.

"When did you hear?" I asked.

"That the old man wanted you collared? I got a 'confidential' on the printer about four o'clock. But then a cancellation came through." He smiled. "Reading between the lines, someone in London must have decided that the old man had gone completely batty. Then, after an hour or more, the same message was repeated. This time with the names of both the D-G and the Deputy on it." He looked at his carpet. "It's not grease, is it?"

"It's water," I said.

"If it's grease or oil, tell me now so I can leave a note for Tarrant to do something about it before it soaks in."

"I told you, Frank. It's water."

"Keep your hair on, Bernard."

"So I'm still on the arrest list?"

"I'm afraid you are. Your ruse with your friend Werner Volkmann didn't fool the army very long."

"Long enough."

"For you to do a bunk, yes. But Captain Berry got the devil of a rocket."

"Captain Berry?"

"The provost captain. I hear the commanding general wants him to face a court. Poor little bugger."

"Screw Captain Berry," I said. "I have no tears to shed for MP captains who want to throw me into the slammer." I looked at the clock on the mantelpiece.

Frank saw me looking at it and said, "They won't come here searching for you."

"What's it all about, Frank?"

"I was hoping you'd tell me, Bernard."

"I went to see the old man and reported all that stuff about Bret Rensselaer and the bank funds."

"I thought you were going to abandon all that nonsense," said Frank wearily.

"Did they tell you what the charges against me might be?"

"No."

"Were they planning to hold me here, or ship me back to the U.K.?"

"I don't know, Bernard. I really don't know."

"You're the Head of Berlin Station, Frank."

"I'm telling you the truth, Bernard. I don't bloody well know."

"It's about Fiona, isn't it?"

"Fiona?" said Frank, and seemed genuinely puzzled.

"Is Fiona still working for the Department?"

It took the wind out of his sails. He drank some of whatever he was drinking and looked at me for what seemed a long time. "I wish I could say yes, Bernard. I really do."

"Because that's the only conclusion that makes sense."

"Makes sense how?"

"What would Bret Rensselaer be doing with umpteen million dollars?"

"I can think of a lot of things," said Frank, who was not very fond of Bret Rensselaer.

"Money. You know what a tight rein the Department keep on their cash. You can't really believe Central Funding let millions out of their sight and forget who they'd given it to."

"Ummm." He smoked his pipe and thought about it.

I said, "That sort of money is stashed away in secret accounts for payouts. For payouts, Frank."

"In California?"

"No. Not California. When I talked to Bret in California, no one except the Americans was getting agitated. It was when I traced the money to Berlin that the excitement began."

"Berlin?"

"So they didn't tell you that? Schneider, von Schild und Weber, right here on the Ku-Damm."

He touched his mustache with the mouthpiece of his pipe. "Even so, I'm still not sure . . ."

"Suppose Fiona's defection was the end of a very long-term plan. Suppose she is doing her own thing over there in East Berlin. She'd need lots of money, and she'd need it right here in Berlin, where it's easy to get to."

"To pay her own agents?"

"Good grief, Frank, I don't have to tell you what she'd need money for. Sure. For all kinds of things: agents, bribes, expenses. You know how it adds up."

Frank touched my shoulder. "I wish I could believe it. But I'm Head of Station here, as you just reminded me. No one would be planted there without my say-so. You know that, Bernard. Stop fooling yourself; it's not your style."

"Suppose it was kept very tight? Bret Rensselaer as the case officer . . ."

"And the D-G getting direct authorization from the Cabinet Office? It's an ingenious explanation, but I fear the true explanation is simpler and less palatable." A puff at the pipe. "The Berlin Head of Station is always informed. Even the D-G wouldn't defy that operational rule. It's been like that ever since your father's time. It would be unprecedented."

"So is having a senior employee arrested at the airport," I said.

"The D-G is a stick in the mud. I know him, Bernard. We trained together in the war. He's careful to a fault. He just wouldn't go along with such a hazardous scheme."

"To get an agent into the Stasi at the very top? A trusted agent at committee level? That's what Fiona is now. You told me that yourself."

"Now, calm down, Bernard. I can see why this scenario appeals to you. Fiona is rehabilitated, and you have taken on the Department and penetrated their most jealously guarded secret."

And, he might have added, made Bret into Fiona's colleague instead of her paramour. "So what is your explanation?"

"A deadly-dull one, I'm afraid. But after a lifetime in the service, you look back and see how much time you've wasted chasing bizarre solutions while the true answer was banal, obvious, and under your nose the whole while."

"Fiona leaving her home and children and going to work for the Stasi? Bret embezzling millions in departmental funds and sitting in California pretending to be penniless? Prettyman reassigned from Washington and his wife told he was dead? Uncle Silas telling me what a wonderful fellow Dodo is, while getting on the phone to have him roughed up and silenced? Except I got there first. A warrant issued for my arrest because I tell the D-G about it? Is this the deadly-dull explanation that has the ring of truth?"

Frank looked at me. This was the first mention I'd made of Silas Gaunt's duplicity—I'd not even told Werner—and I watched Frank carefully. He nodded as if considering everything I'd said but showed no surprise. "The last one certainly does," he said grimly. "I tore it off the printer myself this evening. Do you want to see it?"

"The old man wants me held because he's frightened that my inquiries are going to blow Fiona's cover. They got me to California just so that Bret could persuade me to forget the whole thing. They sent Charlie Billingsly to Hong Kong because of what he might have seen on the computer about Bret's bogus companies. They gave Cindy Prettyman a nice job in Strasbourg to keep her quiet. They panicked at the idea of Dodo loudmouthing their secrets, and chose Prettyman to lean on him."

"It's all very circumstantial," said Frank. But I had his attention now.

"I suppose they are desperate, but I didn't realize how desperate until I landed here. When I took my questions to the D-G, they couldn't think of anything to do with me except to put me in the cooler while they worked out how to shut me up."

Frank looked at me pitifully and said, "You'd better sit down, Bernard. There's something else you should know."

I sat down. "What?" I said.

"It's not like that. When the second teleprinter message came through, I phoned London for clarification. I thought . . . under the circumstances . . ."

"You spoke to the D-G? This afternoon?"

"No, but I had a word with the Deputy."

"And?"

"Sir Percy told me in confidence."

"Told you what?"

"They've opened an Orange File, Bernard."

"On me?"

There was still a chance for him to say no, but he didn't say no. He said, "Ladbrook is coming on the plane tomorrow."

"Jesus Christ!" I said. An Orange File is only started when someone in the Department is accused of treachery and *prima facie* evidence has already been collected against him. Ladbrook is the senior interrogator. Ladbrook prepares the prosecution.

"Now do you see?" Frank asked.

"You still don't believe me, do you, Frank?"

"I don't dare believe you," he said.

"What?"

"I'd rather believe that you were guilty than believe that Fiona was over there playing a double game. Especially if you have started tongues waggling. Have you thought about what you are saying? Have you thought what it would mean for her if they tumbled to her? You'd face prison, but if she got to committee level and betrayed them they'd . . ." He stopped. We were both thinking of Melnikoff, who'd reported back to one of Silas's networks. Over a dozen eyewitnesses had watched Melnikoff being pushed alive into a factory furnace. The KGB had wanted it talked about. "Be careful how you declare your innocence," said Frank. "You could be signing your wife's death warrant; whether what you say is true or not true."

I sat down. It was all happening too quickly. I felt like vomiting, but I got myself under control and looked at my watch. "I'd better get out of here." I hated this room. All the worst things that ever happened to me seemed to happen in this room, but I suppose that was because when something bad happened to me I came running along to Frank. I said, "Do you think Tarrant . . ."

"I gave Tarrant the evening off. Is there anything . . . ?"

"You've done your bit already, Frank."

"I'm sorry, Bernard."

"What's wrong with them all, Frank? Why can't they just call the dogs off?"

"Whatever the real truth may be, you'll never get a completely clean bill of health. Not after your wife defected. Surely you can see that."

"No, I can't."

"Whether your alarming theory is right or whether it is wrong, the Department still can't risk it, Bernard. There were voices who wanted you sacked within hours of her going. They get the wind up when you start nosing around. It scares them. You must see how difficult it is for them."

I got to my feet. "Have you got any money, Frank?"

"A thousand sterling. Will that be enough?"

"I didn't reckon on being an Orange File. I thought it really was some sort of mistake. Some overzealous interpretation of the old man's suggestion . . ."

"It's here in the desk." He found the money quickly, as he'd found the tumbler and the ice and the bottle of Laphroig. I suppose he'd had everything ready. He walked with me to the front door and looked out into the Berlin night. Perhaps he was making sure there were no men on watch. "Take this scarf, Bernard. It's bloody cold tonight." When I shook hands with him he said, "Good luck, Bernard," and was reluctant to release my hand. "What will you do now?" he asked.

I looked at the skyline. Even from here I could see the glow from the floodlights that the DDR used to illuminate their Wall. I shrugged. I didn't know. "I . . . I'm sorry . . . about the marks on the carpet." I nodded my thanks and turned away.

"It doesn't matter," said Frank. "As long as it's not grease."

A Note on the Type

This book was set in a digitized version
of a type face called Baskerville.
The face itself is a facsimile reproduction of
types cast from molds
made for John Baskerville (1706–1775)
from his designs. Baskerville's
original face was one of the
forerunners of the type style known to
printers as "modern face"—a "modern"
of the period A.D. 1800.

Composed, printed, and bound by
The Haddon Craftsmen, Inc., Scranton,
Pennsylvania

DESIGNED BY CLAIRE M. NAYLON